A SISTER'S COURAGE

When her mother passed away, Meg Parker was forced to sacrifice her chance at love for the sake of her brothers. She hopes she will be able to live a full life once again after her father remarries. Lady Alice Langton is travelling the Yorkshire Dales, spreading the suffragette message along with Florence Brookes. Meg decides to flee her old life and joins the two women as their maidservant. When Meg is reunited with her old flame, she is hesitant about her feelings for him. It's not until Florence's actions land them in jeopardy that Meg realises she must find the courage to make a heartbreaking choice.

A SISTER'S COURAGE

A SISTER'S COURAGE

by

Catherine King

Magna Large Print Books
Long Preston, North Yorkshire,
BD23 4ND, England.

British Library Cataloguing in Publication Data.

King, Catherine
    A sister's courage.

    A catalogue record of this book is
    available from the British Library

    ISBN   978-0-7505-3911-1

First published in Great Britain in 2013 by Sphere

Copyright © Catherine King 2013

Cover illustration © Colin Thomas

The moral right of the author has been asserted

Published in Large Print 2014 by arrangement with
Little, Brown Book Group

X 000 000 048 8637

Magna Large Print is an imprint of Library Magna Books Ltd.

Printed and bound in Great Britain by
T.J. (International) Ltd., Cornwall, PL28 8RW

Acknowledgements

I should like to thank novelist Leah Fleming for sparking the idea for this book and short story writer Della Galton for her help with developing the story. I should not have been able to complete it without Lesley Guest Swire, a friend from Rotherham High School, who lent me her copy of *Shoulder to Shoulder*. Thank you, Lesley. My thanks, also, as ever, to my agent Judith Murdoch and my editor Manpreet Grewal for supporting me through to the end with understanding and patience. And thank you, Megan Davey for suggesting my heroine's name! Good luck with your studies.

Chapter 1

Deepdale, Yorkshire, late Spring 1905

Bright sunlight streamed into the warm kitchen and Meg felt her excitement bubbling. She hoped Jacob would be at the Mission today and she looked forward to spending time on her appearance before she went out. She could hardly wait to see him again.

'My, that was a grand dinner, Meg.' Her father scraped back his chair and stretched out his legs.

'Thank you, Father.' Roast beef and Yorkshire pudding with fresh greens from the garden was his favourite Sunday dinner and she hoped it had put him in a good mood. He wouldn't be happy when she told him she was going out. She stood up and said, 'I'll get on with the washing-up now. Would you like a cup of tea?'

'We'll have it later, love. My roly-poly pudding hasn't gone down yet.'

That meant tea in the middle of the afternoon at half past three and Meg wanted to be at the Mission Hall by then. Meg loved her father. He had been a faithful husband to her late mother and was a good parent to all of his three children, even though her brothers had long since left home. As youngsters, the boys never went short of school uniform or shoes and Father still worked hard at the quarry all week so he always had 'something for a rainy day' when they needed it. But, as the only girl and the baby of the family, Meg had found that her brothers' night-school fees came first. She had grown used to her mother's gentle excuses when it came to her schooling.

The boys, in turn, had done well to pass their exams and gain positions as shipping clerks for the White Star Line in Liverpool. Father was proud of their achievements and set them up in decent lodgings with a good suit of clothes each. He had, Mother explained, to do the same for each of his sons. It was only fair. As a consequence, Meg's mother had taken a job at the local textile mill to help out with the housekeeping. Then she had put in a good word for Meg as soon as she was old enough to leave school and they had worked together in the checking room as well as at home. This had made it much harder for Meg when Mother was taken from them a couple of years ago. But Meg had been strong for all of them and kept the household going during those dark days. She had been seventeen at the time. Mother's loss had been a great shock to all of them but especially to her father and Meg worked hard to run things exactly as Mother had for him.

Father was wedded to his routine. Meg thought she had done the right thing by trying not to change any of it when Mother died. But she had noticed lately that he was becoming more set in his ways and dependent on her and she began to worry that she might grow old as a spinster daughter looking after her ageing father. She was already nineteen. Her friend Sally, who was the same age, was engaged to be married.

Meg cleared the table and washed up in the scullery while Father enjoyed a pipe of tobacco in his easy chair by the kitchen fire. The casement clock in the hall chimed. She dried her hands and said, 'Well, that's all done for today. I said I'd meet Sally to help out at the Mission Hall this afternoon.'

'Don't you want to give me a hand in the garden?' Father sounded hurt. 'Your mother used like sowing seeds on a sunny day.'

I'm not Mother, Meg answered silently. She felt disloyal because she knew how much he had loved her mother. She had loved her just the same and, even two years after her loss, whenever she thought about her a tear threatened. Meg made an effort to pull herself together. Why don't I tell him about Jacob? she thought. She knew the answer. Because there's nothing to say yet, and there never will be if I can't get out and meet him on a Sunday.

'Isn't Sally walking out with a young man?' Father queried.

'She is. Robert's a clerk in the municipal offices.'

Father nodded with approval. 'She's done well for herself.'

Meg cheered up at this comment. At least Father would approve of Jacob. He'd been at the grammar school with Robert and now he worked in a lawyer's office in Leeds. But in the summer he came out to this part of the Dales on the railway train every Sunday, even when it rained.

'They won't want you tagging along, will they?' Father added.

13

'Robert will be cycling with the Clarion Club until teatime.' So will Jacob, she thought and dreamed for a moment about seeing his smiling tanned face and bright blue eyes later in the day.

'There'll be a Clarion Club in every town soon,' Father commented.

'Well, so many folk have bicycles nowadays. Sally and I have been asked to help with the teas at the Mission Hall. They're busy on a Sunday afternoon now the days are longer.'

'Haven't you enough to do here, after a week at the mill?'

More than enough, Meg thought. She never grumbled as a rule. Sally had been taken on at the mill at the same time as her, straight after they'd left school. They had to work long hours but the money was good and sometimes they got best-quality cloth cheaper than from the market because the loom had produced a flaw in the bolt and it couldn't be sold to a warehouse. Meg made most of her own clothes and was looking forward to wearing her new blouse this afternoon.

'We are raising money for the chapel roof,' she explained. He couldn't argue with that, she thought.

But he sounded disgruntled. 'I see. What time will you be back?'

Meg's heart sank. She decided to stand her ground. Father would have to get his own tea today. 'I don't know. We might go for a walk by the river afterwards.' With Robert and Jacob, she added silently.

Father made a grunting noise in his throat and Meg hoped he wasn't going to be difficult. She

14

stifled her mounting impatience and went on, 'I've made your favourite lemon-curd tarts. I'll leave them on the kitchen table under a teacloth. There's a full kettle on the range and I've put the tea in the pot ready for you.'

'You've made up your mind then.'

'Don't be like that, Father. I don't go out in the week. By the time I've walked home from the mill, cooked a meal and tidied round, it's too late to do anything else.' Not that there was anywhere exciting to go in their small market town, Meg thought. Her life revolved around working at the mill and looking after Father.

Nonetheless, she felt guilty. Father was lonely without Mother and he suffered more on a Sunday because it had been their family day together for over thirty years. He saw no reason to change the habits of a lifetime, and neither had Meg until Jacob came along.

'It'll be Sunday afternoon on my own again,' he muttered.

Meg didn't know what to say to cheer him. She stood up before she weakened. 'I'll just go and get changed then and I'll be off.'

She put on her Sunday-best skirt in a lovely maroon colour and shoes with heels, and then piled her long fair hair up under a jaunty little hat adorned with a maroon ribbon, sticking it firmly in place with a couple of her mother's hatpins. She had wanted to look like a Gibson Girl since she had seen a sketch and article in a journal. It was a popular fashion with all the young women at the mill. Meg had spent her evenings making an intricate white blouse with a high neck, a

15

pleated tailored bodice and full sleeves with deep fitted cuffs. Satisfied with her appearance she went down to the kitchen, picked up a tin box tied with string and called cheerio to her father in the back garden. He didn't reply.

Sally was waiting for her outside the Mission Hall. Until now, Meg had not been to the Mission Hall as regularly as this since before she started work. When she was little, her parents used to take her and her brothers every Sunday afternoon for an hour's Sunday school. Father believed strongly in education and was proud that neither of his boys would be a quarryman like he was. Now, her eldest brother, Charley, was married and had gone to work in the Canadian office of the White Star Line. Albert, her other brother had talked of a new India office in his last letter. It suddenly occurred to Meg that Father was not only missing her mother, but also his sons. Another pang of guilt at leaving him on his own tugged at her heart.

Sally wore a Gibson Girl blouse too, but her skirt was dark blue. 'The hall isn't open yet. What's in the tin?' she asked.

'I made a few tarts for Robert and – and Jacob, if he's here.' He'd said he would be but, even so, Meg was nervous and her stomach was churning.

'Oh, he will be. Robert says he's quite taken by you.'

'Really?' Meg felt a thrill of anticipation run down her back. Jacob belonged to a different Clarion Club from Robert, but this little market town in the heart of the Yorkshire Dales was popular with cyclists escaping grimy towns and

16

cities in search of fresh air. In summer, the early train from Leeds was packed and the guard's van full of bicycles.

'I saw a notice in the post office about setting up a Clarion Club for girls,' Meg commented. 'Are you interested?'

'Not really. I was going to tell you later. I'll be moving to Leeds. Robert's landed a job with the Corporation and found us a house to rent so we are definitely getting married this summer.'

'Oh, how exciting! You are lucky.' Meg was really pleased for Sally and Robert. But she would miss her friend at the mill. First her family and now her friends were moving away.

'You should join, though,' Sally suggested.

'I haven't got a bicycle.'

'I'm sure you can find one languishing in somebody's wash house.'

Meg warmed to the idea. 'And I can easily run up a divided skirt with that wool worsted from the market.'

'Like Mrs Dawson,' Sally giggled, 'pedalling along the High Street.'

'Ssshh, she'll be here in a minute.' Meg looked around for the lady in charge of teas at the Mission Hall on Sundays and commented, 'She's late with the key this week.'

Sally wandered away, scanning the fells basking in hazy sunshine for a sign of the cyclists on their way back. Meg lapsed into thought and wondered what her father would think. Lady bicyclists were considered, at best, to have independent ideas or, at worst, to be radicals or suffragists. But a bicycle would be really useful to her. She could get home

17

from the mill quickly and be able to carry home end-of-the-day bargains from the market. She wondered how much she would have to pay for one. She caught up with Sally and said, 'I think I might see if I can find a second-hand bicycle. Will you ask around for me?'

'Robert might know somebody.'

'Where have they gone today?'

'Swallowdale.'

'Oh, not too far, then. Here's Mrs Dawson at last. She's pushing her bicycle; she must have a flat tyre.'

A group of Mrs Dawson's Mission ladies had gathered and waited patiently while she wheeled her bicycle and its heavily laden handlebar basket around the back. She stowed it safely in the scullery before returning to open the front entrance. Mrs Dawson was limping, Meg realised as she followed the last of the ladies into the hall and placed her tin box on the floor by the small stage. She and Sally set to work arranging trestle tables and wooden benches in long rows ready for the ramblers and cyclists. It was hard work so the older ladies were glad of their help. Besides, Mrs Dawson wouldn't let 'young girls' near the food and drink preparation. Meg heard her giving orders to her helpers. One of the older ladies came over with cleaning cloths to wipe down the tables.

'It's not like Mrs Dawson to be late,' Meg commented.

'She's got a bad knee,' the lady said. 'She had to push her bicycle all the way here. The doctor says she's got to ease up a bit.'

'Do you mean she will give up her Mission

18

work?' Meg had thought that Mrs Dawson was a permanent fixture on the ladies' committee.

'It's time somebody else had a chance to run things.' The lady's tone was critical. 'We felt sorry for her. She came back home as a widow to look after her ailing sister. When the sister passed away she had empty days to fill so we invited her on to the committee and now she's taken over. We were glad to have her at first, but you can have too much of a good thing.'

'I suppose she's lonely,' Meg said. 'Where are her children?'

'She doesn't have any.'

'Oh, that's a shame.'

Mrs Dawson had taken up her position at a small table by the door to take the money when walkers and cyclists clattered in, hungry and thirsty from their outing. Her selected servers stood behind a wooden counter making up the enamel plates of potted-meat sandwiches, buttered scone and fairy cake or jam tart, baked at home by Mrs Dawson and her chosen helpers.

When the hall was ready, Sally went outside to look for Robert. Meg followed her to the door and asked, 'What shall I do next, Mrs Dawson?'

'Go and help with the copper in the back. If the water's ready you can fill the teapots.' She stared at her for a moment before adding, 'You don't want to be spoiling that nice blouse. You'll find a clean pinny in my bicycle basket.'

'Thank you, Mrs Dawson.'

The big enamelled teapots were so heavy when full of water that they had extra handles above the spout for lifting. Meg put coal on the fire

19

underneath the copper and added more water from the pump at the sink. Then she took off her apron and went to stand with the other ladies behind the counter in the hall.

She scanned the benches for Jacob. Sure enough, he was sitting with Robert, enjoying his tea. He noticed her and waved. Meg's heart somersaulted and she waved back. Sally sidled up beside her and murmured, 'He's here, then.' Meg felt a tingle of pleasure run down her spine. She remembered their first meeting outside this very hall.

Robert had introduced Jacob to his fiancée and her friend and Meg was immediately attracted to Jacob. They had chatted about the villages he'd cycled through, which Meg knew well. Jacob was handsome and sociable with dark hair and bright blue eyes that crinkled at the corners when he smiled. He had told her that he had a position in a legal office but that was all she knew about him, except that she'd taken an instant liking to him. He'd said how much he loved Deepdale and they had discussed whether the railway was a good thing or not for the Dales.

Mrs Dawson distracted Meg from her dreaming as she arrived at the counter with her cash box ready to take money from those who were hungry enough for a second round of tea. Jacob rose to his feet and came over. He handed payment for two more teas to Mrs Dawson and scanned the remaining plates. 'Any more with lemon-curd tarts?' he asked.

'Lemon-curd tarts?' Mrs Dawson queried. She appeared to be offended. 'I didn't ask for lemon-curd tarts. We don't do them as a rule.'

'Oh!' Meg exclaimed. 'I left them in a tin...' She looked around quickly for her tin, which she spied under the counter, opened and empty. 'Oh,' she repeated, 'they were mine, Mrs Dawson. I made them for my father's tea and – and – I brought some with me.' She looked at Sally, who had put her hand over her mouth to stifle her giggles.

Jacob smiled at the row of ladies in front of him and went on, 'They were very good. We both said so. May we have them again next week?'

'We'll see,' Mrs Dawson replied, handing him two plates with sandwiches, scone and a jam tart.

'I'll bring your mugs of tea over,' Sally volunteered, and went to talk to Robert.

'The lemon-curd tarts did look very nice,' one of the Mission ladies commented.

'I made the lemon curd myself,' Meg added.

'I suppose you want paying for them?' Mrs Dawson answered.

'Well, no, not really, they were for...' She stopped.

'You have to be paid for the ingredients now they've been sold,' Mrs Dawson stated. 'How many did you bring?'

'A dozen.' Jacob was in lodgings and she'd thought he might take them on the train back to Leeds.

Mrs Dawson opened her cash box and began to count out coppers.

'No, honestly, Mrs Dawson, I don't want paying for them.'

'The Mission always pays it way.'

'Well – er – well...' Meg's mind was racing.

21

'Actually you could do me a favour instead.'

'What kind of favour?' Mrs Dawson sounded defensive.

Meg looked at her expectant face. 'I'm looking for a second-hand bicycle. Do you know anybody with one for sale?'

'For you?' Mrs Dawson asked.

'Yes. We might be having a girls' cycling club here.'

'Indeed?' Mrs Dawson appeared to approve. 'I'm thinking of selling mine. The doctor says I have to get rid of it.'

'Can I have a look at it, Mrs Dawson?'

'It's worth more than a dozen lemon-curd tarts, my girl.'

'Oh yes, of course. I didn't mean–' Meg began.

'You'll have to wait until I've had my committee meeting after we've done. Go for a walk or something.'

Oh dear, she would be late home and Father would be wondering where she was. But she wanted a bicycle. 'All right, Mrs Dawson,' she replied and went over to join her friends.

Later, Jacob suggested that he and Meg take a different path from Sally and Robert. He leaned his bicycle against a stone wall and turned his face to the sun. 'You're lucky to live in these parts.'

'There's not much work though,' Meg commented.

'I know, but I wish I still lived here.'

'Are you from round here, then?'

'My father is gamekeeper up on Ferndale Moor. I used to help him in my school holidays.'

'Weren't you at the grammar school with Robert? Ferndale is a long way from the grammar school.'

He smiled at her – she adored his smile – and continued, 'I had lodgings in the week. I'd won a scholarship, you see.'

'Good for you.' Meg had inherited her father's admiration for learning. 'They said that I could have gone on to the girl's high school if I wanted.'

'Didn't you want to?'

'I did actually,' she said. She remembered her excitement when the headmaster had asked to speak with her father and her disappointment when Mother explained that it would cost too much money. She had accepted Father's decision at the time but now she experienced an unusual sense of frustration that she was stuck in this town working at the mill for ever. She added, 'But I have two brothers and they came first.'

'That's a pity.'

Yes it is, she thought, and liked him for saying so. She said, 'Well, if I had gone to the high school I wouldn't have met Sally in the mill,' and smiled.

'Or me,' he added seriously.

That cheered her and she thought again how much she liked Jacob. 'I have to go back to the hall before Mrs Dawson locks up,' she said. 'She might be selling her bicycle and I want one.'

'Is that so? Which model is it?'

'I don't know.'

'Well, how much does she want for it?'

'I don't know.'

'You'd better let me take a look at it for you.'

'Would you?'

'Of course I would. Although I reckon Mrs Dawson will have bought the best, don't you?'

'Probably,' she agreed with a grin.

'Come on then, let's go back.' Jacob pushed his bicycle with one hand and offered Meg his free arm. She linked hers with his and it felt comfortable.

But Meg stopped suddenly when they approached the Mission Hall as she recognised a familiar figure talking to a couple of the Mission ladies' husbands. They were waiting for the committee meeting to finish.

'Oh dear,' Meg muttered with a sinking heart. Surely he could have spent his Sunday afternoon without her? She hoped he wasn't going to make a fuss just as she and Jacob were getting on so well. 'My father's here,' she said.

Chapter 2

'Really? Where?' Jacob's alert eyes followed Meg's gaze.

'Over there with the others.' Reluctantly she unhooked her arm from Jacob's and said, 'Wait here.'

'Why? I should like to meet him.'

'He doesn't know about you yet.'

'Don't you think he ought to, then?'

Jacob looked hurt so she rushed on: 'I don't want to upset him. Oh, I'm sure he'll take to you but it's just that he – he depends on me so much since Mother died and he misses her. He doesn't want me going out on a Sunday. He's lonely, you see.'

Jacob didn't look pleased with her little speech but he appeared to accept it and said, 'I'll wait here for you.'

Meg gave him a grateful smile. She didn't want her father to blame Jacob in any way for keeping her out. It was very important to her that Father approved of him. 'I'll see what he wants,' she said and quickened her step. It wasn't that she didn't wish Father to meet him. It's just that she would like to prepare him first. But there was no sense in avoiding it now, because everyone at the Mission Hall had seen her with Jacob so she had to tell Father about him before anybody else did.

'Hello, Father.'

Her father turned round. 'I thought something had happened to you.'

'Is everything all right?'

'The house is so empty without you. I wondered where you were.'

Meg suppressed a sigh and raised a smile. 'I'm on my way home now. I was just waiting to have a word with Mrs Dawson. She's the lady in charge.' Meg looked around for her and saw Jacob approaching slowly. He stopped a few yards away, caught her eye and began to examine his bicycle chain.

One or two ladies wandered out of the hall, called cheerio and left. The next one headed straight for her husband and said, 'Mrs Dawson's giving up the chair at last.' They linked arms and walked off with their heads together.

'Where is this Mrs Dawson, then?' Father asked.

'She'll be locking up. She wants to sell her bicycle and I was thinking of buying it.'

'What do you want a bicycle for?'

'Well, for–' Meg stopped as Mrs Dawson came round the corner of the hall with her bicycle. 'Here she is now.'

Father frowned in the sunlight. 'Who did you say she was?'

'Mrs Dawson.'

'I know that face.' Father gazed at Mrs Dawson. 'She's Edith Braithwaite that was. Bossy Braithwaite we used to call her. What's she doing here?

'She's in charge of the ladies' committee.'

'Aye, that sounds like her, right enough. Come on, Meg lass, let's be off before she sees you.' Father took hold of her arm and propelled her forward.

'Oh, but I've been waiting to have a look at her bicycle,' Meg protested.

'You don't want a bicycle.'

Yes I do, she thought, so I can get home much quicker from the mill to put your tea on.

'Look sharp, lass.' Father twisted his head to look back as he propelled her forwards. 'She's talking to that big lad who was hanging about. Bicycles are for lads anyway.'

'It's a girls' bicycle,' Meg commented, turning to look for herself. They were out of earshot but, short of calling out to Jacob and making a show of herself, Meg felt helpless. The last thing she wanted was a scene outside the Mission Hall giving the wrong impression of Jacob to her father.

'What happened to Sally?' Father asked.

'She and Robert went home.'

'So why didn't you?'

'I told you! I wanted a closer look at Mrs Dawson's bicycle.'

'I'll not have you hanging about places like this on your own. Folk'll get the wrong idea and you never know what types have come out for the day from Leeds.'

'Mrs Dawson used to live in Leeds,' Meg said pointedly.

'Don't get cheeky with me,' he replied. 'You know what I mean.'

Yes she did, and whilst she appreciated that her father cared for her welfare, she felt stifled by his presence. She was nineteen, not nine, and quite capable of taking care of herself. She walked on patiently working out that if she settled Father at home with a cup of tea she could hurry down to the railway station and see Jacob before he went back to Leeds. 'How do you know Mrs Dawson?' she asked.

'We went to the same school when we were nippers, same as everybody else around here.'

'Is that all?'

Father's boots crunched on the dry stony ground as he quickened his step. 'I'm parched. Let's get home and put the kettle on.'

Meg knew better than to press him further. She'd find out why he was reluctant to answer some other time. Her concern at the moment was to get to the station before Jacob's train left. Twenty minutes later, she poured Father a second cup of tea and said, 'I'm just going to run down to the railway station to see if Sally is seeing Robert off.'

'Doesn't he bicycle home?'

'It's twelve miles, Father, and the Leeds train stops at his station.'

'Don't be long.'

'Oh, I might go back to Sally's after and say hello to her mother.'

'What time's supper then?'

'Will half past seven be all right?'

'Aye, I'll do a bit more in the garden.'

Meg heaved a sigh of relief. Everything was back to normal for Father so he was contented. She went upstairs to tidy her appearance and dab on some scent.

Jacob was waiting for her at the top of Station Hill and she ran to meet him. 'How did you know I'd get away?'

'I didn't. I just hoped but I would have waited until I heard the train whistle at the junction.'

'I'm sorry about my father. He worries about me when I'm out on my own. Thanks for coping with Mrs Dawson for me.'

'It's a good bicycle and it's worth what she wants for it. I asked her to give you first refusal.'

'Oh, did you? Thank you, Jacob.' His broad smile melted her heart and she so much wanted to kiss him that it hurt.

'I can lend you the money if you like,' he added.

'There's no need for that. I'm well paid at the mill and there is very little to spend it on in Deepdale.'

He put his head on one side and gazed at her.

Then he took her arm gently and drew her into the shade of yew hedge. 'May we say goodbye here? The platform will be crowded today.'

A thrill of anticipation ran through Meg. Did he want to kiss her? She hoped so.

'I won't be with the Clarions next Sunday,' he said. 'I am overdue a visit to see my parents.'

Meg's disappointment must have shown on her face because he went on quickly, 'I can cycle up to Ferndale from here so I'll be on the early train as usual.' He looked tense, she thought.

'Shall I meet you when you arrive?' she asked.

His face relaxed a little. 'Please. And will you tell your father about me? I really like being with you, Meg, and I want to talk to my parents about you.'

'We haven't known each other very long,' Meg cautioned.

'I don't need any longer to know that you're the girl for me.'

'Oh.' Her heart turned over. She had hardly dared hope that his interest in her might be so deep. 'I feel the same about you. I haven't met anyone like you before.'

His smile returned and he let out a light sigh. 'I thought so. We're meant to be together. I shall ask my mother to invite you for tea at Ferndale.'

'I should like that.' She thought of how she would break her good news to Father and added, 'We don't need to rush things though, do we?'

'Well, no, but I may be moved on from the Leeds office later this year.'

Meg's eyes rounded. She was unsure of what to think except that this did seem to be rushing

29

things. 'What do you mean? Where will you go?'

'Oh heck, I wasn't going to say anything until I had spoken with my parents about it. It's not certain yet but it's an opportunity for me to get on and I want you to be part of it. I love you, Meg.'

His beautiful blue eyes penetrated hers with a longing that she realised matched her own.

'Jacob, I love you too. You are everything I have ever wished for in a man.'

He glanced around. 'No one's about,' he said. 'May I kiss you?'

He didn't wait for an answer and Meg's knees were in danger of buckling underneath her as he lifted her chin and covered her mouth with his. The fluttering inside her made her legs tremble until she felt his arms encircle her body and hold her close. He had kissed her before, on the station platform amongst a chattering public clamouring with bicycles and haversacks. This was different. This was a deep and passionate capture of her mouth and mind. She was so close to Jacob's body, so aware of his strength and resilience. Her hands explored the breadth of his shoulders and narrowness of his waist. He pressed her soft and pliant form against his so that she was in no doubt that she aroused his masculine need. Thrilled and frightened at the same time, she knew what this meant and was relieved they were in a public place for she realised that she could never refuse him. She loved him and she wanted him to love her in return.

He was breathing deeply and tracing the shape of her back and waist. His hands found the curve of her breasts and she groaned. He released her suddenly and stepped away. His eyes had darkened and there was a flush on his cheeks. Meg's face burned so she guessed she looked the same. 'You want me as much as I want you,' he murmured.

Meg couldn't speak. She nodded her head, wide-eyed and breathless.

He grasped her again, holding her head against his chest and nuzzled her hair. 'How shall I wait until next week before I see you again? My parents must know how much I love you. I shall insist that I take you with me when I visit next month.'

Meg wished she could quell the thumping of her heart and find her voice. She heard the steam whistle of the train as it approached the old turnpike crossing. And then the distant rattle of metal wheels on metal tracks. Only a few more moments of bliss!

He bent forward and gave her another briefer kiss. 'I hate saying goodbye to you. It is such a long time before I can see you again.'

A cold hand clutched at Meg's heart. 'W-why is that?'

'It's a whole week until next Sunday. I wish you lived in Leeds.'

'So do I,' she replied, but it might as well have been Canada for any hopes that she harboured.

'Goodbye, my beautiful Meg, until next week.'

'Next week,' she croaked at last and watched him wheel away his bicycle and mount it for the last hundred yards to the station. It was several minutes before she felt recovered enough to walk back to prepare her father's Sunday supper.

The following week Meg tried, several times, to find the right moment to tell her father about Jacob. But he worked long hours at the quarry and if he was in a talkative mood after eating he took himself off to the local inn for a glass or two of beer. On Saturday, the quarry shut early at one o'clock and Father came home for dinner calling in at his favourite shops on the way for a few weekend treats. Meg finished at the same time at the mill and she had continued her mother's practice of calling at the fish fryer in town and buying battered cod and chips for dinner. As she hurried home with her hot newspaper parcel she rehearsed what she would say about Jacob.

When they had eaten, her father sat back with the remains of a glass of bottled beer and said, 'I called in at the butcher as usual. You'll find a piece of belly pork in the meat safe for tomorrow.'

'That's nice. What have we from the garden to go with it?'

'I'll have a look in a minute. You're not going to the Mission again tomorrow, are you?'

Well, Jacob wouldn't be there, but she could still give Mrs Dawson a helping hand with the teas and make her an offer for her bicycle. However, there was a mild pleading in Father's tone that made her hesitate and she replied, 'Not if you don't want me to.'

'You want to watch that Edith Braithwaite, she'll have you doing all sorts for her if you're not careful.'

'Mrs Dawson, you mean? I don't mind when

it's for a good cause. Mother taught me how to stand up for myself.'

'Aye, your mother had her head screwed on all right, especially with the likes of Edith Braithwaite.'

'Did Mother know her?'

'We were all the same age.'

'Mrs Dawson didn't work at the mill, did she?'

'Not her. She got a bit above herself and went off to Leeds to work in one of them big shops. You wouldn't do that to me, would you, Meg love?'

Meg didn't know how to reply as several scenarios that might involve her moving to Leeds tumbled through her head.

Luckily for her, Father had more to say and went on, 'D'you know, I never thought I'd get over losing your mother like that. And I don't think I ever would have done without you, Meg love. What with the boys doing so well and moving away, I've only got you now.'

Meg gave him a nervous smile and wished he hadn't brought up her mother's death. 'I miss her too, Father,' she said.

'You've got me, haven't you? We've got each other. That's what families are all about, aren't they: being there for each other?'

'Yes, Father,' she agreed and realised that with Father in this mood she would have to wait until another time to tell him about Jacob. And, Meg admitted, there was some truth in what he had said about Edith Dawson. She added, 'I won't go to the Mission tomorrow. I can help you in the garden instead.'

Father beamed at her fondly and finished his glass of beer. 'That'll be grand. You're a good lass to me, Meg love. Your mother always said you would be. Even when she was taken right badly she told me I hadn't to worry. She told me that you'd always be here for me.'

Meg remembered how her mother had fretted when she was too poorly to look after the house. It was all a blur now because Meg's overriding memory was one of distress that she was going to lose her darling mother. Towards the end, the mill gave her time off to nurse her mother and neighbours rallied round to help. Even then Mother's main concern was that Father's dinner would be on the table when he came in from the quarry, and that his shirt collars were pressed and his shoes polished. *He's a foreman now, Meg, and he has a standard to keep up*, her mother had said.

'Don't fret yourself, Mother,' Meg had assured her, 'I'll look after him.'

He'll be lost without me. Promise you'll look after him, Meg. Promise me.

'Of course I promise you,' Meg had replied. It had not occurred to her at the time that this meant for ever, as long as Father was alive. But what else could it mean? Who else was there to look after him? She was his only daughter and it was her duty. She had given her promise and her dying mother had expected her keep it.

But that was before she knew Jacob and when she met him from the early train the following day, his first anxious question after he had kissed her was, 'Did you tell him?'

'I'll do it today,' she replied.

He smiled and placed his arm around her shoulders, giving them a gentle squeeze as he pushed his bicycle up Station Hill.

'Which train are you catching tonight?'

'Oh, it'll be the usual one. I don't want to be too late back to my lodgings.'

'You'll be spending more time on your bicycle than with your parents.'

'My father is meeting me with a horse on the edge of the Ferndale estate. It'll be better suited for crossing the moor. Can you ride a horse?'

'I've never tried. I don't know if I can ride a bicycle yet either,' Meg laughed.

'Well, make an offer for Mrs Dawson's soon or you'll never know.' He kissed her lightly, checked a few things on his bicycle and placed one foot on a pedal. 'Will I see you tonight?'

'I'll wait for you by the yew hedge.'

'That'll spur me on.' He leaned towards her, kissed her again and pushed off, heading towards the old packhorse route to Ferndale.

She watched him until he was obscured from view by the crowd of ramblers and bicyclists streaming away from the railway station. Then she took a short deep breath and walked home with a firm purpose in her mind. I'll tell Father at teatime, she thought, after a couple of hours in the garden when he's sitting down with a pot of tea and my own scones freshly baked this morning. She'd tell him why she was going to the station and leave him to ponder as she went to meet Jacob.

The garden needed both of them, Meg thought

as she and Father tackled weeds between the vegetable rows. She sat on her heels and wiped her brow with the back of her hand. The sun was already sinking in the sky but it was still warm. Gosh! It must be way past teatime! Most of her neighbours had gone indoors. She stood up quickly and dusted down her sacking apron. 'Cup of tea, Father?' she asked.

'I'll just finish this row,' he replied.

'Don't be long then,' Meg called as she went into the scullery to scrub her hands.

She cleaned herself up, put on a fresh blouse and was going downstairs when she heard a knock at front door. A smartly dressed lady holding the handlebars of a bicycle stood outside.

'Mrs Dawson?'

'Good afternoon, Meg.'

'Good afternoon. How is your knee?'

'Much better now I've given up this thing, thank you. I'm sorry you couldn't stay to talk last week and you weren't at the Mission today so I've brought my bicycle here to show you. The young man last week asked if I would give you first refusal.'

'Oh, well, yes, that's very kind of you but' – she glanced over her shoulder – 'it's not really convenient today. My father–'

'That will be Albert, won't it? Albert Parker. I thought I recognised him last week. Is he in?'

'He's in the garden.'

'Splendid. I'll wheel this round the back. I expect he wants to take a look at it for you.'

'Oh, he was just finishing...'

But Mrs Dawson was already pushing her

bicycle down the road to the end of the cottages where she could walk round to the gardens. Meg bit her lip, made the tea and put out an extra cup and saucer and tea plate on the kitchen table. Then she hurried outside to find her father standing with his mouth open in the middle of his vegetable patch and Mrs Dawson wheeling her bicycle up the garden path. He glared at Meg but didn't follow Edith.

'Tea's made, Father,' she called as cheerily as she was able.

'What a pretty cottage and garden you have here, my dear. How cosy it is for the two of you. Shall I leave this here?' She leaned her bicycle against the wash-house wall. 'I have to get rid of it, you know: doctor's orders.'

'My father isn't totally convinced I need it, I'm afraid.'

'You leave him to me, my dear. I shall persuade him.'

'Oh, I don't think you will. I mean, he doesn't know you very well, does he?'

'Of course he does! We grew up together in Deepdale.' She clasped her hand to her throat. 'Oh dear, he probably hasn't told you. He won't mind, you can take my word on that.'

'If you say so.' Meg was torn between her father's opinion of Mrs Dawson and her certain knowledge that if anyone could persuade her father of the value of a bicycle to a twentieth-century young woman it would be Mrs Dawson. 'Will you come in for some tea?'

The clock chimed the hour as her father came through from the scullery, suitably cleaned up for a visitor and thankfully on his best behaviour. Meg would have to leave within the next five minutes or she would miss Jacob. She poured the tea, handed round the scones and passed the butter and jam. Father cooperated in silence and without a smile for anyone.

'Father, I should be really grateful if you would take a look at Mrs Dawson's bicycle. It would be very useful for me to get to and from the mill and bring home shopping from the market.'

'Bicycles are for boys,' he responded.

'Oh dear me no, Albert,' Mrs Dawson replied. 'They are for everyone these days. When I lived in Leeds–'

Meg interrupted by standing up to add more hot water to the teapot. 'Father, I just have to go out for half an hour.'

'Go out? Now? Where?' The look of shock – or was it fear? – on his face, made her waver.

'The – the station.'

'What for?'

'S-Sally will be there seeing Robert on to his train. I shan't be long. Will you wait for me, Mrs Dawson?'

'Of course, dear.' Mrs Dawson picked up a scone laden with butter and jam and smiled at Meg's father. 'Oh my, this jam is lovely, Albert, and I know my jam. Are the raspberries from those canes I saw out there?'

Meg's father was proud of all his garden produce and, for a moment, seemed to forget his fear. 'Indeed they are, Edith. I had a good crop last year. They are a new strain...'

Meg saw her opportunity and slipped out

38

through the front door before Father had a chance to stop her. She felt so guilty at leaving him with someone he detested that she almost turned back. But she didn't, because she could see Jacob waiting by the yew hedge scanning the road for her and probably wondering what had become of her. He came towards her as soon as he saw her.

'What's happened? You looked flushed. You've not had a row, have you?'

Not yet, Meg thought but said, 'Mrs Dawson's visiting! She arrived with her bicycle. I – I've left her having tea with Father and he can't stand her.'

'She was asking me about you and your father last week.'

'Was she? What did she want to know?'

'I think she just wanted to confirm he was the Mr Parker she knew as a girl.'

'Is that all?'

'Not exactly. She asked whether there was a Mrs Parker in the household.'

Meg closed her eyes in horror. 'He'll never forgive me for leaving him alone with her. Jacob, I have to get back straightaway.'

'The train will be here soon, anyway. Look, you will buy the bicycle, won't you? I can't get over next Sunday but' – his blue eyes danced with joy – 'my parents have asked me to take you to visit them quite soon and we could cycle up to Ferndale together.' He grasped her shoulders and squeezed them. 'They want to meet you, Meg. Isn't that wonderful?'

Meg caught her breath. Jacob must be sure about his feelings to take this step forward in their relationship. 'Yes it is. You don't think you are rushing things with them, do you?'

'Maybe.' He shrugged, but his excitement could not be dampened. 'I'm over twenty-one and I have a proper salary with – with a future.' His eyes began to shine as he went on, 'This is just the beginning for us, Meg. I want you to be part of my life. You want that too, don't you?'

'You know I do.' But her own excitement was marred by wondering what it would mean for Father. This wasn't just about leaving him alone on a Sunday. Jacob's office was in Leeds, like Robert's, and there was no question about Sally moving there after her wedding.

Jacob picked up on her caution. 'You do love me, don't you?'

Do I ever, she thought. She worshipped him and sometimes her body ached with a desire to match his. 'I love you more than I can say,' she whispered, reaching up to wind her arms around his neck and adding, 'Kiss me, my love.'

He did not need an invitation and their mouths and bodies locked with the deep and increasingly familiar passion that she craved. He was breathless when his lips left hers and he whispered, 'It'll be two weeks before I see you again. Dear God, how will I survive?' His voice was hoarse and his eyes were fiery and she wished they could stay there holding each other for ever. Their bodies didn't separate until the steam whistle from the approaching train penetrated their fervour. Then he was gone, turning to give her one last wave before disappearing into the clamouring throng at the station.

Chapter 3

Meg ran all the way home and arrived, panting, at the front door. She took a few deep breaths and marched in purposefully to find Mrs Dawson sitting alone at the kitchen table. Through the kitchen window she could see her father inspecting the bicycle in the back yard.

'You persuaded him?' Meg asked.

'Seems so, doesn't it?'

'What did you say?'

'He's a man. They are all the same. You just have to point out to them how much nicer their life will be and they eat out of your hand.'

'Is that so?' She couldn't imagine her father eating out of Mrs Dawson's hand.

'You just tell them what they want to hear. It always works.'

Meg wasn't sure about that but she didn't argue. 'Well, if Father approves I'll buy it from you. Jacob told me how much you want for it.'

'Is that the young man's name? He's quite taken by you, isn't he?'

That's what Sally had said, Meg thought with amusement. 'Do you think so?'

'I know so, my dear. Don't let that one slip through your fingers, like I did your father.'

'I beg your pardon, Mrs Dawson?'

'He hasn't told you, has he? We were sweethearts when we were kids. Oh, don't look so

41

shocked. It was before my Arnold came on to the scene.'

But not before Mother, Meg thought, if they had all grown up together. 'As I said,' Meg responded, 'I want to buy your bicycle.'

Mrs Dawson nodded her agreement. 'Well, with you being Albert Parker's daughter, you can have it for less than I asked from that young man. And I've included my bicycling clothes. They're folded up in the basket.'

'Thank you, Mrs Dawson. That's very generous of you.'

Father came indoors, wiping his hands on an old rag. 'It's a good enough little machine. But you'll have to keep it in working order yourself. I'm not spending my Saturday afternoons mending your punctures.'

'Of course, Father.'

Mrs Dawson stood up. 'If that's agreed, then I won't keep you.'

'I'll get your money.' Meg dashed upstairs to the tin box she kept under the bed and counted out the notes and coins.

When she returned her father had gone out into the garden again and Mrs Dawson was watching him through the kitchen window. Meg paid up and showed Mrs Dawson to the front door. 'What will you do with yourself now you've come off the Mission committee?'

'I can fill my days well enough,' she replied lightly.

'Good luck.' Meg watched her walk off with only a trace of her limp. She did appear to be able to get her own way when she wanted. Meg could understand why some people didn't like her, especially when she started bossing them around. But, Meg thought, she seemed a cheerful soul and didn't appear to mind lending a hand.

Meg was smiling to herself at the way Mrs Dawson had changed her father's mind when he crashed into the back kitchen with his face like thunder and shouted, 'Don't you ever do that to me again!'

Meg was stunned. Father was normally a mild-mannered man. 'Do what, Father?' she asked.

'Leave me alone with *her*. She's a menace to mankind, that woman is.'

'Don't be silly. She means well.'

'Does she now? How do you know that?'

'She came all the way round here pushing that bicycle to show me.'

'Aye and she'll have her feet under the table before you can say "Jack Robinson". She always gets what she wants, does Edith Braithwaite, never mind anybody else.'

Meg had to agree but didn't say so. 'She's Edith Dawson now, Father.' His behaviour towards her was irrational and Meg guessed it was more to do with past history than her bicycle so she added, 'Anyway, what does it matter if others get what they want as well? Her bicycle is a bargain and now it's mine.'

Father let out an exasperated grunt and went back to his garden. He and Mrs Dawson must have parted on very bad terms all those years ago. She was surprised he still bore her a grudge and wondered again what had happened between them.

The bicycle was all Meg expected and she adored it. She soon learned to balance and pedalling became easier with practice. It gave her a little extra time and freedom without distracting her from her responsibilities at home. She made new clothes suitable for a lady bicyclist and had a fresh topic of conversation with the other women at the mill.

Christine at the mill had been a close friend of her mother, even though Christine was a few years younger. She had a large growing family of her own and had taken Meg under her 'mother-hen' wing at the mill after Meg's mother had died. Meg often wondered how Christine coped with her job at the mill as well as her husband and children. The following week, Meg asked Christine if she knew anything about her father and Mrs Dawson when she had been Edith Braithwaite.

'She was more my sister's age than mine,' Christine told her, 'but they talked about her a lot because she was so pretty and she had her pick of the lads. She was pushy too, always wanting the best for herself. Well, no one blamed her for that because a girl's got to think of her future and all the ambitious lads and lasses looked outside the mill and the quarry to get on. She set her cap at your father right enough, until she realised that he wouldn't budge from the quarry.'

'Mother always said he liked working there.' He still does, Meg thought.

'He didn't have the same drive as Edith but he couldn't see it for himself, so when she upped and married Arnold Dawson he was a broken man until your mother saw her chance and picked up

44

the pieces.'

'Oh, I didn't know that.'

'It was all a long time ago and a lot of water has gone under the bridge since then but I don't expect your father has forgotten.'

'No, he hasn't. He doesn't like Mrs Dawson at all.'

Christine put her head on one side and raised her eyebrows. 'Are you sure about that?'

'Yes,' Meg replied.

'Then I should keep a close eye on him when she's around if I were you,' Christine responded.

Meg was mildly offended by this apparent criticism of her daughterly concern and responded sharply, 'Well I always do. I promised Mother I would.'

Her Sunday at Ferndale with Jacob loomed large in her mind and she was at her wits' end thinking of what to say to Father about it. Meg had never once failed to cook her father his Sunday dinner since Mother had died. She considered asking Christine to invite him to theirs, but Christine already had a houseful. There was Sally's mum and if Sally and Robert were visiting her they would welcome him and speak well of Jacob. Satisfied that this seemed like a good solution, she focused her attention on making a bicycling skirt to go with her smart Sunday coat and hat to wear on the day.

The following weekend she gathered her courage and raised the subject over fish and chips and a bottle of beer on the Saturday.

'I've been invited to Ferndale for the day one Sunday.'

'Ferndale Lodge out on the moor? I know the mason there. He comes to the quarry for his stone.'

'Not the Lodge, Father. I'm going to the gamekeeper's cottage.'

'Who do you know from up there?'

'The gamekeeper's son was at the grammar school with Sally's Robert. They both belong to Clarion Clubs and go bicycling together.'

'Oh, well, you are Sally's best friend so it's nice of them to ask you. Is that what all this bicycle business is about?'

She was pleased he was concentrating on his dinner and did not see the guilty look on her face as she let his misunderstanding pass. 'Yes. Do you mind me going up there one Sunday?'

'It's a long way for an afternoon but you've got young legs.'

'Oh, I'll be out all day.'

'All day?' His tone was indignant. 'What'll you do about my dinner?'

'I'll arrange something for you. Sunday is the only day for visiting folk.'

'Aye. Your mother and me used to go for tea though.' She noticed Father frowning at her. 'I suppose it's about the wedding.'

'Wedding?'

'Aye, you said Sally was getting wed in the summer. Is this friend of Robert going to be his best man?'

The notion had never occurred to Meg. Sally and Robert didn't even know about her visit to see Jacob's parents and her mind raced. She didn't want to speak about Jacob while her father's mind

46

was on weddings! She coughed over a chip. 'I – I don't know but now you come to mention it...' She left his unanswered question hanging in the air and after a few seconds asked, 'Will you be all right on your own for a day?'

'I'll have to be, won't I? But I'll miss you. I've nobody else now so don't make a habit of it.'

'Of course not, Father.'

She had not exactly lied to him, Meg thought as she washed up later, but at least he knew that Jacob existed in her life. She tried not to feel guilty but she just wished Father hadn't mentioned Sally's wedding. It was her own fault for saying Jacob was a friend of Robert's instead of a friend of hers. Now she couldn't ask Sally's mother to give Father his Sunday dinner as he would find out about her – oh Lord – her deception. That's what it was, Meg thought, and she knew it could not go on.

The following Sunday she was meeting Jacob for tea at the Mission and she suggested that Father walk over to meet her as he had done before. She planned to introduce him to Jacob properly.

'Will that Edith Dawson be there?' he demanded.

'I expect so. She's not in charge any more but she likes the company.'

'I'll not bother, Meg love. I don't want her to get the wrong idea.'

Meg hid her surprise. After his behaviour when she brought the bicycle round and her comments to Meg she was perfectly sure that Mrs Dawson knew exactly how her father felt about her. 'Well, I want to meet Sally. I shan't see much of her after the wedding when she's living in Leeds.'

'Aye, Leeds is a long way from home for the likes of her. What will her poor ma do on her own?'

Sally's mother had been widowed for a long time and had brought up Sally by doing cleaning and washing in better-off households. She had an independent nature and was perfectly capable of looking after herself and filling her time usefully. Rather like Mrs Dawson, Meg thought. But no one expected a man on his own to look after himself. Wives did the cooking and laundry and housework. Or daughters, of course, Meg thought. Even if a man hadn't either, a widower on his own with a regular wage would soon find someone to marry him. However, Father wasn't living alone and Meg suddenly had a dreadful vision of spinsterhood as her father's housekeeper stretching out in front of her and it wasn't what she wanted. She had an idea and said, 'Why don't you go round and see Sally's mum one day?'

'What do I want to do that for?'

'You could take her some leeks from the garden.'

'She's very welcome to some of my leeks if she wants them. You can drop them round to her on your bicycle.'

Meg suppressed a sigh. 'I'll ask Sally, then,' she replied and gave up on the conversation.

On Sunday Jacob was very excited because his parents had written to confirm that his father and sister could get a whole Sunday off together and their visit was planned.

'We're going next week, Meg,' he enthused.

'We'll take the bicycles up to the edge of the moor, leave them in one of the hides and Father will meet us with a horse.'

'I – I've never ridden a horse,' Meg admitted.

'I'll take you on mine. You'll be quite safe. Have you got a waterproof cape in case it rains?'

'Mrs Dawson gave me hers.'

'That was good of her.'

There had been several items in the basket that Mrs Dawson no longer needed. Meg didn't mention the flannel bloomers, which had made her giggle when she unfolded them. But she had used the fabric to make a lining for her new bicycling skirt.

'Jolly good. Take a warm coat for the horse because it can get cold up there, even in summer.'

The following week went very slowly for Meg. On the Saturday she asked Father to bring a piece of brisket and got up very early on Sunday to leave it braising with vegetables in the bake oven. Father was already out in the garden, picking and cleaning fresh vegetables to take with her. He wrapped them in newspaper and placed them in her basket.

'Thank you, Father,' she said.

'Me and your mother always took something with us when we visited and they'll not grow much in that poor soil up on the moor.'

'There's apple pie and a fruit cake for you in the pantry.'

'Don't be late back.'

'No, Father.' She hurried off to meet Jacob from the train. Robert was with him but he was bicycling with the Clarions and meeting Sally later. Meg persuaded herself she had told only a half-lie to her father but it gnawed at the back of her mind until she and Jacob had left Deepdale behind and were climbing towards the mist that shrouded Ferndale Moor. Then she became increasingly apprehensive about meeting Jacob's family.

Mr Wright met them as arranged. He was tall and smartly dressed in tweeds and knee-high leather boots. Meg would have known they were father and son simply by looking at the pair of them together. He seemed pleased with the vegetables and tied them securely to his horse.

Jacob formed a stirrup with his hands so that Meg could hoist herself in the saddle. Thank goodness for her divided skirt, she thought. She shuffled forward to give him room to mount up behind her. While Mr Wright checked over the saddle fastenings and reins Jacob put his arms around her and whispered in her ear, 'Are you comfortable?'

'Yes, thank you.' She nodded. 'I hope you're not going to gallop,' she added.

'Maybe a canter,' he replied. His arms tightened about her as he took the reins from his father and urged his horse forward. 'Mmm,' he murmured appreciatively, 'this is nice.'

Yes, it was, she thought. She could feel every movement of his arms and body as he manoeuvred his horse skilfully along the moorland track. A bright sun burned away the mist and Jacob pointed out landmarks that Meg had heard of until the gamekeeper's cottage came into view. It was a substantial stone-built dwelling of two storeys and had a wide front door flanked by windows each side. Smoke curled up from the chimney until it was blown away by the cold east wind. The cottage had a barn and stables at the back but no garden of any sort in sight. Meg noticed that there were pretty lace curtains at all the windows. Beyond the outbuildings, and much nearer to Ferndale Lodge in the distance, a cluster of estate workers' cottages sheltered in a dip in the moorland.

Mr Wright helped Meg down and said, 'I'll stable the horses, Jacob. Take Meg inside out of this wind. Your mother and Ruth will be in the kitchen.'

'Who's Ruth?'

'She's my sister. I don't think I've said much about her to you yet.'

'No, you haven't,' Meg replied, wondering how old she was and what she was like. At least she would be closer to her own age than his parents.

The large square kitchen had a low ceiling with small windows and a mouth-watering smell of roasting meat. Mrs Wright emerged from a pantry with a mixing bowl covered by a teacloth in her hands. She placed it carefully on a scrubbed deal table and wiped her hands on a towel tucked into her apron ties. Jacob took Meg's elbow and pro-pelled her towards his mother.

'You must be Meg,' she said. She stared at her for a moment and appeared to approve. 'How do you do, dear,' she said.

'I'm very pleased to meet you, Mrs Wright. Thank you for inviting me.'

'You look a bit nithered. Jacob, the fire's going

51

in the parlour. Take Meg to warm up; your father has put out sherry in the dining room.'

'Will you have one, Mother?'

'Let me get the Yorkshires in first then I'll come through with your father.'

The parlour was another square low-ceilinged room with a large fireplace flanked by a couple of comfy sofas and chairs that had seen better days. 'Where's Ruth?' Jacob said to the empty room. 'I expect she's laying the table for dinner. Let's surprise her.' They went out into the hall and across to another room.

A polished dark wood table had been laid for dinner with polished cutlery and glass. The sherry was standing on a matching heavy wooden sideboard. It was beautiful furniture, much better than any Meg had seen in town. As she walked towards the fire she ran her fingers over the waxed surface.

'Lovely, isn't it? It came from Ferndale Lodge when they refurbished in the arts and crafts style. Mother prefers this old-fashioned dark furniture and looks forward to a chance to use it. Normally we'd eat in the kitchen.' He glanced around. 'No Ruth here either. She probably can't get away until later. She works up at the Lodge. Mother did too before she married Father.'

Meg stared at the relative opulence of her surroundings. Jacob's family were servants but compared to her own situation they were well off. 'Has your father always been a gamekeeper? she asked.

'Born and bred to it, here at Ferndale. Actually, he's more of his lordship's steward these days. He's got younger men keeping an eye on the land

and game. Let's go and have that glass of sherry.'

He poured Meg a sherry and then went to look out of the window. 'Here's Ruth now. She's walked down from the Lodge.'

Meg sat by the fire with her glass. 'I'm looking forward to meeting her.'

She was younger than Jacob and as pretty as he was handsome. At nineteen Ruth was the same age as Meg. She had a responsible position as head parlourmaid at the Lodge and held an ambition to be housekeeper one day. Over dinner she chatted on about their daily routines and how easy it was to keep an empty house in spotless condition. But when the grouse shooting started in August she would be forever cleaning up mud from floors, furnishings and linens. 'You'd think they'd know better than to keep their boots on indoors,' she said.

'Now then, Ruth, don't criticise your betters,' her father warned.

'I don't think they are our betters,' Ruth stated.

'Not at the dinner table, dear,' her mother responded.

'Why not? What do you think, Meg? Are they better than us because they were born richer?'

'I – I really don't know, I have never met anyone who is very rich.'

'You've never been in service?'

She shook her head. 'I'm afraid not.'

'What do you do then?'

'I work in the textile mill in Deepdale.'

Ruth stared at her and said, 'You're a mill girl? You didn't tell us that, Jacob.'

'Why should I?' Jacob replied.

'Well, because you're going to be a fancy lawyer.'

'Do be quiet, Ruth,' her mother interrupted. 'You really must learn to curb that tongue of yours if you want to be a housekeeper. Would anyone care for another roast potato?'

Meg exchanged a glance with Jacob and he smiled. She guessed it was to give her confidence but she didn't have a problem. She wasn't ashamed of her background. In fact she was proud of her family and what they had achieved. Like many modern young girls she agreed with Ruth that being rich didn't automatically make you any better than anyone else; or worse than them, for that matter. She wondered why Jacob had not mentioned being a lawyer before. Was this the new opportunity he had mentioned that was such a secret until it was settled? Why hadn't he told her about it? She had assumed his position in Leeds was similar to Robert's working for the Corporation.

When the meal was over, Meg volunteered to wash the pots, an offer that was accepted as long as Ruth helped her. Mrs Wright came in to help put away, then she made a pot of tea and laid a tray to carry into the parlour.

'How long have you worked at this mill?' Ruth asked Meg.

'I've been there since I left school. My mother worked there and she got me the job. I met my best friend Sally there.'

'But Jacob said you were clever. Didn't you want to do anything else?'

'There wasn't any choice where I live. It's a

good job.'

'But even so–'

Mrs Wright interrupted, 'Ruth, carry the tray in for me. I'll bring the teapot and Meg can take the hot-water jug. Jacob and his father are outside having a chat; I'll just give them a call.'

Meg volunteered to wait until the refilled kettle had boiled for extra hot water and Mrs Wright took Ruth into the parlour with her. The kitchen window was open and when Meg heard raised voices from outside she stood stock-still. They were talking about her.

'It pains me to say so, Jacob, because she is a lovely lass, but your sister has a point.' This was Mr Wright's voice. 'She's not for you. You're moving up in the world. You'll sup with gentry. Lawyers don't wed mill girls.'

'I'm not fully qualified yet.'

'It's only a matter of time. Life will be very different from here when you're in London. Does she know that?'

London? No, she doesn't know that, Meg thought.

'I haven't mentioned it yet.'

'Well, you'd best get on with it because it's a big step for a mill girl. Didn't you say she looks after her widowed father?'

'He's not an invalid! He's lonely, that's all. It's only two years since his wife died. He'll soon meet a widow of his own age.'

'It won't work, lad. You'll meet a different sort of girl in London, one with a bit more...'

'A bit more what?' Jacob sounded angry. 'Money? Connections? Breeding?'

'Don't raise your voice to me! I only want what's best for you.'

'And I want Meg! Can't you understand that?'

'Yes I can, but you're not thinking straight, lad. Your brains are in your trousers where she's concerned.'

Meg heard an exasperated sigh from Jacob and his father went on: 'Yes, I see from your face that I'm right. You're my only son, Jacob, and a chip off the old block. I can read you like a book. It's not that we don't like her. She's bright, I grant you, but she is only a mill girl.'

'I know she loves me.'

'Of course she does! You're a good catch for her! For God's sake, don't get her in the family way or you'll be ruined. She'll bring you down to her level and all that education will have been wasted.'

'If you weren't my father, I'd hit you for saying that.'

'Yes, well, the truth will hurt. But I mean it, my lad. If you take up with her, doors will close in your face and that will break your mother's heart.'

Meg felt her own heart beginning to thump with anxiety as the voices faded. Jacob's parents had been so kind to her! Yet all the time they disapproved of her. She couldn't face them. She sat down on a kitchen chair while the kettle bubbled away on the range.

Chapter 4

A few minutes later Jacob came into the kitchen looking for her. She jumped to her feet and grabbed a potholder for the kettle.

'I'll do it,' he said, picking up the hot-water jug. His face was angry.

'Is everything all right?' she asked.

'Family stuff,' he replied. 'We'll make a move straight after tea.'

She nodded in agreement. The visit hadn't turned out as well as either of them had expected and Meg had no idea what to say or do to make it right.

Their journey on horseback to the bicycles was silent and after saying their goodbyes to Jacob's father, they said little to each other until they reached the proper road though Deepdale.

'Why didn't you tell me about going to London to be a lawyer?' she demanded.

'It wasn't certain until quite recently. Have you got anything against lawyers?'

'Of course I haven't. I just wish you had told me sooner. I wasn't prepared for some of the things your family said.'

'Don't take any notice of Ruth.'

'It's still a lot to take in all at once.'

'Everything is happening quickly for me as well. But I wanted my family to meet you.'

'And approve of me,' she added and then

stated, 'Well, they don't. They don't like me at all.'

'They don't know you as well as I do. They'll come round.'

Meg turned down the corners of her mouth and shook her head slightly. 'They won't.'

'I don't need their blessing.'

'Yes you do. They are your parents, Jacob, and they have a point. You haven't been totally honest with me about what you do and what your future will bring.'

'Does it make you feel any differently about me?'

'Of course not! I love you, but–'

'But! Why is there a "but"? You either love me or you don't.'

'That's not fair! You ought to have told me about London.'

'I couldn't, at least not until I was sure.'

'But now you are.'

'Yes. They want me down there next month. Oh, do say you'll come with me, Meg. I need you to be there by my side.'

'You need me? What are you saying, Jacob?'

'Darling Meg, you know how much I love you. Do say you'll come.'

'Come as what, Jacob?'

His face distorted in pain. 'Oh, Meg, please try and understand. I'll still be learning and won't be able to afford a wife until I am qualified.'

'Come as what, Jacob?' she repeated in a raised voice.

He stared at her. 'Oh good Lord no, Meg, not that. I'm not asking you to be my *mistress!* I should never ask that of you. I simply want you to be with me in London. I don't mean live with me, not until we're married.' He stopped for a second to draw breath and then went on, 'You will marry me, won't you?'

'You know I will. There is nothing in the world I want more.'

He seemed relieved and his mouth descended towards her to kiss him. She pulled back from him and murmured, 'But I didn't know you were going to London.'

'I didn't know myself until recently, but I'm really looking forward to it. You can leave the mill and come with me! There are hostels for young ladies, or lodgings if you prefer, and you will easily find a post, a better one than the mill, in a store or even an office.'

Meg realised that Jacob had already given their future some thought. She was flattered but would have been more pleased if he had talked to her about it before they went to see his parents. She said, 'I'd need training for both those positions and there is nothing wrong with working in a mill. I have experience of mill work.'

He didn't reply and his silence echoed in her head as a death knell to their relationship. She searched his eyes for a glimmer of hope but there was none. 'You agree with your parents, don't you?' she went on. 'You don't have to say it. I can see it in your face. A mill girl does not make a suitable – a suitable wife for a lawyer.'

'You are only a mill girl because your mother was one before you and there is no other work for you to do in Deepdale! If you had gone to the high school you would be on your way to becoming a teacher by now!'

If, if, if! He was probably right but she was who she was and he had always known that. 'I'm sorry to disappoint you and your parents. I have never claimed to be anything other than a Deepdale mill girl.'

'But you could be anything you wanted.'

'No I couldn't! I can't just drop everything and do what I want!'

'Why not?'

'Because I have other people to consider.'

'What people?'

'My father. I can't abandon him. I am all he has. I'm his only daughter and it's my duty to look after him. He has no one else!'

Jacob looked shocked. 'What about me? What about our future together?'

'I thought it would be here, in Leeds.' Even the idea of moving to Leeds was giving Meg a problem. She wondered if it really had not occurred to Jacob that she, truly, was not in a position to leave home.

His mouth turned down at the corners. 'Surely your father is aware that one day you will marry?'

Meg hunched her shoulders. 'I don't know. Not yet, I suppose. It's too soon after losing Mother.'

Jacob frowned. 'You told me it was two years. He's not ill, is he?'

'No. But he does need me.'

'So do I, Meg. This is a big step for me as well as you and I've got to take it. I'm not likely to get such an offer again.' He began to plead with her: 'Meg, Meg, you said you loved me! I wouldn't have asked you if I weren't sure of that. I know you're the one for me! You have to come with me.'

If only it were that easy, Meg thought. How could she leave her father, who depended on her so much, to fend for himself? She couldn't, she simply couldn't. 'I can't go to London with you, Jacob,' she said. 'Please try and understand.'

He looked bewildered, as though he hadn't heard her properly. But he said, 'I understand well enough. You won't even talk to him about us! You are choosing your father over me.'

She inhaled to deny it, that it was not as straightforward as he thought, and found that she was unable to form the words. She loved them both but she had made a promise to her mother and she had a duty to her father. She let out a sigh and responded, 'Yes, I suppose I am.'

'Have you any idea how much that hurts me?'

Meg saw the rawness in his eyes and felt like crying herself. 'It hurts me too! I don't want to lose you.'

'Then find a way to come with me!'

She hunched her shoulders. If Father were rich he could afford a housekeeper. But even that wouldn't be the answer because another woman trying to be her mother would only upset him. He wanted Meg to look after him. It was so different in her mother's day when a daughter married a boy from their home town, and sometimes lived in the same road so they were never very far from their parents. Meg had no answer. 'I do love you, Jacob,' she said.

'Not enough, it seems,' he replied.

His words stung her to the core. 'That's not fair! You have to understand my situation!'

His face had darkened with despair. 'All I understand is that I love you and I am prepared to go against my parents' wishes to be with you.' His voice cracked as he added, 'Why won't you do the same for me?'

'It's different for a daughter! It's breaking my heart to say it but I can't leave my father.' She shook her head and repeated, 'I can't.'

Jacob's face twisted in anguish before her eyes. The only time Meg had seen such grief in a man's face was at her mother's funeral when Father had wept. But Jacob did not dissolve into tears. The set of his jaw hardened and his lips hardly moved as he spoke. 'You should have talked to him about us, Meg, and told me sooner. You knew how much I loved you.'

'But you'll come back, won't you?' Meg asked anxiously. 'We can write.'

He was shaking his head. 'My life will be in London.'

A cold fear gripped her and the chill spread through her body. 'You still love me, don't you? It will break my heart never to see you again.'

'Men have hearts that break as well. If you won't come with me, I think it's best not to prolong the agony.'

'No, don't say that!'

'You've made your choice and it's not me.'

Meg shook her head wordlessly. Why couldn't he see she had no alternative?

'I really thought you loved me,' he muttered.

'I do,' she croaked.

'No.' He sounded sad. 'You'd fight for a way for us to be together if you did. I thought I'd found my soul mate in you. I can see now that I was mistaken.'

The train whistle sounded and he turned away from her. 'You're not!' she protested. 'I want to be with you; with *you*, Jacob.'

He hesitated and looked back. 'You gave me false hope, Meg. I cannot forgive you for that.'

Her eyes must have shown her desperation. She couldn't make him any promises if she couldn't even think of a solution. She was trapped.

'This is too painful,' he went on. 'I shan't come over to Deepdale again. Goodbye, Meg.'

She sagged against the yew hedge and groaned. She could not even see him through the blur of her tears. The sun was sinking in the sky. How could a day that had started out so well end so badly? She had been so full of hope and joy this morning and now her life was in tatters. Why did it have to be like this? Why did Mother have to die? It was not her mother's fault but she could see no way forward as her tears spilled out.

'Are you all right, dear?' A woman had stopped on the adjacent path.

She pulled herself together. There would be time enough for tears in the loneliness stretching ahead of her. She brushed away a few stray leaves on her skirt and noticed a trailing bootlace.

'Just doing up my laces,' she answered and bent down to hide her flushed face. The woman walked on and a few moments later Meg emerged with an aching heart and an angry brow pushing her bicycle. It's not my fault either, she thought.

It's not fair.

She approached the back garden. Father was bending over a bucket off water washing soil off newly dug carrots. He heard the gate open and looked up. 'There you are, my lass. Make us a cup of tea, would you?'

'Can't you make it yourself for once in your life?' she snapped. She wasn't contrite. He was to blame! It was all her father's fault! She stalked past the tool shed towards the wash house and almost knocked down Mrs Dawson with her bicycle.

'That's no way to speak to your father, young lady.'

'What are you doing here?'

'My, my, you sound as though you need a cup of tea yourself. Shall I make some for you both?'

'What are you doing here, Mrs Dawson?' Meg repeated irritably. The last thing she wanted was Father in a bad mood because of this woman. She went indoors for the wash-house key.

Mrs Dawson was holding her bicycle when she emerged. 'This nearly fell over. You should be more careful how you leave it.' Meg could not trust herself to say anything civil and fumbled with the door lock. Mrs Dawson spoke to her back. 'I half expected to see you at the Mission today. I asked around and someone said they'd seen you heading up the fell this morning. That's a fair pull. Did you have a good day?'

She wanted to say 'Mind your own business', took a deep breath instead and demanded, 'What do you want?'

Mrs Dawson pushed the bicycle into the wash

house. 'I don't want anything. We had some teas left over today and I brought one round for your father. He's been quite anxious waiting for you to come home.'

Meg imagined the mood her father would be in after Mrs Dawson left and said, 'Well, I'm here now so you can go.'

Mrs Dawson raised her eyebrows at Meg's tone. 'He's just digging a few carrots for me, if that's all right.'

Probably just to get rid of you, Meg thought but said, 'You can wait in the kitchen if you want.' She locked up the wash house and went indoors to take off her bicycling clothes.

Meg took her time, hoping Mrs Dawson would have gone when she came downstairs. But the older woman called her from the bottom of the stairs. 'Tea's made, Meg. Your father is waiting for you.' Meg grimaced at her expression in the mirror and went down to the kitchen.

'He wants to hear all about your day, don't you Albert?' Mrs Dawson said.

'Well, I don't want to talk about it.'

'Remember your manners, Meg. We have a visitor,' her father responded.

'I'm sorry.' She knew she didn't sound sorry but she just wanted this tea over so she could go upstairs and cry.

'I won't stay long, Albert,' Mrs Dawson said.

'You stay as long as you like, Edith,' her father answered firmly. 'And you, young lady, will behave yourself.' He reached for a scone as Meg sat down at the table. It was laid with the best white cloth and matching napkins, knives, and the best tea plates, cups and saucers off the dresser.

'Did you lay the table, Father?' she asked.

'Your father told me where to find everything,' Mrs Dawson answered.

After a couple of minutes of silence, Meg looked from one to the other and made an attempt to be polite. She said, 'I am sorry, honestly. I don't feel very well, that's all. It's been a long day and I'm tired. I'm going upstairs to have a lie-down.' A half-truth, she thought. She felt like a wounded vixen running to earth to lick her wounds. She saw Mrs Dawson raise her eyebrows at Father and his mouth turn down at the corners in a kind of conspiratorial exchange. Something had gone on between the two of them this afternoon. She had no idea what and at that moment didn't really care. All Meg cared about was her own broken heart and how she was going survive without Jacob.

Shawbridge, Yorkshire

'Mr Melvil is here with his motor car,' her mother called.

Florence Brookes checked the tilt of her hat in the hall mirror and waited for her mother to emerge from the drawing room. Her father, looking uncomfortable in his starched collar, rose from a hall chair with the help of his silver-topped cane. Her mother's housekeeper, in a neat black dress and trim white apron, hurried from the back kitchen to open the front door when she heard the heavy brass knocker fall against it.

66

Florence's father had built this four-square red-brick house with a tiled roof and tall chimneys on the gains from his prosperous shops in Shawbridge High Street. Brookes Villa had a long drive down to a coach house with stabling for two horses, a tack room, hayloft and upstairs accommodation for his outdoor servant. The household was run by three indoor servants who lived in the attics, which were reached by a winding back stairs. They had a housekeeper, a cook and a houseparlourmaid who doubled as personal maid to Florence and her mother. The housekeeper also had a daily woman to do the scrubbing and a washerwoman came in once a month for the laundry.

Florence enjoyed the comforts of her father's prosperity, although she still remembered her childhood years when Father had only had one shop and they had lived in rooms above it. Brookes Villa was a whole mile away from the High Street and, sometimes, Florence missed the bustle of town life on her doorstep. She smiled at Mr Melvil's chauffeur as he settled her in the motor car. There was plenty of room for the three of them in the soft leather seat, even though her mother was quite stout. Her father was a small wiry man. But he was 'sharp as a ferret', Mother had warned her during Florence's younger years.

Florence was excited. They were going to the Grand, the best hotel in Shawbridge, for luncheon with Mr Melvil, who had been staying there with his mother and father these past few weeks while he looked for premises in the area. The possibility of a Melvil's chemist shop in Shawbridge had caused a flurry of interest in town and Florence appreciated that her father's influence on municipal growth had ensured this invitation. With her mother's encouragement, Father had provided well to prepare Florence for such occasions.

He had paid for her to attend a small private school where she had learned discipline, respect and good manners. And little else, she now realised. This had been followed by a whole year in a ladies' academy in York to add elocution, deportment and household management to her repertoire. Yet she had had to use all her charm to persuade Father to let her attend the afternoon lecture programme at the Mechanics' Institute to improve her knowledge of literature, art and science. Heaven forbid that her father might ask her about the content of some of the lectures! He had old-fashioned views on the education of girls and he was a strict parent. But he was generous towards his wife and daughter and liked nothing more than to accompany them dressed in their fashionable gowns and hats to local gatherings.

If Florence was excited, her mother was beside herself with pride. She had confided in Florence that her dearest wish was for the town's mayor to be present. The luncheon was private so the local newspaper would not be in attendance but she was sure it would be reported. A Melvil's chemist shop in the High Street was an important addition for any small town.

Florence had not ridden in a motor car before, nor had her mother and father. They normally travelled in Father's carriage, a small light affair that needed only one horse, and most of Father's deliveries from the shop were done by bicycle. However, he kept a heavy horse and cart for his bulkier items from Brookes' Provisions or Brookes' Hardware and he was considering a motorised vehicle to replace it. Shawbridge was expanding and trade was good.

The Grand was familiar to Florence and her parents. At seventeen, when she had finished at the academy, Father had held a proper ball there for her and invited everyone of importance in Shawbridge. As a consequence, Florence had begun to receive invitations to luncheons, dinners and the occasional ball. She had thick brown hair and an attractive face, strong rather than pretty, and was much in demand as a partner. But she had not yet met anyone who threatened to capture her heart. Not, that is, until she met Bradley Melvil at a reception given by the mayor. As soon as Florence saw him she was captivated by his cool grey eyes, light brown hair and full set of whiskers. He carried himself like a soldier and stood head and shoulders above the other gentlemen.

They were shown into a private dining salon, glittering with chandeliers, crystal and china, and were greeted formally by Mr and Mrs Melvil and their son Bradley. Florence was delighted to be seated next to him for luncheon. The mayor's wife was on the other side of him and the town clerk's daughter on the opposite side of the table. Florence noticed her lingering glances at Bradley Melvil and experienced an uncharitable sense of superiority towards her. But every lady's attention was quickly diverted to a small gift-wrapped package nestling on top of her linen table napkin.

Mrs Melvil, seated opposite her husband, caught Florence's eye, picked up her own package and pulled at the ribbon bow. Florence smiled and copied her. Soon all the ladies were wreathed in smiles at finding a small bottle of Nouveau nestling in a silk-lined box.

Mr Melvil senior had made his fortune from chemist shops in the South Riding towns and he held a patent for a scent that he had developed in his experimental workshop. It was called Nouveau so that everyone would think it was French and its fresh flowery perfume and affordable price made it very popular with women of all ages who had a little money to call their own. It had made Mr Melvil a wealthy man. Florence's father had tried to buy it to sell in his shop but Mr Melvil was firm in his conviction that customers had to visit a Melvil's chemist shop to purchase it. It was this exchange that had opened up the possibility of a Melvil's in Shawbridge High Street, which was regarded by the mayor as something of a triumph for the town.

The old blacksmith's forge next to the post office had closed down after the owner had died. The bicycle had reduced his farrier trade and his sons were more interested in machines than horses. The opportunity to sell the premises to Melvil's had been their dream come true and they had already split the proceeds and left Shaw-bridge.

Florence turned to her dining companion. 'This is a lovely gesture, Mr Melvil.'

He smiled. 'I'm pleased you think so. It was my

idea. May I compliment you on your hat, Miss Brookes?'

'Thank you, Mr Melvil. We have an excellent milliner in the High Street.'

'And two very good tailors, I have noticed.'

'Yes, they are branches of the same family.'

'You do not have a theatre, though.'

'Good heavens, no! I'm sure the mayor would never allow a music hall.'

'I was thinking more of plays.'

'Plays?' Florence repeated thoughtfully, reflecting on the ones she had travelled to see with her academy teachers. 'We have festive entertainments in the Mason's Hall, but nothing that approaches the productions in Sheffield or Leeds. But we are a small market town with a growing population so perhaps that is something for the future.'

He did not reply and Florence's mind raced to keep the conversation going. She added, 'We have a lecture programme in the Mechanics' Institute and we have had a speaker on Mr Shaw's plays.'

'Did you attend? How large was the audience?'

Florence felt slightly snubbed. She did not wish for Bradley Melvil to go away with the wrong impression of Shawbridge and went on, 'I did. We are not totally uncultured, Mr Melvil. We have lectures on literature, science and – and even politics. The organiser is the daughter of a retired professor.'

Her tone must have been challenging for he responded, 'Please forgive me, Miss Brookes. I was not criticising. But I shall be a resident here to set up our new shop.'

'You will?'

'This is a new location for Melvil's and I shall be responsible for its launch.'

'If your Shawbridge branch is a success then a Melvil's chemist in every town in Yorkshire must be your next challenge.'

'You have an instinct for business, Miss Brookes.'

Florence blinked. No one had said anything remotely like that to her before. She had expected charm and flattery from Bradley Melvil, but never this kind of comment. Was it a compliment? Her mother would not think so, nor her father. Their ambition for her was to be pretty, charming and cultured enough to make a good marriage. Since they had moved from living 'over the shop' Father had forbidden her to even stand behind the counter in either of his shops, let alone go into the storerooms at the back. Mother and she could visit him but only when dressed in their finery and they were allowed to sit on the mahogany chairs he provided for his more aristocratic customers.

Bradley Melvil must have noticed her surprise because he went on, 'I am sorry. I did not mean to offend you.'

'You haven't. I am aware that if I had been a son I should have been ... actually' – she gave a short laugh – 'well, actually, I should have been keeping the shops open today so that Father could be here.'

'Then I am very pleased you are a daughter and we have met under such enjoyable circumstances.'

He *was* flattering her. She smiled and met her mother's eyes at the other end of the table. Who but Florence would notice Mother's almost imperceptible nod of approval in her direction? Well, perhaps the town clerk's daughter opposite her, who seemed resigned to her conversation with a young gentleman that she already knew.

The ladies took their after-luncheon coffee in the hotel lounge in the old-fashioned way leaving the gentleman in the private dining room to discuss commerce and politics. The ladies talked of fashion and weather until their menfolk appeared. When they did, Florence watched Bradley Melvil covertly while she engaged other young ladies and gentlemen in conversation. He circulated skilfully, charming each guest, young or old, in turn until she thought he was deliberately avoiding her.

One or two carriages were announced and Florence's father came over to say that Mr Melvil's chauffeur was ready to take them home but that she may stay longer if she wished.

'Will you send the carriage later for me?' she asked.

'No need, young Mr Melvil will bring you. Did you know he has his own motor car for when his father and mother go back to Sheffield? Mother says you are not to hurry home under any circumstances.'

Eventually, Bradley Melvil was free of other guests and was standing beside her. 'Thank you for waiting,' he said. 'Will you have tea with me? I've ordered a tray in the hotel lounge.'

Florence went off to the ladies' lavatory behind the hotel dining room and sat on the polished wooden seat in the mahogany and brass cubicle for longer than she needed. Was Bradley Melvil really interested in her? She could hardly believe it. He had just about everything her mother and father would want for her – and more. She tidied her hair and opened her gift bottle of Nouveau, dabbing a spot behind her ears and on her wrists. Then she adjusted her corset to plump up the visible part of her breasts and pushed down the lace neckline trim to a minimum. She immediately pulled it back into place, mindful of the value of modesty, and took a deep breath.

Florence walked confidently towards Mr and Mrs Melvil and their son, seated comfortably around a low table in the corner of the Grand's comfortable lounge. Both gentleman rose to their feet as she approached and Mrs Melvil was smiling. Florence relaxed and settled in the vacant chair.

Mrs Melvil, a woman rather like her own mother, stood up beside her husband and said, 'Do forgive us, Miss Brookes, but my husband is rather exhausted and we shall take tea in our suite.'

Florence responded with a slight bow of her head. 'It was a delightful luncheon party, Mrs Melvil, quite the best our little town has seen.'

'Thank you. Good afternoon to you.'

'Good afternoon, Mrs Melvil.' Florence turned to her husband and repeated, 'Good afternoon, Mr Melvil.'

Mr Melvil did indeed look tired and his cheeks had a yellow tinge to their pallor. Bradley Melvil remained standing until his parents had gone and then took the chair opposite Florence where his father has been seated. He commented, 'It has been a hectic week for my father.'

'He is fortunate that he has you to take the reins for him.'

'And Mother, until my younger brothers have finished their education.'

'You have brothers! How lucky you are!' When she was a child, Florence had often dreamed of being part of a larger family, but knew that would never happen now, unless – unless... She stopped to think. It had not occurred to her until now that she could, one day, acquire brothers and sisters by – by *marriage*. Good heavens, she chastised herself, Bradley had only asked her to stay for tea! But why had he singled her out, when he must have so many ladies to choose from in Sheffield? 'Do you have sisters as well?' she queried.

'I'm afraid not. Poor Mother is surrounded by gentlemen.'

A waiter brought the silver tray of tea. Florence had noticed him at luncheon. He was a handsome fellow with slicked-down black hair and a twinkle in his eye, very smart in his black tailcoat and starched white shirtfront. She had deliberately not made eye contact with him at any time, but even so his manner seemed too familiar as he unloaded the tray and handed out gilt-edged bone-china tea plates with tiny linen napkins. 'That will be all, Sandy,' her host said.

Sandy? He knew the waiter by name? Oh well, she supposed he and his parents had been staying at the Grand for a few weeks and probably received special attention from all the staff.

'Shall I pour the tea, sir?'

'Thank you, no.' Bradley Melvil's tone was firm.

'Very well, sir,' the waiter replied. Florence gained the impression he felt slighted and he hesitated before turning away.

'Sandy is very obliging. He is our personal butler during our stay,' Bradley explained. 'My father tips him well.'

'I see.' Except that she didn't. If one of Father's counter assistants had shown similar petulance towards a customer he would have been sent to work in the storerooms, if not dismissed.

'He means well,' Bradley Melvil added, 'but I want you to myself. Will you be Mother and pour?'

'Milk or lemon?' She lifted the heavy silver teapot.

'Lemon, please. May I call you Florence?'

'You may, if I may call you Bradley.'

'Yes, of course. I wonder, do you enjoy concerts, Florence?'

Tea with Bradley Melvil lasted an hour and a half and by the time he had driven her to Brookes Villa and escorted her to the front door, Florence's mother was on pins and needles with curiosity. She was in the entrance hall and helping the housekeeper take Florence's wrap before Bradley had driven away. 'Your father has gone to close the shops so we're having a late supper. Come into the drawing room and tell me everything, dear. Who else was there for tea?'

'Only the Melvils and they went to their suite early.'

'Really? They left you alone with him?'

'We were in a public room at the Grand, Mother, and Bradley is a gentleman.'

'Bradley? Oh, Florence, does he want to know

you better?'

'I believe so.' Mother's excitement was infecting Florence. It was true. Bradley Melvil was interested in forming a relationship with her. With *her*. Not that she didn't think she was worthy of him, but he was very attractive and very wealthy, as well as being educated and cultured. For the first time, Florence appreciated the true value of her ladies' academy training. 'He's very interesting, Mother. He wants to make his home here.'

'He wants to settle down here? That means he *is* looking for a wife. You know, his mother hinted at such a thing at luncheon. She remarked that Shawbridge was a good place to raise a family and she wanted nothing more than that for her eldest son. I should have asked if she meant Bradley.'

'She did, Mother. He is the eldest.'

'Oh, my darling child, I'm all of a flutter.' She went to the door and called her housekeeper from the back. 'Bring the sherry now, please,' she asked. 'It will calm me down before your father comes home. You know how he hates me to chatter at mealtimes. When will you see him again?'

'He is having a private dinner at the Grand a week on Saturday and he has asked me to help him host it.'

'Florence, I think I'm going to faint.' Mrs Brookes sank into a nearby chair.

The housekeeper brought in the sherry tray. Florence took it from her, poured her mother a small glass, handed it to her and said, 'Bradley wants my advice on the guest list because it is a dinner with a purpose.'

This calmed her mother before she sipped the sherry. 'A purpose? What kind of purpose?'

'He wishes to gather around him people with similar tastes in literature and music. He wants Shawbridge to have a theatre for concerts and plays.'

'That may not go down very well with some folk I can name. You say he wants you to help?'

'I know all the local people and which ones will be sympathetic.'

'You do indeed, dear.' Mrs Brookes pondered this thought and murmured, 'I believe he feels he must give you a test before he commits himself. But I know he has no worries at all. You will make him an excellent wife.'

Chapter 5

Deepdale

'I see you've put yourself down for overtime again, Meg.'

Christine was in charge of the women in the checking room at the mill and responsible for drawing up the rota. She was pinning the list to a noticeboard while they were eating their sandwiches for dinner.

'Christmas is coming,' Meg replied by way of explanation.

'I thought you might want to get off early some nights.'

'No, thank you.'

'Not even for the Mission social?'

'No, thank you.'

'All work and no play makes Jack a dull boy.'

'Don't you mean "Jill a dull girl"?' one of her workmates laughed. 'Leave her be, Christine. She's allus a misery guts these days.'

'No I'm not,' Meg protested.

Christine came and sat beside her. 'Is everything all right at home, love? It's a big change for any lass.'

'You said I ought to keep an eye on her. You saw it coming.'

'Didn't you?'

Meg shook her head. She had been too wrapped up in her own grief to notice at first. But the signs were there, from that day: from the Sunday she had returned to find Mrs Dawson – Edith – in the garden with Father.

She never did find out what had happened while she was away, except that when she challenged her father about Edith the following weekend he had been surprised.

'I thought you didn't like her?' she had said.

'Whatever gave you that idea?' he had replied.

Meg hadn't argued with him because he was clearly flattered by Edith's attentions; she hadn't wasted any time in getting her feet firmly 'under their table', just as Father had predicted. Meg hadn't reminded him.

At first, Meg didn't need to bake every week because Edith came over every Sunday with her own tarts and scones, enough for all week as well as tea. Then she started to bring a hotpot or a pan of stew 'to save young Meg cooking in the week'. When the summer evenings arrived they began to go for walks and call at a public house for a glass of beer and Father's face took on a permanent ruddy colour. By September everyone at the mill knew about them but Meg had been too wrapped up in her own misery. She was very careful to avoid the Mission Hall and the river because her memories of Jacob in those places were too painful.

One Sunday in September Meg came in from a solitary walk on the fell at the back of their house. Edith was already busy and called out, 'Close the back door, Meg. There's a draught and I've got the oven door open.'

Meg inhaled a mouth-watering aroma of roasting pork wafting from the kitchen to the scullery. It was a typical Sunday now. Edith had taken over from Meg in the kitchen. She came over in the morning as though she had always cooked their dinner. Meg tried to be pleased for Father because he obviously liked it when Edith told him what to do and organised his life for him. But Meg found her overbearing and thought it best simply to stay out of her way to avoid any friction.

That Sunday both Edith and her father had been particularly jovial and Meg wished she could be cheerful with them. But Sundays were the worst because Sundays reminded her of Jacob and the agony of her dilemma. It made her angry that he hadn't understood her difficulty with Father and even angrier that he had thought she had deceived him. She tried to convince herself that he did not love her as much as he had declared. He could not have loved her, surely, or he would not have let her go so easily. The only person who seemed aware of her grief was Christine at the mill, for Sally was too wrapped up in her own wedding and new life in Leeds. Meg missed talking with Sally, especially on a Sunday.

'Where've you been today?' Father had asked her on that memorable day. He was already in from the garden and washing his hands in the scullery.

'Walking.'

'Has your bicycle got a puncture?'

'No, I've just gone off bicycling for a bit.'

'You could have helped me in the garden.'

'I will this afternoon. Move over, I want to wash my hands.'

Edith called from the kitchen, 'I hope you two are hungry.' She beamed as she lifted a golden-brown Yorkshire pudding from the range. 'I fetched a jug of ale from the pub. Bring it through from the scullery, Albert.'

The table was laid for three and Father carefully poured some into each of the tumblers.

'Come and sit down, Edith. We'll tell her now.'

'Tell me what?' Meg queried as she slid into her chair.

'We've been thinking about this for a while now. It's been a few months since I met up with Edith again and, well, there's no sense in keeping two houses going and paying two lots of rent when we can manage with one.' He leaned across the table and took hold of Mrs Dawson's hand. 'I've asked her and she's said yes.' Father was smiling as he

81

went on, 'We're going to get wed and live here.'

Meg's eyes widened. Father was going to marry Edith! She was surprised into silence. She knew Father enjoyed Edith's company, and her cooking, but she had never imagined her father would *marry* again. Well, what had she thought would happen? Nothing, she realised, because she never thought of anything except her own loss these days or she would have seen it coming. But it was only just over two years since Mother died! Marriage meant, well, as he said, living together. Living here, just as he had with Mother.

'Say something then, lass.'

All she could manage was a weak 'W-when?'

'Michaelmas Day,' Edith answered briskly.

'But that's the end of this month!'

'Yes, dear. The banns were read out in church today. Would you like to be my maid of honour?'

'Say yes,' her father prompted.

'Yes,' Meg echoed.

'Congratulate your father as well,' Edith encouraged.

Meg obeyed. She didn't know what was happening to her life. Everything seemed out of her control.

They chinked their glasses and drank. But Father added, 'You could look a bit more pleased. I don't know what's wrong with you these days, Meg.'

Meg had pasted a smile on her face. If it had all happened six months earlier, she would have been free to follow Jacob to London. She had wanted to scream.

It was over two months after the wedding now,

but since that day she had wanted to tear up her life and throw it away.

'Come on, Meg, do cheer up. There's no point in dwelling on what you can't change.' Christine's voice roused her from her memories.

'I know,' she agreed.

'You get on all right with Edith, don't you?'

Meg nodded. 'It was quite difficult when she first moved in. Some of Mother's things were around and she moved them all.'

Edith had cleared the front bedroom of her mother's memory. She asked Meg which items she wanted for her room and put the rest in a box in the loft. If her father objected he didn't say anything. He told Meg he wanted Edith to make the house 'her own'. So she did. Father was not totally henpecked by her. He did stand his ground occasionally but Edith was a persuasive woman and anything she could not have sooner, she managed to acquire later. Meg recalled a comment from one of the Mission ladies about her new stepmother. You can have too much of a good thing, she had said. Meg agreed.

Christine seemed to understand. 'It's hard for you, love,' she sympathised, 'but she is the lady of the house now. You owe it to your father to be nice to her.'

'Oh, I am. Honest, I do try.'

'They get on well together, don't they?'

Too well, Meg thought. She had assumed Father was past what the mill women called 'all that' because he and Mother had given up years ago. At least, for a couple of years before Mother died, Meg had not heard the bed springs as she had as a child. But then Edith moved in with the ring on her finger and her own ideas. Cries and squeals accompanied the creaking bed now.

It wasn't that she objected. Her father was a man like any other. But every time she heard them it reminded her of how it could have been for her with Jacob and she wanted to scream at her loss. She took to putting the pillow over her head to drown out the noises and wished the cottage were bigger.

Christine went on, 'You can always come round to us if things get too bad at home.'

'Oh, we're all fine, thank you.'

But Christine didn't appear to believe her and frowned. 'You're not still moping about that Leeds lad, are you?'

Meg glanced at her. She was a very perceptive woman. 'He's gone to London. He – he won't be coming back.' Not to her, anyway. With the benefit of hindsight, she could see that she had let Jacob down. At the time, she had been too angry and too proud to write to him, not that she knew where he was now. He was gone. Her heart felt as though it were crumbling every time she thought about it. She had made a huge mistake and it was too late to put it right.

'Oh, I see,' Christine commented. 'You were very fond of him, weren't you?'

Meg couldn't trust herself to answer. Christine added, 'Well, there's plenty more fish in the sea, I tell my girls.'

I don't want anyone else, Meg thought, but said, 'You're right. He couldn't have cared much for me anyway or he wouldn't have upped and left like that.'

'That sounds more like the Meg I know. Why don't you go back to helping at the Mission Hall on Sundays?'

Meg didn't reply. Memories of Jacob at the Mission on Sundays were too painful for her. She wondered how long she could keep up her pretence that she was getting over him.

Christmas Eve was a freezing cold day but Edith was sitting on an old chair in the back yard plucking a goose. Its long neck lolled languidly down from her lap. She had spread an old sheet on the ground to catch all the feathers for a new pillow. Meg put away her bicycle and went indoors to start grating stale bread for the sage and onion stuffing.

Father was sitting by the kitchen fire warming his feet. He'd been out collecting holly and mistletoe to decorate the front room. 'Are you and Edith going to the midnight carol service?' she asked.

'It's too cold to sit around in a draughty church. Edith's had a barrel of ale sent from the brewhouse. I'm tapping it tonight.'

Meg had noticed the small barrel set up in the scullery. Since Father had married there was more money in the household because Edith had an annuity from her first husband and she was a generous lady. Father enjoyed a glass or two of beer with his dinner and it showed in his ruddy complexion.

'She's made a grand pork pie an' all. Have you seen it in the larder?'

Meg had and it was impressive, made in a

proper raised pie mould with a crisp golden crust. A half-ham on the bone was simmering on the range to eat hot tonight and have cold for the rest of the week. They were certainly going to have a good Christmas this year. The quarry and the mill had closed for two days and they had plenty of coal in. Meg left her father and Edith before a banked-up fire in the front room to walk to church.

She enjoyed the midnight service, sang heartily and afterwards chatted to folk she hadn't seen in a while. But the frost was keen on the ground and parents had stockings to fill before they could go to bed so no one lingered. Meg let herself in and locked the door behind her. The remnants of supper littered the kitchen table but Edith had left her a tray of pork pie and pickles. She was hungry and it was tasty. The ale was good too and she drank a glass. Life could be worse, she thought. She had to forget about Jacob if she could, put her mistake behind her and try to move on. Father had and, despite Meg's misgivings about Edith, he appeared to be enjoying his new life. She filled a stone warming bottle with hot water and went upstairs to bed.

She was roused the following morning by Edith's voice calling across the landing. 'Meg! Meg! Come quick.'

She hurried into the main bedroom. Edith was standing in her nightgown gazing at the sleeping form of her father. 'I can't wake him. You try.'

'Father!' Meg shook his arm and raised her voice. 'Wake up, Father, it's Christmas Day.'

His skin felt cold to the touch and he did not

move. Alarmed she pulled down the sheet to watch his chest rise and fall. 'Pass me your hand mirror, Edith, the one off your dressing table.'

Meg held it in front of her father's pallid lips and waited.

'He isn't, is he?' Edith anguished. 'Oh, not again, it can't happen to me again.'

Meg stared at the still cold body. The room around her seemed to recede into dimness and there was a monotonous drone in her ears. Her father was dead. She couldn't move. The mirror slipped out of her fingers and landed on the eiderdown.

Edith sagged on to the bed. 'Whatever shall I do?' she whispered, grasping Meg's arm. 'Oh, whatever shall I do?'

The room gradually came back into focus for Meg as Edith tugged at her arm. She put her hand over Edith's and found her voice. 'I – I'll have to fetch the doctor.'

'He can't do anything for him now. Neither can I. Meg, it's Christmas Day.'

'You'll have to get dressed, Edith,' Meg suggested. 'Go downstairs and make up the fire.'

Meg pulled on her bicycling skirt and a thick jumper. She picked up the wash-house key from its hook in the scullery and went out into the frosty air, a thousand questions tumbling through her mind. The doctor's housekeeper answered the door and she explained her fears. The lady was so sympathetic that Meg's tears began to flow. 'Come in, my dear,' she said. 'I'll make you a cup of tea.'

'I can't. Edith – that's my stepmother – is on

her own.'

'Very well, dear, the doctor will be along as soon as he can.'

Meg hardly remembered the rest of the day except that Edith seemed to be coping better than her. Edith seemed to mope rather grieve. Meg was distressed. She cried on and off all day. She had loved her father dearly and he had had so much to live for. Hardly a word was spoken between them. The doctor arranged for an undertaker to call and take her father's body to the chapel of rest. One or two neighbours came out on the street to see what the fuss was when folk should be eating their Christmas dinners. Edith's goose languished in the meat safe untouched. Instead of cooking, she sat in the kitchen feeling sorry for herself. As Christmas Day wore on at a snail's pace, Edith grew more morose. By mid-afternoon Meg felt a hunger pang and made a pot of tea and some ham sandwiches. Edith roused herself to fetch a tin of her mince pies from the pantry.

Meg tried to make her feel better. 'He enjoyed these last few months with you,' she said. 'He had that at least.'

'I should've had longer with him. It was nice having a man around again. The bed will be so empty without him.'

Meg hadn't realised that the bedroom was so important to Edith and didn't know how to respond. Meg had no experience to draw on and for a minute longed for Jacob by her side. Jacob could deal with any situation, even one he had no knowledge of. But Meg was sympathetic. Perhaps Edith had felt the same loneliness when she lost her first husband and recognised it? Meg did her best for Edith but she needed someone to help *her* through this as well. She needed Jacob. His memory brought on her tears again.

The vicar called on Boxing Day to offer his condolences and arrange a date for the burial. The day after Meg sent a telegram to Charley in Canada and another to Albert who had been moved from Liverpool to the India office. Neither had been at the wedding and neither would be able to attend the funeral either. However, Edith roused herself enough to organise a wake at the Mission Hall.

It was well attended. Even the quarry manager and his wife came, as well as many of his workmates, one of whom knew Edith from her younger days. Meg thought Edith was genuinely sorry to lose her new husband but she seemed to soak up all the attention as a grieving widow rather too readily.

Mr Taylor had been a long-standing work-mate of her father and they occasionally shared a glass of beer at the inn after work before going to their respective homes. Meg had met him several times but did not share her father's liking for the man. He was friendly enough so she never knew quite what it was that irked her. Too friendly, perhaps, she considered as she watched him approach her and Edith to take his leave.

He smiled at Meg, and she realised it was his smile she didn't like. It was too simpering for a man and his eyes moved up and down as though he were sizing her up. She was thankful that he spoke to Edith. 'I'm the quarrymen's representative on the welfare committee. May I call round one evening next week, Mrs Parker?'

'I won't be needing welfare, thank you. I can afford my rent and Meg gets good wages from the mill.'

'The quarry is your landlord so if you want to stay in the house, I have to transfer the rent book into your name. There is also the matter of the Friendly Society.'

'Oh?' Edith became more interested.

'We had a scheme at the quarry. Albert paid into it regularly.'

'Oh!' repeated Edith. 'I see.'

'I have to explain it all to you, Mrs Parker, and there are papers to sign.'

'You'd better come round for your tea, then.'

'That's very kind of you. Would Wednesday suit?'

He smiled at Meg again and walked away. Edith leaned over and whispered, 'Bring me some neck o' mutton from the butcher's on your way home from the mill on Tuesday. I'll make a hotpot for tea.'

Hotpot was one of her father's favourites and Edith had enjoyed cooking for him. As Meg wheeled her bicycle out of the wash house to go to the mill on Wednesday morning, Edith came out with some empty beer bottles. 'Stop at the inn on your way home and get these filled with dinner ale, and if the egg man calls at the mill, bring me another dozen. I'll make a custard tart for pudding.'

'We haven't heard what Mr Taylor has got to say yet, Edith.'

'It's good news, though, we know that much.'

Meg pedalled away to the mill and when she arrived home that evening the house was sparkling clean and a mouth-watering smell wafted from the warm kitchen. All credit to Edith, Meg thought, for the house did always look nice these days. Edith was a homemaker and Meg had to admit she had made a comfortable and very pretty home for Father; and herself, of course. But Meg was never in any doubt it was Father Edith wanted to please. Meg took off her boots and washed in the scullery and then went upstairs to tidy her hair and change her dress. 'I'll set the table when I come down, Edith,' she called.

'Well, hurry up, I want to have a wash and change myself.'

Mr Taylor came to the front door, which had a small lobby where Meg hung up his hat and coat before showing him into the front room. He carried a leather document case, the kind that senior clerks used, and held on to it firmly. The house had a small hallway with a door to the front room and another beyond the stairs that led to the back kitchen. 'Please sit down, Mr Taylor. Will you have a glass of sherry?'

'Sherry, eh? I thought a milk stout might be more your taste.'

'Edith has always liked a sherry before her tea.'

He glanced around the room and pulled his mouth down at the corners in an expression of surprised approval. 'I know how much your father earned. The mill must be paying its lasses well these days.'

'This is all Edith's work. She made it lovely for

91

my father.'

Edith came through from the kitchen, carrying a small china dish of toasted nuts. 'Good evening, Mr Taylor. Tea will be another few minutes.' She placed the dish on her polished side table. 'Try these while you wait. Meg, love, pour me one of those, will you?'

'You live well, Mrs Parker.'

'I got used to it with my first husband and Albert liked it too.' She took her glass of sherry from Meg and said, 'Meg, talk to Mr Taylor while I finish cooking.'

'Albert must have come into a legacy or something,' Mr Taylor commented.

'Oh no, it's Edi – that is, Mrs Parker's. She has a widow's pension from her first husband's works. He was in the offices.'

'I see.' He laid his document case on the table and looked at it. 'Aye well, apples only fall where there's an orchard.'

So Edith was right, Meg thought. Mr Taylor had brought good news. Nonetheless, she wished he wouldn't look at her so openly, as though he were inspecting her, although he seemed to approve of what he saw.

'Did Mrs Parker make you that frock?'

Meg was proud of her needlework and sat up straight to show off her handiwork. 'This is my own sewing, Mr Taylor. My mother taught me.'

He stared at her and said, 'Very nice.'

Meg felt uncomfortable in his presence. She tried to work out why and couldn't find an answer. Perhaps it was something to do with her grief. She changed the subject. Father had liked

92

his job at the quarry and she talked of his happy times there.

'He was a good foreman, right enough.'

Edith's voice from the kitchen called them through and Meg led the way. 'You sit here, Mr Taylor,' Edith said, drawing out the carver chair at the head of the table.

Meg wished she hadn't. She'd being doing well until then but that had always been Father's chair, right from her being a little girl, and seeing another man settling comfortably in it caused her throat to constrict. Didn't Edith realise the significance?

Meg watched her treat Mr Taylor like an important visitor – well, she supposed he was – pouring his ale and serving him the best pieces of meat from the stew. She had put the vegetables in dishes for them help themselves instead of serving them straight on the plates as she usually did. Meg was hungry and happy to let Edith and Mr Taylor talk as she ate. But she listened and watched. Edith made a fuss of him and smiled when he complimented her. He was very charming. There was no doubt that he had 'a way with the ladies', as Mother would have said. His eyes were everywhere, including on Meg more times than she considered polite. Edith either didn't notice or found this acceptable for she kept filling his glass, which Meg thought was foolish.

Meg cleared the table and did the washing-up in the scullery while Mr Taylor talked about the business of the evening; when she had finished, Edith was signing documents on the table.

Mr Taylor collected them together in his leather

case. 'Mr Parker used to pay his rent in the office when he collected his wages. I can call here for it, if you like, and save you from having to come up to the quarry every week.'

'Thank you, Mr Taylor,' Edith replied. 'What day will it be?'

'I do rent collecting on Saturday mornings. This part of town is at the end of my rounds.' He looked across at Meg. 'The mill finishes early on a Saturday, doesn't it? Do you come straight home?'

'I usually bring in fish and chips for our dinner on my way through town,' Meg answered.

'Well, if you're calling at dinnertime, Mr Taylor,' Edith said, 'Meg can bring some for you as well next week. That will be nice, won't it? Saturday will be just like it used to be.' Meg didn't think it would be and suppressed a sigh. She avoided Mr Taylor's eyes and was glad when he left and Edith volunteered to show him out.

Chapter 6

They had half an hour for dinner at the mill and Meg put a few coppers into a tin for tea and milk so she had a hot drink with her bread and cheese. The egg man called most days as he was a relative of one of the overseers and was always welcome for a cuppa. He took eggs to the quarry, not to the labourers who wouldn't be seen dead doing shopping for their wives, but to the owner, who bought a whole basket at a time and took them home on his lorry.

Meg asked the egg man if he knew Mr Taylor in the offices at the quarry.

'Mr Taylor? Don't mention his name to me. Got my cousin's lass in the family way, he did, and him a married man an' all.'

'Take no notice of him, Meg love,' Christine said. 'Nobody was sure who the father was, least of all the lass herself.'

'But it could have been Mr Taylor?'

'Well, so she said, and he does have a roving eye. But he was a grown man and she were nobbut a kid so I can't see it meself.'

And he had a wife, according to the egg man. Meg didn't know whether that was a good thing or a bad one as far as Edith was concerned. Meg knew Edith was missing her father as much as she was, but it wouldn't do to cause a scandal in their small town. Besides, Mr Taylor had a respectable position at the quarry so he certainly wouldn't want to be the subject of any gossip. Meg tried not to think ill of him. He was just being nice to a recently bereaved widow and her stepdaughter, that's all.

'Do you know Mr Taylor?' she asked Christine. 'I mean, what's he like?'

'I can't say I know him. I just know *of* him, y'see. Ee, lass, you have to be careful when you've just lost someone. You miss 'em a lot when you're grieving and do things that you wouldn't normally do, if you know what I mean.' Christine gazed at her seriously. 'Men can take advantage of that, y'know. He's not caught your eye, has he, lass?'

'Good Lord no!' she said, but thought, I'm not so sure about Edith, though.

Christine smiled and went on, 'Anyway, you're young and pretty and you'll soon find someone. Maybe that gamekeeper's lad will come back from London?'

Meg shook her head. 'I wasn't the one for him and his parents didn't like me. He'll have bigger fish to fry now, I expect.'

'Shame,' Christine commented.

Yes it is, Meg agreed silently and suddenly felt tearful and depressed. She gulped down her tea, shook away the crumbs and stood up. 'I'll pack my bicycle basket now. I want to get away as soon as the hooter goes today.' The others thought she had gone, but she had to stop just outside the door, put down her eggs and tie up a loose boot-lace. She heard them talking about her.

'I do feel sorry for young Meg. She lost her mam and then her sweetheart and now her dad has gone too.'

'Such a lovely lass an' all.'

'I expect she'll find a fella one day to look after her.'

'Not round here, she won't. There's no young 'uns her age left now.'

Meg was cross with them for gossiping about her, but they were right. There was nothing to keep young folk in town any more. The mill wasn't taking on any more women and workers didn't leave because there was nowhere else. Now Sally was gone, she was the only young one left. The others liked her and were kind, but they had their husbands and children to think about.

Well, Meg thought, she didn't need any 'fella' to look after her. She could take care of herself. She had decent wages and a nice home with Edith. They didn't have much in common but they rubbed along well enough and once a month on Sunday Sally and Robert dropped by when they were over to see her mother. That would come to an end soon, Meg inwardly sighed, with Sally expecting her first already. Well, Meg decided, I'll go and see them in Leeds. Why not? Everybody travelled around these days, except the stick-in-the-muds who wouldn't leave their own homes.

Had Jacob thought she was a stick-in-the-mud for not wanting to leave? Whatever he had thought she knew now that she had been wrong to refuse to go to London with Jacob. It had been the right decision to stay at the time because her Father had needed her and Jacob's father wouldn't have given him permission to marry anyway. Jacob had said he would go against Mr Wright's wishes but, in her experience, that was never a good idea. You had to win your parents round somehow. As it was, Jacob had given her up because of her decision. She closed her eyes and could still see his face, tight-lipped and angry when he said it would be best not to prolong the agony.

She wondered what might have happened if she had followed him to London but failed to find work in a shop or office. Jacob had said he couldn't afford to marry her. She'd have been destitute in London and a burden to him. His mother and father had been right. Jacob wouldn't have wanted her when he started mixing with the gentry in his new position. Then where would she have been on her own without the fare to come home? She'd have been scrubbing floors or worse to save up the money.

There had been too many things against them and not enough 'fors'. So why was she convinced that she had thrown away her only chance of real happiness? Why, oh why did she keep torturing herself by thinking about him? She couldn't stop herself, that's why, and her heart crumbled a bit more every time she thought of him.

Meg was pleased she had her job at the mill to keep her occupied now that Edith took care of the house. The wages came round on Saturday and she celebrated with buying dinner on the way home. It seemed like normal again to have three newspaper parcels in her bicycle basket. She passed Mr Taylor on the way, collecting rents from other quarry houses in town, but he didn't see her. Edith had the big meat plate warming in the oven for Meg to put the dinner on while she put away her bicycle. As Meg went upstairs to take off her hat and coat, Edith was coming out of the big front bedroom looking clean and tidy. In fact her hair looked as though she were going out for the day. She had on a blouse she only wore for special occasions, and – Meg peered closely at her face – she had a touch of rouge on her lips.

'What is it, Meg?' Edith demanded. 'Have I got a smut on my nose?'

'No, you look lovely, Edith.'

Edith smiled. 'Thank you, dear. Will you put out some of my pickled shallots? I don't want vinegar on my fingers.'

'I'll be down in a tick. Is the kettle nearly boiled? I'm parched.'

The rent book was on the table at her father's place with the money inside it and before long there was a knock at the door. Edith patted her hair and bustled through the front room to let him in, leading him into the kitchen.

'Well, Mrs Parker, may I say how fetching you look today?'

'Thank you, Mr Taylor. Your rent's on the table.'

He sat down, counted the money and entered the amount in the rent book, putting his initials in the end column. 'Are you sure you can manage this between you? It's not as though you have a man's wage coming in.'

He sounded really doubtful and Meg began to worry. 'The quarry doesn't want the house back, does it, Mr Taylor?' she asked.

'Not as long as you can pay the rent.'

'I'll have my money from the Friendly Society soon,' Edith said. 'When do you think that will be?

'It can take a month or two.'

'Don't you worry about us, Mr Taylor,' she assured him. 'You sit there and enjoy your dinner. Have you many more calls to make?'

'This is my last one but I have to get my money bag in the safe at the office before it closes to-night.'

'You've plenty of time then. I thought I might show you the garden after dinner.'

Meg joined them in her father's vegetable plot when she had finished the washing-up. Edith was pulling a few weeds and Meg realised how untidy it had become in the short time since Father died.

Mr Taylor turned when he heard Meg approach and said, 'Here she is. Mrs Parker was just saying what a help you are to her, but this is a lot for a young lass to take on.'

'Well, I shan't grow quite as much as Father, but it's a shame to let it run to weeds.'

'Why don't I give you a hand on a Saturday? I'll have a couple of hours of light after my round even in winter.'

'Oh, would you? I'd be so grateful,' Edith responded.

Meg was cautious. 'But we couldn't pay a gardener, Mr Taylor.'

'I won't need paying if you give me my dinner. I'd have to go to the inn otherwise.'

'Won't your wife have tea waiting for you at home?' Meg asked.

Mr Taylor's untidy eyebrows shot up. 'My wife? I haven't got a wife.'

Meg wanted to ask what had happened to her, but Edith interrupted. 'Meg, why don't you show Mr Taylor Albert's tool shed while I rub up a few scones for tea?'

Meg's heart sank. Edith was doing exactly the same for Mr Taylor that she had done for Father and she recognised a similarity to her own behaviour when she lost Mother. She and Father had not wanted their routines to change. It had been a comfort to them for their days to go on as they always had and Edith, she realised, was doing just that. Meg was torn between sympathy for Edith's loneliness and her suspicions about Mr Taylor. She decided to give him the benefit of the doubt until she'd spoken to Christine again.

Her father's tool shed was a small stone-built outhouse that had been an earth privy, now sealed off, before the landlord had built a wash house and flush privy in the back yard. It didn't have a window so it was dark and dank. Father had built a bench across the end for potting and he had an oil lamp for the winter months. Meg held open the door for Mr Taylor to go in.

He peered in and said, 'All very neat and tidy. After you, dear.'

'Well, there isn't much room for two.'

He gave her a firm push. She was so surprised that she stumbled and ended up next to the bench to keep her balance. The door clicked shut and she was engulfed in black.

'Mind the threshold, dear,' Mr Taylor said. He was very close to her and she could feel his breath on her face.

'Open the door! I can't see a thing.'

'Me neither. Oh, is that you?' He had put one hand on her arm and was tracing the shape of her waist with the other.

Horrified, she felt his fingers stroke the curve of her breast.

'Mr Taylor!' She pushed him away.

'Oops, my dear.' He seemed to overbalance and lean against her more, pressing his body on hers so that her back was hard against the bench and a stack of clay flowerpots went over.

'I am sorry,' he said. 'I lost my footing in the dark. That is you, isn't it?'

101

He was pretending to be confused. She was sure he was pretending because as he spoke his hands were roaming up and down the front of her body.

She shoved him aside and cried, 'Get off me!' Hot and flustered, she fell against the door and pushed it open to escape into the fading daylight. So much for giving him the benefit of the doubt!

He righted the stack of flowerpots and wandered outside. 'I'm sorry, my dear. I couldn't see what I was doing. No harm done, eh? The flowerpots didn't break.' He smiled in the weak simpering way that she hated.

She didn't want him to call her 'my dear' either. She wasn't his 'dear'. She wasn't anybody's 'dear' and she was upset. She wanted her father back and tears threatened. 'Don't you ever do that to me again,' she spat.

This seemed to amuse him and he strolled by her as though nothing had happened, inspecting the rows of vegetables and picking up stones as he progressed. Meg took a few deep breaths and waited until he had gone indoors before she followed. Surely Edith would see him for what he was and not take up his offer? She made her excuses and went upstairs to do some sewing in her bedroom until he had left. The aroma of fresh-baked scones hot from the oven made her mouth water but Meg stayed in her room. When Edith called her down for tea, she said she had sewing to finish for the next day and she'd have hers later.

Eventually, she heard Mr Taylor leave through the front door, but finished her sewing before she came down. Edith's scones were a delight and it was so late when Meg ate hers that she had them with her bedtime cocoa. Edith was in a very buoyant mood.

'Isn't Mr Taylor a charming man?'

'You seem to have taken a shine to him, but you hardly know him.'

'Oh, I can tell he's a gentleman. He is so helpful and it will be handy to have a man calling on us to keep an eye on things. There's so much a woman on her own can't do, even you, my dear.' Edith gave Meg a hesitant smile.

'He's not a home bird like Father and Christine at the mill says there's gossip about him.'

'I'm sure that's all it is. People will talk because he's on his own.'

Meg wanted to tell her about the tool shed, but she was embarrassed by the incident and Edith would think she was being silly. So Meg took another angle.

'He knows you're coming into a bit of money, Edith. You must be careful.'

'He's on the welfare committee, dear! He must have given cheques to widows before, and helped them out until they're back on their feet again. It's part of his job and there's no harm in him doing a bit of gardening for us in return for his Saturday dinner.'

Meg had to agree. Jobs at the quarry were hard to come by as it was known for treating its workers and their families well. Mr Taylor was probably doing no more than his employer required of him and he had been very apologetic about the tool shed. It was just that Meg did not think he was sincere: not about the incident; not about anything really. She just didn't like him. But clearly Edith did.

The following Monday she asked Christine about him.

'He's older than he looks for a start because he dyes his hair. There was talk at one time that he might have been a bigamist. You see there was a rock fall at the quarry – oooh, over twenty years ago now – and a young man was killed. It was the quarry's fault and his widow had two bairns so the quarry gave her a settlement. That's what started the welfare committee and the Friendly Society. Mr Taylor was a foreman then and sharp as a sack o' razors. He emerged as the boss's favourite for promotion to the office to organise it. He also moved in with the young widow and her children when she got her cheque.'

'You mean he married her?'

'That was it. Everybody thought they'd got wed when they went to visit her parents. The trouble started when they set up house together. Mr Taylor, him being the rent collector an' all, couldn't keep his trousers on where other women were concerned and she got fed up with him so she upped and left with her kids and her bank account.'

'So it's true. He really doesn't have a wife.'

'Well, folk thought he had for a time, but after she left he said he'd never married the young 'un. Mind you, he only told folk that because he wanted to wed this other woman who was older than he was and a bit of a battleaxe. Her husband had been in the Friendly Society and everybody thought Mr Taylor had turned over a new leaf when he did marry her. That was until she died of the cancer not long after. Them that didn't know him thought he'd been kind to her. There were others who knew better. Take my advice and watch yourself with him, my lass.'

'It's Edith that I'm worried about.'

'What, your Edith? Edith Dawson that was? She can take care of herself well enough, can't she?'

Meg shrugged. 'I suppose so.'

Meg tried to talk to Edith about Mr Taylor but Edith did not want to listen. It was obvious that she wanted a replacement for Meg's father in the house she had made her home and Meg was worried about her doing something rash that she would later regret.

'He's a widower and he wants a bit of company,' Edith argued. 'What's wrong with that?'

'Nothing,' Meg was forced to agree.

'He's on the staff at the quarry, you know. He gets a monthly salary so he's not after my money.'

'Well, what is he after, then?' Meg queried. She realised immediately that she should have thought before she spoke.

'Meg, love, you're a grown woman! You've not been wed like I have but you do know about these things.'

'You don't want to be the centre of gossip, Edith.'

'He knows that and neither does he.'

'But if he keeps coming round here people will talk.'

'Look, Meg love, you're beginning to sound

bitter. I can understand how you felt about that Leeds lad going off without you. He would have been a good catch for any Deepdale lass. But you can't let it eat you away for ever. If I didn't know you better I'd say you were jealous of me.'

Shocked that Edith had even considered she might be, Meg's mouth dropped open. 'Good Lord no! I'm worried about you. Mr Taylor has a history with – with women.'

'And I've buried two husbands so I know what I'm doing. Folk my age always have a past. You don't have to worry about me. I know how to get what I want.'

Meg couldn't disagree with that. 'But what do you want, Edith?'

'Well, a ring on my finger for a start, before there are any shenanigans.'

Meg felt better about that because she was sure that Mr Taylor was not the marrying sort and maybe he would get tired of labouring in the garden for his Saturday dinner. But that didn't cheer her for long because she was convinced that Mr Taylor was working towards more than a meal for his services. Meg did not sleep easy that night.

Shawbridge

Florence sat bolt upright in the front seat beside Bradley as he allowed the rumbling engine of his motor car to stall. The night air was cold and she clutched her fur wrap closely around her neck. A light from a lamp in the hall of Brookes Villa glowed through a stained-glass fanlight over the wide front door of her home.

Since their first dinner together last spring, with sons and daughters of other town merchants and tradesmen, Florence and Bradley had been 'walking out together' and last weekend he had made her an offer of marriage. Bradley had opened his shop in the old forge and gathered a small group of supporters for his newly formed theatre society. Florence had invited Miss Preston, who organised the lecture programme, to join them but she did not have spare time to contribute and had even expressed concern that Florence might be distracted from her afternoon meetings.

'Not at all,' Florence had assured her. 'Bradley has enough like-minded fellows to help him.'

'I had assumed you were as interested as he in the theatre?'

'I shall welcome the addition to Shawbridge.'

'But you prefer, dare I say it, politics and history?' Miss Preston suggested.

'Is that so terribly unfeminine? Your lectures do make me think more about life outside the High Street.'

'And encourage you to ask more questions. We have another suffragist speaker in the New Year.'

'Oh, how wonderful! What will she talk about?'

'Well, actually, she is raising money for a project to take her message to mill towns and villages in the Dales as a kind of travelling speaker.'

'How adventurous of her,' she had replied. 'I shall look forward to it.'

As Bradley drove her home in his motor car, Florence mused on how brave the suffragist must be to break free from the expectation of being a wife and mother and looked forward to her talk.

'Florence, do pay attention when I'm speaking to you.'

'Oh, so sorry, Bradley, I was thinking of the lecture.' Underneath her chin, she could feel the shape of her emerald and diamond ring beneath her glove. He had proposed formally last week over dinner at the Grand. She had expected it. He had not considered any other girl in town and he said that he loved her. She had accepted him – what girl wouldn't? – so why didn't she feel happier? She pasted a smile on her face and turned to him. 'Thank you for bringing me home, Bradley.'

He made no attempt to climb out of the motor car to open her door and help her out. 'What was your lecture about this week?'

If she thought he was truly interested she would have invited him indoors for a nightcap to discuss it. Instead, she said, 'May I tell you another day? I am rather tired and Father will be waiting up for me.'

'Very well, Florence.' Now he helped her down as she expected. 'You are happy about our engagement, aren't you?'

'Of course, darling.' She emphasised her response by stretching up to kiss him lightly on his cheek. His skin was cool and smooth above his neatly trimmed beard and moustache. She would have felt happier, though, if he had drawn her into his arms and returned her chaste peck with a passionate kiss. 'Are you?' she asked lightly.

'I am delighted, my dear. Your mother has accepted Mama's invitation for luncheon at Melvil

Hall on Sunday. I travel to Sheffield on Saturday and will meet you from the railway train. We must set a date for the wedding.'

Mother and Father would be thrilled for she had told them all she knew about the Melvils' grand house on the Derbyshire side of Sheffield. Their own detached villa was substantial, in the best part of Shawbridge with a large front garden behind wrought-iron railings, but Bradley's family home was much larger and well placed in its own grounds. It had been built for a former king's mistress, sold off when he died and now belonged to the Melvils.

Bradley escorted her to the front door, which opened as if by magic as she approached. 'Thank you, Mrs Jackson,' Florence said as the housekeeper put out her hands to collect her fur wrap, coat and gloves and stow them in the closet. She reached up to unpin her hat, watching Bradley return to his motor car, crank the engine to restart it and then drive away.

'Has Bradley gone back to the Grand?' Mrs Brooke appeared at the square entrance hall from the door to the drawing room.

'He has.'

'Then close the front door, dear. There's a dreadful draught in here. We'll have our cocoa now, Mrs Jackson.'

'He told me about the invitation to Melvil Hall.'

Her mother's eyes sparkled. 'Isn't it exciting? He brought it with him and I have already written a reply. Your father is so proud of you.'

Florence did think she had done rather well by

gaining the affections of such a handsome, eligible bachelor. A good match was what her upbringing and education had prepared her for, and Bradley was most certainly that. Even Florence was aware of envy amongst her mother's contemporaries on the town's committees.

'Did Father speak with him about extending his premises?'

'I believe he did. Why?'

'Well, Bradley did come here to establish Melvil's chemist in a prime position. I thought at first he might be more interested in Brookes' shops than me.'

'Florence! How ridiculous. You are beautiful and intelligent and talented, why shouldn't he fall in love with you? You tell her, Mr Brookes.' Florence's father had joined them in the hall and walked into the front drawing room where a large fire burned in the grate. Mr Brookes took up his usual position in front of it with one hand resting on the carved mahogany mantelshelf.

'You leave the business to me, Florence, and concentrate on looking pretty,' he said. 'You'll be set up for life wed to a Melvil.'

'They are such an attractive couple, don't you think, Mr Brookes?' her mother enthused. 'Didn't I say to you if you want our daughter to marry well you must send her to that York academy?'

Father nodded. He had a self-satisfied expression on his face and answered, 'It was worth the expense, right enough.'

Florence gave her father a weak smile. She had wanted for nothing in her upbringing and in her father's eyes, his investment had paid off. She wished she felt more enthusiastic about her future with Bradley. She believed she would if he were more – more – well, more loving towards her. She could hardly talk about it to her parents. They were Victorians through and through. She said, 'But I wonder if my dowry is more attractive to him than I am.'

Father did not return her smile. He said, 'Now then, lass, where did you get that idea from?'

'I – I'm not sure that Bradley really loves me.'

'What? I think the size of that ring on your finger is proof enough, my girl. Fellows from families with his wealth don't make a commitment to marriage lightly.'

She stretched out her hands to the flames and watched the jewels flash in the firelight.

'Your father's right, dear,' Mother added. 'The Melvils are worth more than we are any day, much more. And I most certainly hope that his behaviour towards you is respectful. I mean I do worry about the influence those theatrical *bohemian* types might have on him. I am very glad to hear that he isn't like them.'

Florence smiled at her mother's concern; she always described any kind of improper behaviour as 'bohemian'.

'He is always a gentleman towards me,' she said, and that was her grumble. She would have welcomed a 'bohemian' divergence or two. Bradley was simply not passionate enough for her, she thought. She sighed unconsciously. She would have to wait until after marriage for that. Perhaps she ought to be grateful that he respected her virtue enough to wait. She considered asking her mother about proper married love, but knew Mother would have a fit if she did. She wished she had a sister to talk to.

Father cleared his throat. 'These lectures you're so fond of, Florence, I don't consider they are the kind of thing a Melvil will want his wife caught up in.'

Florence was astounded. 'But they are interesting, Father. I enjoy them.'

'Enjoy them? He told me you have suffragists to speak. I won't have a daughter of mine listening to those – those women. They're troublemakers and criminals.'

'No they are not! They have strong beliefs, I grant you. You should listen to them before you condemn them.'

'Florence! Do not speak to your father like that her mother exclaimed. 'Anyway, you'll be far too busy for lectures, dear, after this weekend. Do you know what is involved in getting married? You'll need a dress, attendants and invitations. Bradley is talking of building a house for you, a brand-new house!'

'Be quiet, Ethel,' her father snapped. He returned his wrath to Florence and said, 'I forbid you to go to any more lectures at the Institute.'

'But we have had very few lectures on suffrage, Father!' she protested. 'We have a different speaker every time.'

Her father glared at her. 'You will do as I say.'

Florence was cross with her father for speaking to her as though she were a naughty little girl. 'This is Bradley's doing, isn't it?' she protested. 'You wouldn't have known anything about it if he hadn't taken me there and then come back here. What else have you been cooking up with him behind my back?'

'That is enough, Florence. You will go to your room.'

Go to her room? 'I'm not a child any more, Father,' she protested. 'I'm a grown woman, soon to be a married woman, so please treat me like one.'

Her mother appeared mortified at her outburst and Florence knew that if she didn't obey her father, Mother would be dreadfully upset. And she felt suffocated by all this talk of the marriage and the Melvil money. So she left the warm drawing room and dashed upstairs to the relative chill of her bedroom, passing Mrs Jackson in the hallway.

'Your cocoa, Miss Florence,' Mrs Jackson called after her.

'I don't want it, you have mine.'

She realised now why Bradley had been so insistent on taking her to the meeting in his motor car. It was for the same reason he had asked her to be hostess at his first public dinner at the Grand. Mother was right in her initial observation. He was testing her and checking up on her. He could have asked her about the lectures and she would have told him. But he hadn't, he'd had to see for himself and that meant he didn't trust her to be honest with him. Was that any way to start married life together?

After a while she calmed down and returned to the drawing room. 'I'm sorry, Father,' she said. 'But it's too soon to be talking of the wedding and the new house. It's overwhelming me.'

'I told you not to rush things, Ethel,' her father said.

'Well, I'm sorry too, I'm sure,' her mother answered. 'I was only thinking of your father's reputation in Shawbridge. He has to give you a good send-off.'

'I have decided to ask Bradley for a long engagement.'

'That sounds sensible to me, lass. It'll give me and your mother plenty of time to organise a grand do for you,' Father said.

'Will Bradley agree, dear?' Mother asked. 'You don't want to be putting him off.'

'She has the ring on her finger, Ethel.' Her father sounded impatient. 'We'll sort it all out on Sunday. That's why we've been invited.'

Chapter 7

Langton Park, near Shawbridge

'Prudence has settled down well to being your wife.' Alice stretched the fingers of her right hand and gazed at the rows of leather-bound books, neatly arranged in tall bookcases lining the walls. She was in her brother's study writing invitations to a charity fund-raising cocktail party to be held at Langton Park. *Earl and Countess Langton request the pleasure of...* Strictly speaking, she thought, Prudence ought to be doing this now.

'Prudence adores the house and has endless ideas for refurbishments,' he replied.

Alice smiled at her brother, pleased that her pretty sister-in-law had found useful interests to occupy her time.

Charles continued, 'She has her own money, of course, but I have given her the income from Grandmama's trust fund as well. Grandmama spends hardly any of it now she is bedridden.'

'I didn't know that Grandmama had a trust fund.'

'It was her marriage settlement. Strictly speaking it's not a proper trust, but Father accounted for it separately and I have continued to do the same.'

'It must be quite substantial.'

'It is. Her father and uncles were bankers. Of course, she married before the law about one's wife's income came into force.'

Alice's mother had told her about the Married Women's Property Act. It ensured that women kept their own money when they married instead of having to give control to their husbands.

Charles went on, 'All of Grandmama's wealth became Grandfather's on her marriage. She was a jolly good choice in that respect. Grandmama's fund has kept Langton going for years.'

'Had you considered setting up a trust for me, Charles?'

He raised his eyebrows. 'You don't need one. Langton Park has accounts at all major suppliers and you can have anything you want, you know that.'

'Anything at all?'

A guarded expression crossed his brow. 'Within reason, sister dear.'

'Well, I should like to have money of my own, actual cash in my – in my pocket.'

Charles could not have appeared more shocked if she had asked to learn to use a typewriter. 'Alice, dearest, how dreadfully middle class. Where do you get your ideas?'

'Must I be forced to tell every shopkeeper that I am Lady Alice Langton?'

Charles's expression told her that was a request too far. 'Of course you must! And be proud to!' he thundered. 'They all know who you are anyway, do they not?'

'Perhaps they do but there are other people who do not. I should like to attend the afternoon lecture programme at the Institute in town.'

Charles gave a short laugh. 'What nonsense, Alice. Why on earth do you want to go to lectures? I had three years of them at Oxford and believe me they will bore you.'

'I am not you. I have not had the benefit of attending university,' Alice pointed out. 'I might find them interesting.'

Alice saw that this reminder of his more youthful days had distracted her brother. 'Ye-e-s,' he mused, 'I remember one or two bluestockings who insisted on studying with the gentlemen. Good heavens, you don't want to be one of them, do you?'

No she didn't, but if she did Alice couldn't see anything wrong with that and began to feel irritated with her brother. She replied, 'I might. How shall I know if I haven't tried?'

Her sharp tone caused Charles to frown. 'Then go if you wish. Have them send the bill to me.'

'Must I? I should prefer the anonymity of paying the entrance fees with cash.'

'And I should prefer you not to.'

'You sound more like Father every day. This is the twentieth century, Charles.'

Her brother made a disapproving grunt. 'I blame that Pankhurst woman from Manchester. Stirring up trouble and assaulting police officers indeed! We should bring back the stocks. A few days of public ridicule would put a stop to her antics.'

'The magistrate did send her to prison.'

Charles shook his head. 'This is what happens when you let wives keep their money.'

'I'm quite sure Prudence will never let you down in that respect.'

'And neither will you.' That sounded like an order to Alice and she raised her eyebrows. He added firmly, 'You will remember my position in the Riding.'

'So what will you do about my own bank account?'

Charles ignored her persistence and took a small key from his desk drawer to unlock a cupboard in the pedestal. He lifted out a cash box and raised the lid. 'How much do you need?' He counted out several large white banknotes and slid them across the desk. 'Keep them well hidden. I do not want you set upon by thieves.'

'Thank you. May I take the motor car?'

'Briggs is very busy. Prudence uses him a great deal for her social calls and shopping.'

'Perhaps you would prefer that I walk to the

village and catch the horse bus to town?'

'Now you are being silly.'

Actually, she wasn't. Alice fancied she would enjoy riding on an omnibus. 'You are making it difficult for me, Charles.'

'Well, perhaps you'd better not go. I cannot have you wandering around town on your own and forgetting that you are Earl Langton's sister.'

As if I could, Alice thought. She was losing her patience. She was not a child, she was twenty-six and quite capable of looking after herself.

'Then let Briggs take me! I need to begin re-building my life. Much as I love living with Grandmama in the Dower House, she is now too frail to enjoy my readings and conversations.'

Charles frowned. 'I see. Do you need another nurse for her?'

'No. Thank you. We manage very well and I have a rota of local women to sit with her and call for the nurse if necessary.'

'You have villagers looking after Grandmama!'

'They are her former servants or their daughters and Grandmama knows them,' she explained. 'She insisted, so that her nurse and myself may have more free time.'

'Well, if you have time on your hands, why not visit Mother in London? She writes that the London stores make a big show for the festive season.'

'I cannot *leave* Grandmama! Darling Charles, don't you understand? She is nearing the end of her life.' The words caught in her throat causing a tear to spring into her eyes. Grandmama had had a good life until she became old and frail. But it did not make the prospect of losing her any easier to bear.

'I do know that. My physician told me so when I came back from honeymoon and he presented his bill. That was more than six months ago and she is still with us.'

Grandmama was a fighter, so Alice understood her brother's ironic tone. She said, 'Nevertheless, I ought to start thinking about my own future.'

For the first time in their conversation her brother appeared interested. 'You know, you are still beautiful, Alice, and not too old to marry. There are some decent fellows coming back with fortunes from our colonies in India and South Africa...'

At the mention of South Africa, Alice's eyes clouded and Charles rose to his feet. 'Oh God, I'm sorry, old girl.' He stood next to her for a moment and added. 'I thought you would be over Hugo by now.'

Alice agreed with Charles and had believed she was. But sometimes, when she was feeling especially vulnerable, Hugo's memory would catch her out and tears threatened. I'll never get over losing him, she realised but said, 'I am. It's just that it's December and – and December will never be the same for me.'

She had met her beloved Hugo during her coming-out season, had fallen in love with him and had looked forward to becoming the wife of an army officer. He had been a fine soldier and had relished the challenge of war in Southern Africa, only to be cut down when the Boers forged through the British lines at Colenso to lay siege to Mafeking. Seven months later, as everyone had cried tears of happiness to celebrate the relief of Mafeking, Alice had mourned her loss.

Charles squeezed her arm gently. 'I'll see what I can do about a decent dowry for you.'

It was a kind thought but marriage was the last thing on Alice's mind. She had tried to replace Hugo in her affections. She had accepted invitations to race meetings, shooting parties and hunt balls across the nation. But no matter how tall and strong and handsome, no gentleman had ever come close to replacing her darling Hugo.

I don't want a dowry, she thought irritably, I want my independence, my own money and – and I want a bicycle so I don't have to ask for the motor car and be quizzed about where I am going every time I want to go to town! Charles was not mean with money but her own bank account would give her a freedom from questions that she did not have at present, or ever would. Their mother had a trust fund from her own father which would revert to his family when she died, which meant she had nothing to leave to Alice.

Why hadn't Alice's father set up a trust for her? She knew the answer. It was because he assumed she would marry and the sum would be part of her marriage settlement. But she didn't marry before Father died and so she was dependent on the generosity of her brother.

It was strange, Alice thought as she looked at the banknotes in her hand. She could have almost anything she wanted yet sometimes she felt that she had nothing at all that was her own. Independence was all about money. It wasn't the amount you had but what you did with it, she reflected, and it crossed her mind that, with cash in her hand, she was able to go out and buy a bicycle now.

She hesitated only because Charles would not approve of his sister riding around the estate and village dressed like a shop girl. Her own deep-rooted sense of propriety stopped her. The family had always been well respected in the Riding and Charles worked hard not to tarnish their reputation. She was his only sister, older than he, and he never questioned his duty to take care of her. The least she could do in return was to support him in the Riding and not be the cause of any gossip, however much this might irk her. She gave an irritable sigh and asked for the motor car to take her into town at the earliest opportunity to enrol on her lecture programme.

The following week Briggs drove her into Shawbridge for her first lecture. It was a cold, dank December day overcast with cloud. She asked Briggs to stop the car well away from the Institute and she sat in the back of the Rolls-Royce staring at the imposing red brick building. A few people, mostly ladies, approached and walked up the steps. One arrived on a bicycle and carried it with some difficulty up the steps. A porter came out and helped her to take it indoors.

'Wait in the motor car, Briggs, I'll walk from here.'

'His lordship says I must stay with you at all times, my lady. You get all kinds of ruffians going in there.'

'You are referring to night-school classes. This

is afternoon and the room will be full of ladies for this lecture.'

'I just saw a – er – a working man go in, my lady.'

'Yes, I noticed him too.' He wore a suit of clothing but he was most definitely not a gentleman and a frisson of anxiety stirred in her breast. 'Perhaps he was a policeman, Briggs?'

'Policemen wear a uniform, my lady.'

Alice pushed aside her concern and responded, 'As do you, Briggs, so please do as I ask and stay here.'

'Very well, my lady.' He climbed out and opened the door for her.

Alice breathed a sigh of relief. She had enrolled as Miss Langton last week. It was a fairly common surname originating from the Langton estate and village and spreading through the Riding over a couple of centuries. She did not wish to be conspicuous and had dressed soberly, as if she were visiting the vicar and his wife in the village to discuss an estate bereavement.

When Alice approached the steps, a motor car drew up and the driver climbed out to open the door for his passenger. He was not wearing a uniform although he was dressed expensively in tweeds, eye goggles and gauntlets. His passenger was very pretty and also well dressed in a costume and matching hat. She caught a little of their conversation.

'Thank you, Bradley. I shall catch the tram later.'

'I won't hear of it. What kind of gentleman am I if I do not escort you home? I shall be here for you in one hour and a half precisely.'

Alice went through the double doors into the entrance hall clutching her new leather notecase. She was directed to a room set out with rows of chairs facing a table raised on a platform. The gas lights hissed already as there was very little natural light. Some women were already seated and others were standing in small groups engaged in conversation.

She chose a seat near the front in the middle of the row, sat down on the hard wooden chair and opened her notecase. The lady who had arrived in the motor car had followed her in and took one of the vacant seats next to her. Alice gave her a brief formal smile, which she returned and held out a gloved right hand.

'I'm Florence Brookes.'

Alice shook hands with her. 'Alice Langton. Have you been to one of these lectures before?' she asked.

'I have indeed and I wouldn't have missed this one for anything.'

Miss Brookes seemed excited and, unsure why the lecture was special, Alice replied, 'This is my first, although I am looking forward to all of them.'

'The speaker was there, you know.'

'Oh!' Alice had read her programme and knew the topic was Mrs Pankhurst's recent address in Manchester and the aftermath. 'How thrilling! Do you think she saw the arrests?'

'I hope so,' Miss Brookes replied.

The lady who had enrolled Alice stood up on the platform. She had had a short conversation with her when she enrolled and told Alice she was the daughter of a university professor, now retired, and had worked as his assistant since she had finished her own education. She continued to help him with writing his books. The lecture programme had been her idea. Her father was a regular speaker but today a woman sat beside her on the platform looking down at her notes on the table. Silence descended on the murmuring audience and Alice turned her attention to the lecture.

Alice's knowledge of Mrs Pankhurst and the recent incident in Manchester came from newspaper reports. She had tried to open a discussion on the topic at one of Langton Park's formal dinners. Charles had closed down her conversation immediately with comments such as *Well-bred ladies should know better* and *This is what comes of letting wives keep their money.* Even Prudence raised her eyebrows at that one but had smiled prettily and asked him about the hunting this year. However, one of the guests offered a response: a gentleman who was advising Charles on his parliamentary duties in the House of Lords. He had said, *Actually, my lord, it was Dr Pankhurst who started it all. His wife and daughters simply carried on the work when he died.* Alice had spoken with him in the drawing room later and it was he who had told her about the lecture programme.

Alice was spellbound by the lady speaker and the passion and courage in her speech. She was so captivated that, when they were having refreshments at the end, Alice picked up a leaflet, brought by the speaker, about the association she represented. She read it with interest.

'Are you thinking of joining, miss?'

She was not used to such familiarity and blinked. It was the slightly shabby-looking man that she and Briggs had noticed earlier.

'Are you?' she parried.

'Dear me no.' He shook his head. 'They wouldn't let me in. I'm lucky to be here today.' He was local and spoke like one of the servants or villagers. She smiled and moved away, grateful that Miss Brookes was nearby. 'Do you know that gentleman?' she asked.

'I haven't seen him here before, but then I haven't seen an audience as big as this before either. Did you enjoy your first experience?'

'Very much, thank you.'

'The next one is Egyptian Archaeology. Will you be here?'

'I hope so.'

'Do you have far to go?'

'Langton.'

'Oh, that is a long way out of town. You'd better hurry if you want to catch the last omnibus, unless why don't I give you lift to the market place? My – my friend has a motor car.'

'Yes, I saw you arrive. That is very kind of you but someone will meet me.'

They had to wait in the entrance hall while a few ladies took their bicycles outside and Alice asked, 'Do you know where I can buy a bicycle in Shawbridge?'

'You have certainly asked the right person for that!' Miss Brookes laughed. 'You can purchase one from my father's shop. He's Brookes' Provisions and Hardware, in the High Street. Father prides himself on being able to supply any item you request.'

'Really? How splendid. Do you know anything about bicycles?'

'No, but Father does. Call in one day and he'll advise you. Miss Langton, did you say? I'll tell him to expect you.'

The raucous sound of a klaxon came from the roadway. 'Must dash; see you at the next lecture.'

Alice was one of the few ladies remaining in the entrance hall. Through the open doors to the steps she noticed a uniformed policeman standing outside and Briggs watching for her on the other side of the road. She waited for the organiser and speaker to walk away. As they went by the speaker pushed another leaflet into her gloved hand. 'Do consider joining our cause, miss. Goodnight.'

'Goodnight,' she replied and followed them down the steps. Briggs hurried across the road.

'Come along, my lady. His lordship would be very angry with me if I let anything happen to you.'

'Briggs, what can happen to me at a lecture?'

'I had a word with that policeman. He was keeping an eye on the meeting. He doesn't want any suffragists stirring up trouble in Shawbridge.'

Alice saw his reasoning. 'Well, for goodness' sake don't say that to his lordship. It was a peaceful meeting.'

Briggs opened the door of the motor car and asked, 'Straight home, my lady?'

'Actually, no. Do you know where the High Street is?' she asked.

'Yes, my lady.'

'Drive me down there.'

'Very well, my lady.'

'Brookes' consisted of two large shops side by side, with groceries and provisions in one and hardware in the other. She stared at the plate-glass windows displaying a variety of goods, a few of which were visible in the fading light. When they reached the end of the High Street, Briggs said, 'Shall I take you home now, my lady?'

'Turn around and drive along the High Street again, Briggs. I want a second look.'

'Very well, my lady.'

'It was a truly interesting lecture, Grandmama. The speaker actually knew Mrs Pankhurst and her daughters, and she explained how they became devoted to their cause.'

It was a whole week since the lecture but the first time Alice had felt Grandmama was alert enough to enjoy her report. Alice waited for a response but saw only fatigue in her grandmama's eyes. The old lady waved her hand in a negative gesture that showed she wished to rest. Alice smiled but inside she was crying. Grandmama was fading. The nurse came in with a tray of Benger's liquid food and a letter.

'Good morning, Lady Alice. This note came for you a few minutes ago from Langton Park.'

'Thank you.' She picked up the small envelope and opened it. It was from Charles requesting her presence at luncheon that day. She bent towards her grandmama and said, 'Charles wishes to see me. I shall be back for tea.' Then she hurried away to change wondering who else might be there.

As it turned out she and Charles were alone because Prudence was taking luncheon with a friend in Harrogate. Alice prepared herself for 'family business', probably about Grandmama. She was seated alone in the lofty dining room at Langton Park for a full ten minutes before Charles appeared. He did not look pleased and he was carrying a newspaper which he waved about in the air.

'Alice, this will not do.'

Surprised, she remained calm and responded with a polite, 'Good morning, Charles. How are you?'

'Never mind that, what about this!' He brandished the newspaper under her nose and then dropped it in front of her on the table. 'Are you deliberately trying to embarrass me? Mother will be mortified.'

Alice picked up the newspaper, which was a weekly publication that served most of the Riding. There was a photograph of her on the front page. She had seen it before. It was the picture of her taken a long time ago to mark her engagement to Hugo and had been kept in the files of the newspaper office for future use. When it had first appeared, a photograph of Hugo in his army officer's uniform had been by printed alongside hers and that memory was painful. She read the headline and her fingers scrunched the page as she did. *Lady Alice Langton Joins the Suffragist Cause.*

'It's not true,' she protested, 'why on earth would they write that?'

'You were present, Alice,' Charles snapped.

It was an article about the lecture she had attended recently and it was clear from the words that the journalist had been present. The shabby man, she realised, who had painted a word picture of the meeting's audience but had reported only on the more radical ideas of the speaker.

'Really, Alice!' Charles went on. 'Is this what I am paying for? These lectures are a cover for insurgents and communists. I cannot have the Langton title associated with them.'

'Don't be ridiculous! It was only one meeting.'

He leaned forward to emphasise his words. 'So was the Manchester riot and – and – those – those – I cannot refer to them as ladies – those *women* were arrested and put in prison after that. Our chief constable had a man on duty all evening outside your meeting. Who knows what might have happened if he had not been there?'

'Charles, it was just a lecture.'

'I don't care. I won't have you going there again. As Lord Langton's sister you have a reputation to uphold.'

'Does that mean I may not seek to broaden my thinking and have views of my own?'

'Not those views! I thought your lectures were to discuss art and music.'

'And science and politics.'

'Good heavens, what do women want with science and politics? Can't you do needlepoint at home instead?'

'No I can't and you are being silly!'

Charles did not reply as his butler came in with the soup and he waited until he had served them. 'You may leave us,' he said, before shaking out his napkin and replying, 'You have no cause to speak to me in such a way. You are mixing with the wrong kind of people and I forbid you to go to any more of these so-called lectures. The organiser is the daughter of a *communist*.'

'He is not a communist. His life's work at the university has been to study and write about philosophy.'

'You will do as I say, Alice, and the matter is closed. Shall we enjoy luncheon?' He picked up his spoon and tasted the soup. 'Ah, leek and potato, my favourite.'

Alice inwardly fumed as they drank their soup in silence. She had no intention of arguing with Charles as she knew she could not change his views. He wouldn't have known about the lectures if she had not told him for she had paid with the cash he had given her. However, it made her more determined than ever to negotiate some kind of independence from him. His mood improved when pork chops with baked apple arrived and after some discussion of the weather and his breeding pheasants he seemed to relax.

'Have you given further thought to a bank account of my own?' she ventured.

He pushed aside his plate. 'You have not inspired my confidence to do so,' he replied.

Alice pursed her lips to stop them trembling with anger.

'If Father were alive he would have agreed with me.'

'I am not convinced of that. He made no provision for a trust in your name.'

Alice closed her eyes to gather her courage, but

her words were strangled. 'My settlement was to be a wedding gift. He trusted me to manage my own affairs.' However, Father had died before had done anything about asking his lawyers to draw up the papers.

Charles was silent for a few minutes and she believed he genuinely sympathised with her. It had been difficult for both of them to lose their father so suddenly, but Alice had not been very close to him. To lose Hugo not long afterwards had been devastating for her. Alice had loved Hugo with a devotion that devoured her and she was a broken woman after his death. The newspapers lauded him as a hero and Charles had said she ought to be proud of him. But she would rather he had been less courageous in battle and still alive to love her.

Eventually Charles said, 'Have you thought any more about marriage? I've put word out about your dowry and Prudence is organising house parties for the shooting season with you in mind.'

'You make me sound like one of her charities.'

'Now that is enough, Alice. I – we do want to please you.'

'Then let me have my own bank account.'

His butler came in to take away their dirty plates and bring in hot plum pie.

'Very well, Alice. I shall contact my banker if you give me your word that you will not attend any more of these lectures.'

'No, Charles, I shall not, nor shall I allow you to bully me.'

'It is my duty to look after you.'

She refused pudding, placed her napkin on the

table and rose to her feet. 'If that is your last word on the matter I shall return to Grandmama.'

'Why must you be so obstinate? I mean what I say about your position as my sister. I shall instruct Briggs not to take you into town in the motor car without Prudence.'

Alice did not trust herself to remain civil towards her brother. 'Good afternoon, Charles,' she said, and left.

A brisk walk back to the Dower House gave Alice a chance to calm down. That settles it, she thought. I shall definitely buy a bicycle and see what my dutiful brother thinks of that when Brookes' present their account!

Chapter 8

Deepdale, Spring 1906

It began for Meg when Mr Taylor organised a regular railway excursion to Skipton on Saturday afternoons for quarry workers and their families. He said she was entitled to free tickets as the daughter of a former employee and she saw it as a polite way of avoiding his Saturday-afternoon visits. He said she could take a friend and she asked Edith to go with her.

'Mr Taylor suggested it,' Meg explained, 'so he will understand that we can't give him dinner any more.'

'It's more for the younger folk, dear. No, you

take one of your friends from the mill. You girls work hard all week and it's good for you to get away. Here, I'll give you some money to treat yourselves to tea in a café.'

'If you're sure you don't mind.' Meg hesitated before adding, 'Will you be all right on your own with Mr Taylor? He can be, well, very forward for a rent collector.'

'Oooh, I think I can take care of myself at my age, dear.'

Meg felt slighted. She had had Edith's best interests at heart and did not want Mr Taylor taking advantage of her. 'What will you do for your dinner?'

'Now then, don't worry about me. You take your fish and chips straight to the railway station with the others. I'll have a bit of supper ready for you when you get home.'

'All right, if you're sure.'

Edith smiled in that satisfied manner she used when she got her own way. A free ticket and tea paid for meant that Meg could actually buy some of the things displayed in the shop windows. She searched for a suitable gift for Edith – something she couldn't get in Deepdale – and returned tired but cheerful, grateful for hot soup and an early night. It became the highlight of her week and she looked forward to Saturdays, to finishing early at the mill and to eating her dinner out of a news-paper with others on the excursion. She found friends to partly fill the gap that Sally had left and started to think of Mr Taylor in a different light.

Spring was cold in the Dales. Edith always lit the front-room fire for her when she arrived home chilled from the railway train. At least she thought it was for her, but when she found Mr Taylor installed in the armchair with a glass of stout by his elbow and his legs stretched out in front of the fire, she experienced her first doubts.

'Good evening, Mr Taylor,' she said as she unpinned her hat and shook off the rain. 'Is Edith all right?'

Her answer came through the open door. 'Is that you, love?' Edith called from the back kitchen. 'Sit yourself down. I'll call you when it's ready.'

'Come and sit down then, Meggy, m'ducks,' Mr Taylor said. His faced was flushed from the heat of the flames. 'Have you had a nice time?'

Nobody ever called her Meggy. Mother liked Megan, the name on her birth certificate, but she had been Meg to everybody all her life. 'Yes, thank you,' she answered. 'It's very kind of you to keep giving me these tickets. I hope I'm not depriving anyone else.'

'Not at all, m'dear.'

She noticed he watched her as she took off her coat. 'I'll take this upstairs and go and help Edith in the kitchen.'

'Edie doesn't need help. Leave her to it and come and sit by me.'

'Is something wrong?'

'No. I just want to talk to you.'

As she climbed the stairs, delicious aromas of a Sunday roast wafted under her nose. Why was Edith cooking a roast dinner on a Saturday night? What would they eat tomorrow? It didn't make sense to Meg. It occurred to her that Mr Taylor had stayed all afternoon and an anxiety took hold of her stomach. Something was afoot and her old doubts about him surfaced. She tried to push them from her mind. Edith was too sensible to be taken in by his ways, wasn't she? Meg's stomach knotted. She couldn't be sure.

The front-bedroom door was slightly ajar as usual. It was Meg's habit, taught to her by her own mother, to tidy her bedroom and make her bed before she left for the mill and, as Edith was an early riser and went out with a jug to walk half a mile for fresh milk for breakfast, she did her room too before she went downstairs. Meg, feeling guilty and ashamed of herself, peeked in. She felt sick. It served her right for being nosey, she thought. But if she was worried before, she was frantic now.

The neatly made double bed was tumbled and creased, and – and there was a smell. She wanted to cross the room and open the window. She had lived with two brothers and she knew that men smelled different from women. Her heart began to thump. There was a Macassar stain on the pillow. Mr Taylor used Macassar on his hair and Edith had made antimacassars for the front-room chairs. She stumbled across the small landing to her own bedroom and sank on to the bed.

Edith and Mr Taylor? Was that what these Saturday excursions were about? She had known that Edith had rekindled her father's vigour and had been pleased for him. Edith had as good as told Meg that her own appetite for the bedroom had not gone away. She covered her eyes with the heels of her hands, and blew out her cheeks. She wished she hadn't peeked. She didn't want to know, just

135

as she hadn't wanted to know about her father and Edith, even though she could hear them from her bedroom. She tried to be rational about her feelings. She had been pleased for her father and Edith; they were married and appeared to love each other. But Edith and Mr Taylor? Edith had money and Mr Taylor had a questionable past with widows. Perhaps Edith had not heard about his reputation? Eventually, she stood up, tidied her hair and face and went downstairs.

'Meggy-y-y.' Mr Taylor greeted her as though she were his long-lost daughter. 'Meggy, come and sit by the fire with me. Edie's doing the roast tonight.' He leaned over the arm of his chair and picked up a dark brown bottle. 'You'll have a glass of stout with me, won't you?'

There were glasses on the side table by his elbow. One was almost empty. He refilled it from the bottle and then opened another. Edith didn't normally cook on Saturday nights, not after fish and chips at dinner, but the smell was appetising and the cold had made Meg hungry. She took the stout and sat opposite Mr Taylor by the fire. 'Is it your birthday?' she asked.

'You're a sharp one to be sure. No it's not, my little one. But Edie and I are celebrating.'

He wasn't drunk but he was certainly tipsy. They weren't celebrating the Friendly Society cheque because Edith had that already and it was safe in the bank. He – he – oh dear Lord, he was grinning – no, *leering* at her! She avoided his eye and sipped her stout. On an empty stomach, the alcohol spread quickly through her veins, but it was warming rather than cheering.

There was absolutely nothing wrong with Edith and Mr Taylor enjoying each other's company but this was her home too and she had a nasty suspicion that Mr Taylor had given her the train tickets deliberately to get her out of his way. Perhaps that was what Edith wanted too? Meg began to feel uneasy and drank her stout more quickly than was wise.

'Steady on, Meggy, m'lass, you've not had anything to eat yet.'

She half smiled and placed her glass on the floor. 'What are we celebrating then?'

Mr Taylor raised his voice. 'Edie! Edie ducks, come here a minute.'

My goodness, he had a loud voice when he shouted. When Edith came into the front room, Mr Taylor stayed seated and raised his arm. Edith took his hand and stood beside his chair. She was flushed and beaming from ear to ear.

'Has he told you, love? We're going to get married. Saul – that is, Mr Taylor – will move in and live here. Won't that be a treat?'

Meg didn't know whether to be horrified at the notion of living with this man or pleased that at least he had offered Edith marriage while he bedded her and spent her money. Edith was obviously happy but Meg was sorry that she had felt able to replace her father so quickly. She pasted a beam on her face and lied, 'I thought something was going on between you two. I'm very happy for you, Edith.' She picked up her glass and raised it in the air. 'Congratulations, Mr Taylor.' She might have added, 'and welcome' if he had been anybody else. But she hadn't liked

137

him from the start and now she despised him for manipulating her out of the way as he had.

'You can call me Saul now, like Edie does.'

'You've never called me Mother, have you, dear, and Saul sounds much better than Father.'

Edith meant well but she might as well have driven a knife through Meg's heart with those words. Neither of them came even close to being the wonderful people her parents had been.

'Supper's ready. I hope you're hungry after your fish and chips. Saul brought us a joint of venison.'

'Best cut, it is. The gamekeeper had it sent over from Ferndale for me doing him a favour. He needed a special bit o' stone for some work on his cottage.'

Ferndale. Meg closed her eyes for a moment and the knife in her heart twisted again. Jacob's father had supplied Edith's celebration meal. Her hunger pangs receded but she said, 'I'm starving. I must have walked miles in Skipton today.'

'And you've given me a very hearty appetite, Edie,' Saul replied, standing up with a wink. He picked up the remaining full bottles of stout, leaving the empty ones to litter the front-room carpet.

Meg took a moment to gather her strength before she followed them into the kitchen. They were happy, she told herself, and why shouldn't they be? Just because she had let her one chance of happiness slip through her fingers there was no reason to begrudge Edith another opportunity.

'We could have had this for our Sunday dinner,' Meg commented.

'No need, there'll be plenty left over for you,

love. Me and Saul have been invited out tomorrow. Someone he knows from the quarry.' Edie gave the gravy a stir; then she turned to face Meg and added, 'Saul's stopping here tonight.'

Meg detected a challenging tone in her voice and mentally braced herself not to show her true feelings about Saul. 'That's nice,' she said. 'I'm pleased for you, Edith.' She saw Edith let out her breath and realised that her stepmother had been concerned about Meg's response so she added, 'You deserve to be happy.'

This seemed to cheer Edith no end. She lowered her voice. 'He's a few years younger than me, you know, and – and, well, you know, he likes the bedroom side of things a lot.'

'As long as you do, too,' Meg whispered.

'Oooh, yes.' Edith smiled and looked pleased.

Meg smiled back and took the spoon out of her hand. 'Shall I finish the gravy while you see to the vegetables?'

The house was surprisingly quiet that night apart from Saul's snoring. Meg couldn't sleep, not because a creaking bed kept her awake, but because that one mention of Ferndale had resurrected thoughts of Jacob. She continued to miss him and the familiar empty yearning in the pit of her stomach returned and wouldn't go away. She didn't know what to do to stop it when she thought of him, except perhaps copy Edith and find someone else take his place. But Meg didn't want another man. She wanted Jacob.

As the clock ticked on she went over and over their parting words. *Don't give me false hope, I couldn't bear it.* There was no going back for him.

She had lost him through her own actions. The distant church clock chimed four and, exhausted, she drifted into sleep. A couple of hours later the creaking bed from Edith's bedroom woke her.

Edith decided to wait a few months after Meg's father died before she married Saul. But Saul stayed every Saturday night. Meg dreaded having to spend her free time at home with him in the house. The cheap Skipton excursions had ceased now the railway was busier with summer visitors so Meg found somewhere to walk or cycle with anyone who was willing on Saturdays after work.

'You don't seem very happy about me and Saul,' Edith commented early one Saturday morning as Meg ate her breakfast.

'But I am. Why should you not find happiness and enjoy yourselves? I'm pleased for you both.'

'Well, you don't have to go out *every* Saturday when the mill closes. Saul wants to get to know you. I'm sure he thinks of you as a daughter. He often mentions you.'

'Does he?'

'He keeps asking me what you do of a Saturday and Sunday.'

'Do you think he wants me to leave?'

'Quite the contrary, dear, he thinks *you* want to and he would like you to stay home more when he visits.'

'Really?'

'We could have tea round the front-room fire, like a proper little family. I'd like that. I know he can't replace Albert, God rest his soul, but our lives have to go on, love.'

Meg sighed inwardly. She knew that well enough too. Saul must be aware that he could never replace her father in her affections. Surely he didn't want to? Perhaps he simply wished to please Edith, who wasn't totally insensitive to Meg's feelings.

'All right, I'll come straight home and bring fish and chips like I used to.'

'Thanks, love.'

Meg was secretly pleased that Edith and Saul welcomed her back as she was really fed up of not being able to get on with her sewing on Saturdays. Christine at the mill seemed relieved too when she told her.

'I know it's difficult for you, lass,' Christine said. 'But you want to find yourself a sweetheart, that's what you want to do.'

Easier said than done, Meg thought. She was twenty now and most of the eligible young men had left for the industrial towns or big cities. The only ones she met were too young or already spoken for, or, heaven forbid, had a wife and a roving eye. These were the worst. They seemed to think because she didn't have a ring on her finger that she was fair game for 'a bit of fun' and when she gave them short shrift they were rude and called her names.

So, she made a special effort to have a pleasant Saturday afternoon and evening at home with Edith and Saul.

'Meggy.' It was Saul's way of welcoming her. He was in the kitchen and he advanced towards her with open arms.

She dodged his advance and placed her parcels

of hot fish and chips on plates already warming in the oven and said, 'I'll just go and put my bicycle away.'

'I'll do it for you when I'm out in the garden later. Come and give your Saulie a hug.'

'Where's Edith?' she queried but her words were muffled by Saul's worsted waistcoat as his arms surrounded her. He placed his hands on her back and pulled her close so that she could feel the imprint of his gold watch chain on her breasts. It was no different from the hugs her mother and father used to give her and she still had her coat on but it was the way his hands moved that made her stiffen. They roamed over her back as though he was assessing her shape. He pressed her too close to him, squashing her against his chest. His hug went on a few seconds too long for her comfort.

'My, you're a fine lass, aren't you? A right fine lass.'

She pushed away from him, blinking and managed a faltering smile. 'Is Edith all right?'

'She's in the outhouse looking for her pickled cabbage.'

'Oh, I know where it is. I'll go and show her.' She escaped into the scullery before he could protest. The back door was open and Edith was in the yard with a jar of yellow piccalilli in her hand.

'The cabbage is on the top shelf at the back. You need the stool to reach it. I'll get it for you.' Meg rushed past her, glad to be in the fresh air once again. She found the red cabbage and stood in the yard trying not to think the worst of Saul. It was just his way, she reasoned, and she had to fit in with both of them for Edith's sake. But she hadn't liked how he had held her and … and she suspected that he had liked it much too much.

The kitchen was cosy and warm and Edith had cut bread and butter to have with their fish and chips. Meg made a huge pot of tea, which she topped up with hot water halfway through the meal.

'I've a bit of custard tart if you fancy something sweet,' Edith said as she poured more tea. She picked up the milk jug and stared into it.

'Have we got enough milk for tomorrow?' Meg asked. 'I could walk to the farm and fetch some.'

'I've plenty, thanks. You could do a bit in the garden if you want.'

'What needs doing?'

'Shed could do with a tidy,' Saul said. He looked directly at her. 'Me and Edith generally go for a lie-down after Saturday dinner.'

'Right. Garden it is for me then,' Meg replied, a little too hastily. She didn't want to be in the house if they were upstairs together. The garden was far enough away. 'I'll come in and get the tea ready when it gets dark. Shall I light the front-room fire as well?'

'Saul'll do that afterwards, won't you, love?' Edith smiled at him and he grinned back.

Meg realised that they were both already looking forward to their 'lie-down'. She stood up and said, 'I'll just change my dress.'

This is how it's going to be, she thought as she prepared for an afternoon in the garden, so I'd better get used to it.

Saul had made some changes to the garden but

143

most of it had been dug over before the winter so it was at least tidy. The shed was another matter. It was a tumble of tools and her father's old armchair and little table were covered in dried soil dust and bits of rusting metal. Meg welcomed her task and became absorbed in restoring it to her father's little haven. She cleaned the tools and put them where they belonged, took the chair outside and went over it vigorously with a stiff brush. The fabric was threadbare but it was comfortable with good padding and upholstered wooden arms. The table was rickety and she resolved to ask Saul to strengthen it.

When she had finished she sat down in the armchair and surveyed her work with satisfaction.

Daylight was fading fast and, although there was an oil lamp, Meg thought it would be a waste to light it now. She was wondering if Edith and Saul would be up again when the door opened and Saul stood in the doorway framed by the darkening sky.

'Are you still here?' he queried. 'You must be waiting for me.' He stepped inside and closed the door behind him.

Chapter 9

Meg stood up immediately and tried to squeeze round him.

'Not much room in here for two, is there?' Saul commented as he barred her way. 'Nice, though, isn't it?'

'Let me out, Saul. I have to get the tea on.'

'It's not time yet. Come here to your Saulie for a bit.' He put an arm across her shoulders and propelled her towards him. 'There, that's a lot better, isn't it?'

'No. Let me go.'

'Oooh, I thought we were friends now. Proper friends.' His arm was firmly across her back, holding her in place and his other hand was now stroking her cheek. 'Soft as silk,' he murmured. 'I bet the rest of you is too; all over as soft as silk.'

'Stop it, Saul. It's not right.'

'What's not right? We can be friendly with each other, can't we?'

'Not like this. Let me by so I can get out.'

'Not yet, Meggy. This is too nice.' He heaved her closer and his hand slid from her face down her neck to her blouse. 'Isn't that nice, Meggy love?'

'I said stop it!' She pushed his hand away with her one free arm. The other was trapped by her side and squashed up against him. 'You're supposed to be marrying my stepmother!'

145

'She won't know if you don't tell her, and she won't believe it if you do.' His hand was snaking down her body following the shape of her waist to her hips and then back to her – her breasts, where he squeezed each one in turn. 'Oh,' he groaned, 'my, what a handful, so round and firm, just how I like them. I've had my eye on those little beauties since I first noticed 'em.'

Meg gave up trying to push him away and stretched to pick up a trowel from the table. 'I'll hit you with this if you don't let me go!'

'Meggy! That's no way to treat your future stepdad,' he reproached her. 'Don't be like this. We don't want you turning into a bitter old spinster, do we? Everybody knows that all you need is a bit of loving from a fellow who knows what he's doing, and I'm that fellow.'

Her fury at this comment unleashed an un-known strength in Meg and she threw down the trowel and broke free, bursting out of the shed door into the twilight. She didn't know what she was most angry about, the fact that Saul was betraying her stepmother without qualm, or that his words had touched a nerve. She let out a sob. Was it really that obvious she so desperately missed Jacob?

It was true and that was why it hurt. She couldn't bear to think of Edith and Saul enjoying themselves together in the bedroom because she wished, desperately, that it could have been her and Jacob. But Saul was an idiot if he thought he or anyone else could help in this respect. Nobody could help her. No one was ever going to come anywhere near to replacing Jacob in her heart. She could not even contemplate any relationship, let alone an intimate one, with another man. Not yet anyway and perhaps never. Was Saul right? she anguished. Was she destined to be a frustrated old spinster? The notion hurt her and it hurt a lot.

She pulled herself together and went indoors, wrestling with whether to tell Edith about Saul's behaviour or not. Edith would of course be devastated but better she knew now than after the wedding when his roving eye would continue to stray. The difficulty was that Meg had no doubts that Saul would deny any improper behaviour towards her. He'd say he was just trying to be a loving stepfather and he was such a charmer where Edith was concerned that she would believe him.

Edith would be hurt unnecessarily and it would sour Meg's relationship with her. Besides, Meg wondered whether she was making more of this than it warranted. What if Saul was right and other folk thought she was turning into a frustrated spinster? If she complained about him it might confirm their doubts. She tried to calm down.

Saul must have received her message of rejection loud and clear. He'd be stupid to try it again. But he was a man who was used to success with women and who had a good opinion of himself as a result. She decided to ignore Saul's behaviour and put on a brave face for Edith's benefit. The three of them had to live together in harmony. It might be awkward for a while until they settled down to a new routine but they would all have to do some adjusting, she thought.

Meg strived to avoid Saul's hugs when he greeted her. But usually Edith was present and she didn't want to cause a fuss. He would soon be her stepfather and expected to welcome her as his daughter. So she smiled and allowed him to put his arms around her in a manner that made her feel decidedly uncomfortable.

Edith and Saul married quietly and afterwards Meg had the distinct impression that Saul had been talking to Edith about her. Saul was in the kitchen when Meg came in from the mill but Edie was upstairs and Saul took advantage of her absence. He grabbed hold of Meg and pulled her into a corner so quickly that she overbalanced and fell against him, clutching at his clothes to stop herself falling.

'Put him down,' Edith laughed as she returned from upstairs. She stood in front of them both and went on, 'You must forgive her, Saul love. Meggy is thrilled to have a proper little family again. Me, too. I am so lucky to have found a fellow willing to look after both of us. Any other man would have wanted my stepdaughter married off and out of his way. But I told him straight, Meggy, my love, I said to him, this is Meggy's home for as long as she wants it.' Edith looked enquiringly from Saul to Meg and back to Saul and added, 'That was the right thing to say, wasn't it?'

Meg thought this was an odd little speech to make and wondered what conversations about her had taken place. It crossed her mind that Saul knew how little she thought of him and as she had rejected him he might have wanted her to leave. Saul gave his answer by standing between them and putting an arm around both and squeezing. 'What man wouldn't be happy with two gorgeous women like this at his beck and call? I'm the lucky one here.'

Edith giggled but Meg found it hard to raise a smile. Saul had clearly coloured Edith's opinion of her and it was becoming more and more difficult for Meg to say anything about his unwelcome behaviour.

With two wages coming into the house and Edith's nest egg for a rainy day, Meg was more comfortably off than she had ever been with her own flesh and blood. But she was unhappy and no amount of the best cuts of meat and bottles of stout on a Saturday and Sunday could make up for that. Edith encouraged Saul to drink all evening and at first Meg considered advising her against this. But then Edith would suggest it was time for bed and, when they all went up together, Meg heard Saul's snoring before she went to sleep herself. She suspected Edith had another motive for getting Saul drunk. They all got a good night's sleep, although Saul made up for it in the morning and Meg often woke to grunts, squeals and creaking bedsprings.

But one Sunday Meg woke very early without disturbance and went down to see if the range fire in the kitchen was still glowing. Two minutes later, Edith was by her side fully dressed with her boots in her hand.

'There's no need to go out for milk this morning,' Meg said. 'We've got plenty in.'

'I want some horseradish for the beef. There's a good root at the back of the allotments.'

'But that's over the other side of town! We'll do without.'

149

'I want a bit of horseradish with the beef.' Edith looked guilty when she spoke, as though telling tales out of school. 'He'll think I've gone for milk. He's told me not to because he likes me there when he wakes up so he'll be cross.'

'Then don't go, Edith. Don't make him angry. I'll go for the horseradish instead.'

Edith shook her head. 'He wears me out in the mornings. It's not all fun, you know, and some-times he's, well, he's too much for me. If I take my time, he'll be dressed and downstairs before I'm back.'

Meg's heart broke for Edith and she forgot about her own criticisms of Saul. 'Why not talk to him about it?' she suggested.

'I've tried but... Oh, you wouldn't understand. Men are men and they have needs – I can't explain it to you. You've not had a husband and I've had three now.'

Edith buttoned on her warm coat and went out to the shed for a garden fork. Meg nurtured the fire into life and added more coal as quietly as she could so as not to wake Saul. Then she went back to her still-warm bed while the fire drew. She snuggled down hoping for a last short snooze before Edith returned and started breakfast.

She was just dropping off when she heard a landing floorboard creak and waited for a second squeak from the fifth stair.

'Wake up, Meggy. It's Saulie.'

She took a breath and held it. He was in her bedroom. She ignored him and feigned sleep until she felt his hand shaking her shoulder. 'Wake up, Meggy. Edie's not here.'

Meg opened her eyes and muttered into the pillow, 'She's gone to dig some horseradish.'

'Oh, she has, has she?' He sounded annoyed. 'You'll have to do, then.' He pulled back the bed-covers and climbed in beside her.

Meg shot up to sitting and attempted to scramble out of the bed. 'What are you doing, Saul? Get out this minute.'

He had caught hold of her arm at the elbow and yanked her backwards so she fell on the pillows. Quick as a flash he placed a hand on her hip and straightened her body on the bed. The crumpled bedcovers pressed into her skin through her flimsy nightdress. It had already ridden up to her thighs and she pushed at the hem frantically to lengthen it. But his body had covered hers and she was pinned to the bed unable to struggle free. The horror of his intention exploded in her head. He had taken off his pyjama bottoms! Her hand, still clutching the edge of her nightdress, was trapped between his hairy leg and her crushed thigh. She wriggled it free, beat her fists against his back and spluttered, 'Get off me, you filthy animal!'

He grinned at her, ignoring her punches. 'I'm doing you a favour, Meggy. You've been wanting this for a while now so stop your struggling and have a bit of fun for a change.'

'This is not my idea of fun!'

'You won't be saying that afterwards. That's a promise from your Saulie.'

'If you don't get off me I'll scream.'

'Who'll hear you? The neighbours'll think it's Edie anyway. You've heard her, haven't you?

You're in fer a treat, my little Meggy. Saulie knows how to give a lass a good time.'

Meg was terrified but the more she struggled the more he bore down on her, ignoring her flailing arms, forcing her thighs apart with his knee.

Meg couldn't believe this was happening to her. She had thought him capable of charm and deception but not – not this, surely not this? He shoved a hand down between their bodies and, oh dear Lord, he was fingering her between her legs.

'Come on, Meggy, give a little. It'll be easier for the both of us if you do.'

'Stop this, Saul. I don't want you. You're raping me.'

She felt him go rigid and his face twisted into a snarl. 'That's a nasty word to use. I don't like lasses who accuse me of that when I know they want it more than I do.' His tone was threatening and his hand had left her private area to fumble with his own which she felt hardening against her skin. 'I'll show you what you're missing, you stuck-up little prig.'

He shoved himself into her, forcing her up the bed until her head connected with the headboard. She squealed in pain and cried, 'Stop it! Stop it!' But it was too late, he had entered her and for a second, one second only, he relaxed his body against hers. 'There. That's better, isn't it?' he muttered and then he seemed to forget her altogether as he closed his eyes and began to pump away at her. Push, push, push, grunting and sweating and dribbling over her face, he went on for ever and she thought that she was dying.

152

Pinned to the mattress by his weight, she remembered thinking that hell would be preferable to this. How much longer? She moaned her protests but he was unaware, he was in a place of his own. Eventually his grunts became more urgent and his thrusts harder and stronger. His breathing was noisy and rattling in his throat until quite suddenly he let out a cry like an animal in pain and pulled out of her so quickly that she wondered what was happening. His seed spilled on to her stomach over her crumpled nightie and exposed skin and he flopped down on her almost suffocating her as she felt him pulsing to a finish.

'You are a beast,' she fumed. 'You're not fit to be living with decent women. Get out of my room.' She didn't expect him to take any notice of her and he didn't.

His eyes were hard and glittering but his mouth was grinning. 'You'll want me back for more. The lonely ones always do. We just have to make sure Edie never finds out.'

'And what if I tell her?' she challenged.

'She won't believe you and if she does she won't blame me because she knows as well as I do that you're desperate for it. I've told her how you rub yourself up against me when I hug you.'

'I do not!'

'We all know you've been frantic for a fella since that gamekeeper's lad moved on. If Edie does find out I'll just say you were jealous of her and you flaunted yourself at me. Edie understands men and their needs so she'll forgive me. But not you, my lass, she won't forgive you. She'll hate you for it and you don't want to risk that, do you?' He leaned forward so that she could feel his breath on her face. 'This is our little secret.'

Her stomach knotted, and the bile rose in her throat and she wanted to be sick. Her flesh hurt where he had invaded her and she wanted to kill him with her bare hands. She felt helpless against his lies and spat out, 'Well, it's not going to happen again!'

'Of course it is, so stop your whining and get your clothes. Edie'll be back soon to get the breakfast on.' He climbed off her and went back to Edith's bedroom without another word.

Meg didn't move a muscle for a long time and her mind turned over and over deciding what to do. Her bedroom was cold and silent. She heard Saul go downstairs and rake the fire. Then Edie returned and a muffled drone of voices came through the floor. She moved one of her legs and felt the damp patch on her nightdress where he had spilled out over her. She suppressed an urge to vomit and bitterness burned the back of her throat.

She couldn't stay in bed all day and wished for the earth to open up and swallow her. What was done was done but it was still difficult for Meg to believe it had really happened to her in her own bed, in her own home. Well, it was no longer her home. It was no longer Edie's either. It was Saul's house now and impossible for Meg to stay there. If she did she was likely to end up killing him, literally. If she had had something heavy to hand by the bed earlier, she would have cracked him on the head with it.

She struggled out of bed eventually and washed

herself all over in a small amount of cold water from the jug on her washstand. She screwed up her nightdress and put it in an empty pillowcase and threw it under the bed as though trying to hide all the evidence. She wanted to blot the incident from her mind, as if it had never happened. If she didn't think about it it would fade from her mind. But every step she took reminded her of her pain, both real and in her head. She applied a special cream that she kept for cut and grazes and it soothed her rawness. She put on clean everything and her bicycling skirt and boots, wrapping a few extra belongings in her woollen shawl. She brushed her hair automatically, sat down to pin it up properly and secured her hat on top of it. She didn't know why at first but as her appearance took shape in the glass she realised she was dressing not for Sunday dinner at home but to go outdoors. Her warm coat was on a hook in the front lobby. She took it and her bundle out through the front door and left them by the stone wall and then went back to the kitchen.

'There you are, at last,' Edie said. She was sitting at the table concentrating on peeling vegetables. 'Have you had a nice lie-in?'

'Yes, thanks,' she lied. 'Did you get your horse-radish?'

'I did. Will you grate it for me after you've had your breakfast?'

'I'm going out.'

Edith looked round and noticed her hat. 'I need a hand with the dinner, love.'

'I'm going out for the day,' Meg repeated.

'Oh. You never said. Are you all right? You look

a bit peaky. Is something up?'

Meg looked away and lied again: 'No, nothing. I forgot to tell you I was going to see Sally's mum today.' It was the first name that came into her head but she knew that Sally and Robert were not coming over from Leeds this weekend.

Edith was silent so after a few moments Meg added, 'Don't wait for me at teatime. Sally's mum is a bit lonely these days and I'll stay over if she asks.' That part was true, she thought, and it was the best she could do in her present state. 'You don't mind, do you?'

'I suppose not. Do you want some bacon before you go?'

'No, thanks. I don't feel like any.'

'I hope you're not sickening for something.'

'I'll get my bicycle then.'

'You're not leaving now, are you?'

'It's a nice day. I thought I'd bicycle the long way round.'

'Oh.' Edith sounded disappointed. 'It's just the two of us all day, then.'

'You are happy with – with...' Meg couldn't bring herself to say his name. '... with him, aren't you?'

'Of course I am! Don't take any notice of me. Saul isn't in a very good mood. I was a bit out of sorts first thing but I'm fine now.'

'Where is he?'

'He's had to go and collect a rent. They were out yesterday and he won't wait for it until next week.'

'Well, if Sally's mum asks me to stay over I will, so don't worry.'

Edith didn't look happy about this but simply replied, 'You're a grown woman, Meggy.'

'Cheerio, then.'

'Ta-ra, love.'

Meg went out of the back door and collected her bicycle. She wheeled it round the end of the terrace to the front and stowed her belongings in the basket. She must have made her decision to leave before she dressed, but could not remember exactly when. She had thought of nothing except scrubbing this morning from her memory.

Her only choice was to leave this house, and the man who dominated it, behind her. She glanced up at the eaves, at the roof that had sheltered her all her life. It used to be her home and now it was a place of grief and misery for her. Neither of the occupants really loved her. She must go and live somewhere else. But she had no idea where that would be.

Chapter 10

Langton Park

The atmosphere at the Dower House was subdued as Grandmama's life was ebbing away and Charles insisted that his physician stayed with her at all times. He was accommodated in a spare bedroom. Alice sat for hours simply holding her grandmother's hand. The physician watched closely from the foot of the bed. The nurse stood at the opposite side from Alice and waited. She had observed such scenes before.

'Not long now, my lady,' he said as Grandmama's breathing rattled weakly in her throat.

'Shall I fetch his lordship?' the nurse suggested. Alice shook her head. 'He could be here now if he wished.'

The room was hushed as they all strained to hear the next rattling breath. It did not come. After an interminable silence, Alice looked wide-eyed at the physician. He picked up Grandmama's blue-veined and bony wrist, frowned and shook his head. 'Her ladyship has gone, my lady. I am so sorry.'

Unconsciously, Alice nodded her head. Such a grand old lady, she thought. She'd lived an interesting life to the full, from her adventurous European childhood to enjoying her father's banking wealth. But it was not the money or the title she had married that made her grand, it was her vigour and her zest for life. If I can be half the woman she was, Alice thought, I shall be satisfied.

'Shall I send a servant to tell his lordship, my lady?' the nurse added.

'I shall go myself.' Alice placed her grandmama's hand gently on the bed sheet and stood up. 'I shall be quicker on my bicycle.'

Until now, Alice had kept her bicycle for going to the village or further afield to Shawbridge and had not ridden it up to the Park before. She leaned it carefully against the wall, adjusted her skirt and went in to deliver the distressing news. The butler opened the door to the drawing room at Langton Park and announced, 'Lady Alice to see you, my lord.'

Charles rose to his feet. He was frowning and Alice thought he must have guessed her mission. 'What on earth do you think you are doing, Alice?' Before she could reply he went on, 'You were riding a *bicycle*, for heaven's sake.'

He must have seen her arrive. 'I was in a hurry, Charles. Grand–'

'Then you ought to have sent one of the servants.'

'Oh, Charles, do let me finish.' She stared at him and spoke clearly. 'I am sorry to have to tell you that Grandmama passed away at twenty to three this afternoon.'

'Ah, I see.' He stretched out a hand towards her. 'Come and sit by the fire.' He pressed the bell push on the wall. 'You're trembling. You need a brandy.'

Prudence, who had been sitting quietly by the fire, also stood up, took her hand and led her to a chair.

'Thank you, Prudence.' Alice let out a huge sigh. Her hands were shaking and in an effort to control herself she had been holding her body rigid. Now she was in danger of breaking down into tears.

Prudence said, 'We were expecting it, Alice. She was very old. Order tea, Charles, tea is much better at these times.'

When the butler arrived to take his orders, Charles asked him to fetch his steward immediately to the library. He bent over to kiss Prudence on the cheek. 'I'll leave you two ladies together.

Tell Alice about your plans, dearest.'

His wife murmured, 'Of course, darling,' and patted the couch beside her. 'Come and sit by me, Alice.'

Alice did not have much in common with Prudence but she felt better after the tea. Her numbness receded. Prudence droned on about her refurbishment ideas and Alice only half listened until she realised that her sister-in-law was talking about the Dower House.

'You will have to live with Charles's mother in London while we have the alterations done,' Prudence said. 'But afterwards the Dower House will be much more comfortable with plenty of room for you both.'

Poor Grandmama was hardly cold in her bed and Prudence had the builders in! She and Charles must have been talking about it for days. 'Electricity and a telephone will bring the Dower House into the twentieth century, don't you think?' Prudence added.

Alice had to agree. Grandmama's cook would appreciate a new range in the kitchen and she herself would welcome running water and a flush lavatory upstairs, but she said, 'Shall we wait until after the funeral before we discuss it further? It hardly seems appropriate now.'

'If you wish. You were very close to Charles's grandmother, weren't you? But Langton Park goes on.' She smiled weakly.

Alice stood up. 'I must get back. The servants at the Dower House will need my support.'

'Charles will speak to them later. There will be changes, of course.'

Alice did not trust herself to respond. If she had to move out then so would the servants and she wondered what Prudence had planned for their futures, if anything.

'Shall I ring for Briggs to take you back, Alice?' Prudence asked.

'I don't need the motor car, thank you. I have my – that is, I have a bicycle.'

'Dearest Alice, I do so agree with Charles about this. We cannot have Earl Langton's sister pedalling about the estate like some servant. It will not do. Briggs will drive you back to the Dower House.'

'I'd rather walk,' Alice replied firmly.

She had no desire to upset Prudence or indeed herself by openly going against Charles's wishes so she pushed the bicycle until she was out of sight of the drawing-room windows and rode it the rest of the way.

The Dower House servants had gathered in the kitchen and Cook's largest teapot was on the table. There was a general shuffling when Alice entered until she said, 'Please, all of you, don't get up. We are all very sad. Do try and keep to your routines. It will help.' She managed a smile. 'You still have me to look after.'

One or two muttered, 'Thank you, my lady,' although they were red-eyed and subdued. A death meant change for any household.

After the funeral, Alice was surprised that the Langtons' family lawyer asked her to assemble the Dower House servants as he read Grandmama's will.

'I didn't know that she had made one. I thought

all her money was tied up in the estate and surely the Dower House contents belong to Langton Park too?'

'Indeed they do, but the Dowager Countess did have money of her own. It was left to her by her father's family after your grandfather passed away.'

'I didn't know.'

'No, not many people were made aware. Your father and Charles knew of it, of course, but not how much.'

How thoughtful of Grandmama to leave her money to the servants! They were returning to the Dower House for their own wake anyway. 'I'll just go and tell them to gather in the dining room.'

'You too, Lady Alice.'

'Do I have to be there? I'm expected at Langton Park.'

'We shall wait for you.'

'I do not wish to prolong their suspense. I'll send my apologies to Charles and Mother with one of the gardeners.'

Alice's gaze wandered around the dining-room table, taking in the serious faces of the Dower House servants. The women looked dour under their old-fashioned black hats while the men were uncomfortable in stiff white collars. When the lawyer began reading out the long list of bequests she was not the only person in the room to gasp. Grandmama must have had a considerable inheritance of her own at some time to be able to leave so much money! The equivalent of five years' wages meant that none of the servants need worry about being dismissed as part of Prudence's modernisation.

'…and finally, the residue to my beloved granddaughter, Alice, in recognition of her kindness and devotion in my latter years…'

'Really?'Alice was so surprised that she spoke suddenly and out loud. A murmur of appreciation rolled around the room.

'Quite right, too,' someone muttered.

'Well, I don't expect there's much left after her generosity to you. I am so pleased for all of you, because there will be changes at Langton Park. But now you will have a safety net. Good old Grandmama.' It was an impulsive little speech but Alice meant every word. She raised her eyebrows at the lawyer and shrugged. His serious face smiled a little.

'If I may, I should like to request a private audience with you, my lady?'

The housekeeper stood up. 'Into the kitchen, all of you. We shall raise a glass to the late Dowager.'

'Or even two,' someone added.

Dear Grandmama, Alice mused as the servants filed out, closing the door firmly behind them. This was absolutely typical of her and she loved her even more for her secrecy.

The lawyer did not waste any time. 'The late Dowager explained her wishes to me. She wanted you to have some independence from his lordship.'

Alice gazed at the wall behind the lawyer's head and murmured, 'She understood me.'

'She has left you a considerable sum. Her father's family were bankers and two of her brothers remembered her when they passed on.

163

Her capital has accumulated and she had stock in banking which is now yours so that you have an income as well.'

'I shan't know what to do with it,' she exclaimed. 'I am so accustomed to having everything being paid for by my father or my brother.'

The lawyer smiled. 'I am sure you will after some thought.'

An income? An income meant true independence and Alice asked, 'How much is it?'

'Well, you could buy a house and motor car and keep several servants comfortably.'

Alice gave a short nervous laugh. 'I don't need a house and servants!'

The lawyer looked down at his documents and spoke quietly. 'The Dowager Countess thought that one day you might wish to think about it. She thought a motor car would be useful to you.'

Yes, it would, Alice thought. The Dower House was now her mother's first home and Charles would expect Alice to live there too, which was fine as long as Mother stayed in London. But the arrival of a grandchild would be certain to bring her home to Yorkshire.

'Does his lordship know about this?'

'Not yet, my lady. My duty here is to the late Dowager and her beneficiaries. However, I should imagine that word from the servants will spread quickly.'

'Quite. I shall tell him before he hears it from his valet.' She stood up and the lawyer scrambled to his feet to open the door for her. 'There is one other thing before you leave. Would you have a word with the servants about taking care of their money? I'm sure most of them do not have bank accounts. Good afternoon.'

Alice walked slowly through the grounds to Langton Park thinking that, for the first time in her life, she had real choices about her future.

Shawbridge

Florence searched for a fault in Bradley's behaviour and could find none. His manners were perfect and she could not wish for a more desirable escort. She valued his protection of her virtue. She was the envy of other single woman in Shawbridge, for not only was he a gentleman in every way, he was handsome and always impeccably dressed. They dined frequently at the Grand and, as a couple, never failed to turn heads. Tonight was no exception.

But sometimes Florence was unsure that he really loved her. Bradley seemed steadfast in his devotion and decision to marry her, yet he had taken her side against both sets of parents when she had suggested an extended engagement. She had, during that time, been prepared to indulge his desires for married love if he had asked her. But he didn't and Florence became impatient for the experience. She began to question the wisdom of a long engagement.

The maître d'hôtel at the Grand led Florence to the best-placed table in the dining room and Bradley rose to his feet as she approached. He stepped forward to kiss her on the cheek.

'My darling, you look exceptionally beautiful in

165

that gown.'

She sat down. Silver and crystal glinted against white linen in the light cast by an electric chandelier. The maître d'hôtel shook out her napkin and draped it across her knees. In the middle of her table setting she saw a small leather box tied around with ribbon. 'Not another gift, Bradley. I am quite spoiled by you.'

He smiled and she acknowledged a thrill of anticipation as it ran through her. He was so very handsome and his consistent wooing had continued after they had announced their engagement. Of course he must love her! She was sure that she was in love with him. Who would not be charmed by such dedicated devotion? The gift was another piece of amethyst jewellery. A pair of teardrop earrings to match the brooch and the dress ring he had already given her.

'I should never have dreamed of wearing this colour but Mother, like you, has commented on how well it suits my dark hair and eyes.' She had ordered a smoky-grey gown with overskirts in a similar lilac colour for a forthcoming ball and had chosen a plain bodice to show off her brooch. She slid her hand across the tablecloth towards him, hoping he would do the same, but he did not notice so she withdrew it quickly.

He looked up from studying the menu. 'Are you hungry?'

She nodded, having learned that Bradley was known as a 'gourmet' and ate well at every dinner.

The maître d'hôtel had disappeared to be replaced by Bradley's favourite waiter, who knew all his personal likes and dislikes and, Florence noticed, dressed impeccably for his position. Bradley turned and smiled at him. 'We shall have trout followed by cutlets. We'll start with Crème Dubarry soup, and perhaps a sorbet before the venison.'

'I can't eat all that, Bradley.'

'You must look at and taste all of it, Florence. When we are married we shall entertain important guests and you need to know the standards I expect in my household.'

She saw the sense of that and sat back while he chose the wines. She had not eaten since breakfast in preparation for this evening, but even so, she would have to leave significant amounts. Since their engagement, she had been studying Mrs Beeton's *Book of Household Management* and her main concern as Bradley's wife was engaging competent staff. She said, 'I shall have to employ a chef from the Grand. Do you think they will let one go?'

'A London agency will find you a suitable candidate.'

Florence felt nervous about this aspect of her future life. If Father had let her work in the shops she would have had more experience of dealing with servants instead of only her notes from the ladies' academy and Mrs Beeton's useful guide. She enjoyed the reading and was a quick learner. It was the actual 'doing' that filled her with dread. Bradley had already chosen a site and an architect for their home.

'Your mother is anxious for us to give her a date for our marriage,' she said.

'Mother will have to wait. I have found an

167

empty building that is suitable for my theatre.'

'That is splendid news! Where will it be?'

'I have not signed the papers yet, so I cannot say.'

'Not even to me?' She felt slighted that he did not fully include her in this aspect of his life.

'You must not be difficult about this, Florence. My theatre is important to me.' He glanced at her face and must have noticed her hurt expression for he added, 'Shawbridge needs a proper theatre, dearest. Your father's shops will benefit too, you will see.'

'I did not mean to criticise. When I am your wife surely I shall be as involved as you are?'

The soup arrived and, unusually for Bradley, he did not pick up his spoon and inhale the aroma immediately. 'I do not think so,' he replied. 'Giles will be moving here to advise me. You remember Giles, don't you?'

Thankfully, he didn't expect her to reply because, actually, she didn't remember him. She hadn't met him. He was a friend of Bradley from London who was closely involved in the theatre project. Bradley continued, 'Anyway, you will be far too busy with your household and social duties.'

Perhaps, she thought. There will be children too, of course. She said, 'We have not talked of children yet.'

'No, not at the dinner table, dearest.'

'But my parents have indicated their wishes for grandchildren quite strongly. Unlike you, I do not have brothers and sisters.'

'Please stop this discussion, Florence.' He

glanced sideways at the waiter, who was standing to attention with a serious expression on his face. 'We are in a public place.'

Florence had understood that hotel servants, like those in private households, were the souls of discretion, under threat of dismissal. However, it seemed that Bradley expected her to behave as a lady, and an old-fashioned lady at that, who may look every inch a woman in public but was never allowed to discuss anything that signified she was a complete woman, let alone a twentieth-century one.

'I am so sorry.'

'You have time to learn. I shall be devoting much of my time and energy to my theatre project over the coming year. We shall not marry until the project is completed.'

'Oh!' Florence had not anticipated a whole year before their marriage. 'You wish to wait that long?'

'I felt sure you would be content with this arrangement as it was your idea to extend our engagement,' he pointed out.

Florence noticed the waiter smirk. She saw the corners of his mouth turn down and this made her more angry than embarrassed. What had it to do with him anyway?'

'Our parents will be unhappy,' she said. 'Should we discuss it with them first?'

'It will not make any difference to my decision. We shall not marry until the theatre is finished.'

'Well, I suppose I may occupy myself furnishing our home when it is built.'

'No, you must leave that to me. I do not want

provincial styles and shall instruct an interior designer.'

Florence felt snubbed. She would have consulted catalogues and perhaps journeyed to London. However, Bradley wanted the best so she asked, 'Then what am I supposed to do for the next year?'

'You may occupy yourself as you do at the moment, of course. Now shall we progress with dinner?'

Florence was cross but she did not wish to make a scene in public and sighed inwardly. As the meal advanced Bradley conversed more with the waiter than with her about the food. Her anger simmered. She controlled it well and in the silences while they ate she considered her options. She chose a time when the waiter had gone to the kitchens.

'Bradley, dearest, may I not join your theatre committee and help in the project?'

'Good heavens, no! You are a lady!'

So it was a gentlemen-only club, the same as her father's group of shopkeepers who met regularly in Shawbridge. Well, women had their committees too. She said, 'Then I am sure you would not object if I took on a project of my own while your time is taken up with the theatre?'

'What have you in mind?'

'I don't know yet. You may be certain I shall not cause you any embarrassment. Well, not any more than I do at present.'

'Now that is unfair, Florence. You are beautiful and clever. You do want to be my wife, don't you?'

'I do, which is why I ask for your approval now. Perhaps I could take up some charitable cause?'

'What an excellent idea. I should be proud of you.' He smiled, she saw again why she loved him and they finished their substantial dinner amicably. Perhaps he would be less critical when they were actually husband and wife?

A charitable committee was a challenging ambition for they were chaired by the likes of Countess Langton and populated by ladies of good standing in the Riding. Women like Florence and her mother stayed home, ran the household, bore and brought up children and supported their husbands in whatever they did. Their contribution to charity consisted of helping with church or chapel fêtes and fairs. However, the ladies who attended the afternoon lecture programme were different and they might know of an opportunity that would meet with Bradley's approval.

Florence had stopped talking about the lectures to Bradley and her parents because they invariably met with disapproval and they assumed she had given them up. She found excuses to go into town when they were held and as long as she kept away from the High Street, neither her parents nor Bradley were any the wiser.

The next meeting was a Leeds speaker from the women's suffrage movement. To avoid another disagreement, Florence was extra careful about her secrecy. She and Mother occasionally took Father's pony and trap into town to take refreshment in the winter gardens tea room where they conversed with several ladies who had not been interested in them before her engagement to

Bradley. On the day of her lecture, Florence told her mother she was meeting an old friend who was secretary to a university professor and she would join her in Father's shop afterwards. Mrs Brookes accepted this as part of Florence's expanding social circle.

Florence was pleased to see familiar faces in the audience and looked forward to talking to them afterwards. She was not prepared, however, for the lady speaker, who mesmerised her with a plan for what she described as 'taking the message to ordinary women in the Yorkshire Dales'. Florence felt the atmosphere become charged with her enthusiasm and excitement buzzed through her. She wanted to be part of this, to contribute in any way she could and this lady was appealing for volunteers to help in her mission.

After the vote of thanks, there was the usual display of pamphlets and a request for those interested in helping to stay behind for a few minutes. A small group clustered around the speaker as she described her idea and Florence's excitement gave her butterflies in her stomach. She realised that she was not the only one. Miss Langton was present again and they exchanged a wide-eyed look of approval. Of course there was the perennial question of money to fund the idea and this was difficult for Florence. Father gave Mother what he called 'spending money' for their outings so she could not do much without his knowledge and agreement. Her initial enthusiasm waned. Mother would never agree, Father would be mortified and she dreaded Bradley's reaction. Others must have felt the same because one or two wandered away but Miss Langton lingered and seemed anxious to say something.

'I can fund it and I want to,' Miss Langton announced.

Everyone's attention focused on her. 'I have money and free time,' she went on.

Florence really wanted to be a part of this and spoke without thinking further. 'I have a year before my marriage. I want to help.' She pushed to the back of her mind the disapproval and arguments she would face at home. She had never been so excited about anything before!

'Women are our future,' the speaker responded. 'The twentieth century will show the country what women can achieve when they have *choices*.' She exchanged a nod with the organiser. 'Come for tea with the professor on Sunday. Thank you, ladies. Thank you.'

Miss Langton collected her bicycle from the lobby and fell into step with Florence as they left. 'I think we shall get along very well and I am looking forward to our adventure.'

'Me too.'

'Are you sure your fiancé will not object?'

No, she wasn't, but he need not know all the details and anyway, Bradley was more reasonable than her parents about the need to occupy her time. 'My father might be difficult. I am not yet twenty-one. But they will certainly approve of tea with the professor and his daughter. What will your family say?'

'I am fortunate to be independent of them,' Miss Langton replied. 'But I shall tell them I am taking a long vacation in the Yorkshire Dales to broaden my education.'

'Gosh, that's terribly fashionable, isn't it? I think I might say that, too. Oh, I see you have one of the latest Raleighs.'

Alice was very pleased with her bicycle purchase. 'Yes. I took your advice and your father supplied it. I am going to see him now to have a basket fitted to the handlebars.'

'Then I shall meet you there in a few minutes.'

'We'll walk together.' Miss Langton smiled at her and continued to push her bicycle.

'I'll introduce you to Mother,' Florence replied.

Mrs Brookes was waiting for Florence in the provisions shop but she had her back to the door and was talking to Mrs Stacey, the housekeeper for their much-respected town physician, and one of Father's best customers. 'Would you mind waiting a moment until my mother is free?' she suggested.

'I'll go next door first for my new basket.'

'You will come back?' Florence asked anxiously. Miss Langton's poise and vowels would help enormously, in securing Mother's approval of her new venture. Alice nodded and wheeled her bicycle to the hardware shop while Florence examined her father's new range of preserves. She was aware that her mother had stopped chattering.

'Did you see who that was?' Mrs Stacey exclaimed. 'Miss Brookes, come over here at once and tell me what she said to you!'

Mrs Brookes turned round but Miss Langton and her bicycle had disappeared. 'Was it the professor's daughter? Florence has attended one or two of her lectures. I can't say I approve but...'

Mrs Stacey was not listening to her. She was far more interested in Florence. 'How do you know Lady Alice?' she insisted.

Florence glanced around. There was no one else in the shop.

'Lady Alice Langton?' Mrs Stacey insisted. 'She was outside with a – with a *bicycle.*'

'That wasn't Lady Alice. That was Miss Lan– Oh! You do mean Miss Langton, don't you? No, that wasn't Lady Alice. Miss Langton told me that her family hails from the south of England.'

'Well, her mother does. But I know Lady Alice Langton when I see her. She called on my employer several times before the old Dowager passed on. I must say, though,' Mrs Stacey continued, 'she looked more like a lady then than she does today.'

'Are you sure it was her?' Florence's mother queried.

'Of course I am. What is she doing in town with a *bicycle?*'

Mrs Brookes joined the interrogation. 'Was she speaking to you, Florence?'

'It isn't her, Mother. I met Miss Langton at the lecture programme.'

'I remember that,' Mrs Stacey said. 'There was a bit of a to-do in the local paper about her. She went to one of those suffragists' rallies.'

'It was a lecture, that's all,' Florence argued with a sinking heart.

Her mother raised her voice and repeated, 'Was she speaking to you, Florence?'

'She has brought her bicycle to the shop to have a basket fitted,' she explained.

Florence thought her mother's eyes were going to pop out of her head. 'Excuse me, Mrs Stacey,' her mother said and disappeared through the door at the back of the shop. Mrs Stacey hurried outside in the direction of Brookes' Hardware. Florence raised her eyebrows at her father's provisions assistant behind the mahogany counter and followed. She was in time to see Mrs Stacey curtsey and say, 'Good afternoon, your ladyship.'

'Good afternoon, Mrs Stacey.' Miss Langton was sitting in the chair Father provided for customers. She smiled but said nothing more and eventually Mrs Stacey turned to the counter where a young gentleman assistant waited patiently to serve her. Florence approached her friend and asked, 'Is it true? You are Lady Alice Langton?'

'I am afraid so. I'm sorry I deceived everybody, but I have really enjoyed being plain Miss Langton.'

'I don't know what to say,' Florence murmured. She had realised that Miss Langton was quite well to do because of the way she spoke. Florence had put some of that down to being from the south of England. Also Miss Langton wore beautiful handmade boots that were obviously costly and far too good for bicycling, she thought. There were wealthy families in the Riding with fortunes made from manufacturing but she had never considered Miss Langton to be one of *the* Langtons, from Langton Park.

Mrs Brookes came bustling in from the storeroom at the back of the shop. Florence noticed that she had tidied her hair and adjusted her hat and carried one of the best cushions from the other shop. She handed it to Miss Langton and curtseyed. 'Your ladyship, are you quite comfortable in that chair? My husband, that is Mr Brookes, is attending to your bicycle himself. May I offer you a cup of tea?'

'Thank you, no. But I should like to speak with you about a journey I wish to make. I should be very pleased if you and Mr Brookes will allow your daughter to accompany me. She will, of course, be paid a stipend.'

'My daughter?' Florence's mother repeated faintly.

'The professor has recommended an itinerary and your daughter has indicated that she is available to join me. We shall not travel far, but Miss Brookes would be away from home for the summer months.'

Florence watched her mother make an effort to pull herself together and reply. 'I am sure Mr Brookes will have no objection, your ladyship. Where – where will you go?'

'The professor's daughter has suggested touring the towns and villages of the Yorkshire Dales. Miss Brookes would act as my companion and secretary and she is quite enthused by the idea.' Miss Langton's eyes swivelled around to Florence.

Florence gave her mother a serious stare. 'You know that Bradley is keen for me to have my own pursuit while he is occupied with his theatre project. I need you to persuade Father.'

'Don't you worry about him, my dear. How could he refuse you a position as companion to

Lady Alice Langton? It is such an honour for you. Bradley, too, will be delighted. Of course Florence may travel with you, my lady.'

Florence allowed her mother and, a few minutes later, her father to be charmed by Miss Langton into agreeing to their daughter embarking on this journey with her. She was aware that her parents had assumed they would travel in first-class compartments on railway trains and hire carriages or motor cars to transfer them to inns and hotels. She did not enlighten them on the selected mode of transport and, when she imagined it, her excitement overwhelmed her.

The recommended means of accessing the more isolated valleys and fells of the Yorkshire Dales, with their rutted cart tracks and narrow bridges, was a horse-drawn caravan. It had proved to be an economical and effective method of reaching ordinary women working in isolated textile mills and factories. The challenge thrilled and inspired Florence at the same time. Miss Langton appeared to be more reserved about it but Florence believed she felt the same and could not wait until Sunday when the planning would begin.

Chapter 11

Meg had never felt as alone as she did on that dreadful Sunday morning when she turned her back on her childhood home. It was too early for calling, not that Meg could have faced anyone who knew her. She bicycled around the quiet streets, every movement a reminder of what Saul had done to her, until the church bell rang and she turned her front wheel in that direction.

She didn't attend church as a rule. Her parents had been chapel and Meg was indifferent to both. But she had to go somewhere and not many would know her in the church. She leaned her bicycle against the churchyard wall and went inside. It was stone cold inside but a bright morning sun lit up the stained-glass window over the altar. The enormous pane was a beautiful work of art, a myriad of colours, and it gave her strength.

She slid into an empty pew at the back. One or two churchgoers nodded as they walked past her and the vicar beamed from his pulpit. He had a good congregation. She opened her hymn book at the right page and tried to sing. The notes croaked in her throat and her tears threatened to erupt. The vicar's sermon was not very long but she had no idea afterwards what he had said.

Her mind was a blank. She kept reliving the morning's events and wondering if people could tell what had happened just by looking at her. She had coins for the offertory and the sidesman smiled as she gave to his collection. When the service was over, the vicar made of point of speaking to her as she left.

'It's Miss Parker, isn't it?' She was surprised he knew her name. He went on, 'Welcome. I hope I shall see you here again.'

She nodded silently and went to fetch her bicycle.

'Meg! Wait a minute!'

Meg turned and recognised a familiar figure running to catch up with her. She braced her shoulders and managed a weak smile. 'Christine!'

'Good God, Meg, what's wrong? You look ill!' Christine clasped her hand to her mouth. 'Listen to me, blaspheming on a Sunday in the churchyard!' She rolled her eyes upwards. 'Do you think He'll forgive me?'

Meg thought briefly that He would. Christine was a good-hearted woman with not a selfish or malicious bone in her body. Christine peered closely at her face and went on, 'What is it?'

Meg felt tears threatening and turned away, 'No, nothing. I – I'm tired, that's all.'

Christine put a hand on her arm to prevent her walking away. 'Have you had a row at home?'

Meg nodded and her tears spilled over. She felt such a child, standing there with her head bowed and a concerned Christine putting a comforting arm around her shoulders.

'Come here, love,' Christine murmured. 'It can't be as bad as all that.'

Yes, it can, Meg thought. It was all her fault.

She had ignored Saul's advances and given him the benefit of the doubt for Edith's sake. She couldn't blame Edith for falling for Saul. But she had despised him before they married and now she felt murderous towards him. How could she say all that to contented, clean-living Christine? Saul had made her so dirty she was embarrassed to face one of her best friends. She tried to stem her tears but it was impossible and she began to hiccup between her sobs.

Christine led her to a quiet corner of the churchyard and they sat on a large rectangular tombstone, warmed by the sun. 'I know it's hard for you, living with them two in what used to be your own mum and dad's. But we all have our arguments, love,' she murmured. 'It'll blow over.'

'It won't,' she gulped. 'I'm not going back.'

A young voice behind them whined, 'Mam, Mam!'

Christine waved her arm and replied, 'Wait over there for me. I'll only be a minute.'

Meg inhaled raggedly and looked up. 'I'm all right. You get off home with your family.'

'I'm not leaving you here like this. You're in a bad way. Come home with me.'

'Oh, I couldn't. You've enough on, with your own.'

'We always have a houseful so one more won't be noticed. You'll just have to muck in with the rest of us.'

At that moment, the idea of 'mucking-in' at Christine's house with her boisterous tumble of children was preferable to roaming the streets. 'Can I?' she asked.

Christine stood up, took her hand and pulled her to her feet. 'Let's be having you, then.'

'I – I'm on my bicycle.'

'I don't think you should ride it, feeling as you are now. One of mine'll wheel it for you. Where is it?'

Christine sorted the large group of children waiting for her, sending one of the older ones to fetch the bicycle. As they walked to the far side of town several went off to their own homes until only three were walking between them.

'I've left the three eldest at home helping their dad with the dinner,' Christine explained. 'It's my treat on a Sunday. He does the cooking while I occupy the youngsters.'

'And a few others as well as your own.'

'Well, it gets them out of their mams' way for a while. Listen, you mustn't tell anybody that my husband cooks the Sunday dinner. He'd never live it down at the quarry if his mates found out. But he likes roasting a joint o' meat and you'll love his baked potatoes.'

Meg thought that she would love simply being with them and, as they walked, her tears dried. Life goes on, Edith had once said. Not always in the way you want it to, Meg thought, but there was no point in feeling sorry for herself. What's done is done and she had to put it out of her mind. But she could not, no matter how hard she tried, and an anger raged in her breast that she found hard to quell.

She mustn't let it show. She must push it away, deep down and out of sight. It would be her secret. Her secret. The words rattled around her head: *our little secret*, Saul had called it. She felt dirty and worthless as she recalled his sneer.

Christine's three eldest children, two boys and a girl, were grown up and had jobs; the boys worked at the quarry with their father and Clara had just started at the mill. The three youngest ran ahead of Christine and Meg to tell their father about their visitor.

'Will he mind?' Meg asked.

'Lord, no! With eight of us filling the house on Sundays, he'll hardly notice another one.'

The house was a decent size. One of the reasons Christine worked at the mill was to afford the rent and food and coal needed for her large family. A fire roared away in the front room as well as the kitchen range and a mountain of greens sat in an enamelled bowl waiting to be boiled. An appetising aroma of roasting meat filled the kitchen and scullery.

'This is my friend Meg from the mill,' Christine said to her husband. 'Me and Clara'll take over the vegetables now. Fetch a jug of ale from the inn and take the lads with you, out of our way.'

When the men and boys had gone and the younger girls were settled in the front room with sewing, Christine rolled up her sleeves and put on a pinny. 'You'll give us a hand, won't you, Meg?' She didn't wait for a reply but handed her an apron and went on, 'Hang your coat behind the scullery door and mash the turnips for me.'

Meg was grateful for something to do. Nine of them squeezed around the big kitchen table sitting on chairs, a bench and stools while Christine's husband carved up a shoulder of mutton and

Clara went round spooning vegetables from the cooking pans on to the plates. The children drank water with it but the grown-ups had a glass of ale, which Meg found welcome. It was lighter than the stout she was used to and was a better choice with dinner, she thought.

She helped with washing the pots afterwards and dreaded the time when she would have to leave. No one seemed to mind that she had little conversation, but Christine's eldest son tried to cheer her up and, prompted by his father, suggested, 'Can I show you my bicycle? We could go for a ride before it gets dark.'

He was a tall, fine-looking young man, a year or so younger than Meg, and spoke to her as though she was one of his sisters. He took hold of her hand and moved towards the back door.

'*Don't touch me!*'

He dropped her hand as though it were a hot coal, raised his eyebrows and looked at his mother. 'Dad said I ought to see Meg safely home later,' he explained. The kitchen fell silent.

Meg stared at him, wide-eyed, and then at Christine. 'I – I – I'm sorry,' she stammered. 'I didn't mean – I didn't want...' Meg looked down, unable to explain her rude behaviour. 'I – I think I'd better go now,' she finished.

Christine stared at her. 'Would you boys go out into the garden with your father for half an hour?' she asked mildly and a moment later added more loudly, 'Now, please.' Her daughters remained, surprised into silence until their mother sent them all into the front room. 'Sit down, Meg,' Christine said and drew out a chair for herself. Her eyes seem to see straight through her. 'What happened, love?'

Meg sat on the edge of her chair and shook her head, unable to find any words.

Christine went on, 'Is it summat to do with Saul Taylor?'

Meg's throat constricted at the mention of Saul's name and she felt sick. When she was forced to think about him a blackness enveloped her brain and she was aware of a monotonous far-away drone in her ears so that she could not think straight. Christine continued to stare. 'You can tell me, you know.'

'I c-c-can't,' Meg choked. 'I c-can't t-tell anybody.'

Christine stood up, walked around the table and stooped to put a gentle hand on Meg's shoulder. 'Poor child,' she whispered.

After a few minutes of Meg's shuddering sobs Christine murmured, 'You can stay here with me for as long as you want.' Meg was so grateful that tears overwhelmed her again. Christine stood there, stroking her hair and soothing her until she felt better. 'I'll make up the couch in the front room for you. Don't worry about my boys. They're good lads, all of them, and they'll do as I tell them.'

'Oh heck!' Florence wailed, 'the stove's gone out again.'

It was such a messy business refilling the oil reservoir that she felt inclined to kick it. The small cast-iron monstrosity with its vertical pipe poking out of the roof of the caravan had become her *bête noire*. She had volunteered to take charge of it as she knew nothing about caring for horses and Lady Alice did. So Lady Alice fed and watered Hector while Florence, well, Florence did her best but she really had very little experience of looking after herself.

Neither had Lady Alice and, in spite of looking aghast at some of Florence's efforts, she was unfailingly grateful. Lady Alice had common sense and a pioneering nature. She might be a titled lady but her face had glowed underneath her practical felt hat when she had first taken hold of Hector's reins. Florence had smiled to hide her nervousness as she climbed up beside her in front of their wooden caravan. They had followed the river valley to the Dales, stopping where there were factories and mills that employed women.

Florence opened the top half of the caravan's rear door and inhaled the fresh air. The hills were shrouded in mist and heavy dew hung everywhere. She shivered and reached for her cream woollen shawl to wrap around her shoulders. Father had given her money for her travels with Lady Alice and when they reached Deepdale she was going to buy another one, larger, thicker and in a more suitable colour. She grinned to herself at the idea. Mother would be horrified to see her clothed like a mill girl. But she had to keep warm when the sun went down. Lady Alice had brought a fur cape, which, somehow, was not out of place on her in the caravan when she opened her mouth. Her aristocratic vowels and use of the word 'one' left Florence in no doubt that they were from different backgrounds. Lady Alice tended to comment that one's breakfast was cold, one's hat was warm but one's feet were wet. However, it sounded decidedly odd coming out of the mouth of someone clothed in a farmer's waterproof overcoat and felt hat, as Lady Alice was when she went outside to feed Hector.

However, Lady Alice was every inch a respectable lady when she gave her speeches from the back steps of the caravan to an often small and always suspicious audience. Her appearance called for a flat iron for pressing skirts and a kettle for steaming hat feathers, tasks which fell to Florence.

Oh Lord, the stove! She must get it going again. Why had Florence never been up in time to watch mother's maid-of-all-work at home? She covered her long skirt with a brown drill apron, rolled up the sleeves of her cotton blouse and pulled on her oldest pair of leather gloves. The smell of the oil made her feel ill and she prayed, quite literally, that the wind would not blow out the flame.

Alice climbed up the rear steps of the caravan and opened the lower door. 'Jolly good show, Miss Brookes! I can see smoke coming out of the chimney.'

'It'll take a long time before it is hot enough to boil the kettle, I'm afraid.'

Alice sighed. She hadn't realised how physically hard it would be to feed and groom a heavy horse. Hector was not as huge as some of the shires she had known at Langton Park, but he was bigger than her hunter. A brisk rub-down after her morning ride had been her only contribution to grooming. Hector was a gentle giant but he ate such a lot, which one had to heave around and prepare! Her cheeks were red from the effort and she was starving hungry. But there was no sideboard with devilled kidneys, bacon and eggs in the caravan.

'Put the porridge on first,' Alice suggested.

'Good idea.'

Miss Brookes had soaked the oats in water overnight, at her suggestion. Alice knew that much from seeing a pot on the kitchen range in the Dower House. She had never set foot in the basement kitchens at the Park. But as mistress of the Dower House for Grandmama, Alice had visited the cook-housekeeper in her kitchen with late-evening requests. Often this was for a special nightcap after dinner and she had been intrigued by the servants' activities.

The cast-iron housing of their small stove was already beginning to warm and Miss Brookes asked, 'Shall we reach Deepdale today?'

'Yes, if the weather holds. There is only one mill, but it is market day tomorrow and I shall speak to farmers' wives and daughters in the square before we move on to the mill. Hector is itching to get going already.'

After porridge sweetened with honey and then hot tea, Alice harnessed Hector to the caravan and they set off. As the morning wore on, a bright sun broke through the low clouds, burning them away and revealing the wild crags and fells of the Dales.

'What a beautiful view!' Miss Brookes exclaimed.

Alice pulled on the reins and Hector slowed to

a stop. 'I have been through here before,' she said. 'I hadn't realised when we planned our journey that Deepdale is on the road to Ferndale Moor. Do you see the high ground over to the right? It belongs to the Earl of Redfern and is the best grouse moor in this part of the Riding. My brother and I have attended shooting parties at Ferndale Lodge.'

'You won't be taking the caravan there, will you?'

'I hadn't thought about it until now. But I have brought my shotgun.'

'You have?' Miss Brookes's voice was high with surprise.

'It's in the large storage locker, the one that goes across the front.'

'Oh, I never open that one. It has all the cushions and bedding piled on it.' After a moment Miss Brookes frowned and went on, 'If you didn't know we were going near a grouse moor, why did you have to bring your gun?'

'You do not need to worry. I am sure we are both quite safe. I have a list of villages, inns and farms for overnight stops. But with a farmer's permission I could rid him of a few rabbits and pigeons. I'm a very good shot and we'd have fresh meat for dinner.'

'Who – who would prepare them for us? I have no idea what to do with either.'

'Me neither. It was an impulsive – and silly idea.'

Miss Brookes was quiet for a moment and then said, 'I'll make a start on vegetables for soup. Give me a minute to clamber in the back.'

Alice considered that Miss Brookes was not enjoying this adventure as much as she was and wondered what she could do. She waited until she heard Miss Brookes call through the partition behind her head and then urged Hector forwards.

Florence did her best amidst the clattering pots and implements that swung about on hooks over her head. The cooking facilities were as rudimentary as Florence's skills, so a whole Wensleydale cheese and a smoked ham both wrapped in muslin were destined to provide luncheons while they were on the move. They had good provisions stored in rectangular wooden boxes that served as seats. Lady Alice had said they had to eat well and a Leeds store had delivered boxes of supplies. If only Florence knew what to do with half of them!

Fresh milk and eggs were easily come by from the farms they passed on their way. Bread was more difficult outside of towns as farmers' wives didn't bake to take to market as a rule. If Florence were lucky, a thrifty housewife would part with a crusty cottage loaf for a sum far in excess of its value. The caravan raised a few eyebrows but exploring the Dales on foot or bicycle was a popular pursuit these days and eccentrics were by no means unusual. As well, Lady Alice was clearly received as 'a better class of traveller', a situation that she exploited shamelessly. Florence, however, had more difficulty in coping with their new lifestyle.

'There's an inn in Deepdale. Would you care to stay there for a night or two?' Lady Alice asked her when they stopped for luncheon.

'You are very generous, Lady Alice, but no, thank you. I want to do this.'

'That's the spirit.' Lady Alice smiled. 'Nonetheless, if we are well received at the market and the mill, we shall have dinner in the dining room at the inn.'

'Well, I can't say that I wouldn't welcome roast beef and Yorkshire pudding, followed by apple pie.'

'Your stews are very tasty.'

'No they are not.'

'No, they are not,' Lady Alice agreed. 'But you are very, very good at giving me notes for my speeches.'

'Do you think so?' Florence was flattered. They had a collection of books and pamphlets about the suffragists' cause, which she enjoyed reading.

'You have a gift for choosing the right words for my audience. That is very helpful to me.'

'I learned from my father. He makes his living from selling goods to ordinary folk and he can be very persuasive about new products. I wanted to help in the shops as Mother used to, but Father wouldn't hear of it. He wants only for me to make a good marriage.'

'Oh, I know how you feel. It's as though one is not capable of anything else.'

'Well, we must show them that we are.'

'Indeed we must,' Lady Alice replied. 'How many leaflets have I left? Shall I ask for more to be sent on to the post office?'

'You have enough. But you have to remember that you are a long way from the city. Deepdale people are traditional folk at heart and mill owners don't care for outsiders who make trouble. We may not be welcome.'

Chapter 12

Christine lived quite close to the mill and Meg walked with her to work in the morning. 'Are you sure you don't mind if I sleep on your front-room couch for a few more nights?' Meg asked.

'I said so, didn't I?'

'Yes, but you have enough on with your own family.'

'You'll get yourself sorted soon anyway. Won't Edith be worried about you?'

'I've written a note for her.'

'Well, if you have to take it over there, you might as well talk to her.'

'I can't. Not yet.' Meg heard a tremble in her voice and her heart began to thump. 'Saul will be there. I'm giving the note to a neighbour who works in the packing shed.'

Christine didn't reply.

Meg added, 'I'll ask around for lodgings somewhere.'

'Don't do anything in a hurry, lass,' Christine commented.

Meg could not be sure whether Christine approved of her plan or not and they walked on in silence until others joined them, also heading for the mill. Two or three were already outside the large gates, clustered around a poster pinned to the solid wood. Christine stopped in front of it. 'Hey, look at this, there's a public meeting outside the mill tonight.'

'It'll be about one of those unions for the men.'

'No, it's for us. Look, *Mothers, daughters, sisters: come and listen to how you can change your life.*'

'Oh, it's that "Votes for Women" crowd,' Meg commented. 'I don't think it's for the likes of us.'

'It says it is. It says it's a travelling display of the work of Dr and Mrs Pankhurst and a talk by Lady Alice Langton.'

'Travelling circus, more like, made up of well-off women with nothing better to do. It's all right for them. They've got time and money to waste. The rest of us are too busy earning a living.'

'Aye, you're right,' Christine responded. 'But it might be interesting.'

'Well, I'm not interested. Some of them have been in prison, you know.'

Christine lowered her voice. 'That's why it could be fun.'

Meg was not convinced. 'The mill owners won't like it. I'm surprised the constable is letting them stop in Deepdale.'

'Perhaps he doesn't know. This notice wasn't here yesterday. Look, they'll be outside the mill when the hooter goes.'

'No harm in going to listen, I suppose.' Meg shrugged and thought, It might take my mind off other things.

The day at the mill, more than anything, helped Meg to cope with her distress. She sank into the routine and welcomed the banter and the gossip of the other women. But the torment was always there, ready to bubble up and explode until she felt that she would burst.

Word spread quickly about the meeting but most of the women declared they were not going. They agreed with Meg. *The mill owners won't like it.*

'The speaker is a proper lady,' Christine argued. 'She's one of them anyway, so she's not going to start a revolution.'

At the end of their working day, a sizeable group collected around the rear of a wooden horse-drawn caravan, situated a short distance away from the mill gates. A well-dressed woman moved amongst them, greeting them with a smile and pushing a leaflet into the hands of anyone who would accept it. She wore an embroidered sash diagonally across her body. Meg couldn't see all of it well enough to read what it said.

'Are you Lady Alice Langton?' Meg asked.

The woman shook her head. 'That's Lady Alice, on the caravan steps.'

About twenty-five yards away, Meg noticed the town constable standing to attention and gradually a few men gathered around him. She knew some as the husbands of her fellow workers. Others she did not recognise and concluded that word must have spread outside the mill.

Lady Alice had a strong voice and was about five minutes into her speech before male voices from behind her began to shout: 'Rubbish!', 'Get back to your sewing!', 'What does your fellow say to that?' and 'I bet she hasn't got one.'

In spite of her initial resistance Meg was inter-

194

ested in the speech and so she looked over her shoulder and snapped, 'Be quiet, will you? I can't hear.' She noticed the men had moved closer and the constable was doing nothing to stop their interruptions.

Then the comments became more personal, not about Lady Alice, but within the audience. One woman retaliated, 'Shut your mouth, Alfred Jones, or I'll shut it for you.' Another man came back with, 'Are you going to let your missus talk to you like that? I wouldn't stand for that.' The man identified as Alfred marched forward and took hold of his wife's arm. 'Come on, lass, I've heard enough. We're off home now.'

His wife shook him free. 'Oh, get off me and go back to yer garden. I'll come home when I'm good and ready.'

Her action was greeted with a murmuring and minor ripple of applause. Lady Alice stopped her speech for a moment and said, 'Well spoken, madam. One should have choices in one's life.'

But Alfred Jones had a group of men around him, urging him on. 'Aye,' he yelled, 'and men should do the cooking and the washing!'

'Well, why not? Women go out to work as well.'

'I suppose you want us to have the bairns an' all!' Alfred retaliated.

'Now then, Alfred,' the constable interrupted. 'That's enough.'

Other women were resisting their husbands as they moved forward to take them home. The constable added, 'Come on, ladies. We don't want any trouble, do we?' But no one took any notice and anyway it was too late. The arguments had started. A few scuffles broke out. One or two men and women became alarmed and walked off quickly.

Christine turned to Meg and said, 'Come on. Let's go home.'

'You go,' Meg answered. 'The men started it and I want to see what the constable does.'

'Don't. You might get arrested.'

'I'll keep out of sight behind the caravan.'

'Well, don't be long. I'll save you some tea in the oven.'

In the confusion of the scuffles, neither Lady Alice nor her assistant saw Meg sneak around the side of the caravan to where a large horse was tethered and grazing. He lifted his neck, swung his large head in her direction and snorted.

'Easy, boy,' she murmured, but he wasn't startled, he was simply curious. She hid behind him and watched.

Lady Alice was looking on with a helpless expression but the other lady was more interested in what was happening. The constable approached the latter and said, 'You've had your say. Now pack up and move on. Deepdale doesn't want troublemakers.'

The lady assistant sounded angry 'We are not causing the trouble! It is the men who are protesting. Go and arrest them.'

Meg wanted to cheer for her.

'Don't you try and tell me my job, young lady. Now are you going or not?'

'Yes, officer, we are leaving.' Meg recognised this as Lady Alice's voice and the caravan creaked as she climbed down the steps. 'We shall leave first thing in the morning.'

The constable turned and yelled at the top of his voice, 'The show's over. You can all get off home now.'

Meg heard a lot of vociferous arguing, which eventually quietened. She moved cautiously to obtain a better view and saw the constable talking sternly to some local women but he did not arrest anyone. When they had all gone, the mill owner came out of the gates in his motor car and stopped while the constable climbed in beside him. It was as Meg thought. These suffragists were wasting their time in Deepdale. Meg sighed and looked round for the quickest way to the road.

'Oh! You startled me! Good evening.'

Lady Alice Langton was striding around the caravan towards the horse. She had thrown a long waxed farmer's coat over her dress and carried two metal buckets, which she placed carefully on the ground. The horse whinnied as she approached and ambled on his tether towards his food and drink. She stood back and watched him eat. 'He's not easily agitated but our audience made a lot of noise.'

'The men made most of it.'

Lady Alice gave her a second glance. 'They did indeed. Were you hiding from them?'

'Yes, I suppose I was. The mill owner must have warned the constable about you.'

'And he asked the men to come and take their wives home. But why are you still here? Have we persuaded you to join our cause?'

'I can't say you have, but I do think the constable and the men were being unfair to you.'

The lady gave her another interested glance. 'Yes, I know. That is why we must carry on with the cause.'

Meg considered this. 'Even if you do, they won't take any notice of you.'

'Some will. One has to start somewhere.'

'The constable could have locked you up.'

'I wish he had. I wish I had had the courage to ignore him.'

'Are you crazy?'

'Think of the publicity.' Alice picked up her bucket. 'Can you stay for a cup of tea?'

Why not, Meg thought and said, 'Yes, I can.'

'Jolly good. Come inside.'

Meg climbed the steps at the rear of the caravan and blinked at the dim interior. It was larger than she'd imagined and the other lady was fussing around a tiny stove with a kettle on the hot plate.

'This is Miss Brookes. I expect you know that I am Lady Alice Langton.'

'Yes.' Should she have said 'my lady'? Meg considered dropping a curtsey but, somehow, it didn't seem appropriate in a caravan.

'What is your name?' Miss Brookes prompted.

'I'm Meg Parker.'

'Welcome to my travelling home, Miss Parker,' Lady Alice said. 'Can you find a space to sit over there on the cushions?'

As Meg's eyes became accustomed to the gloom, she realised that the interior of the caravan was in chaos. There were handbills and notepaper everywhere. Two flat irons sat in the middle of the floor sharing a piece of sheeting with a pair of glove stretchers, some ribbons and two tin plates that held the remains of a cold meal.

'Do you actually live in here?' Meg asked. She hoped she didn't sound impolite.

'Yes. There's plenty of room. A whole family used to occupy it before us,' Lady Alice replied.

The caravan appeared to be well equipped and it had comfortable cushions and velour seat covers, but it was a jumble of clutter. 'You're not very well organised,' she commented and then added, 'I am sorry, I didn't mean to be rude.'

'We have had worse insults than that! But we were campaigning in the market place earlier and had no time to clear up.'

Miss Brookes added, 'We were not welcome there either.'

Meg was not surprised. She sat on the comfortable cushions and watched with interest as Miss Brookes moved backwards and forwards making afternoon tea. It was beautifully presented in a china cup and saucer and accompanied by a matching tea plate holding several half-scones spread liberally with butter. Miss Brookes handed her a linen tea napkin and asked if she would like jam. The tea was awful because she hadn't waited for the water to boil properly. The scone she recognised as from the baker's market stall in town and it was good. Meg reflected that she could easily have made fresh drop scones on the hot-plate.

'I haven't had time to cut bread and butter either,' Miss Brookes added. 'It's been a busy day.'

There was no sight or smell of any dinner cooking. Both ladies ate their scones hungrily and they had one half left, which they offered to Meg.

'No, thank you, there'll be a dinner waiting for me at – at where I live.'

'Lucky you.' Miss Brookes cut the remaining scone in two and gave half to Lady Alice.

'Do you cook your meals in here?' Meg asked.

'We were going to have dinner at the inn tonight, but I'm not sure we shall be served anywhere in Deepdale.'

'Well, I really wouldn't advise it today. Menfolk in these parts like the women to do what they tell them and not the other way round and as it is market day the ale will be flowing freely at the inn.'

'I see,' Lady Alice responded. 'Shall we eat here instead?'

Miss Brookes's face took on an anguished expression.

'I haven't got anything ready and I'm so hungry.'

'Me too.' Lady Alice sighed. 'Bread and ham again, I suppose.'

Meg gazed again at the chaotic interior of the caravan and grimaced.

'I didn't think that looking after the two of us would be so difficult,' Miss Brookes commented.

Lady Alice put her cup of tea down carefully. 'We cannot continue in this muddle,' she stated. 'We need a maid.'

Miss Brookes's face brightened immediately. 'Oh, Lady Alice! That is a first-rate idea. I should have more time to write.' Then her features drooped. 'Where would we find one out here?'

Lady Alice turned to Meg. 'I don't suppose you know of anyone looking for work?'

Meg's eyes rounded. Most girls went into the mill but those who wanted to go into service usually obtained positions at one of the big houses in the area. Besides, who in their right mind would choose to roam around Yorkshire with two eccentric ladies in a caravan?

'Will you ask at the mill for us, Miss Parker?' Lady Alice asked.

Meg felt cornered. She sympathised with these ladies. They had no idea how to look after themselves but it was not a position she would recommend to anyone. 'That might be difficult,' she answered. 'She would have to believe in your cause.'

Lady Alice looked surprised. 'That is not essential as long as she is not against us.'

'But the men in Deepdale are and daughters must obey their fathers,' Miss Brookes added.

'Indeed they must.' Lady Alice turned her charming smile on Meg. 'Miss Brookes's father had to be persuaded. I found her mother to be most helpful in this respect.'

The mention of parents touched a nerve with Meg. She missed them both dreadfully. She no longer had a family or home to call her own and she struggled to suppress a sob in her throat. She would never get over the shame of what Saul had done to her and could not face the inevitable gossip that would circulate about her. A blush crept over her face as the dreadful memory resurfaced. It would not be long before gossip about why she had left home spread to the mill. She feigned a cough to mask her distress and covered her mouth with her napkin.

'Are you quite well, Miss Parker?' Florence asked. She poured a cup of water from a ewer and handed it to Meg.

'Yes, thank you. A crumb went down the wrong way.'

'Do you think that you can help me?' Lady Alice pressed.

'I don't believe I can. If a mother wanted her daughter in service she would place her at the Grange or Manor House or somewhere similar. In any case, a girl can earn much more than a housemaid at the mill.'

'But that is because they have free board and lodgings in service,' Miss Brookes explained.

Lady Alice added, 'You may inform the mothers that I shall pay the same as the mill.'

'Really?' Meg thought that very generous for a servant.

'I shall, of course, provide a uniform, although I have no idea where I might source the Langton livery out here.'

'The draper in Deepdale supplies suitable dresses and aprons for local servants,' Meg suggested.

'Langton housemaids wear grey.'

'He has blue,' Meg informed them. It was a popular colour for general maids in houses that did not keep a brigade of servants.

Miss Brooke intervened. 'Surely the position is part housekeeper and cook, Lady Alice?'

'You are quite right, Miss Brookes. Blue will be suitable. Do you think you can help us find a girl, Miss Parker?'

Meg considered this and in all honesty thought

not. No Deepdale mother that she knew would send her daughter off roaming the Dales in a caravan, let alone secure her father's permission to do so. Lady Alice's title would not overcome the sheer madness of this escapade. She chewed her lip and looked around the chaos of the caravan. The storage lockers down both sides provided a bed for each of the ladies. A jumble of cushions, books and papers was piled across the front locker. There was likely to be an outside storage locker behind the driver's seat for horse feed. Often, the driver or an older boy would sleep there.

'I'll do it,' Meg said suddenly. She must be as mad as they were but what were her alternatives?

'You will? How splendid. Of course her mother and father may come here and speak with me first.'

'No, I mean, *I* will do it. I'll be your caravan maidservant.'

'You will?' echoed Miss Brookes. 'Can you cook and clean and do laundry?'

'Of course I can.'

'And sew and use a flat iron?' Lady Alice demanded.

'I looked after my father and brothers for several years after my mother passed away.'

'Then you will be perfect for us. When can you start?'

Meg drew in a long slow breath through her nose. It was not too late to change her mind. But what had she to stay in Deepdale for? Family life as she had known it had gone for ever. She could never return to the house that had been her home. A radical change might help her get over that dreadful episode with Saul. But was this too radical? She wasn't even sure she supported the suffragists since they had embarked on their law-breaking activities. The newspapers had started to call them suffragettes. Who knew what they might get up to next?

She had refused to leave Deepdale a year ago and had regretted it ever since. It did not matter that it had been the right and moral thing for her to do at the time; it had been a mistake. If Saul spread rumours about her, as he had threatened in order to cover his own scandalous behaviour, her hopes of a respectable future here were ruined. She ought to leave now, before the questions and the gossip started.

'I need a whole day,' she answered.

Miss Brookes commented, 'The constable says we cannot stay here.'

'I am taking the track up to Ferndale Moor tomorrow morning,' Lady Alice added.

Ferndale Moor. Why must she be bombarded constantly with unhappy memories? She was tempted to change her mind. But she needed a way out and – she gazed at the genteel chaos around her – and this was her chance. She said, 'There's a sheep farm beyond that hill where you can camp for the night. The farmer's wife generally welcomes summer ramblers. I'll catch up with you there.'

'Splendid,' Lady Alice responded. 'Here is my card for the draper. Tell him to present his bill to the bank.'

'There is one more thing. I should like to bring

my bicycle?'

'I'm afraid not,' Lady Alice answered. 'I had to leave mine at home. You may use Hector for carrying.'

Meg hid her surprise that Lady Alice rode a bicycle and her own concern that she had never handled a horse. She shrugged. 'I'll have to leave it at the farm then.' The farmer's wife would keep it safe and she guessed it would be for the summer months only.

'I shall tell them to expect you.' Lady Alice smiled. 'As my maid, you will be known as Parker.'

Meg blinked but did not argue. 'I have to go now. Thank you for the tea and scones.'

'Oh, do bring some more with you tomorrow from that baker in the square,' Miss Brookes pleaded and handed her some coins.

Meg took one last look at the caravan's shambolic interior. What on earth would she say to Christine? She would think Meg had gone mad. Perhaps she had? As she hurried to Christine's in the fading light, she wondered if she had made the right decision. She was unsure whether to be shocked or amused by the life Lady Alice and Miss Brookes led and how it would reflect on anyone associated with them.

One of Christine's children was watching for her and came out to meet her. 'Ma was worried that the constable had taken you,' she said. 'Tell us all about it while you eat your tea. We've finished ours.'

Meg saved the details of her new position until the children were in bed and she had carried a shovelful of hot coals from the kitchen to the front room to get her fire going. Christine urged her not to do anything hasty but Meg was not swayed.

'This isn't hasty,' she answered. 'I have been unhappy at home for a long time and I wanted a change. Now I have an opportunity.'

The image of the caravan's tumbled interior stayed with her through the night, not only as she tossed and turned but also as she dreamed. In the morning she realised that she had not thought about Saul once during the night and that was the moment she knew for sure that she had made the right decision. She went into the mill to give in her notice and asked for wages owing to be made up by the end of the day, said goodbye to her friends and then bicycled to her former home for the last time.

Edith was quiet as Meg gathered more of her belongings and secured the bundles on to her bicycle. 'I'm sorry you don't like it here,' the older woman commented. 'Saul said two women and one kitchen never works but I have tried. Saul, too, has done all he can to be friendly.'

Clearly both had decided that the fault was all hers and Meg did not trust herself to respond without breaking down completely. She added fresh bread, scones and two servant's dresses with four aprons to the weight on her bicycle and began the long slow pull towards Ferndale Moor.

Memories of Jacob and his family flooded back and as she relived the Sunday when her heart was broken she could not stop the tears rolling down her cheeks. But Meg stiffened her back and pushed harder on the pedals. A new life would help her forget. She had so many unhappy events to leave behind in Deepdale: losing her mother and Sally moving away, Jacob leaving, her father's untimely death, and – she choked and coughed causing her to slow – and Saul, the hateful man who had taken her virtue with a total indifference to her feelings.

She saw smoke rising first, coming out of a stovepipe chimney. The caravan was tucked away behind a line of sheltering boulders. Hector stood nearby, secured by a long tether, with his nose in a feed bag. Meg stopped and rested one foot on the ground. The farmhouse and surrounding stone barns looked peaceful. Beyond, the road to Ferndale Moor stretched ahead. A brisk breeze cooled the sunny air. She did not know what life held in store for her any more and a frisson of fear made her shiver. She gave a wry smile. She would not find out by looking on from the outside. She pushed forward on her pedals. It was high time she started a new life.

Chapter 13

'I wish the wind would ease. It keeps me awake at night,' Miss Brookes complained. 'Did you have to come over the top of Ferndale?'

'I know this moor,' Lady Alice replied. 'There are several textile mills in the valley on the other side.'

Meg was sitting on the steps preparing vegetables for soup. She was inclined to agree with Miss Brookes. The caravan was very slow and farms for fresh produce were few and far between. She narrowed her eyes at the hazy horizon. 'If I am not mistaken, my lady, I can see Ferndale Tarn in the distance.'

Lady Alice peered out of the door. 'Excellent. Perhaps you will be able to buy fresh fish.'

If we are not run off the land, Meg thought. The grouse season was not yet under way and Jacob's father would have all his men out protecting his birds. Someone would have spotted the smoke from their camp. When the weather was fair, Meg lit a fire outside, next to the driver's tent that she pitched every night for Lady Alice and Miss Brookes to use for washing themselves in private. They were unbelievably grateful for this simple solution.

'Is that a rider on the track ahead?' Lady Alice queried.

Meg followed the line of her gaze, then put her vegetables to one side and stood up. 'It is, ma'am.'

Miss Brookes came to look. 'What do you suppose he wants?'

'We are on private land,' Alice answered. 'But do not worry. Leave him to me, Parker. Lay a sherry tray and put on your afternoon cap and apron. Miss Brookes, please tidy your books and papers.'

Meg exchanged a glance with Miss Brookes and obeyed silently. Lady Alice had a tendency to behave as she obviously used to at Langton Park unless Meg explained the difficulties. Meg was patient with her. Why should a titled lady have experience or understanding of the practicalities of everyday life?

Miss Brookes cleared her side of the caravan, hiding some of the more radical texts out of sight under a cushion. Lady Alice came inside to check her appearance in a looking glass that Meg had hung at the correct height for hats. She glanced around and nodded. 'I imagine he thinks I am a gypsy,' she said. 'I shall disabuse him. Sit down, Miss Brookes. Parker, wait outside with me.'

'Yes, my lady.' Meg straightened her blue dress, pushed a few stray hairs behind her ears and climbed down the steps.

The horse approached at a canter. When the thudding of hooves slowed, a man's voice called, 'Hey, you over there! You are trespassing on Lord Redfern's land.'

Meg recognised Mr Wright. She had forgotten how much Jacob took after his father. The way he moved and the intonation of his voice brought Jacob's memory flooding back. Dear Lord, would she ever get over him? Lady Alice also stared at Mr Wright as he dismounted and slid his shotgun out of its holster. She seemed to Meg to be surprised until she pulled herself together and replied, 'Simply passing through, my good man. I shall on my way by morning.'

'You'll be on your way as soon as I've searched your caravan. Fetch your husband.' He obviously thought they were poachers.

Lady Alice raised her voice, 'May I have your name, sir?'

Her aristocratic vowels must have registered with him for he slowed his pace and peered at her. 'Wright,' he said. 'Gamekeeper to the Earl of Redfern and you are trespassing on Ferndale Moor.'

'Oh, I am sure his lordship will not mind. My brother, Lord Langton, shoots regularly with Lord Redfern.'

Mr Wright did not alter his expression. Only his ensuing words showed that he had changed his attitude towards them. He pushed up the peak of his deerstalker hat. 'Then you must be Lady Alice Langton.' He acknowledged her with a bow of his head. 'Your servant, ma'am. His lordship is not in residence until the shooting commences.'

Lady Alice smiled. 'May I compliment you on the excellence of your grouse, Mr Wright? Lord Redfern's moor is one of the best in the county. Will you take a glass of sherry with me?'

The gamekeeper was silent for a moment. His sharp eyes took in every detail of the caravan, tent and campfire tucked away in the shelter of an outcrop of boulders. Then he answered, 'Very well, my lady. I do not believe I have seen you as a guest of his lordship in recent years.'

'Do you remember me?'

'You were one of the best young shots I had the pleasure of coaching, my lady.'

Meg stood back as they went inside, then she climbed in after them. Mr Wright appeared not to have noticed her at all, let alone recognised her. The interior was cosy but gloomy after the bright sun. Meg left open the top half of the door and lit one of the lamps while Miss Brookes poured sherry from a cut-glass decanter.

Lady Alice said, 'This is my companion, Miss

Brookes. Shall I take your gun, Mr Wright, and place it with mine?' He seemed reluctant to part with it until Alice held out her hand for it. 'I assure you that I have not taken any of your grouse,' she said. 'Nor shall I. You have my word.'

He nodded. 'May I enquire what you are doing here, my lady?'

'I am on a lecture tour of mills and factories in the Dales for the university. I am encouraging young women to engage in educational studies.'

Meg hadn't heard Lady Alice's work described in this way before. She glanced at Miss Brookes, who seemed amused.

'I see.' Clearly, he did not see, Meg thought. He sounded weary, or perhaps cynical. She felt the same. Farm girls and mill hands had little time for learning once they had left elementary school. He added, 'You're a long way from any mills here.'

'I believe this track will take me down to the textile mills of Crandale in the next valley.'

'It will. His lordship has a tenant on that side of the moor, a sheep farmer.' Mr Wright drew a small card out of his waistcoat pocket. 'Tell him I sent you, my lady.'

'Thank you, my good man. May I remain here a day or so to rest my horse? A brace of fowl would be welcome too. I shall pay you, of course.'

He did not answer her directly. Meg guessed he was tussling with whether to treat them as visiting gentry or common travellers. His face was unreadable as he said, 'Are you planning on using that gun of yours, my lady?'

'I hadn't thought to, not so near to the grouse being ready.'

'Well, I have an excess of waterfowl on the tarn and the nearby warren is overrun. If you spend a day culling for me, you may take what you want for the pot.'

'Thank you, Mr Wright. May I fish as well?'

'I am afraid not, ma'am. Trout stocks are down this year.' He sipped his sherry in silence for a while and then said, 'My lady, forgive me for asking but are you really travelling around in this – this gypsy hovel, without a male protector?'

'I manage quite well.'

'I can let you have one of my lads for a week or so to see you down to the farm. He can sleep in the tent.'

'That is my washroom, sir.'

Mr Wright was perplexed rather than amused. 'I just don't understand why Lord Langton's sister wishes to spend her summer living like this.'

'Perhaps Mrs Wright would understand?'

'I doubt it.' He finished his sherry and Miss Brookes offered him another. 'Thank you, no. I'll be on my way. I shall have to log your presence in my day book.'

'Of course, Mr Wright. But you need not record my name, need you? I should not wish to embarrass my brother.'

'Very well, my lady. In return, may I request that you are off the moor before his lordship's shooting party arrives? They are expected within the fortnight.'

'You have my promise, Mr Wright. What shall I do with the culled waterfowl and rabbits?'

'Leave them where they fall. I shall know when you are shooting and send a keeper and dog to retrieve them for the servants' kitchen. Thank you kindly for the sherry, my lady. One of my lads will drop by every day to see if you need anything.'

'I am quite self-sufficient.'

'So I see.' He retrieved his gun.

'Parker, show Mr Wright out.'

Meg opened the lower half of the caravan door. Mr Wright met her eyes and then he recognised her. 'Miss Parker!'

'Sir,' she acknowledged with a nod and followed him down the steps. She had to ask, she could not stop herself. 'I trust you and your wife are well,' she began.

'We are.'

Meg took a deep breath. 'And Ruth and Jacob, how are they?'

Mr Wright took his time to answer. 'They are both very well, thank you for asking.'

'Is Jacob still in London?'

'He is. Have you given up the mill?'

'Yes. I needed a new start.'

He seemed to approve of this and nodded. 'Well, good luck, Miss Parker.'

'Thank you, Mr Wright.' She watched him with an aching heart as he remounted and rode away. Why had she tortured herself by asking him about Jacob? Why?

Lady Alice stood on the caravan steps and also watched him leave, 'Do you know him, Parker?'

'I was introduced to him once,' she answered and hoped Lady Alice would not probe further.

Lady Alice stayed silent. She stood for a long time on the caravan steps watching him ride away. Then she gave a huge sigh, prompting Miss Brookes to ask, 'Are you missing your comfortable life, my lady?'

'What? Oh, not at all! But I do miss – well, I miss someone.'

'Was it someone very dear to you?' Miss Brookes asked.

'It was a long time ago, but it is so difficult to forget him.'

Normally Meg was not interested in conversation between Lady Alice and Miss Brookes but this time was different. She wondered whom Lady Alice had lost in the past. She sat on the bottom step, resumed peeling vegetables and listened.

'Hugo was in the cavalry,' Lady Alice said. 'Mr Wright reminded me of him in the way he stowed his shotgun and mounted his horse.'

'What happened to Hugo?' Miss Brookes prompted.

'He was killed in the war with the Boers in Southern Africa. He took a shot in the chest and the field hospital could not save him.'

'Oh, I am so sorry, my lady, I had no idea. He must have been very brave.'

'He was,' Alice replied softly. After a short silence, she gave another sigh and added, 'But he is gone for ever and I have to live my life without him no matter how difficult.'

'That's the spirit, my lady.'

Meg agreed silently. She, too, must stop this yearning for someone she could never have. Jacob was gone for ever and she had to live her life without him, no matter how difficult. She had more in common with Lady Alice than she first realised.

'Do you not miss your fiancé, Miss Brookes?' Lady Alice queried.

'Y-y-yes.' Meg thought Miss Brookes did not sound too sure. 'I have not lost him so I do not yearn for him as though I have. I write to him. In fact I write a journal especially for him every day but I cannot post it until I reach Crandale.'

'Does he write to you?'

'He does; every Sunday when he tells me how successful his week has been then he wishes me well on my little adventure and looks forward to our marriage.' Miss Brookes gave a short laugh. 'He calls this project "your little adventure".'

'You have not told him the truth?' Lady Alice responded.

'I am travelling in the Dales as companion to Lady Alice Langton,' Miss Brookes declared. 'He is very happy with that information.'

'He will find out one day.'

'Yes, I expect he will; Mother and Father too.' Miss Brookes was quiet for moment. 'Everyone will be angry with me.'

'You may lose him, Miss Brookes. Are you not concerned?'

'Whatever the consequences, I shall have to bear them.'

'You have courage.'

'Do I? I don't think so, my lady.' Miss Brookes rustled some of her papers. 'Suffragettes are the courageous ones. The more I read about their activities, the more I know that what they are doing is only the beginning. Women will have a proper voice one day, they will have the vote.'

'That is fighting talk, Miss Brookes.'

'Yes, I suppose it is, my lady.'

Meg stood up and added the vegetables to her broth simmering in a brass preserving pan suspended over her campfire. She thought it was an odd kind of engagement if Miss Brookes and her fiancé did not mind being apart from each other for weeks on end. They were not at all like any of the young couples she had known. Well, it was Miss Brookes's life; she shrugged and went inside to clear away the sherry glasses. They had to be washed very carefully in the outside bucket and polished dry before being returned to their velvet-lined wooden box. Meg grinned to herself as she recalled Mr Wright's description of the caravan as a 'gypsy hovel'. It was small and over-crowded but it was certainly no hovel.

Lady Alice gave Meg a generous housekeeping budget and instructed her to select the best-quality supplies from farms along their route. However, crossing Ferndale Moor meant a long journey between farms and Meg relied on salt beef and pork for her ladyship's dinners, which Lady Alice and Miss Brookes ate quite late in the evening. Meg looked forward to a brace of fowl or rabbit to ring the changes when they moved nearer the tarn. With continuing fine weather and sheltered sites, eating dinner out of doors under the stars would be possible.

In fact it was Miss Brookes who became Meg's greatest assistance as she learned the ways of the aristocracy through Lady Alice's expectations. Miss Brookes advised Meg on different courses and table settings for the two ladies, how to open a bottle of wine and make coffee. Both ladies walked after dinner and Meg took her own meal while they were out. She sat on the caravan steps and ate her dinner with one fork, rather proud of the neat and tidy campsite she had created. When they returned, Meg had prepared the caravan for night time, with the ladies' beds made ready, curtains rigged around each for privacy and hot water in the washing tent.

Lady Alice pulled on her farmer's overcoat to check on Hector before nightfall and said to Miss Brookes, 'Parker works very hard to make us comfortable but no one said we had to rough it all the time. Will you reconsider the occasional night in a hotel?'

Meg paused as she lit the lamps and her eyes rounded. Rough it! she thought and spoke without further consideration. 'This isn't roughing it!' she protested. 'You are warm and comfortable and have plenty to eat and drink. Good heavens, you even have brandy to keep out the cold!'

There was a short silence after her outburst. Both ladies seemed too surprised for words. Meg, too, had shocked herself for she had never spoken to either in this way before and chewed on her lip. Eventually, she said, 'I am so sorry, my lady, I don't know what came over me.'

Lady Alice was more intrigued than angry. She looked at Meg curiously and asked, 'Neither do I. Why did you say it?'

Meg glanced at Miss Brookes. 'I am not sure that either of you understand what it is like to be a Daleswoman with a houseful of young children to look after and a husband who has to work from dawn until dusk to afford a roof over their heads, let alone feed and clothe them.'

Neither of the ladies responded. She went on, 'It's just that I don't see what all this marching and rallying and votes for women will do for the likes of them.'

Lady Alice spoke first. 'Then we shall have to teach you. Why don't you come and listen to my speech in Crandale?'

'You pay me to clean and cook for you, my lady,' Meg pointed out.

'And you do it beautifully,' Miss Brookes responded. 'Perhaps with Lady Alice's permission you may spend some of your time reading my pamphlets and books.'

'We are not asking you to join the Society,' Lady Alice added, 'but at least you will comprehend our beliefs. Miss Brookes will revise your daily routines to allow time for study. I cannot preach to textile workers about the benefits of learning if I do not offer it to my own servant.'

'I'll draw up a reading list for you,' Miss Brookes went on. She went over to her book collection. It occupied several precious wall shelves. She scanned the titles and selected a text. 'Start with this one and let me know what you think of it.'

Meg was reluctant to take it from her. She had got out of the habit of reading since leaving school and working at the mill and wasn't sure she wanted to take it up again. But Miss Brookes kept pushing the book at her until she accepted it. So, that night, she wrapped a woollen blanket around her shoulders and took a lamp to bed. She was always the last to retire, waiting until the ladies were settled before disappearing behind her own curtained privacy across the front of the caravan.

It was all very well for women to want the same freedoms as men. But men did not have the babies and homes to look after. That was women's work and no amount of banner-waving and marching could change that. However, she was prepared to learn and so she began her reading.

Meg would have been happy to camp by the tarn for the rest of the summer. The weather was fine and the daylight endless. Lady Alice went out in the morning with her shotgun and came back with wild duck or rabbit for dinner. Miss Brookes read and walked and wrote, and talked to Meg about her reading.

'We shall be moving on to the farm above Crandale tomorrow,' Miss Brookes explained to Meg. 'After then you will learn much more about our work.'

'I hadn't realised it was Dr Pankhurst who started this "Votes for Women" movement.'

'Oh yes. He raised the issue nearly forty years ago. We have him to thank for the Married Women's Property Act, too. His widow and daughters have carried on his work and now they have lots of support.'

'But not in the government.'

'Not yet.'

They reached the farm on market day in Crandale and did not see the farmer or his wife until the couple returned home in the evening. The farmer walked over to the caravan immediately with a newspaper under his arm.

'Lady Alice Langton? I have been expecting you, ma'am. Mr Wright from the Lodge has told me all about you. You are most welcome on my land, but he asked me to advise you that it is not safe to visit the textile mill in Crandale.'

Lady Alice was sitting on a fallen tree trunk cleaning Hector's harness. She straightened and replied, 'I have business there.'

'I shouldn't go, my lady. There's been a bit of a to-do. It's all in the newspapers and the constable has sent for reinforcements.' He handed his newspaper to Lady Alice.

'Thank you, my good man. Parker my maid will call on you and your wife in the morning. Was there anything else?'

'Mr Wright asked me to tell you about the Crandale Arms in the square. It is a very good hotel, ma'am. It used to be a coaching inn.'

'Thank you.'

'You may borrow my wife's trap if you wish. It's just that the Crandale Arms will soon fill up with the grouse-shooting season about to start–'

Lady Alice interrupted him. 'Yes, thank you, I understand.'

The farmer nodded, bid them goodnight and left.

Lady Alice scanned the front page of the newspaper with interest. *Women Textile Workers Threaten Strike*. She read the headline aloud, adding, 'They plan to march on the town hall. It sounds very much as though I should be there.'

Miss Brookes stood up and asked, 'Why are they threatening to strike?'

'The women are complaining that they don't

get paid as much as the men who work in the weaving sheds.' She handed the newspaper to Miss Brookes. 'Read it for yourself.'

After a couple of minutes Miss Brookes said, 'It's on Friday. We have to support them, Lady Alice. Your caravan will attract more publicity.'

Meg had overheard all of this conversation and came slowly down the caravan steps. She was frowning. 'Excuse me, my lady, but Crandale is much bigger than Deepdale and I have been reading about the Manchester riots. A crowd can soon become ugly. The caravan is far too conspicuous. It might attract the wrong sort of attention from a – from a mob.'

'There will be no mob, Parker. The newspaper has printed a statement from the mill women's committee,' Lady Alice responded. 'They have declared that their protest march will be peaceful.'

'It was the men who disturbed the peace in Deepdale, ma'am,' Meg commented.

Miss Brookes added, 'I have to agree with Parker, my lady. All my papers are stored in the caravan. It is too risky to speak from the steps this time.'

Lady Alice did not argue with Miss Brookes. 'Very well. I shall take Mr Wright's advice and stay at the Crandale Arms. But I shall take the caravan with me. The landlord will have space for it in his coaching yard.'

Chapter 14

'Parker, you do not have to come to the town hall with us.'

Meg met Lady Alice and Miss Brookes outside the Crandale Arms. 'I want to, Lady Alice,' she replied. 'I saw what happened at Deepdale. It wasn't fair.'

'If you are determined then stay close to Miss Brookes at all times. I shall be on the steps to welcome the women's committee at the head of the march and make my speech from there.'

Miss Brookes explained as they walked, 'We are anticipating a large crowd. The protest has spread to women in other mills so the constable and his reinforcements will get a surprise.'

But it was Lady Alice who was surprised when a constable barred her progress into the town-hall square. Meg could hear the march approaching on the road opposite them.

'Step aside, my good man,' Lady Alice responded in her loftiest tone. 'I have business at the town hall.'

But the constable was ready for her. 'The town hall is closed for the day, ma'am, even for the likes of you.'

'Nonsense!' Lady Alice attempted to push by him.

'I shall have to arrest you, ma'am. I have my orders.'

Miss Brookes took Lady Alice's arm and turned her away. 'Not yet, my lady, not before you have had a chance to speak. We'll find another way round.'

Meg waited and listened for a few minutes. Then she hurried to catch up with Miss Brookes and said, 'Can you hear the crowd? The police will never keep them all out of the square. We'll go back when the constable is distracted. I'll keep a watch for you.'

Sure enough, all the constable's men were needed to keep the protest marchers out of the square and while they were busy, Meg, Miss Brookes and Lady Alice hurried across to the town-hall steps. As soon as the march appeared, they waved their arms in the air, a huge cheer rose from the marchers and a few women broke away from their police restrictions. The few were followed by more until a steady stream of women flowed into the square, filling all corners. A group of women joined them on the steps and they prepared to make their speeches.

Meg had a good view of the square and she noticed the policemen emerging from a narrow street at the side of the steps and pushing their way through the crowd towards the steps. 'Miss Brookes,' she whispered, 'look.'

Women in the crowd tried to stop them, but the police were not interested in their minor assaults. They were after the leaders, who continued their rallying cries from the steps with the benefit of a megaphone and were rewarded with huge cheers from the crowd.

A burly policeman was the first to reach them.

'Now then, ladies, you've had your say. Tell your followers to go home peacefully and nobody will get arrested.'

The speakers ignored him but within a couple of minutes they were surrounded by several large policemen. Meg, at first thrilled by the excitement of the event, began to feel alarmed. She didn't want any of them to be arrested, let alone herself. Prison was not a nice place to be even for a short time.

One of the policemen made a grab for the megaphone and a scuffle broke out. The front rows of the crowd swarmed up the steps to rescue their leaders and within seconds the town-hall steps were a jumble of squabbling bodies, some falling and being injured in the process. Two policemen seized Meg by her arms and half dragged her up the steps. The town-hall door had opened and she was pushed inside where she stumbled. Another pair of hefty men hoisted her to her feet and shoved her into a tiny anteroom. Others followed her until about a dozen women were crammed into the small space. One or two had very frightened looks on their faces and Meg was feeling the same. Miss Brookes arrived looking very dishevelled with her hat askew and her skirt torn. 'Courage, sisters,' she said loudly. 'Be proud to stand up and be counted for what you believe.'

'What's happening out there?' Meg asked.

'The ladies' committee was persuaded to send the crowd home. Nobody wants to get hurt and they have made their point.'

'I don't suppose it will make any difference to

their wages anyway.'

'Never say die, Parker. Rome wasn't built in a day.'

The door opened and two more women were pushed into the room. Everyone shuffled around to make space for them. 'What will happen to us, Miss Brookes?'

'They can't lock up all of us, the courthouse jail isn't big enough.'

'Even so, I don't fancy a night in there.'

'Yes, I am so sorry, Meg. I didn't expect it to come to this.'

'I don't think anybody did. It doesn't do the reputation of the suffragettes any good at all.'

'Quite the contrary, Parker. This is just what we need to strengthen our cause. I am so pleased we had onlookers to see how disgracefully the policeman treated us. Perhaps our lawmakers will take more notice of us now.'

'They'll certainly do that. What happened to Lady Alice?'

'The chief constable escorted her into the town hall.' Miss Brookes looked around. 'But she's not here, is she?'

'I expect he knew who she was. What about you? Didn't you say you were her companion?'

'No and I asked her not to either. Listen to me, Parker. Do not tell anyone that you know me. I'm in big trouble.'

'Oh no! What did you do?'

'Not much more than anyone else, except that I was persistent.'

'Miss Brookes!'

'Do not look so shocked. I had to do it.'

The door opened at that point and a man called out, '*Parker.*'

'Go on.' Miss Brookes gave her a gentle push. 'I need you and Lady Alice on the outside.'

Meg was horrified. It sounded as though Miss Brookes wanted to be arrested. Meg was escorted across the wood-panelled lobby to another room where Lady Alice was waiting for her. Meg was so relieved to see her that she exclaimed, 'Thank goodness you are safe! Have you been arrested?'

'No, and neither will you be. I told them you were with me only as my servant and I am totally responsible for your behaviour.'

'Thank you, my lady.' Meg glanced over her shoulder. 'I am worried about Miss Brookes. She is locked in that tiny room and seems determined not to be freed.'

'I told her to do as the policemen ordered. But she talked of being arrested even though I tried to dissuade her.'

'What can we do, ma'am?'

'Well, I shouldn't think they will lock her up as it is her first offence. Perhaps she will be fined for breach of the peace or some other such misdemeanour and be back in the hotel for dinner tonight.'

'I hope so.'

'We shall know soon enough. The court is sitting this afternoon especially to deal with the women strikers.'

Meg took her place beside Lady Alice on the public benches in the courtroom. They had not been charged with anything and had had time to return to the hotel lounge for tea and cake before the court hearings. Meg had been able to tidy Lady Alice's hair and hat. A succession of protesters appeared before the magistrate and admitted various offences of disorderly behaviour, apologised to the court and promised not do it again. Most were discharged but two from the mill workers' women's committee were fined. They appeared relieved to be free to return to their families. Miss Brookes was the last to appear and was quite dishevelled in her appearance. But she held her head high as she stood in the dock and listened to the charges against her. The policeman accused her of causing an obstruction and using violent and abusive language to incite a riot. Miss Brookes denied it and said she was exercising her right to free speech in a free country. A ripple of appreciative applause rattled around the public gallery.

Miss Brookes stubbornly refused to retract her behaviour and said she would do the same again. The magistrate was clearly angry with her and rebuked her in the most patronising way, pontificating that a lady of her background and upbringing ought to be ashamed of herself. He gave her another chance to apologise and promise to keep the peace in future. When she refused again he found her guilty and sentenced her to pay a fine of one pound or spend fourteen days in jail.

'I choose the latter,' she stated.

Meg jumped to her feet and yelled. 'You can't go to prison! Pay the fine!' Lady Alice stood up beside her and cried, 'I shall pay the fine!'

The magistrate raised his voice. 'Be quiet or I'll have you removed!' Two court ushers approached

Meg and Lady Alice and they resumed their seats quietly.

Miss Brookes spoke up clearly, 'I am quite able to pay my own fine, sir, and I choose jail.'

Meg and Lady Alice stood up again and spoke at the same time. 'You can't!'

'You can't go to jail!'

'*Remove those ladies before I charge them with contempt of court.*'

Meg and Lady Alice were manhandled out of the courtroom and into the street by a pair of hefty court officials. Bewildered, Lady Alice stared at the courtroom door as it closed in her face. 'I cannot let Miss Brookes do this. She has not thought it through. It will be reported in the newspaper. Her fiancé will hear of it and he will be obliged to break their engagement. She must not take this action.'

'I don't see how we can stop her now, my lady, unless...'

'Unless what, Parker? Speak up. This is no time to be servile.'

'Miss Brookes cannot stop you paying her fine,' Meg suggested. 'Go back inside now. They cannot put her in jail if the fine is paid, no matter who pays it.'

'Parker, how clever of you!' Lady Alice pushed open the courtroom door and marched inside. Her progress was barred immediately by the court officials. 'Let me past, sir. I demand to speak with the magistrates' clerk.'

'Oh, do you indeed?' an usher responded. 'Well, lady or not, I'm not letting you back in here today. Haven't you got any sick people to visit?'

'Come away, Lady Alice,' Meg begged. 'It's no good. Wait until they have gone back to the courtroom and then maybe you can sneak in.'

But the court officials were too diligent and Lady Alice did not have an opportunity to pay Miss Brookes's fine before the courthouse closed. However, as others from the public benches left, Meg did find out that the prison cells were underneath the courthouse building and that there would be an opportunity for Lady Alice to pay the fine in the morning. They walked slowly back to the Crandale Arms.

'I shall dine at eight in the hotel dining room and have a tray in my suite for breakfast, Parker. Would you arrange it?' Lady Alice collected the key to her rooms and climbed the grand mahogany staircase.

The Crandale Arms was extremely busy with visitors travelling north for the shooting. Meg gave Lady Alice's orders to the young man on the reception desk and made her way down a carpeted corridor through several doors until she reached a saloon bar at the rear of the hotel where hotel staff mixed with the servants of guests in residence. She asked for a glass of beer and a plate of stew and dumplings and sat down at one of the tables. Others at the table were, she guessed, maids and valets or chauffeurs to Lady Alice's dining companions in the hotel. They were not local, judging by their dialects, and some had made long journeys from the south for the grouse.

Meg had been allocated to an attic room for her stay, which she was required to share with one of these maids. Although she had nothing against any of them, she felt she would have more peace and quiet for reading in the privacy in the caravan, tucked away in the back yard of the inn. Some of the young men in the bar were lively and their forward ways reminded her too vividly of Saul. A party gathered around the piano for a sing-song but Meg had not the least desire to join in. The memory of Saul's attack was too raw and she still blushed with embarrassment at the memory. She felt soiled by him and cringed as she relived his assault. She wished desperately that she could forget him and worried that people would know what he had done simply by looking at her. So she slipped away during the singing and crept out of the back door by the kitchens to the haven of the caravan and one of Miss Brookes's books.

The night air was cold and still but Meg had oil for the stove and lamps and the bliss of an evening to herself. An occasional creak and groan from the timber and metal of the van as it warmed kept her alert and faint scratching sounds from under the floor told her that she had the company of small animals seeking shelter. But a distinct knocking on the side of the caravan startled her.

A male voice called out, 'Is someone in there?'

She stiffened. Perhaps it was the innkeeper? Oh Lord, he probably checked everywhere for drunks and vagrants last thing at night, especially with a hotel full of influential guests. She held her breath hoping he would move on.

'You have no right to be in there. Show yourself now.'

He sounded like Mr Wright. In fact he spoke with exactly the same hint of local dialect, which was not surprising. But it couldn't possibly be him. He would be at Ferndale Lodge with Lord Redfern's shooting party. Meg bit her lip. Whoever he was, he believed her to be an intruder. If she didn't reply, who knew what he might do? He might have a shotgun with him. 'I am Lady Alice Langton's maid,' she answered.

The silence lengthened. He probably didn't believe her so she added, 'The caravan belongs to Lady Alice.'

'I know. Lady Alice joined our party at dinner and I was introduced to her. She told us that her caravan might be a target for troublemakers. She said it was empty.'

'Well, it isn't. Who are you anyway?'

'Lady Alice asked me to represent her and that is all you need to know, madam. If you do not show yourself immediately I shall fetch a constable.'

Meg hesitated. It was perfectly possible that Lady Alice had met with someone that evening to discuss Miss Brookes's situation. She picked up the lamp and moved to the door. 'Is Lady Alice with you?'

'She has retired for the night.'

Meg drew back the bolts on the top half of the door and opened it a crack. The cobbled yard was dark but the man had brought a lamp, which he had placed on a disused mounting stone so that he was well lit. He was a young, tall gentleman in formal evening dress with a white silk scarf around his neck. He was not wearing a hat

231

and Meg would have recognised his handsome face and thick dark hair anywhere.

What the blazes was Jacob doing here? His father had said he was in London. She closed the door quickly and shot the bolts. She must be mistaken! The light was playing tricks on her!

'Madam,' he went on, 'if you are who you say you are, you were with Lady Alice and her companion today so you will understand her ladyship's concern for her property.' He sounded weary as though he was losing his patience.

It was Jacob! He was here, in the yard of the Crandale Arms, standing a few yards away from her, after months of trying to forget him! She began to shake like a jelly. She could not face him, not now after all that had happened. He wouldn't want anything to do with her now. He had dined with Lady Alice so he had moved up in the world, just as his father had predicted. He was dressed like the other gentry and probably here with them for the shooting.

She had to say something and there was no point in lying. She spoke to the closed door. 'I am Parker, Lady Alice's maid. You can check my name on the hotel register.'

She heard his boots take a few steps on the cobbles. 'What did you say your name was?'

It wasn't a secret. If he was known to Lady Alice, he'd find out anyway sooner or later. But her voice came out hoarse and squeaky. 'Meg Parker. It's Meg, Jacob; from Deepdale. Now will you please go away?' She stood motionless for a minute or two with her ears strained for the sounds of him leaving.

'Meg?' He sounded astonished. '*You* are Lady Alice's maid?'

She didn't answer, hoping he would walk away. After a minute or so he asked, 'Have you got someone in there with you?' He sounded tense when he added, 'I'd put the fire out if I were you. The smoke is a giveaway.'

He thought she had a lover with her? How dare he? Stung by his apparent – and unfounded – accusation she fumbled with the bolts on the top half of the door and flung it open. 'There is no one else here! Come and look for yourself if you don't believe me!'

He was standing closer than she'd imagined, only a few yards away from the caravan steps and holding the lamp in his right hand. Why hadn't he gone as she had asked?

'Is that all you men think about?' she added irritably. She was glad it was dark so that he could not see the flush on her face.

'Meg? It really is you; I can't believe it. You're the last person I expected to see. But what on earth is wrong? Why have you locked yourself away in there?' He didn't sound angry, more puzzled and irritated.

'I'm reading if you must know – and you have interrupted me,' she added pointedly. 'Good-night.'

'Good heavens, Meg, don't be so prickly!'

'Well, what are *you* doing here?' she demanded.

'I told you. Lady Alice was worried about her travelling van.'

'I mean here in Crandale.' Why oh why did he have to turn up now, just when she thought she was over him and making a new start in her life?

'This is my home ground and I was invited to join a shooting party. Look, Meg, it's cold out here. May I come inside and talk?'

'No.'

He gave an impatient gasp so she added, 'Why don't you go back to your party?'

'Why don't you? I hear that the guests' servants are having a grand time of it with the hotel staff.'

'I'm not really one of them.'

'No you're not, are you? Maid to Lady Alice is a huge change for you. What does your father think?'

Father wouldn't have wanted her to go into service, she thought. Eventually, she answered, 'My father died.'

Jacob was contrite, making her feel guilty about her rude behaviour. 'Oh, Meg, how awful for you, I am truly sorry. I know how close you were. If you won't let me in, can I take you into the hotel for a nightcap?'

'No.' She spoke sharply. It was difficult enough for her to deal with this conversation without prolonging it.

'Meg, is something wrong?'

If only I could tell you and you could say to me it's all right and that you still love me and want me. She said, 'Nothing's wrong. I am absolutely fine.'

'Then at least let me see you safely back to the hotel. Several young men are already the worse for drink.'

She dared not let him near her. He was perceptive where she was concerned and he would know that something *had* happened to her. He

234

might even see her for the ruined woman she had become! She needed a locked door between them so as not to risk any chance of showing her true feelings. 'There's no need,' she said.

'Don't be ridiculous!' He sounded angry. 'This is no time to be stubborn.'

'I am quite secure in here when this door is bolted. It was safe enough to sleep in out on the moor–' Meg stopped, realising that she had said too much.

'Do you mean you intend to stay out here all night on your own? That is plain foolhardy.'

'It's better than the alternative in the hotel attic. It is my choice. Now will you please leave me in peace?'

'If that is what you really want.' When she didn't reply he added, 'Whatever it is that has happened to you, it has changed you.'

He did not walk away. She had to be the one to finish the conversation. 'I grew up,' she answered and closed the door before she broke down in tears.

Jacob's presence was a painful reminder of what might have been. She did not want to look back on her mistakes and feel sorry for herself. She must forget all about him. It's just that it was so hard for her. But he was a part of her past not her future. She had no idea what that future might be, but she had to go forward without yearning for him if she was to build a new life.

When he moved to London, he had taken her heart with him and she would regret for ever that she had disappointed him. It was too late to remedy that now. Their lives had moved in different directions. She sat down and gazed at the closed door that separated her from further hurt. She could not look Jacob in the eye as the same young woman he had left behind. Always, always, that dreadful memory surfaced, reminding her of that hateful man who had taken her innocence and trampled on her feelings until they were numbed.

The bolts that locked Jacob out of her life also locked in her foolishness, her embarrassment and guilt, keeping her secret safe from the world. She wondered when the remembered images and pain would go away and longed to be on the road again, with women who did not question her and did not judge her; with work to fill her days and new ideas to fill her mind.

She picked up the book she had been reading. The words blurred in the lamplight as tears rolled down her cheeks. The kettle on the stove was warm. She filled a stone hot-water bottle, curled up with it for company and tried to forget that Jacob Wright existed.

Chapter 15

Florence felt dreadful. She had not slept a wink on her cold hard bed and looked down in dismay at her grubby, dishevelled dress and scuffed boots. She glanced briefly at the other woman in the small smelly prison cell. The woman was pretty but wore cheap clothes and jewellery. The curls in her black hair had matted untidily and she had smudged rouge on her cheeks and lips. Oh Lord, Florence realised, her cell companion was not one of the protesters. She was a woman of the streets!

A prison warder brought some porridge, which was hot and very welcome. He seemed to know the other woman. 'What you done now, Maisie?' he asked.

'Nuffink,' she answered.

'Aye,' the warder said and shook his head.

Florence lifted her head. 'What will happen to me?' she asked.

'You'll stay here with our Maisie until you're moved to the women's prison.'

Oh dear heaven, she would have to share with a prostitute! 'Where can I wash?' she asked. He looked at her as though she had asked for the moon.

When he had gone and the warmth of her breakfast spread through her veins she smiled tentatively at Maisie. 'Why did you do it?' she asked.

'You what?' she replied.

'Whatever it is you've done, why did you do it?'

'You 'eard me! I 'a'n't done nuffink.'

'Why are you here, then?'

'Mind yer own, yer nosey cow.'

Florence did but after a few minutes, Maisie said, 'We don't get your sort in here, as a rule. Are you carriage trade?'

Florence felt a blush rise through her face. 'I'm not a prostitute! All I did was to speak up for the women on strike.'

'What, wi' that lot at t' mill?'

'Yes. Did you hear about us?'

Maisie snorted. 'Yer should know better than ter tek on t' mill owners. They'll allus have the upper hand.'

'But, don't you see, that's why we have to fight them. Women seamstresses work as hard as the men weavers and for just as long hours. They ought to have the same pay.' Florence warmed to her topic. 'Men decide everything for us and it's not right.'

'Oh, give over, lass. Yer can't change things so yer may as well gi' 'em what they want.'

'That's what you do, isn't it? And then different men arrest you and sentence you because they make the laws.'

Maisie guffawed. 'They ain't no different! All men are same, believe me, ducky.'

'Then they are just being hypocritical!' But that's it, Florence thought. The laws were made by men to suit men. It was the lawmakers they had to fight, not the mill owners. She sat down on her bed and thought, Maisie was wrong. It was possible to change things but it took time, too much time, she realised. She understood why the suffragettes had lost their patience.

Maisie had a sneer on her face. 'And I'll tell yer fer nowt that none of 'em like yer ter use big words.'

Florence realised that Maisie had no idea what 'hypocritical' meant and explained, 'Two-faced. The men are two-faced.'

'Not when they pay me fine fer me.' Maisie smirked. 'I'll be out of here before you, ducks.'

The warder came back. 'Brookes, come with me, you have a visitor,' he announced.

He led Florence out of the cell and down a brick-lined corridor with stone flags on the floor. 'He's a solicitor. Do as you're told and you might be released. Let this be a lesson to you, young lady. You should be ashamed of yourself. A well-brought-up lass like yourself cavorting with lasses from the mill – what is the world coming to?'

'The twentieth century, I hope,' she replied.

'A word of advice, Brookes; don't be cheeky to the magistrate or you'll be back in the cells with the likes of our Maisie before you can say "Jack Robinson".'

He took her up to the ground floor where the courtroom was situated and led her into a small wood-panelled chamber. The magistrate was there and Lady Alice with a tall young gentleman in a dark suit and stiff collared shirt. Lady Alice smiled at her but stayed silent. The young gentleman came forward and introduced himself.

'Jacob Wright, Miss Brookes. I am a lawyer practising in London and Lady Alice has instructed me to represent you.'

Florence stared at him. The resemblance was striking. 'You're Mr Wright's son, aren't you? Lady Alice hasn't brought you all this way for me, has she?'

'I was already in the area for the grouse shooting, ma'am. Would you be so kind as to leave all the talking to the magistrate to me? My task is to get you out of here. I am sure you want that too.'

Florence glanced at Lady Alice, who nodded.

She had changed her mind, Mr Wright said. The night in the cells had brought her to her senses and she was willing to apologise for her behaviour and pay the fine.

'No,' Florence squeaked. This was a complete turnabout for her. She looked pleadingly at Lady Alice, who nodded insistently.

Mr Wright asked the magistrate if he might have a chair for her, arguing that a night in the cells had taken a heavy toll on his client. When the usher brought it, Mr Wright gave her shoulder a firm push downwards and glared at her. Florence sat down.

It was all very irregular, the magistrate stated when the proceedings were completed. Florence, through the mouthpiece of Mr Wright, had apologised and was 'bound over to keep the peace'. If she repeated her disgraceful behaviour within five years she would surely go to prison. Meanwhile she was free to go. Florence did not know whether to be relieved that she didn't have to return to that squalid cell, or angry that she was released. Mr Wright took her arm and bundled her out of the room before the magistrate changed his mind.

Lady Alice paid her fine to the clerk at the desk and thanked Mr Wright for his help.

'It is my pleasure, my lady.' He turned to Florence and said, 'You may have lost this battle, Miss Brookes, but you have most certainly have not lost the suffrage war. I wish you well. Now, if you ladies will excuse me, I believe there is a shooting brake waiting to take me to Ferndale Lodge. Good morning to you.' He bowed his head formally and left the building.

Lady Alice gazed after him with shining eyes. 'Isn't he marvellous, Miss Brookes? He is so like my darling Hugo, it's uncanny.' She withdrew a folded newspaper from underneath her jacket. 'And do not be cross with me, Miss Brookes. Look at this. Front-page news! You are famous. Someone took a picture of you being arrested. I am so proud of you. Was it absolutely dreadful in that cell?'

'Well, it was awful. I can't say that I was looking forward to another night in there.'

'Will you allow me to tidy your hair a little? I'm afraid you are quite the celebrity and a welcome awaits you outside.'

Florence stepped into the bright sunlight and blinked. A cheer went up from a crowd of women waiting outside. Some held strikers' placards and 'Votes for Women' slogans.

The newspaper had reported hardly a word about the speeches. But a night in a prison cell for a well-brought-up young lady was a headline story. Florence gave a few words of thanks and a few more about rallying support for 'our sisters'. Good heavens, she thought, one night in the cells had been more effective than all the talking Lady Alice had done from her caravan steps. She turned to Lady Alice and whispered, 'I'm rather tired, my lady. I need to sit down.'

'I've arranged for the hotel motor car to take us back. It's that black one over there.'

'Where's Parker?'

'Oh, I couldn't persuade her to come with me. She is taking the opportunity to clean out the caravan.'

'It's a shame she didn't see this crowd.'

'Yes, it might have cheered her up. I believe that, deep down, she is a very unhappy woman, rather as I was when I lost Hugo.'

'Perhaps she left behind a broken heart in Deepdale?'

'Or perhaps she brought it with her. Talking of hearts, you do realise that your fiancé will hear of this, don't you?'

'I didn't think of it at the time, but last night I had plenty of opportunity to reflect. I'm a criminal, aren't I?'

'I don't wish to alarm you, Miss Brookes, but I have known gentleman break off engagements for less undesirable behaviour, with no possibility of breach of promise.'

'Oh dear me, do you think he will? My parents would be mortified.'

'And you, my dear, how would you feel?'

I don't know, Florence thought. I really do not know.

'Yes, what is it?' Florence answered the rap at the door of Lady Alice's suite. A young hall boy stood in the corridor carrying a silver tray with a card on it. She recognised it immediately, picked it up and asked, 'Where is he?'

'He's waiting in the hotel lobby, miss.'

She had been hoping that Bradley would be too busy with his theatre project to read about striking mill girls in Crandale. Her hopes must have been in vain, otherwise why had he come all this way to see her? She had a sickening feeling that Lady Alice would be proved right and he wished to break off their engagement. She tapped the card against her fingernails. She could not blame him if he did and decided not to behave hysterically. She would leave that to her mother when she found out. Father would be a different matter, though. He would not be happy to lose something that was a culmination of his life's work because of what he would regard as his daughter's foolish behaviour.

And what of me, she thought? How much do I care? Florence realised that she would not be so much upset by her broken heart as embarrassed by being jilted. And it would be frightfully embarrassing for her parents because she was the guilty party. She fingered her engagement ring and prepared to return it.

'Is that all, miss?' The hall boy smiled and stood very still.

Florence pulled herself together. 'Wait a moment.' She rummaged in her dolly bag for a coin and gave it to him. 'Tell the gentleman I shall be down shortly.'

She tapped on Lady Alice's door but she must have been asleep so she wrote a short note, left it in the suite sitting room, then gave some attention to her appearance. She walked slowly down the carpeted staircase as elegantly as she could and wondered how much Bradley knew.

'My dearest Florence.' Bradley rose to his feet, grasped her shoulders lightly and kissed her cheek. A few heads turned to look at them. They were an eye-catching couple but she would have preferred anonymity at that precise moment. 'The country air becomes you. Let us sit down and talk.'

'Thank you. Did you drive here in the motor car?'

243

'I did and I have ordered tea,' he said and led her to a comfortable corner where a small table was laid for afternoon tea. 'Are you quite recovered from your ordeal?'

So he did know about her night in the cells! She answered, 'Yes. Thank you. I would have written to you about it. It all got rather out of hand. Are you very angry with me?'

'Your father is.'

'Did he send you?'

'It was my idea. Ah, here is our tea.' He sat back and watched the waiter transfer the contents of his tray to their table. As usual, his eyes travelled over the young man's attire as though he were examining every detail for a flaw. Apparently he found none for a smile played on his lips. Florence hoped that was a sign of a relatively pleasant exchange to come. Bradley's manners were always impeccable anyway. Florence leaned forward to pour the tea.

'I have consulted with your father and mother and they agree with me about this,' he said as he offered her the plate of sandwiches.

So it was to be bad news. 'I am sorry to cause you so much embarrassment but I cannot say I regret my actions.'

'Your dear mother deserves your apology. You deliberately deceived her about Lady Alice's intentions regarding her mode of travel. It was foolish and dangerous.'

Florence could not argue with that. It was hard work too, but she didn't suppose that counted for anything with her parents. 'I would do it again,' she answered.

'Yes, I believe you would, which is why I am

here. I have allowed you a good deal of freedom during our engagement because I trusted you. But I do expect you to respect my wishes.'

'Yes, I understand and I am prepared for what you are going to say.'

'You are?'

'I … we…' She settled on 'you'. 'You feel unable to continue with our engagement after – after recent events.'

'Well, that is very gracious of you to say so, Florence. It has been difficult for me in Shaw-bridge.' He offered her another sandwich. 'I have spoken to my parents too and they agree.'

Florence's face fell. She liked Mr and Mrs Melvil and felt a pang of guilt at letting them down like this.

'We thought early in the New Year, when trade is slack.'

Florence was puzzled. Why wait until then to announce a broken engagement? 'Surely you don't want to wait that long?'

'These things need planning and preparation.'

'What are you talking about, Bradley?'

'I am discussing shortening our engagement and bringing our marriage forward, of course. What else would we be talking about?'

Florence closed her eyes and shook her head. 'I don't understand. Are you saying that you still wish to marry me?'

'I blame myself for your digression. If I had not been so absorbed in my theatre project you would not have taken the position with Lady Alice. A year was far too long to ask you to wait. We shall marry early in the New Year.'

'We shall?'

'I am taking you home in the motor tomorrow. We leave after breakfast.'

'I can't, Lady Alice is expecting me to–'

'Of course you can. Have no fear, dearest. Lady Alice and I have a common acquaintance in a dear chum of mine from my university days. He will join us for dinner tonight. I have reserved a table in the dining room. I shall explain everything to Lady Alice and Giles will support me.' He lifted the plate of scones and added, 'I am told these are excellent. Do have one.'

'Giles? Is that the Giles you have spoken of in connection with your theatre project?'

'The very same: Giles Waltham. It is time you made his acquaintance.'

'Well,' she breathed, 'this is not at all what I expected.' But, as always, Bradley was orchestrating the evening. She had not met Giles, though she had no doubt he would be handsome, impeccably dressed and with faultless manners, and his task would be to charm Lady Alice into agreeing with Bradley. She lifted up the teapot and smiled. 'More tea, dearest?'

'We shall not linger over tea as we must all look our best for Lady Alice.'

She wondered briefly if Bradley had underestimated Lady Alice. Lady Alice could be as charming as he, but she was also perceptive, a quality overlooked by many who were impressed by her status.

'Were you able to book a room here?' she asked.

'One of the best suites was vacated this morning by a party travelling to Scotland.'

'How fortunate for you.' Florence declined cake and left at the earliest opportunity.

Lady Alice was taking tea in her suite. She rose to her feet anxiously. 'I read your note.'

'He still wishes to marry me. I cannot believe it. He blames himself for agreeing to a long engagement. We are to have a winter wedding instead of waiting until next summer.'

'Then all your fears are unfounded. He must truly love you.'

'I suppose he must. I do wish he would show it more when we are alone.'

'He is an English gentleman, Miss Brookes. Wait until you are wearing your wedding band.' Lady Alice sounded excited for her and added, 'I shall leave you to dine alone with him tonight.'

'You are invited to dine with myself and Bradley, and his friend. You have met Giles Waltham before?'

'Giles Waltham? I cannot recall the name but I may recognise him when I see him.'

'Please say you'll join us. I shall be browbeaten by them without you.'

'I look forward to meeting them both.' Lady Alice smiled. 'Have you seen Parker today?'

Florence shook her head. 'She says she is fully occupied with cleaning, drawing up an inventory and replenishing supplies. When she is not working, the caravan becomes her study and I cannot distract her, nor would I wish to.'

Dinner went far better than Florence had hoped. The gentlemen entertained them splendidly with tales of known theatrical personalities and they even had a serious conversation about women's suffrage. Lady Alice did recall her previous meeting with Giles but did not dwell on it and was totally at ease so that Florence relaxed and enjoyed herself. She began to feel more confident about her forthcoming marriage. Lady Alice suggested they should move to the hotel lounge for coffee, leaving Bradley and Giles to join them later after their brandy and cigars.

Florence sighed as she sank into a comfortable chair. 'Thank you so much for supporting me in this way. I am quite certain now that he will not ask me to release him from our engagement.'

'Would you have been dreadfully upset if he had?'

'It would have been difficult to face Mother and Father.'

'That is not what I asked you.'

Florence gazed at Lady Alice. Her face was very serious and she expected an answer. 'Well, yes, I suppose so. Every girl wants to be married. But I should not have blamed him. He did not propose to a suffragette.'

Lady Alice continued to stare at her in a way that Florence found puzzling and – and worrying. 'Do you love him?' she asked.

'Of course I love him! He is cultured, thoughtful and generous and–' Florence stopped. Lady Alice did not seem to be impressed by her answers so she added, 'I am sorry if you do not like him, but I do.'

'It isn't that I do not like him. I am sure he is all the things you say, but are you passionate about him? More to the point, your instincts are correct. He is not passionate about you.'

Florence frowned. Lady Alice had picked on the very thing that had concerned her about Bradley and her words had touched a raw nerve. 'But you said that would change after marriage,' she responded. 'Forgive me, Lady Alice, you are a spinster lady yourself. What do you know of passion anyway?'

'I know that when I fell in love with my darling Hugo I could scarcely keep my hands off him, and he felt the same. He told me so often before he sailed for Africa. I do not detect anything similar between you and Bradley.'

'A lady does not make the first overtures!'

'Indeed not.' Alice appeared to be agreeing with her. 'However, I'll wager he has not indicated any kind of burning desire for you. I am right, am I not?'

Florence was becoming increasingly agitated by Lady Alice's persistence and tried to lighten the conversation. 'Mother thinks he is being chivalrous. She is half in love with him herself!'

'My dear Miss Brookes,' Lady Alice responded, 'I do not wish to distress you but you will have a very unhappy future if you go ahead with this marriage.'

'Really, Lady Alice! I shall have everything I–'

'Bradley does not love you.'

Chapter 16

Florence would have been extremely angry with Lady Alice if she had not considered this herself in the past. She responded firmly: 'He is not demonstrative in his affections but he has shown himself to be steadfast and – and he must care for me. Good heavens, he has forgiven my transgression!'

'He does not want to lose you.'

'Quite so. Is that not proof that he loves me?'

'Oh, Miss Brookes, I am so sorry but I do not believe it is.'

Florence stood up. 'I'm not listening to any more of this. Why are you set against him in this way? Surely you are not envious of me!'

'I am not. I admire you greatly and I do not want to see you hurt. Please sit down and allow me to explain.'

Florence was undecided whether to go or stay. The decision was made for her when Bradley appeared in the hotel lounge with Giles. She turned to face him and offered her cheek for a kiss. Bradley kindly obliged and Florence felt vindicated. Of course Bradley loved her! 'Shall I order more coffee?' she suggested.

Bradley smiled. 'We shall have a game of billiards before we retire. Giles is leaving early tomorrow and we have business to discuss. You don't mind, do you, Florence?'

'Of course not, dearest.'

'Then we shall see each other at breakfast. I am so pleased to have met you, Lady Alice. Goodnight to you both.' He leaned forward and gave her another light kiss on her cheek.

Florence frowned at their receding backs as they departed for the billiard room. 'I suppose you'll say that demonstrates what you think of him. Well, you are wrong. He is not an aristocrat like your brother. He makes his living in business and it is part of his life.'

Lady Alice did not argue with her. She stood up and said, 'Shall we go to our suite? I think our conversation will be more private there.'

Lady Alice ordered a pot of chocolate and some brandy before they retired. Florence respected her friend but she felt obliged to defend her fiancé and, as soon as she closed the door behind her, she demanded, 'Do you know something about Bradley's family, some – some – yes, of course you do – some misdemeanour from his past?' As she spoke the words Florence wondered if she had hit on the truth. It would explain why Bradley was so ready to forgive her. It gave him the moral high ground where she was concerned.

'Yes and no,' Lady Alice responded. 'Shall we be more comfortable by the fire?'

'Tell me what you know. Our respect for each other is too strong for you to keep this secret.'

'It is not a secret that I knew of before this evening, and I have no firm evidence that I can quote to you. But after tonight's dinner I am certain.'

'It is something to do with Giles?'

251

'Yes and no.'

'Lady Alice! Will you please stop talking in riddles!'

'You have heard of Oscar Wilde?'

'Bradley talks of his plays. He says they are very witty and deserve to be staged more often.'

'Do you know anything of Mr Wilde's personal life?'

Florence shook her head. 'He's dead, isn't he?'

'Yes. He died disgraced and in exile so his work has fallen out of fashion.'

'I was not aware of that.'

'I am sure that Bradley is.'

'Well of course, he loves the theatre.'

Lady Alice took a deep breath. 'He loves other gentlemen too.'

'He enjoys their company, of course, but "loves" is a strange word to use.'

'It is the relevant one here. My dear Miss Brookes, it is clear to me that you do not know everything you should about Bradley.' Lady Alice took another deep breath. 'I cannot sit by quietly and watch you go into this marriage.'

'What do you mean? Did Giles tell you something I should know?'

'He said nothing to me. Yet at the same time his actions told me all I needed to know.'

'Now you are being cryptic and it does not suit you.'

Lady Alice appeared undecided whether to go on, but eventually said, 'There is no other way for you to discover the truth about your fiancé. He will never love you as a husband ought. Bradley loves Giles.'

Florence laughed. 'You have taken too much wine with dinner.' But her laugh subsided when she noticed Lady Alice's concerned expression and added more slowly, 'They are very good friends.'

'I am convinced that they are lovers.'

'Lovers? I don't understand.'

'It has been described as "the love that dare not speak its name".'

Florence could see that Lady Alice was deadly serious and – and she detected pain in her eyes. Florence stared at the ornately designed wall-paper, her mind tumbling over snatched memories of interrupted conversations and guilty glances in her direction ... wicked ... unnatural ... unspeakable. She inhaled to respond but had no words. Lady Alice would not say these things if she were not truly worried for her future happiness. Surely it could not be true of Bradley! He was so attentive and charming towards her!

Lady Alice gave a sympathetic groan and shook her head. 'I found it difficult to comprehend when I read the newspaper reports about Oscar Wilde. He was tried and sent to prison for his crimes. But Langton Park had had a similar scandalous incident below stairs and two footmen were dismissed. I was forbidden to speak of it but servants talk quite openly when they do not know one is listening.'

Florence sat down silently and hid her shaking hands. This was too much to take in. The chocolate and brandy arrived and Lady Alice asked for a maid to bring hot water for washing. She handed Florence a glass. 'You are shocked by my observations. Drink the brandy. It will help.'

Florence gulped at the fiery liquid and it helped to quell her trembling. They were simply observations and yet they explained so much about Bradley and – and his friendship with Giles. Their friendship ran deeper than the theatre project, much deeper. She frowned and grimaced with frustration. 'I *knew* he did not love me. I knew it. But I believed Mother when she said he was being respectful, and that our love would develop after our marriage.'

'Do you think your mother knows?'

'Good Lord no! I am certain she does not. And I am equally certain now that his mother does. She is so very keen for him to settle down and marry.'

'He is assured of respectability if he marries you. But Giles will always be a part of his life and of your marriage.'

Florence raised her head. 'Bradley is in love with Giles?'

Lady Alice's face had a pained expression. 'Gentlemen do fall in love with each other and always have done. Your education probably did not include that aspect of the classics.'

'I can't say it did. But I was watching Giles with you. He was attentive and charming and I thought he was flirting with you.'

'I believe it was a performance.'

'Well, it was a good one if it was! How can you be so sure?'

'Did you not notice how his eyes were on Bradley for most of the time?'

'I can't say I did. I thought Giles was totally

occupied by you. He's rather like Bradley in his attentiveness.'

'You had no notion of their true relationship so why should you look for it? Believe me, it is Giles whom Bradley loves and Giles with whom he wishes to spend his evening.'

Florence wished she could be as sure as Lady Alice. 'But they are very good friends from university days! It is perfectly reasonable for gentleman to play billiards together.'

'And afterwards?'

Florence was stunned into silence at first; then she said, 'You don't think you might be mistaken?'

'I should dearly wish to be for your sake but I fear I am not. They will be together tonight; I would stake my life on it. That makes them criminals.'

'Then who am I to judge them except that – that, well, it's not – not natural.'

'I know of three gentlemen in my brother's circle of friends who are similarly unnatural. Indeed one of them, a peer of the realm no less, proposed marriage to me not long after Hugo died. He promised me wealth and freedom to do as I wished. My mother was very keen but she did not know the truth and my brother did.'

'He told you?'

'When we were children he had joked about the occasional bull or stallion with such tendencies. I did not fully realise the implications of this until Charles dissuaded me from the marriage.'

Again Florence stared at the wallpaper. 'Bradley would not have enlightened me, would he?'

'And risk a scandal, possibly prison? I should think not.'

'Prison?' The horrors of her incarceration were fresh in her mind. 'If you are correct then he has deceived me in the most cruel of ways.' Florence's eyes took on a haunted look. 'I – I cannot marry him.'

'Please do not say or do anything hasty. If you do decide to withdraw from this marriage you must do so in a way that will not tarnish your own reputation.'

'I suppose your people know all about how to do that.' Her tone was caustic and Florence regretted it. 'I am sorry. I know you have my happiness at heart.'

Lady Alice seemed to understand her distress, for she picked up the second glass of brandy and brought it over. 'Drink mine too. It has been a shock for you and this will help you sleep. Your mind will be clearer in the morning.'

'Yes, you're right.' Florence stood up with the brandy in her hand. 'I doubt that I shall sleep anyway.'

'Take a cup of chocolate while it is hot.'

Florence nodded. The rich sweet drink might soothe her. 'Goodnight then.'

'Goodnight, Miss Brookes.'

They retired to their respective bedrooms. Florence sat in her armchair and drank the chocolate and the brandy. The chambermaid brought in a ewer of hot water and fresh towels; then she turned down the bed and pulled the curtains, blotting out the blackness of the night. What if Lady Alice was wrong? Surely gentlemen might share business pursuits and other masculine interests? Her father belonged to a shopkeepers' association that according to him discussed politics and cricket matches most of the time. Florence shook her head. Lady Alice might be wrong. The only person who could confirm her observations was Bradley himself. She would not judge her fiancé on someone else's opinion. In the morning she must arrange a private moment and ask him outright.

Florence shuddered as she inhaled. How could she ask him? What words could she use? And if she were wrong, his response did not bear thinking about. His fury would surely wreck an already shaky relationship between them. What had Lady Alice said? He would not risk her knowing? But if she were to be his wife he must trust her! What was she thinking of? If Lady Alice suspected then others must too! How could she move forward into marriage with this question hanging over her like a large black cloud? She had to know the truth for certain.

The chocolate and brandy did not have the desired effect and, wide awake, she paced around her room. If Lady Alice was correct in her conclusion, she could not marry Bradley. She had anticipated a close, loving relationship with her husband and looked forward to discovering the physical joys that she had read about. The whole of her future had been called into question by Lady Alice's observations, observations that had confirmed the existence of her own worries. She must face Bradley with her doubts and she could not sleep until she had. She pushed aside the heavy drapes at the window and watched the hotel's late diners leaving in their carriages and motor cars. It was not late. If Bradley and Giles were still in the billiard room, she could ask him tonight. Florence checked her appearance in the mirror and crept quietly through the sitting room and into the landing corridor.

A night porter came in from the saloon bar to answer her query at the reception desk. 'The billiard room has closed, miss. Mr Melvil has retired for the night,' he told her.

'Very well.' Disappointed, Florence climbed the grand staircase slowly.

She had formed the words; she was ready to ask him, ready for the truth, ready to discuss their future. Surely he had only just retired? Billiards normally went on for half the night, didn't it? At the top of the staircase she did not turn right for Lady Alice's suite but left for Bradley's rooms at the end of the landing. She tapped lightly on the door.

A minute later Bradley opened it. 'Florence! I thought you were the night porter with our brandy.'

'I should very much like to talk to you.'

'Now?'

'Yes, now. I can see you are still dressed. Would you come downstairs? It is important, Bradley.'

'Is it so important that it cannot wait until morning? This is most unseemly, Florence.'

'I shall not be able to sleep until I have asked you a question about our future.'

'It is not convenient, Florence.' Florence heard a cough behind her in the corridor, and Bradley continued, 'Ah, here is the night porter with our brandy. Goodnight, my dear.'

For Florence it was the moment that she knew the answer to her unspoken question. She held herself rigidly wondering if she had the courage to go through with this. She half turned, took the tray from the night porter and said, 'Thank you, you may go.'

'Give the tray to me, Florence,' Bradley demanded.

She examined the two large brandies on the tray and then raised her eyes to Bradley's. 'Our brandy? Giles is with you, isn't he?'

'Don't be ridiculous!'

Why was his reaction so angry? He and Giles were sharing a suite in the same fashion as she and Lady Alice. Or were they? She searched Bradley's face and realised that she had misjudged his response. She did not see anger in his eyes; she saw fear. Lady Alice was right about her observations but Florence was wrong about his reaction. Bradley was frightened. She had not seen it before, or, if she had, she had not recognised it. He did not want her to know and he was afraid of what she might do. Instead of feeling betrayal and hurt at his deception she was sorry; sorry that a successful and confident gentleman could be brought down so easily by her discovery.

Florence felt nothing but sadness. 'You and Giles are lovers, aren't you? You ought to have told me,' she said.

The look of alarm that crossed his features brought a lump to Florence's throat. He said, 'Would you have married me if I had?' There was pleading in his eyes and her heart broke for him. He was not going to deny it.

She shook her head. 'We shall talk in the morning after all. Goodnight, Bradley.' Florence held her back straight and her head high as she walked shakily down the corridor.

She heard the steady breathing of Lady Alice deep in sleep through her bedroom door and stole silently towards her own bed. She turned down the lamp and lay on her bed staring at the darkness. She was numb, her mind a total blank for a long time, and then she felt her tears welling. She did not try to stop them. She let them flow until she was worn out and drifted into a restless slumber.

Her rest was short-lived. She was awake early to wash, dress and go down to hotel breakfast. She asked the head waiter to seat her and Mr Melvil at a private table and as Bradley approached, hesitating when he saw her, she removed her engagement ring and placed it on the table in front of him.

'Please don't do this, Florence,' he said. He was frowning and looked haggard.

'Sit down, Bradley. I shan't stay long and then you may breakfast with Giles as you planned.' She started well but when she saw the fear in his eyes Florence found it difficult to continue. She had not seen this weakened side of him before.

'What will you tell your parents?' he asked.

She swallowed. 'Now we are no longer engaged, I believe that the way you live your life is no concern of mine, or indeed anyone else.'

'I cannot help being the man I am. I do love you, Florence.'

'I am sure you do in your own way. But I cannot live a lie.' She examined his face, felt a genuine sorrow for him and inhaled deeply. This was the most difficult conversation of her life but she must do it. 'I shall not breathe a word to anyone about last night. Had my education been of a broader nature I should have recognised the signs earlier as Lady Alice did. You were never going to tell me, were you?'

He looked helpless and lost for words and she was torn between irritation that she had been fooled and sympathy for his predicament. She could have been vindictive and cruel but it was not her way and she went on, 'I shall say to Mother that I was obliged to release you from our engagement following my arrest and you were gracious enough to agree to an amicable separation by mutual consent.'

The furrows on his brow lessened slightly.

She finished her rehearsed speech quietly and quickly. 'Your secret is safe with me. I should not wish to be a part of sending anyone to prison. Goodbye, Bradley.' She stood up and walked away without looking back. She did not realise that she was holding her breath until she was safely in Lady Alice's suite. She leaned against the closed door and panted.

'Good heavens, Miss Brookes! Are you quite well?' Lady Alice was sitting at the small dining table in the large bay window that overlooked the market square. 'Breakfast has just arrived.' She lifted a domed silver cover. 'Bacon and kidneys, jolly good show.' She shook out a linen napkin.

Florence took a few deep breaths and joined

261

her at the table. 'I have broken our engagement.'

Lady Alice put down her napkin. 'So soon? A little hasty, don't you think? How did Bradley take it?'

'He was unhappy but I did not give him a choice.'

'You are very brave. How do you feel about it?'

'I am relieved that I have got it over with but extremely shaky. I was very fond of him and I dread returning home to Mother. She will winkle the truth out of me and I have promised Bradley that I shall take the blame.'

'That is noble of you, as well as brave.'

'I am sorry for him. Women are not the only people in our society who are suffering.'

'Do you know, Miss Brookes, I do believe you are a politician at heart.'

Florence put her elbows on the table and rested her face in her hands. Her voice was muffled. 'I cannot go home after this. I am a coward. I shall write to Mother and Father; give them time to get used to my broken engagement.'

'Well, that makes two of us with nowhere to call home in Yorkshire.'

'Surely you will return to Langton Park at the end of the summer?'

'I shall always be welcome at the Dower House, of course. But if I continue my work with the suffrage movement I shall only become an embarrassment to my brother.'

Florence poured coffee for them both and said, 'Will you give it up?'

'I don't think I can now. We must have votes for women.'

'I agree.' Florence put down the coffee pot and stated, 'I want to do more. I can't go back to Shawbridge and be the daughter my parents want me to be. If I try, I shall let them down again because I want to be a militant suffragette like Mrs Pankhurst in London–'

'London?' Lady Alice interrupted. She put down her knife and fork, sat back in her chair and repeated, 'London, why yes, of course, we shall move to London. We shall continue the fight in London.'

'We? I should have to obtain a position somewhere, but I'm sure–'

'Dear Miss Brookes, you have a position already as my companion and secretary. Mrs Pankhurst's daughter Adela is working with the regional committee in Yorkshire. I shall speak with her today on the hotel telephone. Now do have some breakfast, it's delicious.'

Florence spent her morning writing some very difficult letters and covertly watching Bradley and Giles leave for Shawbridge in the motor car. The hotel had become much quieter as another party had left for the grouse moors and the hotel dining room was almost empty when she met again with Lady Alice over lunch.

Lady Alice was troubled. 'I spoke with my brother on the telephone and he is being difficult. He had heard about the strike and my contribution to the speeches. I have not known Charles quite as angry before. He thinks that what I am doing is dangerous and so does Mother. They are insisting I give it up.'

'You will at the end of the summer!'

'It is not soon enough. However, I suggested that I might move away from Yorkshire for a while and he suggested I try Langton Place in London. He wanted me to go there several years ago when he married but I would not leave my grandmama.'

'But that is what you wanted!'

'Well, yes and no. Mother lives there and she has the same opinions as Charles about the suffragettes. If she insists on remaining in London I shall take a lease on a house in Leeds until she leaves.'

'You are determined to go then?'

'Of course, aren't you?'

'Yes, indeed. Will you ask Parker to come with us?'

'Langton Place is fully staffed for maids.'

'She is not just a housemaid, my lady. She has looked after both of us like a lady's maid and recently has been very helpful with keeping my books and papers in order. But more than that, she has the makings of a suffragette.'

'Really? Do you think she will want to come with us?'

'Shall I ask her to have tea with you later and you can discuss it with her?'

'I think you ought to be there too, Miss Brookes.'

'Very well. I shall go and find her after lunch.'

Meg had completed her fettling of the caravan and was pleased with its pristine appearance. She had made a list of supplies to purchase for Lady Alice's approval and welcomed an opportunity to present it to her at teatime. She put on a clean and neatly pressed blue servant's dress and tidied her hair. The hotel lobby was quiet and she padded across the soft carpet to the restaurant. Lady Alice and Miss Brookes were already seated at a table by the window. The Crandale Arms was well known locally for its delicious teas and several other tables were already taken.

'Good afternoon, Parker. Miss Brookes tells me you have been very busy. Do you take milk or lemon in your tea?'

'Milk, thank you, my lady. I have made a full inventory and a provisions order.'

'Excellent. I have been very comfortable with you to take care of me and I should like you to continue in that role.'

'Thank you, my lady.'

'I and Miss Brookes have a proposal for the future. Do help yourself to sandwiches.'

Meg was apprehensive but Miss Brookes was smiling which made her feel easier.

Lady Alice went on, 'The regional organiser has requested that I take the caravan to the East Riding for the remainder of the summer. Whilst I am happy to oblige, Miss Brookes and I have decided that we should prefer to carry on the fight in London.'

'London!' Meg exclaimed. 'Will you take the caravan to London?'

'Good heavens no! I shall leave it in Yorkshire for others to use. I shall reside in Leeds until Langton House in London is ready and I should like to know if you will come with me.'

'You are offering me a post as a maid in your

London house?'

'No, Parker. My brother's housekeeper in London will already have her maids. I should like you to be more of a personal assistant, rather like a gentleman's gentleman.'

Miss Brookes added, 'Only you will be a "lady's lady" for both of us and help with our suffragette campaigns.'

'Are you asking me to join the Women's Social and Political Union and wear the green and purple sash?'

'Let me explain,' Lady Alice replied. 'I do not want ordinary housemaids, or indeed ladies' maids, in the office in my London house. I need someone who understands my work and Miss Brookes assures me that you do. However, I shall not insist that you join the movement.'

Meg pulled down the corners of her mouth as she thought. Her readings and discussions with Miss Brookes had influenced her and, since the mill workers' strike, she had been convinced that the suffragettes were right. Unless women made a lot of noise and trouble for the government the gentlemen would not take any notice of them and nothing would be done. It simply wasn't fair for women not to have a say in matters that concerned them. So she welcomed the chance to continue working for Lady Alice.

In any other circumstance she would have welcomed, also, an opportunity to see London. Dear heaven, not so long ago she would have given anything to be able to travel there! But she did not wish to risk running into Jacob. London was a big city, though, much bigger than Leeds, and it was highly unlikely that she would. And if she did, they had parted on bad terms for a second time so he was unlikely to speak to her.

No one would know her in London. She could put Deepdale and Jacob behind her for good and have a new and different future as a suffragette. Yet one memory was still raw, and a guilty burden every time it surfaced in her thoughts. She could not forget what Saul had done to her and it made her want to weep. She was learning to push him out of her mind, to look forward instead of backward and think about her future instead of her past. But it was not easy. Not yet. She ran her hand across her brow. She could not get out of her head the fact that she was a ruined woman. She was aware that modern women indulged in marital relations before marriage. But they were in love and betrothed, in a joyful state that she had glimpsed once herself and would never know again. She must, she realised, consider a future as a spinster.

Lady Alice offered the plate of scones. 'I understand that you need time to think about my offer,' she said.

'No, my lady, I do not,' Meg replied. 'I'll come with you and be proud to support your cause.'

Chapter 17

Langton Place, London, Summer 1908

There were people everywhere, more than Meg had ever seen before, even at the women's march in Crandale. Motor cars and horse-drawn omnibuses made slow progress along streets lined with fine houses, tall and faced with white stone, built side by side with little space between them. They were arranged in squares with a small park in the middle surrounded by iron railings, similar to those that separated the houses from the pavements.

The motor car drew to a halt and Lord Langton's London chauffeur turned to her. 'Here we are, miss. Go through that gate in the railings and down the steps to the servants' hall. I'm afraid you'll find it a lot smaller than Langton Park.'

Meg had never been to Langton Park but she did not enlighten him. Lady Alice had leased a cavernous red-brick villa and its matronly housekeeper in Leeds for the autumn of 1906. She had donated her caravan and Hector to the East Riding campaign and spent the winter in Leeds holding small meetings in the drawing room or distributing leaflets and making speeches wherever the regional committee sent her. Miss Brookes supported – and occasionally guided – her throughout whilst Meg did her best to look after them both, acting as go-between for the housekeeper.

Adela Pankhurst had persuaded Lady Alice to remain in Yorkshire during 1907 while other more experienced campaigners decamped to London to support the newly established suffragist headquarters and women's parliaments. Meg took this opportunity to watch and listen and learn. She began to write, at first helping Miss Brookes with pamphlets and then on her own, using language and arguments that appealed more to mill girls like herself. There were, however, occasions when Meg reflected that words were all very well but it was deeds that got things done. During this time, Meg often worked side by side with Miss Brookes and they became firm friends. They addressed each other by their first names when neither Lady Alice nor the housekeeper was within earshot.

Lady Alice travelled to London several times and was invited to attend the women's suffrage meeting at the Albert Hall in March of 1908. By Easter, her ladyship had arranged for her mother to return to Langton Park in Yorkshire so that she and her companion and assistant could remove to Langton Place in the early summer. Lady Alice was very excited as she had been asked to make a speech at the Hyde Park rally in June.

Meg wondered how she would fit in at Langton Place. But she was a quick learner and was pleased when Lady Alice suggested she refer to her as Miss Parker instead of plain Parker. 'Although you will live in the servants' hall you will not answer to the housekeeper or butler. You will be responsible to Miss Brookes,' her ladyship had said.

Meg checked that all her bags were unloaded

and crossed the pavement towards the iron railings.

'Miss Parker, wait a moment!'

'Yes, Miss Brookes?'

Miss Brookes was climbing out of the motor car behind Lady Alice. 'I should like you to unpack the trunk containing my books and papers. Lady Alice's housemaids will have no idea what to do with any of it.'

'Certainly, Miss Brookes.' Meg turned to Lady Alice. 'Where shall I find the office, my lady?'

Lady Alice answered, 'Ask the butler or the housekeeper anything you wish to know. Langton Place is small so you'll soon find your way around.'

Meg gazed up at three storeys of Georgian windows topped by a stone balustrade hiding the windows of servants' attics and thought of her former home in Deepdale. Langton Place was not at all small, she thought. She still had much to learn about the aristocracy.

Two footmen dressed in livery walked down the marble front steps to deal with the various items of luggage. The chauffeur quickly isolated Meg's travelling box and placed it at her feet and said, 'Tell the hall boy to leave it by the back stairs.'

She opened the wrought-iron gate in the railings and went down a flight of stone steps to a door that opened as she approached. A young maid, probably no more than fourteen or fifteen, asked, 'Are you Miss Parker?'

Meg nodded and pointed up the steps. 'Can someone bring my box indoors?'

'Come inside. I've saved you some tea.'

'Thank you.' Meg sat at the chair drawn out by the maid, who disappeared to return a minute later with a tray of tea.

'It's a bit stewed by now, but it's hot and wet. The cake is very good, though. It's ginger. Did Lady Alice really live in a caravan on the moors?'

Meg smiled, realising why she was receiving such attention. 'Have you asked the hall boy to fetch my box?'

'Ooops!' The maid dashed out of the room and returned half a minute later. 'He'll take it straight to your room.'

Which is where? Meg wondered. She said, 'I should like to speak to the housekeeper.'

The maid looked disappointed. 'She's upstairs seeing to her ladyship.'

'You're from Yorkshire, aren't you?'

'Yes. My dad's a gardener at Langton Park.'

'How long have you lived in Langton Place?'

'Not long. I like it, though. The housekeeper is my aunty.'

'I see.' Meg sipped her tea. 'Can you tell me where I can find the butler?'

'He'll be chivvying the footmen because it's time to lay the table for dinner.'

Meg stood up. 'I'll go and find him. Thank you for the tea.' She went up the stone staircase and through the green baize door to the front hall where, sure enough, the butler was marshalling his footmen with the last of the luggage. She introduced herself and asked for directions to Lady Alice's office and her own room.

'Ah, you are Miss Parker. Welcome to Langton Place. You will be on the second floor at the rear

271

and Lady Alice's office is in his lordship's library opposite the dining room. I have installed new bookcases for you. Dinner is at eight o'clock tonight. Sherry will be served in the small drawing room at seven thirty. Do you have any questions?'

'Only where I might find you or your housekeeper if I do.'

'The housekeeper is usually in the linen room next to the servants' hall. I can be found in my sitting room at the end of the basement passage.' He smiled. 'Unless either of us is attending to the needs of the household, of course.'

'Thank you.' She headed towards the library and Florence's trunk full of books and papers.

Florence came into the office as the casement clock in the hall chimed six. She flopped down into one of the fireside chairs. 'Meg, you must be as exhausted as I. Have you had tea?'

'One of the maids made me a cup when I arrived.'

'That was ages ago.' She reached forward and pushed a button set in a mahogany surround by the fireplace. 'Come and sit down.' She watched Meg stack papers for a minute and then added, 'Do stop. I want to talk to you.'

A footman came into the room and she ordered a tray of tea. 'Just tea,' she added, 'no cake, and bring it quickly, please. The dressing gong will be sounding in an hour.' She waited until Meg was seated opposite her and asked, 'Do you think you will be happy here?'

'Of course I shall. I am living in a grand house in Mayfair.'

'You always seem so very serious.'

'I think the women's movement *is* serious, Florence.'

'But we shall have a life outside our work, when we may relax and enjoy ourselves.'

'I prefer to read and study.'

'Then I am not sure I have done the right thing by introducing you to my books.'

Florence was pleased to see Meg's reaction to this comment. 'Oh, but you have, Florence,' she protested. 'I truly enjoy my learning and I understand so much more about women's suffrage, injustice and the government. It has made the cause more meaningful.'

'We have much to do. Demand for the penny *Votes for Women* newspaper is increasing. We have to tell people about our marches and rallies, how the police and magistrates are treating us.'

'I believe, from her ladyship's speeches, that she is not wholly in favour of all this vigorous militancy.'

'Do you agree with her?' Florence prompted.

Meg considered this for a moment. 'There are other ways that are more – well, more constitutional.'

'Other ways are taking too long. The men in government mean to crush us and we must challenge them in any way we can.'

'You have a rebellious nature, Florence, which surprises me.'

'Why so?'

'You've had a comfortable upbringing with fewer restrictions than those imposed on Lady Alice's childhood.'

273

'I agree. I've not personally suffered from the deprivations that have inspired many men and women to fight for social justice. I had a loving childhood but even as a young child I felt instinctively that something was lacking in me; that I was, to my father anyway, not the ideal he had hoped for. I did not understand this feeling until my cousin went to school. His education was considered a much more important matter than mine.'

'But you did have proper schooling.'

'My school was carefully selected but beyond the fact that the headmistress was a gentlewoman and the other girls came from well-off families, no one questioned what we learned – or did not learn.'

Meg raised her eyebrows and waved an arm at the bookshelves she had filled with Florence's collection. 'But look at this: you are well educated, more so than Lady Alice.'

'That is in spite of my schooling and not because of it. Making the home attractive was the overriding aim. When I asked Mother why it was not considered important for my cousin to learn the same as me, she laughed at me.'

'My mother would have reacted in the same way,' Meg responded. 'I knew from an early age that it was my duty to become a good housekeeper like her, and that money would not be wasted on my education.'

'Didn't that make you feel angry?'

Meg did not answer her for a moment. She seemed troubled by her thoughts and eventually said, 'I should have liked to have gone to the high school but I was happy helping to run the home with Mother. It was different after she died. I had a duty to look after my widowed father.'

'Just as I felt it was my duty to marry well.'

'I stayed with my father because I loved him. He assumed I would not marry and it did not occur to me that he was being selfish. I was his daughter and it was my duty. But I lost the love of my life and – and more.'

'Sometimes fathers expect too much of us,' Florence commented.

'I could not blame my father. It was my choice and my decision, although I did feel pressured by him.' Meg shrugged. 'It was what daughters were expected to do but I was very unhappy at the time.'

Florence thought that Meg was still unhappy because she sounded so wistful as though the memory made her sad. Florence did not pursue it and said, 'Well, my father made me angry. One night I couldn't sleep for thinking about it, and it was then that I had an explanation of sorts. Mother and Father came into my bedroom last thing to do their customary check on me. I feigned sleep so as not to worry them. Father bent over me and I knew I was not dreaming because I felt the heat of the candle flame until he shielded it with his hand. But I heard him whisper, rather sadly I thought, "It will always be a regret to me that she is not a boy." This angered rather than upset me. Why do men consider themselves so superior to women? I could not answer the question and I am sorry to say that for many years I went along believing that men *were* superior, and strove to be the perfect model for a wife.'

'Then why did you break off your engagement?'

'Men are not superior to us! We can be as strong as they and – and they can be as weak as we are.' Meg's eyes widened at her outburst and she added, 'Bradley betrayed me and that is all I shall ever say on the matter.' It angered her still to think about it and Florence was pleased that the tea arrived and interrupted them. She did not want to lie to Meg as she had to her parents. But it would be awkward to explain to Meg what she and Lady Alice had seen between Bradley and Giles.

Florence changed the subject and began to talk about Langton Place. 'It's a beautiful house, isn't it? Dinner here will be a more formal occasion than in Leeds. The servants expect it and Lady Alice does not wish to cause any gossip. I suggest you wear your blue gown tonight.'

Meg stood up and exclaimed. 'My blue! Good heavens, why didn't you tell me earlier! I shall have to unpack and press it.'

'Sit down and enjoy your tea. I have been supervising the unpacking for all of us throughout the afternoon. One of the maids has prepared your room and you will find everything you need ready on your bed. I've also arranged a fire and hip bath for you. It will be ready as soon as we have finished this tea. Try and make it for sherry in the drawing room before dinner. The butler here is very traditional in his ways and Lady Alice does not wish to upset him.'

The dining room in Langton Place was very grand and Florence had been wise to recommend that

Meg wear her best dress. If she had to dress for dinner every night she would need another evening outfit, if not two. The floor and furniture were highly polished dark wood with a reddish hue. Three places, neatly arranged with silver cutlery, lead-crystal glasses and white linen napkins, occupied one end of the largest, shiniest table Meg had ever seen. An ornate silver bowl full of exotic fruit rested between the settings next to a decanter of red wine. Her chair, when she pulled it out from the table, was upholstered in maroon velvet that matched the floor-to-ceiling window curtains. The room was well lit with an electric chandelier. The servants' basement had electric light too although it did not extend to her bedroom and she noticed a table of oil lamps at the bottom of the staircase for taking upstairs.

Lady Alice looked stunning, and very much a titled lady, in a pale grey outfit of chiffon and lace. Florence was in mauve. Florence waited for Lady Alice to sit down before she did and Meg followed her example.

Florence resumed their drawing-room conversation when the butler had left them to their soup. 'We have to be prepared to go to prison. It is the only way to show the government we shall not give up.'

'Well, many were in favour of more militancy at the Albert Hall in March,' Lady Alice commented. 'They said that the movement has relied on argument for forty years and still we do not have the vote.'

'Arguments are no longer enough,' Florence responded.

'But we have been effective at the by-elections with argument,' Meg pointed out. 'We have influenced men to vote against government candidates and they have lost their seats. The government is worried. They must listen to us now.'

Florence shook her head. 'They may listen, but what will they *do?* Our women's parliaments at Caxton Hall will continue to show them the way. Until the government *acts* we have to keep up our activities. I, for one, will be supporting the militant speakers at the Hyde Park rally.'

'I shall not,' Lady Alice stated and added, 'but there is room for us all; twenty platforms, I hear.'

'Twenty platforms!' Meg exclaimed. 'It must be a huge park.'

'It is. I hope the weather is good as everyone will be wearing their Sunday hats,' Florence said.

Meg gave her a grateful glance. She had time to trim her best straw boater. 'Do be careful not to get arrested, Miss Brookes,' she said. 'The Crandale magistrate bound you over to keep the peace and the London police are treating suffragettes harshly.'

'Oh, there won't be any militancy at Hyde Park,' Florence replied airily. 'I shall save that for Parliament Square.'

Meg frowned. Florence had experienced a night in prison so she knew how dreadful it was yet it did not appear to concern her. The butler came in with dishes for the fish course and Lady Alice began to talk about London fashions. Meg had little to contribute and her mind wandered, thinking that neither of these two ladies had any idea what real hardship was if they thought that 'roughing it' was a few weeks travelling in a caravan in summer with a maid to look after them. At least Lady Alice was being sensible about not smashing windows or chaining herself to railings. But Florence! She seemed determined to be arrested. Meg worried how Florence would survive weeks on end in Holloway jail.

'What about you, Miss Parker?' Lady Alice asked.

'I beg your pardon, my lady?' she answered. Her concentration had drifted from the conversation.

'Should one show one's ankles or not at the Hyde Park rally?'

'I suppose that depends on whether one has a slender ankle, my lady,' she answered.

'How very diplomatic, Miss Parker!'

They all laughed and Meg turned her attention to the summer clothes she needed. She looked forward to searching the markets for fabrics and making new outfits in the basement linen room. Later, she decided on her best white blouse with a high neck and pleated bodice for Hyde Park. It suited her and she had a plain skirt in a dusky pink that fitted well at her waist. She shortened it by a daring three inches and decorated the hemline with bands of lace ribbon to draw attention to her pretty ankles. She wished she could afford a pair of white kid shoes to complete the look but consoled herself with the knowledge that grass stains would ruin them.

Meg knew it was going to be an exhausting day because Lady Alice's platform speech was scheduled early and she and Florence arrived with her. Yet they found far greater support there than they had anticipated and as the day wore on the atmosphere became charged with excitement about the number of women, and men, who attended. Florence's eyes shone and she spent much of the afternoon speaking with the organisers, recognisable by their distinctive purple, green and white sashes. Meg noticed that Lady Alice was tired and searched, without success, for a vacant chair.

'Would you care to take my arm, my lady?' she offered.

'Thank you, Miss Parker. I was thinking about my speech all last night and hardly slept a wink.'

'It went down well with the crowd, judging by the cheering and clapping afterwards.'

'I have Florence to thank for most of it.'

'Oh, look, two people have moved from that fallen tree. Shall we sit?' Meg didn't wait for her reply but unhooked her ladyship's arm and dashed over to reserve the space. It was a substantial log. She brushed way a few pieces of loose bark and stood guard until her ladyship caught up with her.

'Well done, Miss Parker. Do sit beside me. Doesn't everyone look splendid? It reminds me of the summer fête at Langton Park.'

'I have never seen so many flower-trimmed hats,' Meg commented. Her own straw boater was plainly trimmed with bands of pink fabric and lace ribbon to match her skirt.

'Nor so many white dresses, not since I was presented at court. Every debutante wore white then.'

Meg was fascinated by the many and varied outfits and sat in silence for a few minutes until Lady Alice said, 'Miss Brookes will be some time with the committee ladies, I think. Would you tell her I have returned to Langton Place?'

'Yes, my lady.' Meg stood up.

'Do walk back with me, Miss Parker. I should like to take your arm.'

'Very well, my lady.'

Langton Place was not very far from Hyde Park but Lady Alice was quite pale when they arrived and Meg took her straight to her room and then went down to the basement to arrange a tray of tea for her. Her own feet were beginning to protest by now. When she returned, Lady Alice had fallen asleep in a chair. Relieved that her ladyship was simply tired and not ill, Meg left the tray by her elbow, quietly laid out her evening clothes on the bed and crept out. She climbed the stairs to her own room, took off her boots and stockings and washed her feet in cold water from the ewer. Then she buffed her boots, put them on over clean stockings, and went down to the basement to organise a bath for Lady Alice.

Meg's day at the Hyde Park rally had stirred a frisson of excitement in her. She was impressed by the numbers of people attending and it made her proud to be involved in the Votes for Women movement and even more eager to help. What had started with Florence's reading list in a caravan on Ferndale Moor had become a mission for Meg, giving her ruined life a purpose. She continued to work hard at Langton Place, liaising with household staff in support of Lady Alice and Miss Brookes, and spending any free time either reading in the office or making new clothes in the linen room.

The Hyde Park rally was considered a resounding success. As the summer wore on, Meg was able to contribute more to dinner-table conversations with Lady Alice and Florence.

'The militants are doing more harm than good,' Lady Alice complained. 'They are deliberately destroying property. Have you seen the newspapers?'

'Every woman must do what she thinks fit,' Florence commented.

'I agreed with Miss Dunlop's action,' Meg added. 'She is an artist and to stencil a message to the government in large letters *inside* the parliament building was a very clever idea.'

'Well, it *is* the right of his subjects to petition the King so all prosecutions for petitioning *are* illegal,' Florence responded.

Meg smiled. 'It took the janitors ages to remove those words.'

'They sent Miss Dunlop to Holloway,' Lady Alice pointed out, 'and she made herself ill.'

'I think she was very brave to take that stand,' Meg said. 'It was a political offence and she was not a criminal.'

'But she starved herself for four days!' Florence exclaimed. 'She would have died if Mr Gladstone had not released her.'

'But he did, didn't he?' Meg responded. 'He is unpopular enough in the country without having an unnecessary death on his conscience. He is wrong to imprison the militant suffragettes and when he does it is a greater wrong to deny them political-offender privileges. Hunger strike was Miss Dunlop's only weapon.' Meg gave a decisive nod and added firmly, 'I should do the same.'

'I thought you were against the militants,' Lady Alice challenged.

Florence came to Meg's rescue. 'Miss Parker is being influenced by her reading. Mrs Pankhurst said in her manifesto that as we have no vote, we have the right to plead our case in person.'

'And as it is the men in government who have the power, it makes sense to present our case to them directly,' Meg added. 'Don't forget it was a man who drafted the bills about women's rights for Parliament way back in the 1870s.'

'Dr Pankhurst was different. It is a pity that he died,' Lady Alice responded.

'His widow and daughters are carrying on his fight. He had a son, too, who believes in our cause,' Florence said. 'There are many men who support the fight for women's suffrage, just as there are women who are against us.'

'But it is the men who have the power,' Meg repeated.

Florence went on, 'Did you know that Emmeline Pankhurst was a workhouse guardian before she was widowed and afterwards she became registrar for births and deaths in Manchester? In her speeches, she told stories of young girls of thirteen who came to register the births of their babies and in many cases some relative or lodger was responsible for her state. Mrs Pankhurst became frustrated with the fact that nothing could be done for these girls.'

'But the man broke the law!' Lady Alice protested. 'The age of consent is sixteen. He should have been punished.'

Florence shrugged. 'He'd say she told him she

was sixteen.'

'And everyone would believe him because he is a man and she is a just a girl who was asking for it,' Meg added. She stared at the wall as she remembered her own experience.

'Miss Parker?' Florence queried. 'Are you all right?'

'It's just a memory. Something I once heard a man say to a girl who had been – been attacked by him. *Nobody will believe you because we all know you're desperate for it.*' It was not quite the whole truth, Meg thought, and raised her voice. 'I don't see why they shouldn't believe her. Just because he's a man with a respectable job doesn't make him any more truthful or moral than a woman.'

Florence frowned. 'You haven't spoken like that before.'

'No, and I still can't see how giving women the vote will change how wicked men behave.'

'That's what the woman who shared my cell said when I spent the night in Crandale jail. We must change the law and we shall. Our Votes for Women campaign is only the beginning.'

Lady Alice added, 'Well, it can do no harm to give girls more education. Then they will have more choices. What one needs are more men in Parliament like the late Dr Pankhurst who will change the laws in one's favour.'

Meg agreed and nodded silently, but Florence said, 'Or even better, have women in Parliament. If Members of Parliament were women they would have real power to change the laws.'

'Good heavens, you are a radical, aren't you?' Lady Alice said. 'You are spending too much of your time at headquarters.'

'Do you think so, my lady?'

'No, of course I don't. One does support them but some of those ladies are a little too aggressive for one's taste.'

Chapter 18

Several weeks later, in September, Florence and Lady Alice returned home from headquarters subdued by the information they had learned that day. Florence went straight into the library where she found Meg catching up on her reading.

'Heavens, Florence, you look worried. Has something happened?'

'We heard a dreadful rumour today. Headquarters has written to the Home Office to verify that it is true.'

'What kind of rumour?'

Florence unpinned her hat and placed it on one of the desks. 'We have heard the prison governors are resorting to forcible feeding of suffragettes who go on hunger strike.'

'They can't do that. How can you force someone to eat?'

'They are doing it with the assistance of their medical officers. They use a tube passed into the stomach.' Florence gave an involuntary shudder as she spoke. 'It's – it's...' Unusually, she was lost for words.

'It's an operation!' Meg stated. 'Don't you have

to give consent for an operation?'

'Apparently not if you are a prisoner, it seems. We shall see how the Home Office replies.'

Shortly afterwards, in early October, they were having tea in the drawing room at Langton Place when Lady Alice reported from headquarters that the Home Office refused to release any information on the forcible feeding.

'That means it's true,' Florence said. 'It's very worrying. A dozen suffragettes were arrested over two weeks ago in Newcastle and they are still in the cells waiting to be tried.'

Lady Alice added, 'One of them is Lady Constance. She is determined to go on hunger strike. Would you if you were arrested?'

'I should hope I was brave enough,' Florence responded. 'But I don't know how long I could hold out.'

'You mustn't get arrested in the first place, Florence,' Meg said. 'You're already bound over and you'd get a heavy sentence.'

The following morning, after breakfast, Florence burst in on Lady Alice and Meg in the library with the newspaper in her hand. 'So sorry to disturb you but you must see this! *The Times* has printed a letter from Lady Constance in the cells at Newcastle police station.'

'Really? What does it say?'

'It has eleven signatories, all suffragettes awaiting trial.' Florence folded back the newspaper. 'They are saying that they will continue their protest from their prison cells. They are telling the world that they will go on hunger strike.'

'Bravo!' Lady Alice cried. 'Let me see.'

Florence handed her the newspaper. 'Read out the alternatives. Put your pen down, Meg, and listen.'

Lady Alice scanned the letter and said, 'They say the government has four choices: to release them or inflict violence on their bodies–'

'Inflict violence!' Meg paled at the notion. 'That's the forcible feeding, isn't it?'

Florence nodded. 'Well, the Home Secretary has the King's support for it. His Majesty asked Mr Gladstone in August why he did not use known methods for dealing with prisoners who refused nourishment. The King was not in favour of releasing suffragettes who go on hunger strike as it makes them into martyrs and is likely to encourage more.'

'Shame on him,' Lady Alice commented.

'Mr Gladstone assured the King that more stringent and precautionary measures would be taken in future and *we* know he instructed the prison medical officers last month to use forcible feeding.'

Meg groaned. 'What hope have we if the King is against us?'

Lady Alice went on, 'Lady Constance's letter gives two more alternatives.' Her hand went to her throat. 'She says the government could add death to the champions of the cause by leaving them to starve. Heaven forbid! Mr Gladstone surely would not let that happen? I can't read any more of this.' She handed back the newspaper.

Florence took it from her and continued, 'Or, the letter says, the best and only wise alternative is to give women the vote.'

'Of course it is!' Meg snapped. 'Why doesn't the government do that?'

Florence scanned the remainder of the letter. 'If the government yields to the reasonableness of the suffragette demand they will serve their sentences obediently. They have no quarrel with those who may be ordered to maltreat them.'

'They are so brave. I wish I had their courage,' Meg whispered.

'How do you know that you haven't?' Florence responded.

Meg shrugged and picked up her pen. 'We shall need a leaflet of advice on this for anyone risking arrest.'

'I'll ask at headquarters,' Lady Alice replied. 'There is no doubt that hunger strikers will deepen the effect of our protests. Also we shall need everyone's help for the Trafalgar Square appeal later this month. Headquarters wants thousands of leaflets – and people to distribute them.'

'What is the appeal for?' Meg asked.

Florence answered, 'A rally in Parliament Square to gather as many women as possible and rush the House of Commons in the evening. We want crowds and crowds so that the police are overwhelmed.'

'You will not go, will you, Miss Brookes?' Lady Alice cautioned. 'The Home Secretary is having known suffragette offenders followed in secret.'

'Is he?' Meg was shocked.

'He is using special policemen who do not wear a uniform. They are watching those who have been arrested and imprisoned in the past. If you are seen you will be spirited off in a Black Maria.'

'I shall not stay away,' Florence stated.

'Oh, do take care, Miss Brookes,' Meg cautioned. 'Remember Crandale.'

'I was bound over by a man in a man's justice system that I do not accept. I am going to Parliament Square and the House of Commons rush.'

'Then I shall come with you and look out for you,' Meg volunteered.

'We shall all of us go. Then we may look out for each other.'

Meg sat in the back of the motor car with Lady Alice and Florence. It stopped outside Caxton Hall where hordes of women were already gathering for a meeting before the walk to Parliament Square.

'Goodness, look at the crowds. And it's dark already. We must try and keep together,' Meg said.

'At least the gas lamps are lit. Stay close to me, Meg,' Florence suggested.

'Or me,' Lady Alice responded, 'and do, please, call me Alice. We are friends, are we not?'

'Do you mean me as well, my lady?' Meg asked.

'I do and may I call you by your first names? We surely know each other well enough.'

Florence smiled. 'Meg and I use our first names when we are working in the office.'

'Splendid!' Her chauffeur opened the door of the motor car and Meg watched Lady Alice step down to join a noisy crowd. She did not appear any different from many of the women who wore dark skirts, matching jackets and large hats. Meg's hat was smaller and plainer and her jacket did not match her skirt, but there were others who were not so well off and dressed as she was.

The word spread quickly that several hundred medical students had forced their way into the hall early and taken all the seats so that angry women were left out on the street waving their entry tickets. Between them Alice and Florence pieced together what had happened. The Trafalgar Square rally a couple of days ago had been successful and, as Meg listened to snatched fragments of conversation, she realised that it had been too successful. The government had issued a summons to Mrs Pankhurst, her daughter and Mrs Drummond who had spoken from the plinth of the Nelson Monument. All three had been accused of inciting the public to do a wrongful and illegal act and were summoned to appear at Bow Street police station at three o'clock today.

'They didn't go to Bow Street,' Florence reported breathlessly, 'but the police arrested them at our headquarters not two hours ago. They are locked up in the Bow Street cells for the night.'

'They have taken three of our leaders! Our meeting is ruined. It is so unfair and it makes me so angry!' Meg protested.

'Mrs Pethick-Lawrence has been left to speak alone in the hall,' Alice said.

'And we can't get in to hear her because of those silly men,' Meg wailed and then added, 'Listen. What's that?' She heard a cacophony of whistling and calling. 'It's all those young fellows inside. How dare they?' The throng surged forward and someone pushed open a door. The heckling eased a little. 'Hush! Hush everybody,'

Meg cried. 'Can anyone hear what she is saying?'

There was a lull, an unsettling quietness, and then one by one the young men came out. The surprised crowd parted to let them through and before long there were vacant seats for the women at the front.

'What did Mrs Pethick-Lawrence say to them?' Alice asked.

Again it was Florence who came back with the answer. 'She shamed them. She talked of fair play and asked if it was sporting to interfere with women who were struggling to win the freedom which they already enjoyed.'

'Oh, jolly good show!' Alice exclaimed.

'Then she actually appealed to the man who sat nearest the exit to "get up now at once and go out of that door". Apparently, those were her words and he did.'

'Bravo!' Alice enthused.

'And the others are following,' Meg added. 'Look, we shall have our seats after all. Come on.'

The atmosphere inside Caxton Hall was charged with rebellious anger. The government was dragging its feet. There were noisy demands for the women's suffrage bill, which had passed two readings in Parliament, to become law. Eleven women volunteered to take this resolution to the House of Commons with a bodyguard of men, sympathetic to the cause, to escort them. They were ordinary working men, Meg noticed, as angry as their womenfolk about the injustices of the government. Meg and Florence moved into the crowd behind the deputation as they marched forward to Parliament Square.

'Alice, keep up,' Florence called. 'You'll be separated from us.'

'Don't worry about me. Look after Meg.'

'I don't need looking after,' Meg protested and glanced behind at Alice who was totally obscured, except for her large hat, by others surging forward.

Florence reached across for Meg's hand and said, 'We'll find her later.'

Meg didn't agree. 'Can we go back? I can't see her.' Even as she said it, Meg knew that was impossible. They were caught up in a forward movement towards a barricade of constables waiting at the entrance to Parliament Square.

Someone called, 'Rush!'

The deputation with its bodyguard of men gained momentum but the police were ready for them and pushed them back into the crowds. Again they surged forward and again the police repelled them.

'This is no good,' Florence declared, repinning her hat. 'We'll never get through. They are wearing us out.'

Meg tucked a few stray hairs behind her ears. 'The barricade is strongest in the middle. We could try to break through at the end of the line and get behind them.'

'Good idea. Your side is nearest.'

Meg threaded her way though to the edge of the crowd where she was able to catch her breath. 'Can you see Alice?'

Florence stretched her neck. 'I think she's over the other side next to the gas lamp. If it is her, she is quite near the front. She must have had the same idea as you.'

A few tussles broke out as another deputation was turned back. 'They are not making any arrests,' Meg commented.

'I expect they have orders to exhaust us. They ought to know us better than that by now.'

'Well, the constables will be tiring too. Come on, Florence. We'll head for that alley and choose our moment to rush past them.'

'Wait, this looks like a reporter.'

Meg had noticed him before, taking an interest in Florence, and had assumed at first that he was one of the bodyguards with an eye for a pretty girl. She took a closer look. Judging by his suit of clothes he was not a working man. It dawned on her in a flash and fear took over. 'Dear Lord no, Florence, he doesn't have a notebook. Besides, the reporters have good views from the windows surrounding us. *He's one of those secret policemen. He's after you, Florence.*'

Florence inhaled sharply and replied, 'I've thought once or twice that someone has followed me from headquarters.'

'Why didn't you say before? We can't go back and the police are turning nasty at the front. Look, they have made an arrest. Can you see who it is?'

'It's too dark, but I think I can see Alice's hat and it's not her. She has stayed by the gas lamp. I think she's waiting for her chance to advance. I do hope she's sensible. She would never survive jail,' Florence replied.

'Neither would you, and one of the constables is moving towards us. We'll have to escape down the alley. *Go on, will you?*'

'Let him arrest me. I'll take my punishment.'

The constable and the secret policeman were closing in on them and Meg grew increasingly agitated for Florence's safety. 'No you won't, Florence. You haven't done anything wrong. You're a strong voice in the movement and the police just want to make you disappear like they did today with Mrs Pankhurst.' Meg caught hold of her arm and pleaded, 'You have to run. This isn't Crandale. They are cruel to the women in Holloway.'

Florence looked behind them and back towards the constable. 'Well, they're definitely coming this way.'

'The police are after *you*, Florence. You must get away from them. Headquarters needs you. This alley must go somewhere. You'll have to hide if it doesn't. But you must run now!' Meg gave her a push into the alley and out of sight.

For a few seconds Florence hesitated, gazing at the developing scuffles. The constable's progress was halted by a group of angry protesters but they had no similar suspicions about an ordinary-looking man in ordinary-looking clothes. To Meg's relief, Florence turned and ran into the gloomy darkness, leaving Meg to face the man alone.

'Step aside, miss.'

'Who are you?'

His tone hardened. 'None of your business. Now step aside before I arrest you as well.'

'You can't arrest me. You're not a policeman.'

'Oh, you're one of the clever ones. Working girl as a rule, are you? You don't belong here with these toff's wives who have nothing better to do.' He glanced behind him at the constable who had shaken off his attackers and was approaching. He raised his voice and addressed the uniformed policeman. 'She's gone down the alley. Get after her and I'll deal with this one.' He took a rough hold of Meg's arm and yanked her out of the way as the constable sprinted past her. Then he pushed her further into the alley and backed her against the wall. 'You don't want me to arrest you, do you?'

'You can't. I haven't done anything wrong.'

He laughed and pressed himself against her. 'Well, if you're nice to me, I might find you a special cell for the night, just for you and me,' he breathed.

Horror gripped Meg's whole body as he groped inside her jacket for her breasts. She turned her head sideways to avoid his tobacco-laden breath. A few yards away in the street at the end of the alley, she could see women gesticulating and hear them shouting as the demonstration descended into chaos. She took a deep breath and cried, 'Help!' He put a hand over her mouth to shut her up. But he needn't have bothered because no one heard her or even glanced down the alley. If they had they would not have been able to see anything anyway, without the benefit of a gas lamp.

He was a big, heavy man and all the hurt and anguish and shame of being assaulted by a man came flooding back. She tried with all her strength to push him away and when he didn't budge she tried to bite his hand. She nipped one of his fingers as hard as she could.

'You little cat!' he growled.

But he had taken his weight off her so she retaliated in the manner she had read about in one of Florence's pamphlets. He wasn't wearing an overcoat and she brought her knee up sharply between his legs. He yelped and glared at her so she did it a second time with more force. It was the best way, the leaflet had said, to put off a man determined to force himself on you.

She had hurt him. He was groaning, but he wasn't totally incapacitated. She would have escaped if the breathless constable had not returned.

'I saw that,' he exclaimed and took a firm grip on her arm. 'You're under arrest.'

'What happened to the other one?' the man demanded.

'I couldn't see her anywhere, sir.'

'You've lost her, you idiot! God, give me strength. Arrest this one and get her in the wagon. At least she'll pay for what she's done.'

'Come with me, young lady.' The constable's fingers tightened on her arm.

Meg struggled to break free and cried, 'I was defending myself!'

The constable ignored her protests and half dragged her out of the alley and along the pavement towards the Black Maria. He pushed her up the rear steps and inside through the narrow door at the back. The cells either side were full and the constables were packing women into the space in the centre.

Meg was frightened. She had kicked a policeman. She had kicked him with good reason but he was vengeful and she did not know what was going to happen to her. Others must have shown fear in their faces too for a voice near the front called out, 'Courage, sisters!' and a cheer began, first inside the van and then outside, taken up by an unruly and defiant mass. Meg gave a slight nod and a smile to the woman crushed against her, who returned it and said, 'We shall fight on in prison.' Then she raised her voice so the others could hear her and repeated, 'We shall fight on in prison!'

The responding cheer and banging on the wooden partitions and floor gave Meg courage. She was not in this alone and during that night spent in an overcrowded cell of Bow Street police station with similar protesters, she was able to discuss with her fellow prisoners how she would plead before the magistrate.

The magistrate did not listen to her, of course. It was exactly how Florence had described her ordeal in Crandale. She explained that she had a right to present her views to Parliament. She had not done anything wrong and she was assaulted by a man for no reason. He was a policeman, she stated, but he did not wear a uniform. The constable who arrested her gave evidence that she was not with the women's rally, she was loitering in an alley and he believed she was a 'woman of the streets', the 'gentleman' had said he was a reporter and she had attacked him without provocation.

'That's a lie!' she cried. 'Where is he? Why isn't he here?'

Meg was in the courtroom for less than half an hour. Her crime was considered serious and the magistrate sentenced her to six months in jail. Surely more than any of the other suffragettes received? She pursed her lips and flared her nostrils angrily. Her attacker had been a policeman and he had been truly vengeful. It only made her more determined to fight. She raised her voice and tried to explain that he had assaulted her and not the other way around. She *was* a suffragette.

Her protests went unheard and she was hustled off to prison with three other suffragettes without any of them hearing a word from friends in their defence. Meg hoped desperately that Florence and Alice had not been arrested as well. She had not seen them in the Black Maria but it had been very crowded and her three companions could not enlighten her. When they arrived at the women's prison, Meg was placed alone in a reception cell that was similar to the one described by Florence in Crandale.

It was lit by a gas jet housed in a recess in the whitewashed wall and had unpolished wooden floorboards and a plank bed. Washing facilities were tin utensils on a washstand with a tin skilly to relieve herself. She had a square plank fixed to the wall to serve as a table and a wooden chair. There was a small barred window and underneath it a corner shelf with a bible, prayer and hymn book, the prison rules, a salt cellar, some lavatory paper and a slate with slate pencil. A stern prison wardress told her about the prison rules and routines, and showed her how to care for herself in her permanent cell. Six months! Dear Lord, it was a lifetime in this hell-hole.

The wardress gave her a set of coarse prison

clothing. She hated that poorly fitting brown serge dress! The white cap – at least Meg thought it was supposed to be white – sat like a pill box on top of her hair, kept in place by calico ties under her chin. She had no idea what it looked like. She guessed the white was to distinguish prisoners from wardresses who wore dark caps to match their dark serviceable gowns. The following day the wardress escorted her to the cell she would occupy for the remainder of her imprisonment. On that walk she passed other women prisoners, cleaning floors and walls. One, Meg noticed, appeared rather fetching in her prison cap. She had pretty features and had set her cap at a jaunty angle and tied the bows to one side of her chin. The wardress barked, 'Cap!' at her and stood by her as she straightened it.

Meg's permanent cell was similar to the reception cell but it was smaller and had a stone-flagged floor, although it did have a larger window and a small electric light bulb attached to the wall. Hanging on a nail in the wall was a large round badge of some coarse yellow fabric with the number of her cell.

'Put that on the middle button of your bodice.'

It took Meg a few seconds to realise what she meant and the wardress snapped, 'Do it now, Twenty-seven. That's who you are in here.'

She was twenty-seven, a number. She did not even have a name. It was inhuman. Prison routine was strict and the wardresses behaved like army sergeants, or at least how Meg imagined army sergeants behaved. The bed was hard and uncomfortable and she found it difficult to sleep because she could hear other women weeping or calling out in the night. But she must have slept eventually for she was in a deep slumber when she was roused by the sound of boots tramping on the stone floor of the corridor accompanied by an intrusive loud clanging of a hand bell. She opened her eyes to pitch blackness and then suddenly the light came on causing momentary blindness. She washed hurriedly in the tiny basin of cold water with a cake of yellow soap, aware that the rattle of keys and creaking and banging of iron doors was coming closer and louder.

A large iron key grated in the lock of her cell and a wardress flung open the heavy door. 'Empty your slops, Twenty-seven,' she called.

Meg hurried out to join a queue of other prisoners queuing at the sluice. She wondered if she would ever become accustomed to the permanent foul lavatory smell of prison. Her empty stomach heaved. Forbidden to speak, Meg wanted, at least, to glance and smile at her fellow inmates and turned her head.

'Eyes forward, Twenty-seven,' a wardress yelled. It wasn't the same one as earlier but she sounded exactly the same.

Meg waited in line with the others for the command to return to their cells. The next chore was rolling up her bedding, which she dreaded because it had to be done in precisely the way the wardress had shown her. She remembered the beginning: *Fold the first sheet in four, lay it on the floor and roll up tightly.* Yes, of course, the orders came back to her. She just had to roll up the other sheet and each blanket around it, finishing with the quilt.

'Roll it tighter than that, Twenty-seven. Get on with it, then. Unroll and start again.'

Meg obeyed. She was used to obeying but she feared that others would not find the regime so easy, especially when it came to cleaning the tin she had emptied at slopping out and scrubbing her cell floor. Meg's hands were hardened to scrubbing but cleaning her tins made them sore and the cloths they were given were so well used that rags was a better description. Meg would have consigned them to the rag-and-bone dealer without further thought.

Two of the rags were the same brown serge as her prison uniform and concealed in the folds was a piece of bath brick that she had to rub hard on the stone floor to produce brick dust for scouring. She recalled her mother cleaning her cooking pans this way, but Edith had bought patented cleaners in packets from the hardware store and Meg had used similar in the caravan. Distracted by visions of her past life, the neat little house in Deepdale and the loving family she had once known, tears sprang in her eyes. She blinked them back and swallowed. She could not imagine ever returning to Deepdale after this. No one would understand why she had become involved with the suffragettes in the first place.

'Tins, Twenty-seven!'

Meg jumped and mentally shook herself. None of the tins were washed with water. She took one of the rags, moistened it with spit, rubbed it well on her cake of yellow soap and then soaped the tin all over. The same rag was used to pick up her brick dust off the floor and scour the soapy tin. She took the second serge rag to wipe off the resulting sludge as instructed.

After this, the third rag was a luxury: a piece of once-white calico that, by comparison, felt like silk in her hand. This was her polishing cloth and she rubbed at her tins until they were as bright as she could make them, and her arms and shoulders ached.

She was very hungry. She sat on the stool by her table trying to ignore the emptiness in her stomach and listening to the clanging of cell doors as the wardresses worked their way down the block.

Her tins were satisfactory. She knew that because she was not ordered to do them again and a pail of water was deposited on the floor of her cell for the next chore. She washed the table first, then her shelves, then the bed and finally her stool, which she had stood on to reach the back of the shelf. The same water had to be used to scrub the floor too. Meg made a start but felt so weak from hunger that she had not finished before the jangling of keys and the clanging of iron doors began again.

'Where's your pint, Twenty-seven?'

She scrambled to her feet and handed out her metal pint pot. Relieved of a chance to stop, she spread her small cloth – she would have called it a tray cloth – on the table and set out her metal plate. Before long a wardress brought back her pint filled with gruel and left a substantial hunk of bread on her plate. The oatmeal and water gruel was hot but it didn't have any seasoning in it and Meg found it tasteless because she couldn't find any salt in her cell. But she was hungry so she devoured the bread and drank the gruel thankfully, realising that both Florence and Alice would find this regime especially tough. Thick porridge with cream and honey followed by eggs was their breakfast of choice in London.

She returned to her scrubbing and sweated hard to finish it before it was time for chapel at half past eight. This respite gave her hands a chance to recover before her 'Labour Card' sewing tasks began. A shiver of excitement to be out of her cell ran through her and she hoped for a chance to catch sight of a familiar face. But as they filed out in line, flanked by wardresses barking orders to tie up cap strings, stand up straight and not look about or speak to anyone, she realised that even an exchanged smile might be impossible.

However, although Meg had looked forward to the service, she found the experience extremely distressing. The chapel was plain, unadorned apart from an altar table covered by a cloth for the cross and a small organ for the hymns. The clergyman read lessons and they sang together and prayed. But the majority of her fellow prisoners were old, with thinning white hair and gaunt, hollow-cheeked faces. To Meg, they appeared anxious and careworn, broken down by sadness and prison labour. Many wept when the organ played and the singing began. In the lessons, any mention of pitying the sinner or children or love brought on audible sobs from some. They seemed so desperately unhappy that Meg wanted to weep with them. She went back to her cell miserable instead of uplifted and commenced hemming her Labour Card quota of bed sheets with a heavy heart.

Chapter 19

Alice was pleased with herself. She had attended Parliament Square with the intention of being arrested before the evening was over and had deliberately not shared her plan with Florence or Meg. They would have tried to dissuade her. More than that, they would not have let her out of their sight. However, she was concerned when they were separated by the crowd, particularly for Meg, who had not been to as many meetings as she and Florence had.

She threaded her way slowly to the front, made sure the cordon of police constables noticed her in the glow of a gas lamp, and was among the first to physically fight back against their constant resistance. She met their eyes and challenged them with slogans, shouting and waving her arms to encourage others to follow her lead.

Before long her arms were grasped firmly by two large constables who marched her to the waiting Black Maria. She twisted to look over her shoulder and was satisfied that others had taken her place at the front. As she was among the first to be arrested she was pushed into one of the partitioned cells with no window to the outside and could only listen to the cries and jeers of her fellow suffragettes.

She sat on the plank of wood that formed a seat and admitted to herself that she was frightened. But she was determined to see this through. Although she had argued against militant activity she had become furious with the government's refusal to make progress with the parliamentary bill giving women the vote. The time had come to show her true colours, not as Lady Alice Langton, sister of the well-known Earl, but as Miss Langton, suffragette. This notion gave her courage and stiffened her resolve.

Her hat was already battered so she unpinned it and tore away the distinctive chiffon rose and ostrich feather decoration and scrunched them under her boot. She did not wish to appear privileged and for the same reason said very little. She had learned from experience that as soon as she opened her mouth, people knew she was not an ordinary shop girl. However, as she went through the process of committal and sentencing, she became increasingly apprehensive about surviving life in prison. She had hoped, at the very least, to be housed with other protesters, but this was not so. She overheard a wardress commenting that they were keeping the suffragettes well away from each other as the governor did not want any riots in his jail.

Alice felt that being in prison was no different from waiting to die. No one spoke to her save the wardress on her corridor and they seemed to take a pride in the harshness of her treatment. Although Alice tried her best to complete the tasks, she had neither the physical nor mental capacity for heavy domestic work and her constitution was not accustomed to kneeling on and scrubbing stone floors. The wardress ordered her to repeat the heavy chores over and over again until Alice was so exhausted that she was too tired to chew her bread properly. But there was no one to notice and her glimpses of other prisoners were of downtrodden women with dull, lifeless eyes.

By the end of her first day Alice was still unable to meet the wardress's exacting standards in her cell and she was allocated evening cleaning duties in the sluice that made her stomach heave and retch. Her back and limbs were so full of aches and pains that, exhausted as she was, she was unable to sleep and the following morning she felt decidedly ill. She struggled on through the second day of a similar torturous routine and after a second painful and sleepless night she was so stiff that she was physically unable to climb out of bed.

'On your feet, Thirteen.' It was a different wardress but she flung aside her bed covers and wrenched on Alice's arm.

Alice squealed. It seemed that every joint in her body was frozen and every muscle twanged with pain. She made an attempt to stand by pushing against the cold stone wall, but her stiff, aching limbs refused to move. She waited for the next chastisement. Her cell door clanged shut and she was left alone to slide down the wall in a crumpled heap at the end of her bed. She did not know how long she lay there but when the door opened and banged against the wall again, two wardresses entered her cell. At that moment she wanted to die.

'Come with us, Thirteen.'

She remembered thinking briefly, As though I have a choice, before being hoisted to her feet and half dragged, half carried out of her cell through several locked doors until she was vaguely aware of brighter light and smooth painted walls and – and yes, this was a carpet beneath her feet.

'Stand up straight, Thirteen.'

'She may sit.'

This voice was masculine and moments later she felt a chair pushing at the back of her scratchy brown dress. The wardresses left and Alice raised her head to look at the two gentlemen sitting on the other side of an expanse of oak desktop. This must be the prison governor's office and she was on a 'charge' or whatever they called it when a prisoner had committed a misdemeanour. She felt – she was – exhausted, but not so weary that she wasn't able to defend herself.

She had done her best to complete her tasks; so much so that, she realised, she had strained her muscles, at least the ones she was not accustomed to using. Echoes of the stiffness she had experienced when first riding her bicycle sprang to mind and she prepared her response. She had done too much and as she became more used to the prison routine she would improve at her duties.

The older gentleman said, 'This is my prison doctor and it is his opinion that you are too ill to complete your sentence.'

'I am not ill. I am unused to prison routine.'

The governor looked at his colleague who took

up the interview. 'Your brother, Earl Langton, has spoken to me on the telephone.'

Alice's heart sank at the mention of Charles. The governor knew who she was! So much for wishing to serve her sentence incognito. He was the last person she wanted to be involved. How on earth had he found out? She guessed that her friends had realised where she was and had taken it upon themselves to inform him. Well, she couldn't blame them for being concerned about her welfare. But Charles? She was an independent woman now and the less he and Prudence knew about her activities the better. He would, of course, have heard about her arrest sooner or later. She would have much preferred it to be later.

The prison doctor continued, 'His lordship is concerned about the state of your health, as indeed am I.'

'I need time to adjust and I have plenty of that,' she replied. After a minute, she realised that they had not listened to her and why should they? She was their prisoner and she was obliged to do as they ordered.

The governor slid a piece of paper across the desk. It was an official document with an embossed crest at the top. He said, 'You will sign an undertaking not to engage in marches, rallies or any of the Women's Union meetings for six months.'

'It is the Women's Social and Political Union,' she stated.

'Quite. You will see that the document is accurate. By signing you will secure your immediate release.' He handed her a pen.

She would be released? She would be free to return to Langton Place and the ministrations of the servants? She glanced at the paper and took the pen from him. Then she hesitated. Was it the warmth and comfort of the governor's office that helped her befuddled mind to clear? She placed the pen carefully beside the declaration and responded, 'I do not wish to be released. I wish to serve my sentence alongside my sisters.'

Again the two gentleman exchanged looks and the doctor said, 'I insist that you sign, my lady.'

He called her 'my lady'? She was no longer being treated as prisoner number thirteen. They had made up their minds. Well, so had she! She sat back in her chair and said, 'I refuse to sign.'

'Very well.' The governor stood up and her two wardresses came forward to stand either side of her chair.

'On your feet, Thirteen.'

Satisfied that she was a prisoner again and they were taking her back to her cell, Alice rose stiffly to her feet and extended her elbows towards her jailers to be escorted out of the room. However, she was quite weak and began to feel faint as they marched her away. It was not until one of them unlocked a cell door that she realised she had not been taken back to her permanent cell but had been returned to one of the smaller reception cells.

'What is going to happen to me?' she asked.

They ignored her and left her alone in the cell. She slumped on to the hard bed and leaned against the cold wall, closing her eyes and trying to ignore her aches and pains and hunger. She had missed slopping out and breakfast. Why was she here? Perhaps she was being moved to another block. Might it be a punishment block for her disobedience? An hour later – or maybe more, for she had no idea of the time except that it was day – the jangling of keys roused her and another wardress came in with a tray. She smelled proper food and it was heaven! The tray carried a metal mug of hot tea with milk and sugar and – oh joy – an enamel plate of scrambled eggs with bread, which she devoured hungrily and immediately felt better. Then she imagined her fellow prisoners at their scrubbing after thin gruel and dry bread, felt guilty and wanted to cry.

Every movement continued to remind her of her inadequacies as a prisoner. She wasn't ill as the doctor claimed, she was simply useless. She had spent her life having a succession of servants to do her bidding and it had not in the least way prepared her for prison. She massaged the knotted muscles in her arms and legs with her sore hands and determined to keep going.

The next call from a wardress surprised her. 'Visitor for Thirteen.' The wardress stood back to allow her visitor to enter and added, 'You can go in.'

'Florence! What are you doing here?'

'Alice! How are you?' She gazed at her for a moment and added, 'Forgive me, but you do look awful. The doctor warned me you were ill.'

Alice's hands flew to her face and hair. She had no looking glass and must be a dreadful mess. Who would not after a few days in prison? 'I – I've had a few difficulties with prison routine. I'll improve, I promise.'

'You cannot stay in here, Alice. It will kill you.'

'Oh, but I must serve my sentence alongside my sisters in battle. I am quite determined.'

Florence shook her head. 'But what use will you be to us in here? We need you on the outside.'

'I shall not listen to you! That is the argument I used with you in Crandale. The prison governor is afraid of censure for treating an earl's sister in such a degrading way but I shall not take his bribe. I wish to be treated in exactly the same way as other prisoners.'

'I have not made myself clear, Alice. His lordship has contacted his London lawyers on your behalf. If you do not sign the promise they will instruct a physician to examine you for – for soundness of mind.'

Alice's eyes widened. 'Let him.'

'You are aware of what that will mean?'

'He would not do that to me.'

'He will not allow you to serve your sentence.'

Alice heaved a sigh. She did not doubt that Charles would have her certified as of unsound mind and, with a power of attorney, make the decision for her and guarantee her behaviour. Oh, he wouldn't have her locked up in an asylum. But his concern was as much for the family name and reputation as for her welfare and he would insist that she returned to Yorkshire. What woman in her right mind would not seize any chance to escape from this hell-hole?

'Have you spoken to Charles?' she asked Florence.

'A gentleman lawyer called at Langton Place

311

before breakfast. He asked me to help him persuade you to sign.'

'Florence, you are a Judas!'

'Alice, you must listen to me. This gentleman is very clever and persuasive and he is on our side. We need his help and I need your help too. Meg has received a much longer sentence than you.'

'Meg! I did not know that she was arrested as well.'

'But have you not seen her? She was sent here with you.'

'We are kept segregated in different blocks and addressed only by our cell number.' Alice gazed at the bare stone walls of her cell. 'But she would have been at prayers. I did not look for her. We are not allowed to communicate with other prisoners, not even by smiling. It's inhuman.'

'Then come and be with me on the outside to fight for her. Oh, Alice, I am very worried about Meg.'

'But why was she given a longer sentence?'

'I do not know and the governor will not let me see her. But I owe my freedom to Meg. She enabled me to escape arrest. I thought she was coming after me but she didn't. I believe she distracted the policeman so that I could get away.'

Alice nodded. 'That is exactly the kind of thing she would do. She is the strongest amongst us.'

'Yes, she is, and it is her strength that concerns me for she will keep to her resolve. I know she will. Can you not remember the conversation we had at dinner after Miss Dunlop's action inside Parliament? Miss Dunlop threatened hunger strike so she was released. Meg said she would do the same

312

in her position and I believe she meant it. But don't you see – they won't release her! The government has toughened its stance on suffragettes and it has the support of the King. Men can be so very cruel to women who are not obedient.'

'Our jailers are women.'

'They are controlled by men and obey their orders. The prison governor will take a hard line and I do not want Meg to die.'

Alice considered this. 'Meg is certainly a determined young woman. But the routines are backbreaking, believe me.'

Florence nodded, 'They will break her in the end. We must get her out or at the very least have her sentence reduced.'

Alice remembered the wardress who had made her repeat every one of her tasks and realised that there had been reason for her treatment. She had been totally exhausted by the second day, and the routine would continue because that was the purpose of a prison sentence. The gaunt and sallow faces of the other prisoners haunted her. Meg might have been amongst them and sooner or later would be indistinguishable from them.

Florence continued, 'You have contacts and influence, Alice. I need you in Langton Place to instruct the lawyers and secure Meg's release. Please sign. Please.'

'But I shall feel like Judas if I do,' Alice argued. She met Florence's eyes and knew that her anger was simmering.

Florence's tone hardened. 'Well, I do not. My actions are in Meg's best interests. If you choose to interpret them as treachery then that is your decision.'

'Others will see it so!'

'When have we cared for the views of those who do not know or understand us? Meg needs you on the outside. This gentleman – the lawyer who brought me here – will *listen* to us. Please, Alice, you are no good to me as a martyr.'

'Good heavens, I have never thought *that* of my actions.'

'Then think on it now. Others might.'

Alice closed her eyes wearily. 'Have you considered joining the law profession yourself?'

She heard Florence breathe out and then say, 'You will sign? The lawyer told me that it will secure your immediate release. We shall wait for you.' Florence banged on the iron door with the heel of her boot.

After Florence left it seemed a long time before Alice was escorted back to the governor's office. The doctor was not present. She sat in the same chair and the governor performed the same ritual. She signed without uttering a word.

He picked up the document and leaned back in his chair. 'You are very wise, my lady. You don't want to be mixing with the sort of riffraff I get in here.'

'One of my servants is a prisoner here.'

'Who might that be?'

'Miss Parker, Meg Parker. She was present only as my maid. You must release her.'

'I must do no such thing, madam.'

'But she was looking for me, to see that I was safe.'

314

'I should forget her, my lady. Find yourself another maid who doesn't go around kicking policemen.'

Alice's reaction was instinctive. 'Surely not?'

'She's not what I'd call a lady's maid, my lady.' He folded her signed declaration and nodded to the attendant wardress.

The wardress took her back to the reception cell where her own clothes were stacked in a neat pile on the bed. 'Ten minutes, Thirteen. Leave your prison things on the table.'

The skirt of her gown still held the dust from where she had tripped on the pavement and her hat was definitely not fit to be seen. She dressed stiffly and as best she could without a mirror. She was dirty and dishevelled yet she hardly dared think about a bath and clean linen as it felt like a betrayal of the women she was leaving behind.

She slumped wearily on the hard wooden chair. Her head was beginning to spin and her eyes were losing their focus. She did not want to faint and have to be helped away from the prison gate. She took a few deep breaths and stood up again, knocking on the door to be let out. The wardress led her through more locked gates until finally she stepped over the threshold as a free woman once again. It had been a short sentence for her but it had taken its toll. Her legs felt like jelly and she could barely put one foot in front of the other so that she was in danger of tripping over her own feet.

A smartly dressed young gentleman came forward and took her arm. She glanced up at his handsome face and dark hair. 'Hugo, my darling,

315

it's you,' she breathed and crumpled into a heap in his arms.

Alice came round in the motor car. Familiar features swam before her eyes. Hugo! No, it couldn't possibly be Hugo because he was dead and Alice was very much alive. Why had not Florence said that the lawyer was Mr Wright? This gentleman's resemblance to her beloved fiancé as she remembered him was uncanny. Hugo would have been nearly ten years older now, as she was, over thirty and perhaps showing the lines of ageing in his handsome features. This gentleman facing her had no such signs. He was young and vibrant with bright, alert eyes and a well-shaped mouth. A mouth like Hugo's, she thought.

'She's coming round. Pass me your flask, sir.'

Florence pressed the cold silver to her lips and fiery brandy trickled into her mouth. She blinked and roused herself. 'I am not ill. Truly I am not. It was exhaustion from the work and – and a few days of very poor nourishment. Thank you for the brandy, Mr Wright.'

The motor car jolted and Florence handed back the silver flask. 'Mr Wright was sent to the house by your brother's lawyers.'

'Jacob Wright, ma'am. I am Sir Gerald's junior. We have met before.'

'Crandale. I remember.' The warmth of the brandy spread through Alice's body and she pushed herself to a sitting position. 'Sir Gerald, the esteemed Member of Parliament who claims to support the suffragists and yet has done nothing to further our cause. I am surprised he

316

allowed you to represent me.'

'I specialise in constitutional law and I am a progressive. I believe this country will have universal suffrage one day.'

'You have more faith than I.'

'I did not say it would happen tomorrow.'

Lady Alice managed a wry smile. 'Will you come in for some tea, Mr Wright?'

'I am so sorry, my lady, but I am expected in chambers.'

'Surely you have time for a cup of tea with us?'

Florence pulled the woollen rug around her knees. 'I think you should rest. Your brother has asked me to send for his London physician as soon as you return.'

Alice sat back in the comfortable leather seat and closed her eyes. 'I am not ill, I am simply very tired. The doctor may call on me tomorrow.'

'Your mother is waiting for his phone call on the state of your health.'

'Mother is such a fusspot,' Alice murmured. Her aching limbs felt like lead and her eyes would not stay open. 'We must get Meg out of prison soon,' she whispered and drifted into a doze.

She awoke to Florence's gentle shaking of her shoulder. 'We are home, Alice. You are to have a warm bath first, then a light nourishing supper in bed followed by a good night's sleep.'

Alice blinked. 'Where is Mr Wright?'

'He got out when the motor car reached his chambers.'

'Oh.' Alice was disappointed. 'Will you telephone and ask him to call?'

'There is no need. He became quite agitated as

you slept. I do believe he feels as strongly as we do about our cause and asked how he might help with Meg's plight.'

Alice felt better already. 'I shall invite him to dinner.'

'Ah, I have already suggested tea on Sunday. If you feel strong enough we shall walk in the park afterwards.'

Alice forgot her fatigue and stiffness as she looked forward to meeting with Jacob Wright again. She prayed for fine weather. They would walk in Hyde Park where she used to stroll with Hugo when he was in town. It would be as though she were eighteen again, and in love.

Charles's London physician recommended an American lady to help her recovery. She had travelled to England from Minnesota where there was a centre for women's physical culture that studied the beneficial effects of physical exercise on the female form. The lady was of mature years and quite tiny, but her strength was phenomenal and she kneaded Alice's sore muscles, making them hurt more. However, afterwards, Alice was able to move more easily and the lady left her a booklet of physical exercises for women that Alice read with interest. Later, at her request, Florence made her an appointment with a ladies' salon in Knightsbridge that specialised in enhancing one's outward appearance and she purchased a new afternoon dress that showed her ankles from an exclusive gown shop. She asked Cook to come and see her specifically about afternoon tea on Sunday.

On Sunday Alice lunched quite simply on only

three courses and then rested. She was not fully recovered from her prison ordeal and wished to enjoy her afternoon to the full, for the weather was fine. Mr Wright was punctual and the butler showed him into the drawing room.

Alice rose to her feet to greet him, holding out her hand. 'How lovely to see you again, Mr Wright. Please come and sit over here.' He was, if anything, a little taller than Hugo but his eyes crinkled at the corners in the same way when he smiled.

He took her hand lightly but did not kiss it. 'Thank you, my lady. It is very kind of you to invite me into your beautiful home.'

'The pleasure is all mine. Do make yourself comfortable.'

He smiled briefly and sat down, asking after her health and then Florence's, commenting on the weather and finishing, 'Has anyone been able to see Meg Parker?'

Florence answered. 'I have tried but it is impossible. She is considered to be violent because of what they said she did. I am sure it not true, of course, but the magistrate believed the gentleman. We think he was one of the government's special policemen that don't wear a uniform and are following the suffragettes.'

'That would explain it. I have looked at what the court charged her with. The complainant said he was a newspaper reporter and his complaint said that she – she kicked him in a – a delicate area.' Mr Wright glanced quickly from Florence to Alice.

Alice said, 'Please do not be embarrassed, Mr Wright. We are modern women. Meg has not been with me long but we lived in close proximity for several months and I know she would not do such a thing.'

Florence frowned. 'Unless she had a good reason.'

'What do you mean?' Alice queried.

'Oh, nothing,' Florence replied. 'But she has become more militant recently. I have spent hours with her discussing her reading. She is very angry with the government; I am convinced of it. She read such a lot when we were travelling and–' Florence stopped.

'And what?' Mr Wright prompted.

Florence looked uncomfortable. Alice too was curious. 'Florence, do you know something that I do not?'

'No. I was not there. I was hiding and Meg – Meg distracted him when we were cornered. She was worried about what they could do to me after Crandale. Oh heavens, I feel such a coward now but it was her suggestion and neither of us had done anything wrong. It's not as though we openly encouraged others as Alice did.'

'Then why would he lie about it?' Mr Wright asked.

'Perhaps he didn't.'

Alice stared at Florence. Mr Wright asked, 'Why do you say that?'

'I showed her this pamphlet written for – well, for women like us who are out in the world earning a living or similar. We have so much more freedom than our mothers had and – and gentlemen...' Florence looked at Mr Wright. '...some gentlemen do not understand that freedom to

320

earn one's own living does not imply other kinds of freedom.'

Alice frowned, but Mr Wright's face was without expression as Florence continued, '*If* she did do it, it was because he was trying to take advantage of her because – well, because that is what the pamphlet advises if men do.'

Alice's hand went to her throat. Her eyes were wide. Mr Wright was on his feet. 'But why didn't she say that in court?' he demanded. Gosh, Alice thought, he sounds extremely angry.

'Perhaps she did and he denied it,' Florence said. 'Magistrates tend to believe the men, especially the policemen, you know.'

'Yes, and especially when it is true.'

Alice was shocked by this. 'Mr Wright! I thought you were on our side!'

'I am. Meg ought to have had representation. She had mitigating circumstances.'

'Then can you appeal or something and get her out?'

He shrugged. 'I can try but I cannot promise anything.'

'But if she signs the paper as I did?' Alice suggested.

'She won't sign,' Florence stated. 'I know her. She will fight.'

'Do you think so?' Mr Wright queried. He seemed surprised but went on, 'I doubt that she will be offered the opportunity. She does not have Lady Alice's connections.'

'She is my maid. I can speak for her,' Alice responded.

Mr Wright's voice was firm. 'If any one of us is

allowed to see her and speak with her, it ought to be me. I want the truth.'

'You think she did it?'

'What I think is irrelevant. I must know the truth if I am to fight her sentence.'

Florence looked excited. 'You will be able to secure her release?'

'I do not know until I have seen the court papers. I shall send for them immediately. You may be sure that I shall do everything in my power to help her.'

Chapter 20

Meg was desperate for news of other suffragettes whether inside or outside the prison. At slopping out and prayers, if the wardresses were distracted by gossip of their own, she risked their wrath and spoke to other inmates. Most ignored her but she found out that number forty-one had arrived at the same time and she feigned a stumble on the way to prayers to sit next to her.

'Are you a suffragette?' she whispered as they knelt.

The prisoner looked alarmed but she nodded.

'I'm going to ask for political-offender privileges.'

This time number forty-one shook her head. 'You won't get them.'

'Then I'll go on hunger strike. Will you do the same?'

The woman shook her head again, swallowed

and her eyes became shiny. 'I have a child, a little girl.'

Meg reached across and squeezed her hand. 'I wouldn't have asked if I'd known.'

A wardress called, 'Pray silently!' and they exchanged sympathetic glances.

I have no such ties, Meg thought, that leave me in fear of having my sentence extended. I have nothing to lose. But this woman's daughter had everything to gain from a different, fairer future for women. Meg raised her head slightly and swivelled her eyes around the poor, worn-down creatures kneeling and suffering silently. She was young and healthy and had to do their fighting for them. She would start, today. Why not? Meg prayed silently for strength.

She began as soon as she returned to her cell. She stood on the threshold and turned to her wardress. 'I demand to be treated as a political prisoner with her rights and privileges.'

'Shut your mouth, Twenty-seven, or I'll have you in the punishment cell.'

'I am a suffragist and it was my right to petition the King and to defend my honour. It is illegal to lock me up in this way.'

'Get on with your work.' The wardress's tone was threatening.

'No.' Meg ignored her bucket and scrubbing brush and sat on her wooden chair.

The wardress stared. 'Who do you think you are?'

'Meg Parker, suffragette and political prisoner.'

'You are number twenty-seven and a trouble-maker.'

Meg stared back silently and saw the wardress's expression harden further.

'Suit yourself but don't say I didn't warn you.'

The iron door clanged shut and Meg was alone in her cell. She did not move for several minutes. Then she knelt down, took off her boot and smashed the heel on one of the small panes of glass in her window. She replaced her boot, sat on the chair and waited. Although she heard footsteps in the corridor outside she was disappointed that the wardresses did not respond immediately.

It was evening before two wardresses came into her cell, took hold of her arms and yanked her to her feet. Then one produced a pair of heavy metal shackles, placed her hands together behind her with her palms facing outwards and handcuffed them together. They marched her through the chilly, dimly lit passages to another block and pushed her into a smaller cell.

'That'll bring you to your senses.'

She guessed it was the punishment cell. 'I demand to see the governor,' she shouted after them. She heard the key grate in the lock.

The punishment cell was a cold dark room on the ground floor with hardly any useful light. It was empty of furniture but, at about nine o'clock she guessed, two wardresses brought in a plank bed, a table and a chair. One said, 'See how you feel after a night in here,' and left her alone.

It was the most uncomfortable night of her life. By morning her shoulders ached and her wrists were red raw where the handcuffs had chafed against them. A wardress brought food in the morning and moved her handcuffs to the front with her palms facing so that she could eat. This was the most difficult test for Meg because she was hungry. But she had made up her mind. She prayed again for strength and tipped her gruel and bread into the skilly. That night a wardress removed her handcuffs, on Matron's orders she said, and smoothed on some salve. Meg assumed that Matron was the woman in charge of the wardresses.

Her loneliness was the worst of it. She was not allowed out of her cell except to empty her tin skilly and she desperately wanted to have sight of other prisoners, wretched as they were. Most of all she missed morning prayers. She had two visits that day from a wardress with her frugal meals. She took the water and left the food. The following day she had three visits with nourishment that she ignored. She was surprised at how quickly she became accustomed to not eating and that gave her an increased inner strength. Different wardresses came and went so it was the third day before they noticed that she was not eating.

The wardress she had seen most often brought in a tray and slammed it down on the table. Normally she left immediately, but not this time. She stood over Meg and barked, 'Eat.'

Meg looked straight ahead and stated, 'I am a political prisoner and I demand to be treated as one.'

'Eat.'

'I demand to see the governor.'

'Eat.'

Meg gained further determination when the

wardress gave up trying to persuade her. But the following day she was told that Matron wished to speak to her in the doctor's room and two wardresses escorted her out of her cell. In her weakened state Meg shrank back in fear at the sight of so many people with Matron in the doctor's room. There were seven or eight wardresses and two gentlemen that she assumed were the doctors. One of them read from a blue official-looking paper.

'Listen carefully to my words,' he said. 'I have orders from my superior officers that suffragettes are not to be released even on medical grounds. If you continue to refrain from food I must use other methods to compel you to take it.'

Meg was frightened of what might happen to her but she tried not to show it. She remembered the rumour about putting a tube into the stomach. She might die! 'I refuse to take food,' she stated. 'If you force food into me I want to know how you will do it.'

'That is for me to decide,' the doctor replied.

Although weak, Meg's mind was still working and she remembered Florence's words, drafted for a leaflet. She stood up straight and looked him in the eye. If he was a doctor then she was a patient. She took a deep breath and said, 'You have to prove that I am insane and you cannot do that without summoning the Lunacy Commission. Unless a patient is judged insane you cannot perform an operation without her consent. Forcing food into me is an operation – and an outrage.'

He was gracious enough to bow his head, but he replied, 'Those are my orders.'

Two of the wardresses moved aside and Meg saw that, behind them, a sheet had been spread out on the floor underneath a wooden armchair. She glanced around in alarm. What were they going to do to her? The wardresses surrounded her, took her arms and turned her around, forcing her backwards into the chair. Then the doctor came forward, grasped her head by the jaw and forced open her mouth to form a pouch. The other doctor pinched her nose while the first one spooned in a warm milky fluid.

If she did not swallow it she could not breathe! She spluttered it out as best she could. She kicked out and struggled, gurgled and coughed as she choked on the liquid. The doctor closed her mouth and held her jaws together, while the other banged his hand on her back. Although she spat out as much as she could, she was obliged to swallow a small amount that had trickled down the back of her throat. They stood around and watched her as she recovered. She thought that it was over until they closed in on her again and repeated their onslaught. She had not been ready for the first attack and she was less ready now!

Meg tried to scream a protest and this resulted in her inhaling some of the liquid, setting off a prolonged bout of coughing that distressed and weakened her further. The doctor stopped the process and the wardresses stepped away from her as she tried to recover. When her coughing eased the doctor, quite surprisingly, sprinkled her with eau de cologne. But Meg was too weak to care. She felt very faint and her head lolled like a rag doll. She was aware of an exchange of words

327

but could not hear what they said.

The wardresses did not take her back to the same punishment cell but a different one upstairs on the first floor where the light was better and, again, they left her totally alone. The horror of her attack stayed with Meg for a long time. It was unexpected and a complete shock to her and – and, worse than that, it stirred a memory. This was a different kind of attack and with women in attendance, but it reminded her of an assault by a man from her past, an assault she had tried very hard to forget. Her determination to go on wavered and she suppressed a sob.

She must be strong. She must fight on. She thought of her friends at Langton Place. Perhaps they were in prison and being treated in the same degrading manner. They would not give in and neither would she! Meg Parker was made of sterner stuff! She rallied and recovered, and when she had, her resolve to continue her protest was stronger than ever.

She took water instead of food and it helped to quell her hunger pangs. She could survive for longer by taking drink. However, the doctor had told her that the Home Secretary was refusing to release any hunger-striking suffragette, even on health grounds. If she continued with her hunger strike, she must face the fact that she might die in prison.

Florence's advice danced before her eyes and she took comfort in the knowledge that she was not alone in her protest. No surrender! Her sisters on the outside were fighting for her. But could they persuade the Home Secretary to change his mind before one of them had made the ultimate sacrifice?

This cell was hardly any different from the others except that she had more daylight from a larger window made up of many tiny panes. Occasionally she heard voices outside and worked out that this cell overlooked the prison yard where other inmates took exercise. The following morning after breakfast had been left in her cell, Meg decided on stronger measures to avoid being fed again at dinnertime. She heaved at her bed, table and chair until she had wedged them all together against the cell door. Then she sat on the wooden floor and listened as the wardresses tried unsuccessfully to open it. Eventually they sent for male warders who shouted threats to hose her down with cold water. They tried to frighten her by banging metal bars against the cell door. The clanging noise echoed through her head in the most alarming manner but Meg refused to let them in. Eventually, three or four of them forced open the door and crowded into her cell brandishing iron bars at her.

She was terrified of them and held her breath. She was sure her heart had stopped. Dear Lord, this is the end, she thought. One blow would kill her and she had nowhere to run. 'I demand to see the governor,' she shouted. 'These men have no authority to be in my cell and threaten me in this way.'

The wardresses were behind the men and when she said that they came forward and the male warders left. But she worried that they might return.

'On your feet, Parker,' one demanded.

She ignored their request so two of them took hold of her and half dragged her out of the cell and across the corridor to one that she realised immediately was a padded cell. There was no window and the light was encased in an iron cage. But the most overwhelming sensation was the assault on her nose. The lining was some kind of India rubber and the air was suffocating, giving her an aching head. 'Get your things off,' a wardress ordered. They did not expect her to obey and between them they took off her clothes and replaced them with a clean prison night-dress. Then they carried in her bed.

Meg spent one night in her new surroundings before they took her back to her standard punishment cell so she guessed the night in the head-ache-inducing padded cell had only been a warning. The following morning she stood in the middle of her small cell and racked her brain to think of how else she could protest against her treatment. Suddenly a smile lit up her gaunt, shadowed features. She waited until she heard muffled voices from outside her window and then took off her boot. By standing on her chair she managed to break seven of the small panes of glass in the window. She shouted as loud as she was able, 'Meg Parker! Force-fed in punishment cell! Votes for Women!'

'Votes for Women, hurrah!' Their voices resonated around the yard. These women were not suffragettes. They were the worn-down inmates she had prayed with and their cry of support gave Meg such a surge of renewed strength that she felt she could go on protesting for ever.

She experienced a rewarding sense of satis-faction in being taken back to the padded cell. She had reached the stage where it was discomfort and pain that was keeping her alert. The next day, when she refused to eat food in the proper way, the wardresses did not take it away and return with doctors to feed her by force. Instead they left the food in her stuffy surroundings and abandoned her to starve. It was at that stage Meg thought they really were going to let her die and all kinds of memories began to churn through her mind, fumed by the confines of the India-rubber walls.

She did not regret any of her past actions except one. Although she had loved her father dearly, she had made a huge mistake in choosing him over Jacob. If only he and Mrs Dawson had got together earlier, she would have risked an unknown future in London with Jacob. He would have taken care of her. She knew with certainty that he would.

If she had left with Jacob she would not have been trapped into staying with Edith and that awful, awful man who had raped her. The memory of that early-morning assault resurfaced and ugly images loomed large in her mind. She ought to have told *someone* about him. But, with-out any lasting physical injury, who would have believed her? It had never occurred to her that he would do such a vile thing. Indeed she never thought that any man she *knew* could be so cruel.

Until then she had imagined rape to be some-thing violent, perpetrated by a stranger and leaving its victim battered and bruised. She had been totally unprepared. He was on top of her before she could resist and invaded with such apparent ease on his part that he must have believed she wanted him. What could she have done? She knew what she should have done. She ought to have struggled and scratched, shouted and sobbed. Her rape had been a brutal violation that had not involved violence.

As she starved in her padded cell, Meg tried to erase the dreadful memory of that quiet Sunday morning. If she were to die, she would prefer to go with a happier image in her mind and tried to remember, instead, those special Sundays spent with wonderful, irreplaceable Jacob. If she closed her eyes she could float out of the prison, over the Dales, to meet him on the moors at Ferndale...

Her wanderings came to an end later that day when two wardresses took her to appear before a visiting magistrate holding a special court at the prison. Her hearing was brief and she did not deny her misdemeanour. He sentenced her to solitary confinement on bread and water with loss of any accrued remission from her sentence, and a fine of five shillings. Meg smiled to herself. She had not earned any remission and bread and water meant nothing to her. A bowl of aromatic stew might have presented a more difficult challenge!

Meg was taken back to what she thought was a different punishment cell. But the next day, she suspected she might be in a hospital cell, or at least a punishment cell nearer to Matron and the doctors. If they were not going to leave her to die in a padded cell, she guessed they planned to feed her again. This focused her mind and she was ready for them when they crowded into the cell. She quickly took a lot of deep breaths and did not fight them so that she could last longer without being forced to swallow to take a breath.

They treated her just as harshly but as she did not choke or have to swallow she was able to spit out most of the fluid. It was only when they repeated the onslaught for a second time that she struggled and gurgled and was forced to swallow a little. She had also inhaled a few drops, resulting in another exhausting coughing fit that left her weak and hoarse. The wardresses watched her until her coughing subsided and then they left her with orders to mop up the mess. She ignored them and left the sticky smelly fluid on her prison clothes and the floor of her cell.

However, she knew they would return and wondered how long she could keep up her fight without the benefit of nourishment. In her strongest moments, she determined that it would be until the last breath in her body. But in the darkest, weakest times she considered that she might actually die. Mr Gladstone might wish to demonstrate his power over the suffragettes. Meg was nobody of importance. She was not from a family with wealth and influence. If the prison governor wanted to make an example of any of his suffragette prisoners, she was a likely choice.

Meg did not wish to die but she took solace in the fact that, if she had to, it would be for a purpose that she truly believed in. If her actions helped other women have better lives, then her cause was worthy. But she had had her share of bereavement and knew from bitter experience that it was the people you left behind whose suffering went on. She did not want to leave her friends in London or Yorkshire, or her brothers across the ocean even though she had not seen them for a long time. In her moments of deepest depression Meg wept with bitter regret that she had turned away from her beloved Jacob.

Between these bouts of despair she roused herself from morbid thinking. She, herself, had said that the government would not risk becoming more unpopular by allowing a suffragette to die. Clearly the prison governor was worried about her or he would not have resorted to moving her out of the punishment cell and forcing this nourishment upon her. Most of it soaked into her clothes or stained the floorboards of her cell. Every time they tried she took in an absolute minimum. Her body was weakening but she knew that if her mind remained strong, she could win this battle. The prison governor would have to do something.

The knowledge that hundreds of women outside the prison were on her side gave Meg the strength she needed. If only these women had more influence on the government! Their constant protesting was their only power. Dear heaven, this fight was about the lack of power that women had on their own lives! Meg recalled Florence's words and echoed them. *Our Votes for Women campaign is only the beginning.* For Meg in prison, her determined protests were only the beginning.

Chapter 21

'How is she?' Alice met Florence at the front door of Langton Place anxious for her reply. Florence's expression was sombre.

'They would not let me see her.'

'But you have been out all day! I was sure you would have gained access.'

'I could not even get through the gate, let alone see the prison governor.'

Alice regretted now that she had been persuaded to rest at home. 'I should have gone with you.'

'You could not have made a difference. I found out eventually that Meg has been moved to the punishment block and one of the warders at the gate said there was no chance that anyone would be allowed to speak to her.'

'Then she is continuing to protest as a political prisoner?'

'I fear so. Oh, Alice, I was so worried about her that I asked your driver to take me to Mr Wright's offices on the way back.'

'What did he say?'

'He was in court with Sir Gerald. I have left a message asking him to call as a matter of urgency. He may have Meg's committal papers by now and I think we should ask his advice on what to do next.'

Lady Alice experienced a surge of hope for Meg

but also of pleasure at the prospect of seeing Mr Wright. 'Yes, oh yes – oh, well done, Florence. He will help us.'

'I do hope so. Will you be here if he telephones? I should go straight to headquarters and tell them what I know. There will be others protesting with Meg in prison.'

'Very well. I'll ask Cook to prepare a late supper for both of us.'

Alice sat for a while in the elegant drawing room of Langton Place, trying to quell an unusual stirring in her stomach. Jacob Wright was frequently in her mind. She was of course grateful that he was prepared to fight for Meg's freedom. But more than that, she became excited as she waited for his call. She would invite him for lunch tomorrow to discuss a plan. The anticipation bubbled through her. She stood up and wandered around the room, stopping to examine her appearance in a decorative wall mirror.

She was still attractive, not in the first flush of youth but most certainly not showing any signs of ageing in her face. She smoothed her hands over her cheeks and then down the sides of her gown. Riding had kept her trim in her teens but since she had lost Hugo and gone to live with Grandmama she had lost some of her youthful sleekness and posture. Then she remembered the lady who had treated her when she came out of prison. She had left details of physical exercises to practise. Quickly she went upstairs to her bedroom to search for them. While she was there she opened her wardrobe and searched through her dresses for a suitable outfit for tomorrow's lunch.

She heard the telephone ring and went on to the landing to lean over the banisters as the butler answered.

'Very well, sir,' she heard him say. 'I shall see if her ladyship is at home.'

Alice hurried down the stairs. 'Is that a caller for me?'

'It is, my lady, a Mr Wright from his lordship's lawyers. How shall I reply?'

'I'll speak to him.' Alice took a couple of deep breaths to calm herself and walked slowly down the last flight of stairs.

'Good evening, Mr Wright.'

'Good evening, my lady. I have a message from Florence to telephone you. Is it about Meg?'

Alice outlined what she knew from Florence and waited for his response, which did not come immediately.

'Mr Wright? Are you there?'

His voice sounded strained when he replied, 'I have to get her out.'

'Will you help? Please say yes. Come for luncheon tomorrow to discuss a strategy.'

'I am in court all day.'

'The day after?'

'May I call on you this evening, my lady?'

'You would like to meet this evening?' Alice's heart gave a little flutter. 'Yes, of course you may. Will you come for dinner?'

'I have work to finish here and cannot be with you before nine.'

'Then I shall not dine until Florence returns from the suffragist headquarters. We shall have an informal supper so there is no need to dress.'

'You are very kind, my lady. I shall endeavour to be punctual.'

Alice consulted with Cook first and then asked the head parlourmaid to help her dress for the evening. She heard the shrill ring of the telephone as the maid was brushing out her hair and instructed her to tell the butler to take a message. She hoped desperately that Mr Wright had not cancelled and was relieved that the call was from Florence. Florence was not coming back for supper so Alice would be dining informally and alone with Mr Wright. This must be fate, Alice thought.

The hall clock chimed nine and several restless minutes later Alice heard the front-door bell clang. She was on her feet before her butler showed Mr Wright into the drawing room.

'Supper is ready in the dining room, my lady,' her butler said. 'Would you ring when you are ready for the soup?'

'You may serve it now,' Alice replied, 'then you may retire for the night. I shall lock up when my guest leaves.' She poured a sherry for her visitor and handed it to him. 'It is very good of you to call at this late hour, Mr Wright. Do you mind if we go in for supper straightaway? Here, take this sherry with you.'

'Thank you, my lady.'

He was plainly dressed, in a dark suit of clothes, probably those he wore in court, and Alice noticed that he looked very tired. 'I am so grateful for your help,' she said kindly.

He gave her a gentle smile and offered his arm. She took it and followed her butler through to the dining room. The butler disappeared behind a screen at the end of the room to fetch the soup from the dumb waiter. As he placed the soup plate in front of Alice, he said, 'Cook has prepared mutton cutlets and fried potatoes, my lady.'

'Leave them on the sideboard. You may go. We shall serve ourselves.'

'Very good, my lady.'

He left them sizzling in a silver chafing dish and withdrew. Mr Wright picked up his soup spoon and asked, 'Is Miss Brookes joining us later?'

'She telephoned to say that she is dining with a colleague and staying over. She is becoming increasingly involved in affairs at headquarters.'

'I should like to have spoken to her about her visit to the prison.'

'Florence's greatest fear is that Meg will be on hunger strike.'

Mr Wright's face was ashen under the electric light. He must work terribly hard, she thought. He said, 'The Home Secretary has toughened his position on suffragettes. I have to get her out before she damages her health.'

'But if she becomes ill, surely the prison governor will be obliged to release her, as he did with me?'

'I doubt it, my lady.' His tone had irony in it. 'Meg does not have your connections.'

'Are you saying that I was treated leniently because my brother is an earl?'

'Of course you were, my lady. Who is Meg Parker? She is nothing but a mill girl who has tried to better herself by mixing with the gentry.'

'Is that what you think of her?'

'My opinion is not relevant. That is how the governor will view her. He will believe that she should have stayed in her place of work instead of being out on the streets inciting a riot, so she deserves her punishment.' He paused to drink his soup and then added, 'Forgive me, Lady Alice, but Sir Gerald has indicated to me that your brother is not at all pleased with your behaviour or your continued involvement with women who are sent to prison.'

'I suppose Charles found out about my activities from the newspapers.'

'Sir Gerald was obliged to write to him. When I visited you in prison I was acting on your brother's instructions.'

'Well, you are not here because of his instructions now.'

'Sir Gerald does not know that I am here. I shall be obliged to tell him in the morning and he will inform his lordship.'

'And Charles does not want me to continue my involvement? He cannot stop me. I have independent means.'

'His concern is for your well-being, my lady, and – and he can insist that I do not help you.' He paused and added, 'Through his instructions to Sir Gerald.'

Alice groaned. 'Yes, I see how he would insist that Sir Gerald forbids you to work for me. Your position in his chambers will be compromised.'

'It will, indeed. However, I am prepared to pay the price.'

'You must not give up your career, Mr Wright!' Alice cried and added, 'And I cannot go on call-

340

ing you Mr Wright. Please, we are friends here. May I call you Jacob?'

It was impulsive of her and his eyebrows shot up. He seemed undecided so she repeated, 'Well, may I?'

He shrugged his shoulders – he had good shoulders, she noticed, like Hugo's – and answered, 'My London friends call me Jack.'

'Do they? Yes, Jack suits you. Jack it shall be, and you shall call me Alice. Now, Jack, what did you mean by "pay the price"?'

'If I persist in acting on behalf of suffragettes, Sir Gerald may be obliged to let me go.'

She met his eyes across the table. 'You will lose your position? But if I instruct you–'

'Your brother is one of Sir Gerald's most important clients. I cannot be the cause of a difficulty with your family. I shall have to resign.'

'You would you make that sacrifice for me?'

He seemed unsettled by her response and replied, 'You must not concern yourself on my behalf. I – I...' He seemed about to add more but then stopped. 'It will be my decision, Alice.'

She realised he was relieving her of any blame for effectively ruining his career by continuing to act on her behalf. But why would he give up so much for her unless – unless he – unless he cared for her? Her heart turned over as she watched him finish his soup.

'I have connections, Jack. I am sure we can find a solution.' She smiled. 'Shall we have the cutlets now?'

She stood at his side and watched him as he helped himself from the chafing dish on the side-

341

board. He relaxed a little and commented on the excellence of his supper, which Alice enjoyed as well. But he declined pudding and fresh cobnuts for dessert, saying, 'The hour is late and I should return to my rooms.'

'When shall I see you again?'

'I shall telephone you when I have something to report on Meg.'

'When will that be?'

'I may have news by the end of the week.'

'Then come to Langton Place for luncheon on Sunday.'

'Thank you. I shall look forward to that.'

Alice's eyes shone. 'I'll ring for the motor car.'

'Good heavens, no! I am sure your chauffeur will have retired for the night. I shall find a taxi-cab.'

Alice stood on the steps of Langton Place and watched him walk away. From his stature he could have been Hugo over ten years ago when she first met him. Alice smiled to herself. Jack was not a soldier. He was a lawyer, but just as brave as Hugo, she guessed.

She went indoors, bolted the front door and slowly climbed the stairs to her bedroom. She didn't ring for a maid. She didn't want one. Alice wanted to be alone with her dreams. She was falling in love for the second time in her life and planned excitedly for Sunday. In her mind, she went over the evening's conversation again and again. Why would he have come all this way at the end of a day in court if he had not wanted to see her? And why go against the wishes of Sir Gerald if not to please her? But she must not allow his career to suffer! She had no influence with Sir Gerald, but she could speak to Charles on the telephone and ask him to talk to Sir Gerald. Yes, that's what she would do.

Alice slept well and woke early with a start. She had hardly spared a thought for poor Meg as she had entertained Jack to supper. Jack had mentioned her, of course. What had he said? Alice searched her thoughts. She was only a mill girl who had tried to better herself? She wondered, idly, how he knew Meg used to be a mill girl. To her knowledge, no one had mentioned Meg's past to him. Perhaps they had met in Crandale? She resolved to ask him on Sunday.

However, luncheon on Sunday did not turn out to be the intimate meal *à deux* that Alice had anticipated. She had hoped that Florence would accept one of the several weekend invitations that she received from her colleagues at headquarters. But Florence returned to Langton Place. Also, Alice received a telephone call from Charles to say that he was coming to London on Saturday evening. He ordered the motor car to meet him at the railway station and take him directly to his club where he was dining with Sir Gerald.

At breakfast on Sunday morning Charles asked Florence searching questions about the suffrage movement, which she answered knowledgeably and without any sense of guilt. Charles's frown deepened as they ate and Alice wanted him in good spirits so she was pleased when Florence excused herself for the day. She was travelling to north London to visit a group of suffragettes 'at home' for luncheon. The servants came in to clear the breakfast table and Alice asked Charles if she might speak with him alone on a serious matter after her morning walk in the park.

He suggested the library. She rehearsed what she would say during her walk. There was a good fire in the library when she returned and Charles had drawn up two leather armchairs either side of the hearth. He was scanning the new book-shelves and turned immediately she opened the door.

'What have you done to my library?'

'It is my library as much as yours.' She looked up at a portrait of her late father hanging on the wall and added, 'He was my father too.'

Charles glanced again at Florence's collection and shook his head but he came over, kissed her cold glowing cheeks and commented favourably on her complexion.

'I was not ill in prison,' she responded. 'It was only that I could not do the labouring.'

'Prison is no place for Earl Langton's sister.'

'Or indeed for any other woman who has not broken the law.'

He gestured to an armchair. 'Sit down, Alice. Sir Gerald has explained about the protests and the action the police were obliged to take. Of course I have read about the suffragettes in my newspaper but I had no idea of the scale of the militancy. My only consolation is that our mother is safely in-stalled in the Dower House in Yorkshire with – er – more pressing family matters to occupy her. I have managed to protect Prudence from the worst of the news reports but I do not want her distres-sed by a repetition of your disgraceful behaviour, especially not now. I cannot have you associating with these – these criminals, and I sincerely hope you have decided to come home at last.'

Alice groaned inwardly. His views on the suffragettes had not moved an inch. She took a deep breath and fixed a smile on her face. 'Did Sir Gerald mention a Mr Wright, Jack Wright, one of his junior lawyers?'

'No, why should he?'

'He came to the prison to secure my release.'

'I did not imagine that Sir Gerald would visit the prison himself.'

'Jack – Mr Wright – is lunching with us today.'

'Jack?'

'He will be here as a friend rather than a lawyer and I want you to meet him. He – he is a – a special friend of mine.' Alice felt herself blushing and hoped that her brother would put it down to the heat of the fire.

Charles narrowed his eyes. 'How do you mean: "special"?'

Whenever Alice thought about Jack she felt a thrill wash over her and her excitement showed. 'He is a wonderful gentleman and when you meet him you will understand exactly what I mean.'

'I doubt it. You have taken up with some – shall I say some *unusual* people since you inherited Grandmama's fortune.'

'Oh, Charles, I am enjoying my life again. Can't you be happy for me?'

'Perhaps. You have not spoken with such a sparkle in your eyes about any young man since – well, since Hugo.'

Alice smiled. 'I cannot explain it, but I knew as soon as I saw him that he was – he was special.'

'At least you have taken the trouble to inform me beforehand.'

Alice noticed relaxation in his face. He had been cross with her at first but now his features had softened. He really did not wish her to cause any more trouble for the family and the reason came to her in a flash. What had he said about Prudence? He did not wish to distress her? Prudence was young and self-centred. She would not lose a wink of sleep over Alice's dilemmas. It was Charles who was suffering on Prudence's behalf. Alice gave an involuntary gasp as she realised why: Prudence must be expecting a child! He had dined with Sir Gerald yesterday evening to discuss changes in his affairs! And, Alice suspected, Prudence's condition was the reason Mother had chosen to stay in Yorkshire so readily.

She beamed. 'Prudence is going to have a baby!'

Charles blinked. 'How did you know?'

'I didn't. I guessed. You haven't come all the way to London simply to chastise me.'

She had not seen Charles appear so confused before. His expression was a mix of worry and joy and for a moment he was silent. But Alice jumped to her feet, threw her arms around him and hugged him. 'What a clever brother I have! I am absolutely delighted for you both. How is Prudence?'

'Radiant, I am pleased to say. She is having plans drawn up to refurbish the nursery wing, and I am installing two more bathrooms for the guest bedrooms.'

'Mother will be delighted.'

'She is. The Dower House is extremely comfortable now with electricity and hot water. Both dressing rooms have adjacent bathrooms. Mother will insist you are with her for the birth.'

'I shall try to be there, but I shall not come without Meg.'

'Do you mean that gypsy girl you took on when you were travelling?'

'She is not a gypsy! Meg is a mill girl from Yorkshire and she is a jolly useful help to me.'

'She is in prison! How useful is that? If you need another maid, I'll tell Mother to send one from Langton Park.'

'I don't want anyone else. I have Florence – Miss Brookes, my companion.'

'Well, where is she this morning?'

'She is lunching with friends.'

'Really, Alice, she is a servant! You are too lenient with her. Mother would never allow–'

'She is *my* companion,' Alice interrupted. 'Allow me to decide on her duties.'

'Tch. You become more like Grandmama every year.' Alice was pleased with that remark until Charles added, 'Mama should have been firmer with you after Father died.'

She did not argue but repeated, 'I shall not return to Yorkshire without Meg. She is being treated very badly in prison and I must secure her release. Jack Wright has promised to help me.'

'Has he, by Jove? Does Sir Gerald know that?'

'Not yet. I want you to speak to Sir Gerald on Jack's behalf.'

Charles stared at her. 'Why should I do that?'

347

'Please, Charles. When you meet him you will understand.'

He did not answer her but Alice was satisfied that Charles had not refused outright. Jack never failed to make a favourable impression on those he met. She stood up and said, 'Luncheon is at two o'clock. I shall be in the drawing room for sherry at half past one.'

She hurried upstairs to give herself plenty of time to look her best for Jack. This was when she missed Florence and Meg most as she valued their opinions on her appearance. At the same time she would not have wanted either to see the extra effort she was making today. Not yet, anyway.

Jack arrived promptly and Alice was on her feet in the drawing room before the butler announced him.

'Come and sit by the fire.'

Jack rubbed his hands together. 'Thank you, Alice. I walked through the park and the air is cold today.' Jack took a glass of sherry from the silver salver offered by the butler.

'Shall I inform his lordship that your guest has arrived, my lady?' the butler asked.

Alice nodded and picked up her own drink. She settled on a small couch and gestured to Jack to sit next to her. The butterflies in her insides were fluttering again. She tried to ignore them and asked, 'Have you any news about Meg?'

'I went to the prison but the governor will not allow anyone to see her.'

'But did you say you were her lawyer? They must let her speak to her lawyer!'

She noticed that Jack's eyes were troubled and he seemed to be having difficulty in suppressing his agitation. 'I am doing everything in my power and that is my difficulty. I have no power, not real power. You need to be–' He gave a gasp of frustration. 'What does it matter – I do not have the same influence as Sir Gerald!'

Alice frowned. He was normally so controlled and reasoned in his behaviour. Did it mean so much to him to be able to help her in this way? She reached out with her hand to grasp his. 'Don't give up, Jack. I can help you.'

He looked down at her hand and then at her face. She smiled and he seemed surprised but he did not move away until Charles entered the room. Jack stood up immediately and introduced himself. After an exchange of small talk about his health and the weather, Charles picked up the sherry decanter and recharged their glasses before taking a chair opposite.

'Sir Gerald speaks highly of you,' Charles said to Jack. 'I am pleased to have this opportunity to thank you personally for securing my sister's release so quickly. Do you enjoy being a lawyer in London?'

'I do, my lord.'

'You hail from Yorkshire, though. The Redfern estate, I understand.'

'My father is gamekeeper for the Earl of Redfern's grouse moor in the Dales.'

'Do you ride to hounds?'

'No, sir.'

'Shoot?'

'Oh yes.' Jack smiled. 'My father taught me from

an early age.'

Alice watched her brother's face brighten. 'My cousin has a nice little estate in Sussex with some particularly good pheasant drives. It's a favourite of Sir Gerald's. You must join us on our next shoot.'

'Thank you, my lord.'

Alice felt a thrill of excitement run through her and she resisted the temptation to reach over and squeeze Jack's hand again. The butler came in to announce luncheon and the soup was already on the sideboard. Charles waited until they were all served before continuing the conversation.

'Tell me, Jack, how does a gamekeeper's son get to be a lawyer in the first place?'

Alice interceded, 'With hard work, I should imagine, Charles.'

'Of course, but he needs a patron as well,' Charles replied.

Jack did not seem to mind the questioning. 'You are quite right, sir. Lord Redfern helped my father with my schooling and I have been fortunate enough to gain scholarships and bursaries.'

Charles nodded thoughtfully and drank his soup. Alice took up the conversation with questions to Charles about Langton Park and their local village. She wanted information about Shawbridge as well, for Florence, but knew Charles rarely ventured into the town or its High Street.

'Alice will return to Yorkshire quite soon, of course,' Charles stated.

'It is not settled, Charles,' Alice protested. 'I'm sure I should find life at Langton rather tame after London.'

'What about you, Jack, would you find York-shire life tame after London?'

Alice noticed a slight frown on Jack's face and he did not answer straightaway. She thought he was very tactful when he replied, 'I am equally at home in London and Yorkshire.'

Charles went on, 'A country lawyer is not quite the thing though, is it?'

Jack said, 'Does one have to choose? The rail-ways and the motor car have made England smaller than it used to be and there are other avenues of employment to explore.'

'Indeed? Such as?'

Alice was as interested as Charles in Jack's reply but he avoided answering by saying, 'I have not discussed my future with Sir Gerald yet, sir.'

Charles, however, would not be deflected. 'Do I understand from that remark that you are considering giving up the law?'

Alice detected a firmness creeping into Jack's voice when he answered. Nonetheless, he smiled. 'You must forgive me, my lord, but I do not wish to speak further on this matter today.' He turned to Alice and continued, 'This is excellent beef, if I may say so, and I haven't tasted a Yorkshire pudding as good as this since my mother's.'

'Cook is from Langton Park,' Alice replied, but she was as intrigued as her brother about Jack's mystifying remarks concerning his future.

Alice considered that Charles had been favour-ably impressed by Jack. And she – well, she had to admit that she adored Jack. She could not help herself and was thrilled when Charles declined to walk with them in the park after luncheon because she would have Jack to herself. They talked of each other's childhoods in Yorkshire and Alice realised that, as a boy, Jack had spent most of his school holidays at Ferndale Lodge itself working as a beater or loader for visiting guns. She was disappointed when he did not stay for tea, citing the amount of reading he had to do before court the following day.

'Did you like Jack?' she quizzed Charles as they shared a tray of tea by the drawing-room fire.

'He has no family to speak of.'

'But he is well connected through his profession.'

'It is a trade, Alice.'

'Prudence's father is in trade,' she pointed out.

'Her father's brother is a baronet who married a viscount's daughter. But it's not just that. Jack Wright is too young for you.'

'But there aren't any men left of my age! They all found brides while I was looking after Grandmama. I've been left on the shelf, Charles! Jack is the only gentleman who has shown me more than a passing interest. You must help me. He is my last chance for happiness.'

'Dearest Alice, don't be upset by what I am going to say, but are you sure that he wants you?'

'I think he does. He seemed so very keen to have a reason to visit me. As soon as I mentioned Miss Parker in prison, he agreed to help even though it might jeopardise his position with Sir Gerald. Don't you see? He is so very anxious to please me.'

'I can see that he felt he had to find a way to ingratiate himself with you. He is an ambitious young lawyer and you are well connected with independent means.'

'That is unkind of you, Charles. He is hesitant because I am an earl's daughter and he is not wealthy. He is, after all, a Yorkshireman and therefore he is proud. He has achieved his position through his own merits and hard work, and I am sure he would wish to provide for his wife in the same way. You could help him do that if you provided a dowry for me. You said you would.'

'If he is as proud as you say, he may be offended by an offer of money to marry you.'

'Dear me, Charles, I should be offended too if you put it in those terms! Can you not invest in Sir Gerald's practice and persuade him to offer Jack a partnership?'

'I see you have given the matter a deal of thought already.'

'I know that I would be happy with Jack.'

'Are you sure it is not simply because he has a look and stature that is reminiscent of – of...'

'Of Hugo? Do not be afraid to say his name.'

'Am I right?' Charles persisted.

'Is it so surprising that I should be drawn to a gentleman who possesses the same good qualities that I loved in Hugo?'

'I suppose not.'

'I had not considered that I might ever fall in love again. But I have and I cannot waste time if I am to have the same happiness that you and Prudence enjoy.' Only a few years ago, Alice would not have even hinted at marital intimacy in conversation with her brother. But her time with the suffragette cause had changed her. She smiled into his eyes and continued, 'I am older than Prudence and have fewer years left to bear my children.'

'Alice! He has not proposed to you yet!'

'And he never will, not without a little encouragement from you and Sir Gerald!'

'Well, I can't make you any promises but at least marriage and children would take you away from all this suffragette nonsense.'

Alice ignored his taunt. Charles would never change his views. 'Then you approve of him?'

'I shall invite him to dine with me at my club.'

'Oh, thank you, my darling brother. Thank you, thank you, thank you.'

Alice walked with a lightness in her step for the remainder of the day.

Chapter 22

Meg's world had shrunk to the size of her small punishment cell. Resisting the forcible feeding was her reason for being there and she became even more determined she would continue her fight. She was obliged to swallow some of the milk each time because she could not hold her breath for ever. The doctors seemed satisfied that she took something each time for no one really wanted to do it. They were all following orders and they all pleaded with her to eat in the proper way before they began their attacks on her. She scratched the days in her cell wall and each time the door was open or she heard someone pass her cell she shouted out, 'Meg Parker, force-fed in punishment cell.'

Of course the wardresses chastised her but they could not make life worse for her because she had nothing more to lose. This knowledge gave her the will to keep going. She needed that courage for her body was weakening under her enforced starvation. After two more days the doctors moved her again. This time the wardresses told her they were taking her to a hospital cell where, presumably, the wardresses were nurses as well.

Meg survived another day refusing the food that her jailers presented to her without further onslaught from them. On the second day, after she had rejected her midday food, the doctors and wardresses descended on her. They crowded into the cell, filling her with alarm. Two of the women took a firm hold of her and pushed her backwards until she collided with the edge of the bed. She fell on to it. They lifted her feet, laid her out on the mattress and held her down.

Meg tried not to show how frightened she was and protested, 'What are you going to do to me? You have no right to treat me this way. I demand to see the governor.' She knew it was no use because they were sure to be acting on his instructions. But she was not feeling at her strongest and was no match for these women who, she realised, were very experienced at holding down angry, writhing prisoners. The wardresses were hardly ever injured themselves in these spats but a protesting inmate might easily sustain severe bruising or even a sprain.

However, it was not the threat of being hurt that

had the greatest effect on Meg. She was terrified of what they might do to her this time and stopped her struggling in fearful anticipation. Her widened eyes swivelled towards the two men. They had set down a tray on her table and it carried a long coiled tube, the sight of which made her stomach clench with horror. Meg looked at the doctors and wardresses in turn. They all had grave expressions on their faces.

She gathered all her strength, faced the elder of the two doctors and said, 'I forbid you to perform this operation on me. I am not insane and forbid you to touch me.'

His answer was to present her with the tray of prison food and ask, 'Will you eat in the proper way?'

'I shall not touch a morsel until I am granted the privileges of a political prisoner.'

'Will you permit me to examine you and ascertain your state of health?'

Meg considered this request. It was possible that she was too weak to undergo such a drastic method of forcibly feeding her. She agreed and he was thorough in his examination. He listened to her chest and back with a stethoscope. He took her pulse, tested her reflexes and asked her to state her name and date of birth. Then he said, 'You are a young woman with a healthy constitution and sound mind. Will you eat food in the proper way?'

'I shall not.'

'Very well, you leave me no option.'

The assault happened very quickly. She was pinned down on the bed by four wardresses while the younger doctor picked up the coiled tubing from the tray and advanced towards her. She felt her mouth begin to tremble. It was a long thin rubber tube with a funnel inserted at the end. It must have been two yards in length and in two pieces for about halfway along the sections were joined together by narrow glass tubing. Meg felt a dreadful fear swamp her. She tried to hold her body rigid to stem her trembling.

The elder doctor took the free end of the rubber tube and approached her face. She twisted her head sideways but a wardress placed large rough hands at each side of her head and held it still. The doctor spoke to her in a clear and even tone. He was neither angry nor threatening but he said, 'Be aware that I am going to do this and it is better for you not to make it difficult for me.' Then he pushed the hardened end of the tube up one of her nostrils. She was unable to stop a cry of anguish escaping from her throat. The firm hands of the wardresses kept her still. The end of the tubing was scratchy and she felt it scrape along the lining of her nose. It hurt, but the worst of the pain was in her ears as she felt the end of the tube going down the back of her throat. It seemed as though her eardrums were bursting!

The other doctor must have noticed her agony and said something that she did not hear, because the first doctor began to withdraw the tube. Meg might have been thankful if the scraping tube had not given her even more pain. She started coughing and the wardresses released their iron grip and sat her up. A moment later the plate of food appeared again. Hardly able to breathe or speak,

Meg shook her head emphatically.

Her assailants stood back for a few minutes and she recovered enough to look up defiantly at the people surrounding her. To her surprise, she saw that the matron and two of her wardresses were crying. The doctor picked up her wrist again and counted her pulse before repeating his request for her to take food in the proper manner.

'No, I will not,' she croaked.

Her eyes darted about searching for the tubing and she tensed herself in readiness as the wardresses took hold of her for a second attempt. This time the doctor persevered through her pain and when the end of the tube reached the back of her throat he said, 'You must swallow it.'

Meg tried her hardest not to, but spittle collected in the back of her throat and interfered with her breathing. She had to draw breath! If she inhaled before she swallowed she would choke. The pain in her nose and ears continued as she tried desperately not to inhale.

How could anyone do something so outrageous as this to another human being? It was an uninvited invasion of her body, a travesty and a crime. It was as wicked as rape. Images from her past flashed inside her head. The shock, the hurt, the mental and physical ordeal were just as cruel. How could she endure such distress again? How much torment can one woman survive? She wanted to scream her protest, but had no breath in her lungs. Her groans gurgled in her throat.

She knew, they knew, everyone knew that if she did not swallow she could not breathe without choking herself to death. She spluttered and gurgled like a baby. Her physical resistance was waning. Her determination was just as strong, but so was theirs, she realised. Surely if she continued to hold her breath she would faint? But then might she inhale the fluid and die? Were they going to let this happen?

The doctors beseeched her not to struggle and cause herself more distress. They told her they were determined to complete the procedure. For Meg this offence against her body was no different from her rape except that a group of people were involved. She was forced to relive the degradation, shame and shock of that horrendous Sunday morning in this foul-smelling prison cell and her mind and body seemed to close down on her. The fight drained from her as those same emotions twisted and turned through her heart and her head. The room was getting darker, the voices fading away...

She must have swallowed because she had the most horrible pain in her throat and behind her breastbone that snapped her back to reality. The younger doctor stood on a chair and held the free end of the tube fitted with a funnel above her head. The wardress handed him a jug and he poured a large amount of fluid into the funnel. Meg focused her eyes on the glass phial in the middle of the rubber tubing as the fluid ran through it. It had a yellow tinge and Meg guessed it was milk with an egg beaten into it.

In the periphery of her vision the people standing around her bed became incarnations of Saul, all watching the fluid flow into her. When it had drained away into her unwilling stomach a wardress held a bowl of water under her chin while the doctor withdrew the tube. He plunged the end into the bowl and a wardress took it away. Meg felt her stomach contents regurgitate and she retched. Another bowl appeared. She struggled to sit up as vomit spilled out of her. She vaguely registered a taste of brandy in the regurgitated fluid. She felt light-headed and faint and although the pain in her chest was severe, her mind had numbed. She no longer cared what happened to her. She would rather die than undergo this treatment again.

The doctor performed the same thorough examination of her heart and lungs as before. But this time he did not ask her permission and, as Meg seemed unable to move of her own accord, a wardress assisted him. She felt as though she was sinking into an unknown abyss where no one else ventured; she could not stop herself. The wardresses were relatively gentle with her. They sprinkled cologne over her and put her to bed. Meg lay there in the dim light exhausted, in pain and overcome with drowsiness. Yet she was not able to sleep. How long would this inhuman treatment go on? They were determined to test her resilience to the extreme and she was at the edge of her resistance.

She lay motionless, becoming less and less aware of the comings and goings of the wardresses. If they said anything to her she did not hear them. Her eyes were open but she did not see anything, only a silent blackness, stark and cold and lonely. There was no way out for prisoner number twenty-seven.

'You don't mind if I call you Jack, do you?'

'Not at all, my lord, and thank you for a delicious dinner.' Jack Wright had enjoyed dining with Lord Langton at his exclusive London club, but guessed his lordship was coming to the main reason for his invitation. He and Sir Gerald were of the same mind when it came to suffragettes.

'You have made a favourable impression on my sister, Jack.'

Jack's face remained passive. He had half expected to be told to stay away from Alice and Langton Place, or at least to cease to act for her on behalf of the suffragettes. He said, 'Lady Alice is very concerned for – for one of her servants in prison.'

'Yes, she said. She believes you can help to free her.'

Jack did not respond to this comment. He sincerely hoped that he could have Meg released early but he was aware of the government's recent firmer stance on militant suffragettes. His well-schooled cool exterior hid an internal turmoil at the urgency of his task.

'Sir Gerald speaks highly of you,' Charles added.

'Thank you, sir.'

'He says the only thing that's holding you back is your – well, not to put too fine a point on it, it's your lack of connections.'

'Not all of Sir Gerald's clients are peers of the realm, sir. I am building my own list of satisfied clients.'

'It would be easier for you to become a partner with a lord or two on your list.'

'Yes, I concede that.'

'You're an ambitious man. You'll not be satisfied with anything less than a partnership in ten years' time, will you?'

Again Jack did not answer. He wondered if the Earl was going to threaten him with ruin if he didn't stay away from his sister and her suffragette cause. A word to Sir Gerald was all that was necessary. Jack had already considered the possibility and said as much to Alice. Surely she would not have betrayed this confidence?

'Have you nothing to say? I should have thought you would have had an opinion on your own future.'

'My lord, I believe I made my views clear when I came to lunch at Langton Place. Your words are purely speculation. Your lordship dines with Sir Gerald and I do not wish him to hear of my ambitions from anyone other than myself.'

Charles turned down the corners of his mouth. 'You certainly speak your mind. Have you talked with my sister of your future?'

Jack allowed his genuine surprise to show. 'Indeed I have not, sir!'

'Come now, you have dined alone with her and taken walks in the park. She regards you as a friend. Is she not more to you than a client? Be honest with me, Jack.'

Jack sat back in his velvet-upholstered chair. Lord Langton had finally got round to asking him exactly what he wanted to know. 'Yes, sir,' he replied. 'Lady Alice is more than a client. I regard her ladyship as a friend.'

'And how do you regard her as a woman?'

His lordship certainly speaks his mind too, Jack thought. But as the purpose of this conversation became clear to him, he began to relax. His lordship was merely behaving in a fatherly manner towards his sister and was alert to the possibility of fortune-hunters. Jack was comfortable with the truth about his relationship with Lady Alice. They were well acquainted, enjoyed good conversation and shared an urgent concern for a mutual friend. He had nothing to hide. He said, 'I admire your sister, sir. Lady Alice is very much a twentieth-century woman who enjoys the freedom and independence to commit herself to a cause she believes in. If she were my sister, I should be proud of her.'

Jack had to suppress a smile at Lord Langton's startled reaction. He really didn't know his older sister very well at all! But his lordship recovered quickly and demanded, 'Is that all you have to say about her as a member of the opposite sex?'

'Since you are pressing me to be honest, my lord, I am struck by her beauty and grace, and her lack of vanity. It is refreshing in a lady.'

Jack noticed that this answer seemed to satisfy his lordship and confirmed in his mind that this meeting was about any possible romantic interest in his sister that Jack was harbouring.

His lordship gave him a condescending smile. 'She is the daughter of an earl. Are you not surprised that she is unmarried?'

Jack felt as though he had had enough of Lord Langton's prodding and considered excusing himself. But he would be just as concerned about his own sister in a similar situation and he was a patient man. He answered honestly. 'Young women nowadays do not always make the assumption that marriage is their only choice in life. They travel, attend university, follow gainful occupations and–'

'Become suffragettes,' his lordship interrupted.

Jack would have preferred not to discuss the suffrage movement as it inflamed his anxiety about Meg and he needed to keep a cool head. He could not avoid it now. This meeting was about Lady Alice and she was involved. He said, 'Suffragettes are showing great courage, sir, in the face of opposition from the King and his government. Those in prison are having a very difficult time of it.' He hardly dared think of the treatment poor Meg was receiving. It angered him so much his judgement became clouded and that was not good for a lawyer.

'If they break the law, they deserve to be there.'

Jack recognised his own emotional reaction to this statement and drew on all his faculties to suppress it. 'They are not common criminals, sir,' he pointed out. 'It is a political fight and the purpose of their hunger strikes is to draw attention to that fact.'

'You support them, don't you?'

'I am a lawyer. I can see both sides of the argument. But you have, surely, read about the forcible feeding?'

'The prison governor cannot let them die!'

'Their treatment is inhuman and degrading, my lord. It amounts to torture.'

'Hey, steady on, fellow. It's for their own good, you know.'

'But does it not tell us that the suffragettes mean to fight on? With such a show of commitment and strength, they are gaining sympathy all over the country and in that way they are putting pressure on the government.'

'To do what? Give in to their demands? They have brought it on themselves! Well-behaved young women do not march in the streets as though they were trade unionists.'

Jack was feeling increasingly annoyed with Lord Langton's thinking. His lordship had very little idea of how strong his own sister's feelings were for the suffragette movement and absolutely no notion of what poor Meg was enduring in jail. 'They are marching for their beliefs, sir. In that respect they are no different from the Knights Templar who fought the Holy Wars in Jerusalem.'

'There is no comparison!' Lord Langton stared at him crossly for a moment, and then conceded, 'You have a point but do not talk of war to Alice. She lost her fiancé to the Boers at Colenso.'

'I did not know. Thank you for telling me.' Colenso was nigh on ten years ago, Jack thought, and Lady Alice had not struck him as a woman in mourning. But he was relieved when Lord Langton continued this line of conversation.

'It was a great pity for all of us,' his lordship went on. 'He was a fine soldier and a jolly decent fellow. Next time you visit Langton Place, I shall show you a photograph of him. It was taken of him in his captain's uniform before he left for Africa.'

Next time, Jack repeated in his head. He was not banned from setting foot in Langton Place.

Lord Langton continued, 'Alice will not come home until this maid of hers is released so I want you to do all you can to help her. I'll clear it with Sir Gerald.'

Jack was hugely relieved, so much so that he resisted an urge to leave his lordship's club that minute. He was anxious to return and work openly on securing Meg's release.

His lordship gave a throaty grunt that made him sound much older than his years. 'You don't hunt, you say.'

Jack shook his head slightly. 'It is difficult to keep a decent hunter in London, sir.'

'But you are an accurate gun? That is enough, I suppose.'

'A day out on Lord Redfern's grouse moor is a pleasure I have always enjoyed, and the one I miss most of all.'

'Is that so? I cannot offer you grouse near to London but my cousin's pheasant have bred well this year and his tenant farmers are complaining that they are eating the winter crops. Come down to Sussex with Sir Gerald next week.'

'Thank you, my lord.'

Lord Langton appeared to be satisfied with this response and sat back in his chair. 'That's settled then.' He raised an arm casually. 'I'll propose you for membership here. Sir Gerald will second. You need to be able to socialise with your clients.'

Jack's eyes wavered. He was young and un-known and well aware of the value of such an honour. For that reason he ought not to refuse his lordship. But it wasn't in his plans for the future. If he did become a member of a gentleman's club in London, this one would not be his choice. It was for aristocrats and their kind and he was not one of them. Nor did he wish to be – although Lord Langton seemed completely unaware that this might be so.

However, by the end of the evening Lord Langton was in a jovial mood and when Jack took his leave he shook his hand firmly. 'You'll receive an invitation to the country at your chambers.'

'And you have no reservations about my visiting your sister, sir?'

'I don't say I approve of Alice going to all this trouble over a girl she picked up from a Yorkshire mill. However, if anyone is to help her then I'd prefer it to be you. But never forget, Jack, that my sister's happiness is vital to me. If you hurt her in any way, you'll have me to deal with.'

Jack thought that was an unnecessary comment, but understood his concerns and took advantage of his lordship's final approval. 'There is something you can do, sir, to speed up the process. You are in a position to exert your influence at a higher level than I.'

'What d'you mean, Jack?'

'You have a seat in the House of Lords, sir. You have the power.'

'I am no politician. I don't take my seat. I attend when I am asked to be there for a vote. I support the party in Yorkshire and I can't say these suffragettes elicit much sympathy from us. They're communists, the lot of them!'

'You know that is not true, sir.'

'They joined up with the mill workers' strike, y'know.'

'But there are members in both Houses of Parliament who are beginning express concern about the inhuman treatment of suffragettes in prison.'

'I can't do much, Jack. It's the gentlemen in the House of Commons who have the power nowadays.'

Jack felt like a helpless prisoner himself, with his hands tied behind him, trying to fight his way through a whole establishment of men like Lord Langton. He immediately rebuked himself for such self-pitying thoughts as he imagined how Meg was suffering for her beliefs. But his frustration remained – festered.

Chapter 23

'Your correspondence, Miss Brookes.'

Lady Alice's butler stood by Florence's elbow with a small silver tray. She glanced at the envelope on top and recognised her mother's handwriting. 'Take it to the library, please, and tell Lady Alice I shall join her shortly.' Florence was late eating her breakfast because headquarters had telephoned early to speak with her again this morning. She swallowed a last mouthful of coffee, dabbed her mouth with a napkin and took a deep breath.

Alice was already at her desk, reading her own letters. She looked up as Florence opened the door and smiled. 'I do know what all these telephone conversations are about.'

'You do?' Florence realised that she must not leave it any longer to discuss her tour.

'I am on the find-raising committee. I put your name forward for New York.'

'Did you indeed?' Florence responded. She was pleased that Alice appeared to approve.

'Your skills are perfectly suited for organising the information and writing reports for us. You will be such an asset. When do they want you to leave?'

'Not until next year, but if I am to go away on an extended journey, I have to make my peace at home first.' Florence picked up her mother's letter from her desk. 'My parents are begging me to be with them for Christmas. This will be another letter saying that Bradley is a leading light in Shawbridge and that he has not found another girl to replace me.'

'Perhaps the time has come to be honest with her.'

'Yes,' Florence agreed. 'I should like to go home for a few days soon so that I can clear the air with Bradley, too, before the festive season. I am ready to talk to Mother.'

'You will need an assistant in New York.'

'Meg is perfect for the role. I shall not go until she is free. Is there any more news of her?'

'Not since Jack's telephone call last night.'

'I have noticed that he telephones you or calls in person every night.'

Florence noticed Alice sigh. 'I am so fortunate to have met him. He is a brilliant lawyer and a fine gentleman. Charles likes him too.'

Florence was aware that Alice was attracted to

Jack Wright and that Jack found Alice good company. But she was not sure how deep their relationship went. Florence's recent experience of the opposite sex had been a disaster so she was reluctant to comment.

'He is making progress for Meg though, isn't he?'

'He is becoming a thorn in the side of the Home Secretary and the prison governor.'

'Then he will not very popular with them in the future,' Florence commented.

'That is the least of his worries – or mine.' Alice stood up and walked around her desk. 'I didn't tell you last night because I was too upset myself. Jack has gained the confidence of one of the prison doctors. Meg is very ill. The doctor has said it's not only the starvation that has made her physical condition worse.'

'Good God, Alice! What have they been doing to her?'

'It was the forcible feeding. The doctors used a tube and she went into a kind of shock. They are reluctant to give Jack any details and he is going to the prison again today.'

Florence sat down and covered her eyes with her hand. 'Shock? Is he saying she is mentally disturbed?' She felt tears welling in her eyes. 'I really can't stand this much longer, Alice. They must release her now. They must.'

Alice stood up and came over to her desk. 'Brace up, Florence. This is very hard for all of us but it is Meg who is suffering, not you or I. Jack has already consulted a physician who specialises in disturbances of the mind. He will dine with us tonight and explain.'

Florence's anxiety mounted. 'I want to see her.'

'You say that every day. We all do. Jack thinks he can get permission for this special doctor to see her.'

Florence sat down at her desk, feeling helpless. She continued to harbour guilt that Meg had sacrificed her freedom so that she could escape and worried constantly that Meg's health would be permanently damaged. She stared at her pile of letters. It was difficult to work when her mind was so distracted. After several silent minutes Alice's calm voice intervened.

'I am confident that Jack will succeed,' she said. 'I have never seen anyone so determined.'

Florence pulled herself together, reflecting on how comforting she found Alice's support. When Florence was feeling low, Alice was there to buck her up. Since Jack had taken over the fight for Meg's release, Alice had – had – Florence searched for the word: Alice had *blossomed*. She had always possessed a confidence born of her titled heritage, but these days she gave more attention to her appearance. Her beauty, which had not previously been obvious, now radiated. It was Jack's influence on her, Florence realised. Alice was falling in love with Jack.

She wondered how Jack felt about Alice. After Bradley, Florence doubted all her judgements where men were concerned and Jack was particularly difficult to read. He certainly wasn't a cold fish. She didn't doubt that he had emotions although he rarely showed them in her presence. She hoped that he did love Alice in return. Alice deserved to find happiness at last.

The wind and the rain and the cold of late autumn in London did not seem to dampen Alice's spirit as they did Florence's. The lamps were lit by teatime. Florence stood at the drawing-room window with her china cup and saucer and gazed at the overcast sky. 'I hope Jack can find a taxicab in this weather,' she commented.

'I have sent the motor car to collect him. We are dining early.'

Florence was pleased as she was restless for news of Meg. She returned her empty cup to the tea tray. 'I have a couple of things to finish in the office before I dress.'

'Sherry at half past six tonight,' Alice responded.

Only the butler and footmen wore tailcoats in the evening now that Alice ran Langton Place. She could not ask Charles to change their livery. But Florence agreed with her preference for gentlemen to wear the shorter dinner jacket with a black tie. It was less formal and she didn't feel obliged to wear jewels or a tiara, which was just as well because she possessed neither. When Jack dined with them at Langton Place it was an informal affair, although tonight, Florence noticed, Alice looked especially attractive.

She wore an ankle-length beaded georgette gown with two overskirts in toning shades of green, cream kid shoes and a cream feather in her hair. Florence's dress was less ornate in a plain pale blue. It had a square neckline, broad dark blue sash and long lace jacket. 'Do continue, Jack,' she begged him as they settled in the comfortable upholstered dining chairs.

'The physician was very firm,' Jack said. 'He requested – no, he demanded an interview with the prison doctor about Meg and the prison governor has agreed.'

'Oh, Jack, you have been perfectly splendid!' Alice breathed.

'I shall accompany him to the prison tomorrow.'

'Tomorrow! Shall I come with you? Will they let me see her?'

'I doubt it. The physician will demand to examine Meg.'

'I ought to be there,' Alice insisted. 'I am her employer and you are both acting on my instructions.'

'You were once an inmate yourself, Alice,' Jack explained gently. 'It is better for me to represent you.'

Florence added, 'He is right, Alice. Jack has more knowledge of these matters.' She noticed Alice reach out and place her hand over Jack's where it rested on the white linen tablecloth.

Alice nodded and said, 'Very well. I know you will do your very best for me.'

Jack did not move his hand. He replied, 'None of us will rest until she is released. I shall telephone as soon as I return to my chambers.'

Florence saw Alice squeeze his hand but Jack's face was impassive. The butler moved between them to serve. Jack slid his hand away and asked Florence for news from headquarters of other imprisoned suffragettes.

The following day, Jack paced up and down the stark unadorned prison corridor as the physician and prison doctor met with the prison governor. Since he had discovered Meg was in prison he had noted and filed every action, every statement and every relevant public speech concerning her situation. His lack of sleep was beginning to affect his alertness but he dare not lose concentration for a second. After half an hour he was called in to the meeting.

The prison doctor spoke. 'It is my opinion,' he stated, 'that Parker's mental and physical condition renders her incapable of continuing her sentence within the prison confines.'

Jack clenched his fists and he felt a muscle twitch in his jaw. The option of transferring Meg to a hospital for the insane was the one he feared most of all. His breathing became difficult as though a heavy weight was pressing down on his chest. He had not dared mention it to Alice or Florence as they were distressed enough already. But if the worst happened his campaign for her release would not stop, with or without Alice's backing. He had his file of notes and his reports on Meg's treatment could fill a book. Since Lord Langton and Sir Gerald had given their support he had gained other friends in the newspapers and in politics.

He held on to his composure and asked, 'Where will you send her?'

The prison governor replied. Jack saw that he was not happy and guessed he was acting under orders from above when her answered, 'Parker's case and her condition have been reviewed. She will be released into her employer's care.'

Jack had experienced failure in the courtroom and knew the disappointment that it brought and how to cope with it. He had also known success and was aware of the very fine line between the two, so that any celebration for him was usually subdued. He had never felt inclined to whoop with joy until now. At that moment he wanted to dance around the prison governor's office with the consulting physician. He drew on all his courtroom skills to remain perfectly still and expressionless. 'When will that be?' he asked.

The prisoner governor went on, 'As soon as the paperwork is complete.'

The prison doctor addressed his eminent colleague. 'I need your report on her for that, sir.'

The physician replied, 'I shall send it to the prison tomorrow.'

Satisfied with these responses Jack was able to breathe more easily. He said, 'I should like to see her before I leave.'

The prison doctor and governor exchanged glances and the governor nodded. The doctor said, 'I think you should. You need to prepare Lady Alice to receive her.' He stood up and added, 'This way.'

As their footsteps echoed in the empty corridors, the prison doctor explained, 'Parker is in the hospital wing. She refuses to take food in the proper manner and resists all our attempts to feed her. We have resorted to trying Benger's food in an invalid feeding cup with a spout. But she no longer communicates with her wardresses and her pulse and breathing indicate perilous amounts of stress when they approach her.'

He asked the wardress in charge to unlock her cell. Jack realised his own heart rate had increased and he took a deep breath to calm himself. The doctor added, 'She reacts badly to strangers but seems less disturbed by wardresses who are familiar.'

'She knows me,' Jack said and took one last deep breath as the cell door swung open. Meg was sitting on a hard wooden chair beside a small table and staring at the wall. The cell smelled vaguely of an odd mixture of vomit and eau de cologne.

At first, he did not recognise her gaunt shadowed features as the energetic and intelligent young woman he had known in Deepdale. Her beautiful fair hair was hidden by a dingy prison bonnet and her coarse prison dress was ill fitting and stained.

'Meg?' he said softly, but she did not respond. He raised his voice: 'Meg, it's Jacob.'

Her head turned towards the sound and her staring eyes wandered over him. Her lips moved and she whispered, 'Jacob? Jacob Wright?' She leaned forward to examine him closer. 'It is you!' Then she noticed the wardress and doctor and sat back again. 'Why are you here?' Her eyes took on a haunted expression. 'What have they said to you?'

Tears were not something Jacob had experienced since he was a child. The last time he had cried it was in sympathy with his mother and father when he received news of his scholarship to the grammar school. They had been tears of happiness. The tears that threatened him now were such a mixture of regret and anger that they only added to the turmoil of emotion churning his insides. How could such a lively and pretty woman turn into this pathetic shell of a human being?

'They have said you will be released. You can go home.'

Again Meg glanced at the prison staff. 'Is this true?' she asked.

The doctor answered, 'It is. You will be free within the week.'

Meg looked at Jack and he met her eyes. 'I shall return and take you back to Langton Place,' he said. 'Alice and Florence are waiting for you.'

To his immense joy he saw her mouth curve into a small smile and she said, 'Votes for Women, Jacob.'

It was hard for him to smile back through his tears and his face remained serious. 'Votes for Women, Meg,' he replied. Dear God, he thought, he was going to blub like a baby. The doctor ushered him out before he did. As the cell door closed he noticed the smile had remained on Meg's lips and it sustained him until he returned to help her out of the prison gate.

Meg felt light-headed but she insisted on walking up the steps of Langton Place unaided. Jacob was at one side of her, Alice at the other and the chauffeur was behind her. Florence waited by the open door with her arms outstretched. Meg grasped both her hands and allowed Florence to lead her into the drawing room where Meg was thankful to sink into the nearest armchair.

'How are you?' Florence asked.

'Weak and shaky but – but...' Meg gazed up at the worried faces of her friends and added, '...but triumphant.'

Alice wiped a tear from her eye. 'I have had a room on the first floor prepared for you. My brother's physician is on his way to see you. He will tell me what to do to speed up your recovery. Until he arrives you must rest and take Benger's food only. Jack will seek out anything else you need, anything at all.'

'Jack?' Meg queried.

Jacob answered, 'My London friends call me Jack.'

'Do they?' Meg stared at him, tall, handsome and as smartly dressed as any London gentleman she had seen.

Alice went on, 'Jack is the person I have to thank for your release. He has worked so hard for me.'

'Jack,' Meg repeated and met his eyes. In spite of all her efforts and all she had been through her love for him had not diminished at all. In fact, she loved him more than ever, if that were possible. 'Jack suits you,' she said. 'Thank you, Jack.'

She wanted him to smile so that his eyes crinkled at the corners exactly as she remembered, but he didn't. If he had, she would have attempted to throw her arms around him and kissed him regardless of the time and place. She had fewer inhibitions now; prison and starvation had changed her views on life. She was clear about the people and things that were most important to her and about her own ambitions for the future. When she had regained her strength, she thought...

Florence picked up her hand. 'I'll help you upstairs ready for the doctor.'

Meg nodded her agreement and as she slowly got to her feet Jack asked, 'Is there anything you want now?'

She thought for a moment and considered how, with effort and determination, an earlier nasty incident in her life had receded from her mind until a similar horrible experience had resurrected it. Her body had weakened but her will, if anything, was stronger. She raised her head and answered him clearly, 'I want to write it all down before I forget the details.'

Meg had known Jack well in Deepdale, when they were not all that much younger. They had shared likes and dislikes, agreements and arguments and she had known when he was pleased and when he was angry. But he was different now. His facial expressions and careful language gave nothing away. Neither did hers, she imagined, as she gazed at him steadily. Then she noticed a light come into his eyes, the vestige of a smile on his lips. His features appeared to lift and he looked as though he was ... was ... proud, or perhaps just pleased, she wasn't sure, except that what she had said seemed to meet with his approval.

'I'll see to it,' he said.

Florence led her away. Later, the doctor prescribed nothing more than light nourishing food and fresh country air, with a patent tonic wine and daily walks when she felt able. She must not rush her climb back to normality. There were parks in

London for walking but Alice had a better idea.

'I shall take you to Fieldhurst, my cousin's estate in Sussex,' Alice announced. 'The climate is mild compared with Yorkshire and Jack says the colours are beautiful this time of year.'

'Jack says?'

'Actually, it was Jack who suggested Fieldhurst. He was down there recently shooting pheasant with my brother. He and Charles have become firm friends.'

'Will Jack be at Fieldhurst too?'

'Oh no. Since his success with your release he is in great demand with suffragette sympathisers in London.'

Meg was disappointed that she did not see Jack again before she left with Alice for Fieldhurst. However, she took delivery from a London store of a large package that turned out to be a beautiful wooden writing box, which opened to reveal a tooled leather writing slope and contained all the writing materials she needed. There was no message on the card, simply a signature that said, *From Jack*. Meg thought about the thank-you letter she would write to him all the way down to the country in the motor car.

Florence did not come with Meg and Alice to Fieldhurst. She took the opportunity to visit her parents in Yorkshire and 'clear the air', as she described her task. Before she left Florence mentioned her New York plans to Meg and asked her to consider accompanying her when Meg was well again.

As Meg's health improved, she noticed Alice had a girlish excitement about her that had not been present in the caravan, or the house in Leeds. Life in London and working for the suffragette movement had had a positive effect on her and Meg was pleased for her. She said as much to her shortly after they arrived at Fieldhurst.

Fieldhurst was a very pretty estate set in the Sussex Downs where the rolling hills were softer than the craggy limestone outcrops of the Yorkshire Dales. The motor car passed several woodlands abundant with the yellow, orange, red and brown of autumn. The house was about the same size as Langton Place in London but less grand, built in a cottage style of flint and stone with a red-tiled roof. Mr and Mrs Clarke, butler and cook, and a small brigade of domestic servants ran it for Peregrine and Gertrude Price-Fieldhurst, whose four children were away at school.

Alice explained, 'My cousin and his wife are in the West Country at present for the hunting so we have the house to ourselves until the end of the month. Mrs Clarke will look after us.'

The chauffeur unloaded their luggage and Meg bent to pick up her smallest bag.

Alice caught her arm. 'Clarke will take them. You are no longer a servant, Meg, you are my guest. Everyone regards you as a "Votes for Women" heroine, but here you have to get well and let others take up the fight.'

'I am not used to doing nothing,' Meg argued.

'Jack says I must encourage you to write as well as walk. When you feel strong enough, I shall introduce you to some country pursuits. Both Jack and I enjoy the country.'

Jack again, Meg noticed; Jack and Charles, Jack and Alice. A flutter of nervous curiosity stirred in her stomach. She wanted to find out just how close Alice was to Jack but did not know, at that precise moment, how to phrase the question without sounding rude.

Mrs Clarke, small and neat in her black silk housekeeper's dress with its tiny pleated apron at the waistband, came outside to greet them. 'Afternoon tea is in the orangery, my lady,' she said.

'Splendid,' Alice responded. 'Come this way, Meg. We shall walk around the outside of the house. The gardens here are very pretty at any time of year.'

The orangery, to Meg, looked like a huge glass-house sparkling in the afternoon sun. Its glazing bars were painted white and the interior stylishly arranged with tropical plants, Indian bamboo and rattan furniture and piles of cushions. Tea, laid out on a low table, consisted of tiny sandwiches, scones and cakes, attractively tempting for the most jaded of palates. How thoughtful, Meg reflected. Meg's palate was not jaded, but she was following the doctor's advice and not indulging in too much food too quickly. For a second she remembered the Mission teas in Deepdale and her lemon-curd tarts. How far she had travelled since then!

Alice settled into a low chair as though she had come home. 'Country air, country food and country sports are the very best medicine for you. By the time you are strong again my cousin will be home for his weekend shooting party. Charles will come down from London with Sir Gerald, and Jack, of course. Charles says that Jack shoots very well.'

Meg watched Alice's animated features as she spoke and noticed a dreamy look in her eyes as she finished. 'How well do you know Jack Wright?' she asked.

'I met him in Crandale. He helped me get Florence out of prison after the strikers' march.'

'Oh, I didn't know he was involved.' But Meg knew he was there, on his way to Ferndale Lodge for the grouse shooting. At the time, she had been feeling raw and embarrassed about Saul, and unwilling to face Jack. She wouldn't be so hesitant about it now. Men like Saul deserved to be exposed.

Alice continued, 'Well, I didn't know he worked for Sir Gerald until he came to the prison for me in London, but I realised then, of course, that he was the right person to help me with your case. He has been an absolute tower of strength.'

Meg noticed that Alice positively sparkled when she talked of Jack. There could be only one reason for that, Meg realised with a sinking heart. Alice was in love with Jack. Lady Alice Langton, with her wealth and connections, had fallen in love with an ambitious young lawyer whose career depended on wealthy clients with connections. Meg stared moodily at the glossy dark green leaves of the tropical plant behind Alice.

Alice sat back with her cup of tea. 'Jack is a fine gentleman. Don't you agree?

'I do,' Meg answered. 'Has he mentioned that we have met in the past?'

'No,' Alice mused. 'I do not believe he has. Was that in Crandale?'

'I know him from Deepdale before he moved to London. He used to travel to the Dales regularly for the bicycling.'

'Does he bicycle?' Alice looked especially pleased with this information. 'How splendid! I have a bicycle at home in Langton Park. Sir Gerald regards him with favour, you know. His career as a lawyer will be secured with my brother's help and then he will be in a position to – well, to marry me.'

'To marry you?' Meg queried. Her mood sank further. All Jack's help for her had been to impress Alice! Why should he be interested in a former mill girl from Deepdale?

Alice blushed. 'Yes, it is so very exciting, isn't it? Of course it is too early to breathe a word of this to anyone.'

Alice looked so happy that Meg felt guilty at her envious reaction. Alice had everything: a title, wealth, beauty and independence. And now, it seemed, she had Jack. *Her* Jack. Jack would surely be aware of the advantages of marriage to Alice and she wondered if he had proposed to her yet. If not Alice seemed very confident that he would and Meg ought to be pleased for them both. But how could she when she was still in love with Jack herself?

This was just another trial for her to get through. Perhaps she could return to London before the shooting party descended on Fieldhurst? But that would appear so rude after the kindness and generosity everyone had shown her. She must see it through with gratitude and good nature and until then she had to stop thinking about Jack. She must keep her mind full of other things.

She gazed around the lush plants that thrived in this beautiful orangery and said, 'Do you think it would be possible for me to write in here? It is such a peaceful place.'

'That is an absolutely first-class idea; Clarke will organise a table for your writing slope. Jack says that letters to newspaper editors is a good way to start.'

Jack says. Jack's writing slope. How could she hope to ever take her mind off him?

'He also said,' Alice continued, 'that I must ensure you take your daily exercise in the fresh air. We'll go after luncheon and take the dogs.'

Chapter 24

A week later Alice came into the orangery just before luncheon and asked, 'How are you today, Meg?'

Meg put down her pen. 'I am much better, thank you. My appetite is back and I am strong enough to take my afternoon walk alone. I'm sure you have other things to do apart from being nanny to me.'

'Splendid! I thought I'd take a shotgun and walk a little further today. Have you ever handled a shotgun?'

Meg shook her head.

'I guessed not, but I could show you if you wish. It's quite the thing these days for ladies to join in the shooting and I am out of practice. It wouldn't do to let the side down at the party.'

'Are you suggesting that I learn to shoot?'

'It will add interest to our walks, don't you think? Besides, I'm partial to a game pie.'

'So am I.' Meg's mother used to buy wild fowl, rabbit and sometimes venison from a game dealer at the market and make her own raised pies. Meg remembered watching her mould the hot water paste around a stone preserving jar and then tie brown paper round it to keep the shape. She supposed the cook at Fieldhurst had proper moulds for her pies.

Meg's warm and hard-wearing bicycling skirt was still her favourite choice for outdoors in the country. She had made it from tweed bought cheaply from the mill, but the fabric was top quality – the finest wool – and it refused to wear out. It had a divided skirt and she had cut it so that the flaws did not show. She noticed with satisfaction that it had a similar appearance to Alice's shooting skirt. Hers was in Scotch plaid with an inverted pleat in the centre back and front. She wore a matching shooting jacket with roomy pockets and leather reinforcing patches on the shoulders.

'You take this one.' Alice handed her a shotgun in a soft leather case similar to the one that Alice had slung across her back. She also carried a leather cartridge bag across her body. It was a crisp clear day with a cooling fresh breeze. Alice waved to one of the outdoor staff and they set off on foot with Trudy, her favourite spaniel, racing ahead. 'We'll take the track to the copse. It slopes down to a rather jolly little stream. I remember taking picnics there when I visited as a girl.'

The gun was heavy, though no heavier than the bags of shopping Meg used to carry back from the market in Deepdale. She swung her arms and soon warmed up. When they reached the copse Alice slowed to catch her breath. The fallen leaves were thick on the ground and a hundred yards in the track began to slope gently down towards the stream.

It was a perfect haven, Meg thought: utterly quiet apart from the natural call of birds in the trees and the rustling of leaves as an excited Trudy nosed her way through them. Further on Meg heard the gentle gurgling of water and glimpsed part of a red-tiled roof through the branches.

'Is that a cottage down by the stream?' she asked.

'It's the estate pump house, built years ago in the last century and still working. The stream is fed by a natural spring and Fieldhurst water is prized. Visitors from London often take back carboys full of it.'

'May I have a closer look?'

'Certainly. We have to cross the stream and there's a footbridge further down.'

'It's a very pretty building,' Meg commented as they neared. The pump house was built of red brick in an ornate fashion and resembled a small private chapel or schoolhouse. Alice tried the door but it was locked.

'The water is collected in large tanks inside and one doesn't want to be here when the engine is pumping. It is too noisy for conversation.'

'It's very peaceful now.' But Meg was puzzled. 'Where does the water go?' she asked.

'Underground pipes, the same as in London,' Alice replied. 'They take it all the way to the house and stables.'

Meg inhaled the air and felt her body relaxing in the stillness.

'No time to linger,' Alice urged. 'The keeper is sending up a few birds for me. Come on.'

The footbridge was no more than a mossy wooden plank, which needed careful negotiation and Alice took both guns. But once across, Alice found a spot to unload her heavy burden and take the shotguns out of their sheaths. She showed Meg how to load, unload and handle the gun safely and then suddenly stopped. 'That's the keeper's whistle. Hold my second gun. Remember to keep the barrel pointing towards the sky and watch me.'

Meg was nervous but fascinated. Her father didn't shoot but both her brothers did. They had worked as beaters for shoots around Deepdale and had enjoyed their days out. Her heart began to beat faster as she waited in the silence. The pheasant suddenly appeared out of the copse on the other side of the stream and Alice had raised her gun and shot before Meg had time to think. The crack of the shot was deafening. She missed but quick as a flash she pushed her empty gun at Meg and took the loaded one from her as another bird followed. She must have hit it because Trudy raced off to find her prey. Meg struggled with breaking the first gun to reload. Smoke

388

wafted from the barrel and Meg could smell the gunpowder. Alice had reloaded before Meg had finished, and taken another shot. Eventually Meg handed her a loaded gun and Alice waited. The silence lengthened until Alice dropped the butt to the ground. Trudy came rushing back with the dead bird flopping in her mouth. She dropped it at Alice's feet. 'A hen,' Alice commented. 'Small, but definitely more tender than the cock.' Trudy's tail wagged furiously and Meg fondled her silky head.

'Will you try for the next drive?' Alice took a felt pad out of her pocket. 'Put this over your shoulder to dull the kickback. The birds will come from that way.'

Why not? Meg thought. If she was to join in this forthcoming party she needed to present herself well. Her brothers had enjoyed shooting so why shouldn't she? She agreed and waited with a swift-beating heart for the birds to appear. When they did, in her excitement Meg forgot all that Alice had told her but her determination and instinct took over. She wanted to hit her target. Disappointingly, she missed three chances.

Alice took the empty gun from her and handed her a loaded one. 'Follow through,' she said. 'Move your gun with your target.'

Meg did and to her great delight bagged her first bird.

'Good shot,' Alice said. 'A clean kill.'

Trudy rushed off again and this time the bright red on the bird's lolling head indicated a cock pheasant. Alice picked up their bag and looped twine around both birds' necks to carry them home. Meg blew out her cheeks. 'I'm exhausted,' she said.

Alice put the guns back in their sheaths. 'Yes, that's enough for you today.' She waved to the keeper, who had appeared at the other side of the stream. He crossed the footbridge.

'I'll take those, my lady,' he said, relieving her of the guns and cartridges. 'A brace, I see. Cook will be pleased.'

'Thank you, Wilson.'

'Would the lady care to practise with Mr Price-Fieldhurst's new trap?'

Alice turned to Meg. 'What do you say, Meg? It's a contraption that sends up pieces of moulded clay for you to shoot at. It's nearer the house so not too far to walk.'

'Well, yes, I should like to practise,' Meg replied. 'But I enjoy my walks too and I find it so peaceful down here by the pump house.'

'May I suggest the lady does both, ma'am? A walk on one afternoon and a shooting practice on another, perhaps when the pump house is in operation.'

'Perfect, Wilson. Meg?'

Meg nodded. She wanted to join in the shooting party.

'Thank you, Wilson,' Alice said.

'My lady.' Wilson bowed his head and walked off with his load. Meg watched him cross the plank bridge with an easy stride and wondered if she was really ready to take up shooting.

'Wilson will look after you, Meg. Peregrine and Gertrude are arriving in a few days and I shall be busy helping with their preparations.'

The gunroom at Fieldhurst stored wet-weather boots and waxed coats for anyone that fitted them as well as guns and cartridges. Meg took advantage of this and was able to walk alone to the pump house, in comfort, in the rain. There she found a felled tree trunk in the lee of the wind to rest and think about her writing before she walked back. On fine days, if a keeper was available, he found a suitable gun for her and operated the trap for her shooting practice.

A few days later, shortly after the Price-Field-hursts returned home, Gertrude looked up from the letter she was reading at breakfast and said, 'Lady Pearce wants to know if Miss Parker is still here. She has asked specifically to meet her when she comes down for the shooting party.'

Alice explained, 'Lady Pearce is Sir Gerald's wife.'

'Why does she want to meet me?' Meg queried.

'You are a suffragette heroine, dearest Meg,' Alice replied. She raised her voice and added, 'Isn't she, Perry?'

Peregrine's answer came from behind his copy of *The Times*. 'Yes, she is.' He folded down his newspaper. 'Sarah Pearce was something of a radical herself before she married Sir Gerald. Good shot, too. She always goes out with the guns.' He smiled at Meg over the spectacles on his nose. 'My keeper tells me you're not a bad shot yourself, young lady.'

'I've been practising.' Meg glanced at Alice. 'I don't want to let the side down.'

'You won't,' Alice assured her. 'I've seen the guest list and three of those fellows could not hit the barn door.'

'Now then, Alice,' Perry responded, 'they can't all be as good as your Jack.'

'Talking of guests,' Gertrude interrupted. 'Cook needs the final menus soon to do the ordering. Alice, can you help me with them this morning?'

'Of course,' Alice replied. 'What are you doing this morning, Meg?'

Meg didn't answer because she didn't hear. She was thinking about Jack. *Your Jack*, Perry had called him in answer to Alice. This shooting-party weekend was going to be very hard for Meg to endure. Half of her simply ached to see Jack again, to talk to him, to try and explain the past to him. The other half wanted to run away and hide so that she did not have to face the sight of Alice and Jack together. Alice was her friend but much as she loved her, Meg knew that love might easily turn to jealousy and hatred when she saw her with Jack.

'Meg?' Alice repeated. 'What will you do this morning?'

Meg pulled herself together. 'I'll walk down to the pump house.'

'Not writing in the orangery?' Alice queried.

'I want to think. There are no distractions down there.'

The pump house had become a bolt-hole for Meg, to escape from the increasingly hectic household as it prepared for the shooting party. Extra hands were taken on from nearby villages to lay fires, carry coals, dust and clean rooms, as well as feed a large number of guests and their servants for several days. Meg had become apprehensive of the approaching gathering.

'Are you quite well, Meg?' Alice asked one evening as they gathered in the drawing room for pre-dinner drinks.

'Quite well, Alice. Why do you ask?'

'You seem a little nervous. You do not have to be. Perry and Gertrude told me that you will fit in perfectly with their guests.'

It was a kind way for Alice to tell her not to feel inferior. Meg didn't but she could not give Alice the truth about her feelings. Meg simply wished that the shooting party were over. The London group arrived first, not long after lunch, in several motor cars. Charles had friends in his motor as Prudence was in Yorkshire nursing her pregnancy. Jack travelled down with Sir Gerald and Lady Pearce. Meg's writing table and materials had been pushed behind a large monstera plant as the orangery was to be used for afternoon tea while guests were in residence.

At teatime, Meg was hidden in the foliage tidying away the last of her pens and papers when she heard male voices arriving for their tea.

'Really, Jack, what are you thinking of? Sir Gerald is very influential. You cannot turn down his offer.'

Meg froze as she recognised Jack's voice when he replied, 'Sir Gerald is aware of my reasons. He is not happy but he won't stand in my way.'

'You can't be sure of that. You'll never get another position in chambers if you leave now.'

Jack was leaving Sir Gerald! Meg should have showed herself and joined them for tea. She was confident in her pretty blue afternoon dress and it was her chance to speak to Jack before Alice came down. But she stayed stock-still, quietly putting down her pens and listening.

'I have explained to him that I do not want another position in chambers.'

'But you can't give up the law! It's madness for someone of your background.'

'Sir Gerald understands,' Jack insisted.

'But will Alice?'

'Alice? What does Alice know about this?'

'You mean you haven't discussed it with her at all? I warned you, Jack! I warned you not to hurt her. She isn't expecting you to live off her money, you know.'

'Good God, Charles, where did you get that idea from?'

'Well, what *are* you going to do?' Charles demanded.

'It is no longer a secret now that Sir Gerald has been informed.' More voices floated over to Meg. 'Here he is now, with Lady Pearce.'

Meg heard a general exchange of greetings and then the loud voice of Lady Pearce. 'I'm looking for Miss Parker. Has anyone seen Miss Parker? Lady Alice said she was in here.'

Meg hurriedly picked up her pens and a sheaf of papers and emerged from her dense green hideaway. 'Did someone call me?' she said.

'Are you Miss Parker? Jolly good show. Put down those' – she circled her hands in the air – 'notes and come and sit by me for tea. I want you to give a talk to my ladies' group.'

Other guests were wandering into the orangery, admiring the plants and taking cups of tea and plates of cake from uniformed maids. Several looked in her direction. But Meg could see only one of them and that was Jack. He came towards her. 'Meg. Meg. How superb to see you well again. You are quite well now, aren't you? Alice has given me bulletins but I needed to see you to be sure.'

'I am very well, Jack. If anything, I am even stronger than I was before – before prison.'

Jack stared at her seriously. He was about to comment when Lady Pearce grasped her elbow and steered her away. 'I saw her first, young man,' she boomed.

Meg glanced over her shoulder to see Charles's angry face commanding Jack's attention once again. After Lady Pearce had persuaded her that public speaking was as important as newspaper letters and articles if Meg wished for more women to join the cause, several other ladies had clustered around her, curious about her experiences. She was flustered at first, but then interested in their queries. Finally, however, she felt like a fairground side show and reflected that, if she really cared about the women's movement, she must become accustomed to this amount of interest. Eventually she was alone again as guests circulated with their tea and she searched for Jack.

He was talking to Charles and Alice. She wandered by, hoping to catch his eye but he was engrossed in conversation; all three of them were engaged in a discussion. Meg's shoulders sagged as she guessed what it was about: Jack's future, Alice's future, *their* future together. She couldn't bear it. She had come so far since those Sundays in the Dales. She wanted another chance with Jack. She was ready to try again and it was too late.

Meg watched them for as long as she dared without appearing rude to other guests. Their discussion was a serious one, it seemed. But marriage was a serious business, especially when a peer of the realm was involved. Unexpectedly, a sob caught in her throat, and she turned away. A few ladies were already leaving the orangery to rest before dinner and she followed their example.

At dinner she was seated between an older gentleman who farmed locally and a young man who was home from his tea plantation in Ceylon. He didn't actually say it, but Meg soon understood that he was in England looking for a wife. He was personable and charming and it was while he was describing the comfortable existence abroad that Meg recognised, with a surprising certainty, she was not interested in a charmed life of cocktail parties and shooting expeditions, waited on hand and foot by a houseful of native servants. She was, she realised, not interested in being anyone's wife. She qualified that thought: except Jack's, and if she couldn't have Jack she would do without because no one else would ever come close to him in her affections.

She had her belief in 'Votes for Women' to fight for. She had her writing, which was beginning to earn her a small income. If she worked at it, there would be paid lecture tours for her as well. Florence was going to America; why shouldn't she go with her?

During the next course, the farmer was happy

to talk incessantly about his crops and animals, so her attention wandered across the table to Jack seated between Alice and Lady Pearce. Meg frowned. Alice was not happy. Jack was talking to her but his face, infuriatingly, was unreadable. It was impossible to say whether he was pleased or cross. The farmer next to Meg stopped talking to eat and Meg made a general comment, feeling guilty that she had not listened to him as closely as she should.

Dinner went on for far too long and Meg was grateful to escape with the ladies and leave the men to their port and cigars. Alice was by her side before they reached the drawing room.

'It's all going wrong,' she wailed. 'Charles said he would help me but Jack won't listen.'

Meg took her arm and replied, 'I'm sure it's not so bad. You'll feel better after a cup of coffee.'

'I don't want any coffee. I want everything to be as Charles said it would.'

Meg didn't know what to say. She had believed Jack to be ambitious and turning down an offer from Sir Gerald did sound out of character for him. She wondered why and was torn between wanting to find out more and despair at the prospect of listening to Alice talk about Jack.

'Perhaps some fresh air will clear your head?' Meg suggested.

Alice shook her head. 'There's a frost tonight. I shall take my coffee in the orangery.'

Meg didn't really have a choice. Alice wanted to talk and Meg was her friend and confidante. She prepared herself for heartache. Meg checked that no one was lurking in a corner as she had before she sat in a cushioned bamboo and rattan arm-chair opposite Alice.

'I can't understand Jack. Sir Gerald offered him a secure position in chambers with a huge increase in his income and Jack has refused! He could have taken a house – not in Mayfair, I know – but we could have married and lived very comfortably in London.'

Meg thought that Alice was disappointed rather than angry and queried, 'Is that what Jack wants?'

Alice hesitated and frowned. 'Y-yes. I'm sure he does. He said he wishes to stay in London so why won't he stay with Sir Gerald?'

'Perhaps he wants to represent different clients from those who instruct Sir Gerald?' Meg suggested.

'But Charles told me that some of his clients ask for Jack! Charles was sure he would accept. Jack says he has other plans for his future.'

Chapter 25

Meg was curious. 'Did he say what they were?' She had wondered, at first, if he might wish to go back to Yorkshire, but she was wrong. He had told Alice he wanted to stay in London. Whatever his plans were, if she knew Jack, he would carry them through regardless of Sir Gerald or Charles or – she frowned – Alice. Alice was her friend and she hoped he was not going to hurt her. Meg knew what that felt like. It was not like the Jack she had known to play fast and loose with Alice's emotions. At that moment she wanted to find him and give him a piece of her mind for upsetting Alice in this way.

Meg said, 'Alice, he has to be honest with you.' Alice didn't answer so Meg asked, 'What does Jack want to do?'

'That's not the point,' Alice replied shortly. 'Charles has invested heavily with Sir Gerald for Jack's sake. Jack doesn't know, of course, but he ought to be grateful.'

Meg inhaled sharply. Jack probably did know, she thought. No one would have told him but he was not stupid. Far from it, and neither was Meg. 'Alice,' she said, 'Jack would not wish to think that Charles has bought him in any way.'

'He hasn't! It is perfectly acceptable for Charles to give me a dowry. Jack understands that and he should have accepted. He should have. Hugo would have. Why can't he be more like Hugo?'

Meg's eyes widened. She was lost for words. Then she felt desperately sorry for Alice as she realised exactly where her recent happiness with Jack was rooted. Meg couldn't decide whether to speak gently or firmly but she had to say it. Alice was not thinking clearly; she was cross and losing her usual composure, Meg saw. Meg had to calm her down somehow so she copied Jack's way of dealing with disagreements and spoke in an even tone from an expressionless face. She said, 'Jack is not Hugo. He never will be Hugo and you cannot expect that of him. Jack is Jacob Wright. He is his own man.'

Alice slumped in her chair. 'Charles said as

much when I first told him about Jack. Jack looks so much like Hugo but – but he's...' Alice shook her head. 'He's not the same. Hugo would have stayed with Sir Gerald – for me. He would have done it for me.'

'Hugo was in love with you.' It was the wrong thing to say because it implied that Jack did not love her. Meg didn't know why she had said it but the words were out of her mouth before she thought about them.

Alice looked at Meg with tears in her eyes. 'And I was in love with him.' Alice's voice was soft. 'I was so very much in love with Hugo.'

The pain of continuing this conversation was too much for Meg. It was hard enough for her to bear the knowledge that Jack planned to marry Alice. But if he was in love with Alice, Meg wanted him to be loved in return by someone who wasn't looking for the reincarnation of a lost dream. He deserved to be loved for the man he was and not some imaginary ideal existing inside Alice's head. Meg wanted better for her Jack! She felt her control slipping away and said, quite sharply, 'If you love Jack in the same way, you ought to be speaking to him instead of me. Go and find him and talk to him, Alice.'

To Meg's immense relief, Alice agreed, stood up and left. Meg remained alone for a long time in the dimly lit quiet, reflecting on Alice's conversation. She came to the conclusion that they had simply had a lovers' tiff over Jack's career ambitions and they would soon make it up. More guests were due to arrive in the morning for the next day's shooting followed by a grand banquet in the evening. She wondered if they were going to announce their engagement then. Even the thought of it caused Meg's heart to ache with sadness. If only it were her instead of Alice! But Meg was used to coping with pain and grief and heartache. She had had enough practice recently. Many of tonight's diners were tired from travelling and retired early to their rooms. Meg decided to do the same. She asked one of the maids for a hot toddy to make sure she slept.

Breakfast at Fieldhurst was normally substantial but on the day of the shooting party it was enormous. The sideboard in the dining room was filled with heated silver chafing dishes and domed silver serving platters of eggs cooked in four or five ways, kippers, smoked haddocks, bacon, liver, devilled kidneys and cutlets. Field mushrooms from the estate were supplied for a gentleman who requested them and oatmeal porridge for another, while a foreign lady asked for orange juice and a raw egg. Footmen and maids scuttled backwards and forwards with pots of coffee, tea or chocolate and hot toasted bread wrapped in linen napkins to keep it warm. Dishes of butter curls and marmalade made by the cook with fruit from Spain had to be replenished constantly. The atmosphere was jovial, a mood that spilled outside as gentlemen and ladies with their loaders and dog handlers congregated on the shingled area in front of the house.

The air was clear and cold causing breath to condense in clouds. Meg spotted Jack, dressed like most of the other gentlemen in strong boots, tweed plus-twos, shooting jackets and hats, talking to Charles. She searched for Alice. The ladies were easier to spot as there were fewer of them and Meg saw her join her brother and Jack. They appeared to be on better terms than the night before and Meg guessed they had made up their differences. Perhaps Jack had decided to stay with Sir Gerald after all?

Meg should have been relieved and happy for her friend but she wasn't and acknowledged sadly that she envied Alice. But there was no future for Meg in harbouring her festering ill feelings and she had to let Jack go. She wanted him to be happy and if Alice made him so Meg had to release him from his special place in her heart. She *had* to, for his sake, for Alice's sake, and for her own sake. She was pleased when the estate gamekeeper's son, one of the under-keepers who had promised to be her loader for the day, tapped her on the shoulder.

'Miss Parker,' he said. 'You are in the second shooting brake.' He indicated a line of estate motor cars waiting to take the guns to their first drive of the morning.

'Are all these people shooting?' she asked.

'Thankfully, no.' He smiled. 'Many are followers, just out to enjoy a morning in the fresh air. The shoot captain is waiting for you over there. He is doing the draw for pegs.'

Meg drew a tiny ivory stick with a number on it from a silver case, which allocated her peg position for the first drive. A few minutes later, she climbed into the back seat of a shooting brake full of people she had met for the first time yesterday and set off for the other side of the estate.

After the motor ride, her loader carried her guns and cartridges as they tramped across a pasture to a line of numbered pegs below woodland. When the birds came over, disturbed by beaters, Meg was excited and exhilarated by the challenge. The crack of the guns and the smell of the smoke added to her determined mood. She could get over Jack if she really tried. She had to for Alice's sake. They were her friends and if they loved each other she owed it to them to be happy for them.

But that was easier said than done. When the drive was over and she turned to make her way back to the motors she saw Alice with Jack, walking close together and enjoying a joke. Meg wondered whether they would have been so friendly again if she had not suggested to Alice to go and find him last night.

'All right, miss?' Her loader had stopped a few yards in front of her.

She had unconsciously slowed so as not to catch up with Alice and Jack. 'Thank you, yes,' she replied. 'I was admiring the view. Fieldhurst is a very pretty estate.' If she was avoiding them together in the open air surrounded by others, how would she feel sharing a meal with them or a walk in the park?

After the next drive, the motor cars took everyone to an estate farm where a barn had been cleared for refreshments. Mr and Mrs Clarke circulated, offering tiny silver cups of port or sloe gin and there was an appetising aroma of beef broth. Meg's loader stayed outside the barn with the beaters and keepers. Jack seemed to have disappeared but Alice was talking to the tea planter from Ceylon.

Those who were hungry sat at one of the linen-covered tables for a bowl or two of thick hearty soup and slices of cold pie. Meg hovered, undecided about eating. She was not hungry after her large breakfast but it smelled so good.

'Would you like something lighter? Mrs Clarke has some consommé.'

She immediately recognised the voice at her shoulder. 'Jack!'

'I don't know where these gentlemen put all this food,' he commented.

Meg considered this for a moment and responded. 'Well, one or two have very big tummies.'

Jack laughed and his eyes crinkled at the corners exactly as they used to. Then his face straightened and he said, 'Meg, we should talk properly.'

Meg shook her head. 'There's no need. I am pleased that you are so successful in your London life.' She didn't mean to sound sad, but she did.

'There is every need. I know I hurt you when we parted. I hurt myself too but I thought it was for the best–'

'Don't,' she interrupted. 'Don't rake over those particular ashes. It was a long time ago.'

'Not that long. I wanted to talk to you in Crandale but you were too withdrawn. You weren't the Meg I remembered and I couldn't reach you, shut up in that caravan. What happened to you, Meg?'

She wanted to say 'you broke my heart' but it

would have been unfair to him. She had suffered when he'd left her but the rawness she had felt in Crandale was from a different kind of hurt. She said, 'What makes you think something happened to me?'

'You had changed. You were different in Crandale.'

'We all grow up, Jack. The past is just that; it's gone and forgotten.'

'Has it? The prison doctor and Lord Langton's physician thought that for you it was still there, deep inside you.'

'Jack, stop it!' Meg pleaded. She pressed her eyelids shut with her thumb and forefinger. 'I don't want to go back there.'

He frowned. 'I'm sorry.'

'It's over now and I have a new future.' She dropped her hand and managed a smile. 'So have you.' His engagement had not been announced yet so Meg chose her words carefully. 'I wish you every happiness, Jacob. Truly I do.'

His penetrating stare silenced any further comment from her. His face didn't move a muscle.

Clarke's face loomed over his shoulder. 'Would you care for soup, madam? Sir?'

Meg shook her head but Jack ignored him and stated quietly, 'As I have said, we should talk.'

Clarke led Meg to a vacant seat and Jack's attention was diverted by Lady Pearce who had a young man at her elbow anxious to speak to him. A bowl of soup appeared in front of Meg and she made an attempt to taste it. Why did she feel so utterly drained of energy? Was it going to be this difficult every time she met him? The guests either side of her were already engrossed in conversations and she made no attempt to contribute.

Perry Price-Fieldhurst stood up at the head of the table to make announcements about the next drives and Meg was thankful to hear that there was an option to return to the house. As soon as he sat down, she got up and searched for her beater outside. She shook hands with him, passing across a banknote concealed in her palm to thank him, headed for the motor and climbed inside with an aching heart.

She couldn't do this. Alice was her friend. She couldn't carry on, meeting Jack socially and continue to behave normally. She still loved him and that love was, if anything, stronger than before. She had to think. As soon as the motor reached Fieldhurst, she declined tea and a bath and set off walking for her favourite spot. The pump house was quiet. The shooting party was miles away and the wind took away any noise from the soothing gurgle of the brook. She sat on her favourite log and considered her future.

It did not take Meg long to reach a decision. She would leave Alice's employ and sail to New York with Florence to continue her writing in the cause of women's suffrage. From there, if she sold her articles she could save up for a railway ticket to Canada to visit her brother and his growing family. She had a little money put by but needed to earn something for extra living expenses. It was a risk but when had Meg Parker been afraid to take a risk?

Her mind went over and over her plan and her only regret was that she would be leaving the suffragettes' struggle in England. Meg didn't want to do that. She wanted to fight this wretched government and halt the forcible feeding. She wanted to stop men like Saul getting away with rape. She wanted the vote for women and more besides. But giving up this ambition was the price she had to pay for a new start, a new life and a new future.

She shivered suddenly, chilled by sitting still for so long. There was a movement in the trees, a rustle of leaves and cracking of twigs. She turned around expecting to see a deer wandering down for a drink.

'Alice said you would be here. Is there room for another on that log?'

Meg closed her eyes for a second and inhaled. 'Jack, I have said all I want to say to you.'

'I have things to say to you. Are you cold?' He took off his tweed shooting jacket and put it around her shoulders.

The inside was warm from his body and she inhaled again. 'Thank you. Won't you be missed at the shoot?'

'Alice knows where I am. She sent me down here.'

'She did?'

'Charles tried to tell me about Hugo, you know. He showed me a photograph of him but I didn't see the significance.'

'She was very much in love with Hugo,' Meg agreed. 'It was sensible of Charles to explain that to you.'

'Wasn't it? I thought he was telling me how much Alice had been hurt in the past and to be careful with her feelings. Have you seen the picture of him?'

'No, but Alice said that you bear an uncanny resemblance to him.'

'It's true. I had to be very patient yesterday evening explaining to Alice that I am not Hugo and I will not behave as he did, probably not ever.'

His tone was firm enough to cause Meg to glance sideways at him in surprise. 'She was very upset at your decision to leave Sir Gerald,' she said.

'So was Charles. But in the end, it was Alice who understood the better of the two. Women do have a different perspective on life from men, don't they?'

Meg gave a wry grin, meant only for herself. 'They do, and that is why men ought to listen to them more.'

He scratched his temple lightly and gazed across the brook as though in thought for a few seconds. 'Alice and I had a long conversation last night and cleared up one or two mistaken beliefs.'

'I guessed that you had mended the rift when I saw you together today. You seemed, well, comfortable with each other.'

'We are. We are good friends. I admire and respect her and always shall.'

'Well, that is a good basis for a marriage. She does love you, Jack.'

'No she doesn't. She believed for a while that she did, until my behaviour didn't conform to her ideal Hugo. She came to her senses yesterday evening and realised her so-called love was just a whim on her part. Alice was in love with the *idea* of me being Hugo. It would never have worked as a marriage and Charles suspected as much.'

This sounded to Meg as though the engagement was off. 'Oh, I am so sorry, Jack,' she said.

'Why?' he asked baldly.

'You're in love with her, aren't you? Alice was convinced that you loved her because you did so much for her when I was in prison.'

'For *her?*' He shuffled on the log so that he was half facing her, placed his warm hands on each side of her chilly face and turned her head towards him. There was a query in his lovely blue eyes. He didn't speak. He simply looked at her with his unspoken question.

Meg was overcome for a moment. 'You did it for me?'

'Of course I did it for you. I don't love Alice; I love you. I have never stopped loving you, Meg. I was too inflexible with you in Deepdale, too full of my own success, and I expected you to follow me because that's what wives do. You have no idea how much I regretted that afterwards.'

'Oh yes I have. I made a huge mistake by not trying to find a way to be with you. I ought to have come after you when I had the chance, but I thought you would no longer be interested in me – and I suppose I was too proud.'

'Was that the reason you were so difficult with me in Crandale? You were barely able to speak civilly to me.'

The pain was still there, buried quite deep, but Meg froze at the memory. 'No, that was something else,' she said quietly.

'And that something compounded the trauma of your prison experience. Tell me what happened to you, Meg.'

She wanted to because she wanted to tell someone, anyone, about it and she trusted Jack. Or did she? He'd said he loved her but might the knowledge of what Saul did to her sour that love? Wasn't it best to keep these things a secret? *Our little secret.* Those were Saul's words and that's how he – and others – got away with rape. It's shameful, say nothing! So she had buried it. But the damage Saul had done to her had not gone away. She had carried it with her and it had resurfaced when she had been subjected to another violation of her body in prison. Her secret had festered for too long and it was time to lance it.

But it was hard for Meg to find the words. After her silence, Jack added, 'I'm sorry, I shouldn't have asked you. Shall we walk back?'

Her tears threatened and she clenched her fists. 'No. Not yet.' She was strong. She could say it. 'It happened in Deepdale. A man – a horrible man... I was – was – I was violated.'

'Violated?' He stared at her, first in apparent disbelief and then in horror. 'You mean you were raped?'

She nodded. 'My stepmother remarried. It was him.' The pain welled inside her. 'That's why I left Deepdale.'

Jack was so gentle as he held her and murmured, 'My poor darling.' She leaned against him with her face against his waistcoat. The heat of his body warmed her. She gulped a little as she tried to swallow her tears but they flowed insistently. She didn't know how long she sat there. Eventually, he moved one of his hands and then a handkerchief appeared and she half sat up to wipe her eyes and nose. He didn't seem to want to let her go.

At last she said, 'I thought I had put it behind me when I started a new life with Alice.'

His arms stayed around her, holding her close. 'I'm sorry, I am so sorry,' he groaned.

'I was doing well until prison. Then the forcible feeding brought back the memory. It felt like the rape, Jack. It was a violation. You have to stop them doing it.'

'We shall,' he said. He sounded confident and it was a comforting thought.

She was beginning to feel better now. She had lost track of time in the cocoon of his arms but she was safe. More than that, she was loved and it was the best feeling in the world. He whispered, 'May I kiss you?' and she answered by turning her face upwards to his. His lips were as gentle as his arms. He kissed her lightly on her cheeks and forehead and, when her tweed hat fell off, he nuzzled her hair.

'You and me together,' he said. 'We shall do everything we can to make life better for women. I am leaving Sir Gerald to go into Parliament. I shall fight every by-election in Yorkshire until I win a seat.'

Meg sat up properly with wide eyes. 'Yorkshire? Not in London?'

'I know the people there. So do you. Marry me,

Meg, and we'll fight on together.'

'Does that mean we'll live in Yorkshire as well as London?'

'I miss the moors. The Sussex Downs are pretty, but the Dales are my home. You will marry me, won't you?'

'Oh yes, I'm not letting you get away this time. But I am worried about Alice and what she will say. She is my friend.'

'Mine too,' he said. 'However, we talked it through and we are still friends.'

'I suppose I must do the same.'

He nodded and stood up. 'The sun's going down. It's getting chilly.'

Meg stood up beside him, but instead of walking on she reached up to take his head in her hands and kiss him. She kissed him fully on the lips, passionately and deeply. If he was surprised he didn't show it and, judging by his response, Meg guessed that he, like she, wished to make up for lost time.

The publishers hope that this book has given you enjoyable reading. Large Print Books are especially designed to be as easy to see and hold as possible. If you wish a complete list of our books please ask at your local library or write directly to:

Magna Large Print Books
Magna House, Long Preston,
Skipton, North Yorkshire.
BD23 4ND

This Large Print Book for the partially sighted, who cannot read normal print, is published under the auspices of

THE ULVERSCROFT FOUNDATION